HugoSF

HugoSF

a novel

Jeffrey Hannan

 Pohoiki
Press

for Arvin Alipio Muñoz

ACKNOWLEDGMENTS

My endless gratitude to:

My mother, for her support during the bleak times;

Charles Wilmoth, for taking an interest, for encouraging me, and for providing me with my very first audience;

Dorothy Berger - humanist, wit, inspiration and teacher – for ferrying me through some illuminating and challenging formative years;

Peggy Willett, who constantly reminded me that one must do everything for one's art;

Stephen Cox, from UCSD, for his keen technical insights and for wisely encouraging me to abandon my first novel;

Sho Aoyagi, for getting me back on the path and making me confront, as did Hugo, some difficult truths;

Denise della Santina, for suffering through the first draft and gracefully pointing out its tragic flaws;

Don Clark, PhD, for being a wonderful muse, guide, compatriot and friend;

and

Arvin, for being insistent.

Contents

Buckshutem:

My Miraculous Emergence

We begin with a misgiving.

* * *

My initial public offering took place in Buckshutem, New Jersey, back in 1974. I was born on August 9th, the day Richard Nixon resigned and left the White House in disgrace.

Ma was on the sofa in the living room wheezing like the dickens, lying on a towel that was damp with her own broken water. Meanwhile my Aunt Alice sat crouched on the edge of a nearby chair with her face glued to the TV screen. "Ain't it a pity," Alice muttered.

"Christ's sake—," wheezed Ma, barely able to get the words out. She gasped for air then a second later hollered, "Alice—."

"Hang on, Janie," Alice waved a dismissive hand at her nephew's wife. "They're gettin' on the helicopter."

"Sons a—," declared Ma as another contraction consumed her.

Aunt Alice, her eyes transfixed on the Air Force helicopter sitting on the White House lawn with Nixon nearing the top of the steps, pulled a wrinkled Kleenex from the elastic band around the short sleeve of her house dress. She dabbed her eyes as Tricky Dick waved his last goodbye. "Lordy, what a shame."

Doctor Bing, the family doctor and a friend of my Daddy's, was coming in from near Cape May. Daddy had gone down to the end of the long driveway to wait for him.

"They comin' yet?" Ma called to Alice.

"No, I ain't seen 'em yet."

"You ain't even looked!"

"Lordy Lord," Alice shook her head. She rose from the sofa in slow syncopation with the rising helicopter. She banked to the right toward the window, drawing her eyes away from the TV screen toward the long dusty drive that cut a chalky path through the corn field. Within a moment she caught a glimpse of Bing's Chevy Nova coming up the drive: "Oh, I see `em. Here they come."

Breathing crazily, Ma let out a cry. A massive contraction consumed the lower half of her body and she wailed for all the good green cherries to come falling off the trees.

* * *

All that morning Alice had done little to help Ma. She didn't believe that Ma was gonna deliver anytime soon. She scoffed at Ma when she overheard her tell Daddy at breakfast, *"He's comin' soon"* (meaning me), as she sat nearby stirring a cup of dubious tea. Later on she declared, as she watched Ma slice lemon rounds for a pitcher of lemonade, "It's the heat, Janie. Why, you don't even look three days out from havin' that baby."

"It ain't the heat," Ma protested from the kitchen counter. "And you ain't having the kid, I am." Four or five times they went round and around, Alice claiming *"It's the heat,"* or *"You're just upset the President's quit but you don't know it,"* and Ma replying, *"It ain't the goddam Nixons! I can feel `im pushing around wantin' out!"* Around midday Ma hollered, "Go call my husband in the barn, you old bitch! And tell him to get over here and call Dr Bing!" The walls of her gut were rolling and stretching and started to burn as if being singed with fire.

With the Nixons on their way back to California and Alice weeping softly, Ma's lying on the sofa in agony, sweating like a hog in the hock. She'd pulled her flimsy dress up beneath her hips, exposing her round protruding belly and her privates. She'd bent her knees and was pressing her feet against the sofa's arm for leverage against the commotion going on inside her. She was rocking at her shoulders to fight the pain and hang onto her breath, determined that if she had to deliver the baby herself she was gonna do it.

Alice turned away from the TV and surveyed the scene taking place on the sofa behind her. "Lord A-mighty," she cried out, seeing the tip of my right foot piercing the dark confines of my mother's womb. A set of my slimy toes wriggled in brazen, disorderly delight, eager to set foot in the thirsty New Jersey sunshine. Alice stumbled backwards into the TV set and then tripped over a magazine rack and fell to the floor, where she lay clutching the TV stand in disbelief.

In less than a christian minute Dr Bing and Daddy rushed in through the front door. Bing took one look at my mother's face and then at the purplish foot pushing out between her legs. He rushed over and dropped his medical bag on the floor. "Don't push!"

My father, seeing my foot, remarked, "Jesus, that ain't right."

Dr Bing, who wasn't half bad-looking for a 45 year old, salt-and-pepper haired general medical doctor from Grange, deftly placed one hand on Ma's belly and with the other pushed on my foot in order to keep me from coming out. "Alice," he commanded, "get me a pot of hot water. And Dwight, get me some towels."

Alice struggled to get to her feet.

"For God's sake, woman," hollered Bing. He turned his attention back to Ma. "You'll be all right, Janie. Baby's breeched. Gonna be tough we gotta work with it." He grabbed my errant foot and gently pushed me inwards, testing the tension. Then he shook his head in mild dejection. "Not gonna be able to turn him around."

"What's that mean?" Daddy asked as he hurried over to a side cupboard.

"Means we're gonna have to deliver him as is."

"Can't come out one leg at a time!" Daddy said.

Ma let out a cry and Bing, with beads of summer sweat surfing down his neckline, said, "I know that, Dwight." He apologized to Ma then gently pushed my foot back in. "Don't push," he told her. He slid his hand in along with it. "Gonna pull him out by both feet, if I can get hold of 'em."

Alice stumbled into the kitchen muttering something about having *"seen them done somethin' like that with a pig once..."*

Bing persevered, manipulating me both from the curvature of Ma's belly on the outside and from the inside as well. All the while Daddy's getting panicky and reinstating his long lost friendship with Jesus. He watches, sweat pouring down his face and soaking his shirt, dripping on Ma's dress and pooling on the braided rug. The sort of sexy Dr Bing, who's got a wide brow full of sweat and a pair of trim, dark eyebrows framing cobalt blue eyes, is looking intense yet assured. "Kinda got – his other leg – in a knot."

"Oh Lord..." Daddy rocked on his knees beside Ma, holding her hand and looking like he was going to faint.

All of a sudden Bing shouted, "Got 'em!" Bing had grabbed me by the ankles and told Ma to "hang on a second." A bit of blood seeped out from Ma. A thin trail of it slid down Dr Bing's muscled forearm. He took a deep breath then instructed my father to hold a towel beneath us: "There's a good chance the cord'll be wrapped around his neck. Second he's out you gotta hang onto him til I check. Hear me? That cord'll turn into a noose in a heartbeat."

Bing looked Ma in the eyes. She was looking well past worn out. "All right, Janie, it's now or never," he told her. "You're doing great. You get a contraction you just let it go. Let 'im come on out."

Just then a searing contraction shoved me against the fleshy gates. Under the reassuring but tested gaze of Dr Bing, with my ankles bound by his fingers, my chunky legs and waist struggled to debut in Buckshutem County. We all held our breaths in silence. Then with a final determined tug from the doctor, I was yanked fully downwards and out. I alit into the searing light, which sheared the darkness just as a wail from Ma shattered the momentary silence surrounding my miraculous emergence.

"He's out!" called Bing.

"Hot potato," cried Daddy as he shoved his hands beneath me and my slippery skin landed on cloth. "Looks all right, don't he?"

Bing nodded his head gladly.

"He all right?" Ma gasped.

"So far so good," said Bing. "Umbilical cord's ok, God."

Alice returned carrying a roasting pan between the hot pads in her hands. Her face was damp with sweat and her thin black hair disheveled. "Careful," she said as she set the sloshing pot of steaming water down on the floor beside Dr Bing. "It's near boilin'."

"Wet me a towel," demanded Dr Bing. "Come on, Alice, get with it."

"Have mercy…" she implored as she shoved a few towels into the water.

I was draped in my Daddy's arms in a kitchen towel with a print of faded yellow and blue daisies that Alice had picked up at the five-and-dime when they were on special, six for a dollar. Bing pulled a small, turkey baster-like ball and tube from his bag and sucked the mucous from my nose and mouth. "Now take one out and let it cool a second," he told Alice. "Not too hot. And wipe him off good." Alice nervously doused another towel in the water and wrung it out as Bing snipped the umbilical cord attached to my stomach.

"Lemme see 'im," Ma said.

Daddy raised me, swathed in dime store dish towels, to show to Ma. Ma reached out her arms as if to take me. "Baby boy," she grinned.

"Dwight—," Bing interrupted, and there was no uncertainty in his voice: "Hang onto the boy. Alice, call an ambulance. They both got to get to the hospital."

"What's wrong?" Ma asked.

"Just a precaution, Janie. You're bleeding a little, is all."

As soon as he said that a pain overtook Ma on her insides. She called out as another contraction stung her tiny frame. Dr Bing shoved some towels underneath Ma's buttocks and the afterbirth was delivered.

Aunt Alice looked aside and declared grotesquely, "Gonna have to replace that sofa."

Ma grunted.

Bing told Alice to "Get on the phone, woman." He looked tensely back and forth at Ma's face, then the length of her body, then back at her face and over at my Daddy, who was still holding me in his arms and kneeling beside Ma.

"Baby boy..." Ma whispered. Then suddenly she choked and her breathing halted as a gush of blood poured out from between her legs.

"Dammit!" yelled Dr Bing. My father stepped back in a panic, squeezing me against his chest. Dr Bing tossed the bloody placenta towels onto the floor and grabbed a handful of dry ones. Ma's body quivered and she gasped a few times.

For nearly half an hour the good Doctor Bing did everything he could, pressing on Ma's chest to try and keep her breathing, applying shots in her arm with syringes, packing her lap with towels and blowing in her mouth to try and force her lungs to take air, all to no avail. The whole time Daddy and his Aunt Alice hovered nearby in fear. Bing did everything in his power—he had saved the baby, people would later recall—but unfortunately there wasn't a thing he could do for the young wife.

* * *

By the time the ambulance got there Ma had been dead for some time. Dr Bing, looking broke, had collapsed his head into his arms on the kitchen table and wouldn't move. Nearby the overturned TV tray and wrecked sofa, and with the static-y TV news crackling in the background, a distraught Aunt Alice sat in her chair weeping into the sleeve of her dress. Next to the sofa, kneeling by his wife's side, was my Daddy, holding onto me. The new air in my lungs was nearly choked from the pressure of his arms as he clutched me for dear life and smothered me with devastated kisses.

Ugly Bus:
The Rise of Irrational Exuberance

"God, Hugo, how awful." Angela waited for the clanging noise of a cable car going down California Street to abate. "I thought you said your mother lived in Orlando."

"Stepmother. My father remarried."

"Oh. And Aunt Alice?"

"Dead."

"Mh."

"Killer bees," I said solemnly.

Angela looked at me with—well, it wasn't entirely disbelief, it was more like the gentle perturbation of having received too much information in the form of a dubious tale. I could hear a beeping noise emanating from her purse. She took the device out, glanced at it, tapped the screen with a stylus. She stood there in her sexy brown slacks and a soft tan turtleneck and nodded her head gently: "Cool."

It was such a perfect word for the pretty, young, lesbian/bisexualisa that she was: *Cool*. Angela was charming, disarming, smart...she was cool. She was strong-willed and vibrant, like Elizabeth Taylor in *The Sandpiper*, one of the countless California movies my Aunt Alice and I used to watch when I was a kid growing up in New Jersey. She was the sort of girl I wanted to marry: beautiful and willful without having yet become a monstrous drunkard or a bitch. She was the reason I moved to California: I adored her and everything she represented. I wanted to woo her. I needed her. But I could never be with her in that way; she was my closest friend and I was merely her dutiful admirer.

"What's cool?" I asked.

"My two o'clock with Celia. I think she's going to promote me."

"Serious?"

"She's been talking to me about what she wants to do with the company and asking what I want and—. Actually, Dede, our second in command, told me *'in confidence'* the other day that Celia's been thinking of putting me in charge of Development."

"No kidding, that's brilliant."

"Imagine *that*, Hugo Storm. Yours truly, Director of Technical Development for Thrive.com." Angela crossed her fingers for luck. I pulled open the heavy glass door of the modern, grey gothic office building. As she turned to go in, I pleaded, "If she promotes you, please hire me."

"It's web development, Hugo, not sales."

"I don't care if it's janitorial. You've got to help me."

"I know I know. I'll see what I can do, I promise."

I leaned in toward her with seductive breath and whispered into her ear: "*...And will you starve without me?*"

"Don't start."

"*On a hot summer's night would you offer your throat—?*"

"Hugo—."

(I loved it when she scolded me.)

"Shoot pool this weekend?" she asked.

"Definitely."

"Cool."

I waved goodbye to her as a crowd of office workers converged on the elevator banks, obscuring my view and drowning out my words: "Thanks for lunch…"

The lingering rains of winter had ebbed that morning and the sun was out in all its tantalizing briskness. The lure of springtime filled me with a dreamy state of wanderlust which tugged at the disenchantment that underscored my life. All around me the world was undergoing a transformation—optimism soared. I, on the other hand, 24 and filled with promise (unquantifiable though it may have been), felt trapped and helpless in the shadowlands.

As I walked down the hill my beeper went off.

I took it off my belt and looked.

It was my boss.

I did as I would typically do: I groaned.

All around me, San Francisco's Financial District was vibrant, alive, filled with endless work and countless people basking in an era of everything good. Real life had run utterly afoul of my own expectations, though, and now there I was. This was not the California I'd expected, nor life as I'd envisioned it. This was not the land of my imaginings.

I clipped my beeper back onto my belt and with a reluctant sense of duty I meandered down California Street, taking the most indirect way possible to catch the number 15 bus back to my dreaded office.

* * *

I worked in inside sales and support, so I didn't really need a car for work. Considering I didn't own a car, that was a good thing. If I needed one—if I had to drive to a client site, for example—I borrowed Angela's. Otherwise I took the bus.

Riding the bus in San Francisco is like being a fish trapped in a metal cage on the deck of an undulating fishing boat. It's a dank, dehumanizing jaunt that repeats itself throughout the City. Short of breath and writhing, you're jammed in one on top of the other, jarred around backwards and forwards because of all the hills and turns, shoulders banging shoulders, backpacks banging into chests, heels stomping toes, the steamy odor of wet wool, leather and mothballs, the hacking up of morning breath, chewing gum, b.o., sundry bodily scents and bad perfume. There's a certain ring in hell reserved for bus drivers who like to exacerbate the misery of riding these slippery death traps. They're the ones who floor the gas pedal when taking off, driving a g-force wave through the back of the bus, sending old men tumbling down the aisles. For them, every intersection is a life or death choice. It's commonly known in our small city that if you're at a street corner and the stoplight has just turned from red to green, the odds are 1 in 3 that there'll be a Muni bus barreling through the intersection in front of you.

Not long after leaving Angela, I arrived, jostled and disjointed, at the corner of Bryant and 3rd, south of Market Street, locus of the New Media explosion and home of my distinctly antiquated employer, Screaming Software.

The city blocks are long south of Market and they lack any real, distinct charm. They're mostly treeless, one-way, heavily trafficked, grungy avenues of low-rise commercial fronts and one-hour parking meters. Think wind-strewn litter and uninspired grey cement, car repair shops and turn of the century warehouses being slowly overwritten with geeky new modernist buildings. Screaming occupied half a floor in a seedy old brick building on the corner of 3rd Street and an unremarkable alley. Just across the alley was one of the new neighborhood gentrifiers, a cash-rich internet consultancy called Ascend. Fat with IPO funds, Ascend had recently doubled in size after its acquisition of one of its equally glamorous rival players. It occupied an old five story warehouse, recently gutted and lined with windows, its interior spaces opened wide, full of breathing space and light. You could see into their space from the dusty window in our lunchroom. It lay across the alley filled with millionaires in tennis shoes, foozball tables, ping-pong, free snacks and bottled water. I heard they even had soda machines that utilized virtual currency built into cell phones. Everyone sat at long, shared desktops cluttered with elegant laptops and telephone headsets. Through its windows you could see the verve and activity of the place vibrating above the rows of workers' heads, creating a tangible cloud of sensation, a partially controlled chaos that harbingered the winds of market madness outside.

When I was growing up in New Jersey, my only ambition was to get out of New Jersey. Now that I was out of Jersey and living and working in San Francisco, my ambition was to get out of Screaming and go to work for a company like that.

Screaming was a software company that wrote and distributed a sales management program called Viper (so named in order to elicit a sense of speed and tactical efficiency). The software came stored on an installation disc accompanied by a thick user manual, all of it shrink-wrapped in a box whose artwork was designed by an old hippie graphic artist who lived near the Panhandle. Our web-based version was in the works but God only knew if, when, or how it would take off. The days of distributed software were hardly over, but at that point in time the World Wide Web was where it was at. Venture capital had been pouring into Silicon Valley internet ventures for several years and the overflow was flooding the streets South of Market in San Francisco with the potential to raise the fortunes of companies like ours, and those who toiled there, to unimaginable levels.

Depending on whom you talked to, Screaming Software was teetering on the brink of either outright success or utter failure. From my standpoint, we were pretty much making a decaffeinated effort at an internet play, though. A web-based version of our software was in the works but it was ominously behind schedule, and from a functional standpoint it was clinging precariously to that dangerous line between barely workable and slapped together. The die-hard, old-world techie who was in charge of the project didn't know a thing about the web. My chats with the programming staff, and my peeks into their development sandboxes, confirmed as much. On top of that, the company leaders couldn't grasp the concept of putting our product on the internet since the distributed version was doing just fine. All they knew and were repeatedly told was that *"you gotta webify to survive"*, so they did their pathetic best and they followed the rest of their peers headfirst into hypertext space.

My job was inside sales and customer support. My role was basically to sell endless incremental upgrades to our clients and help them out with training and usage, all the while dangling the promise of imminent, internet-based anywhere web virtuality. Viper was a sales tool, which meant I spent my days selling software to salespeople.

(Conceptualize that.)

After getting off the bus I stopped by the Barbary Coast style diner on the first floor of our building for a cup of mediocre coffee to get me through the rest of the day. I made it back upstairs to the office around two o'clock and passed by the cubicles of the programming staff. We all said our hellos out loud. It was a small yet diverse group: Trini was Pakistani, Henry Chinese, Lili Russian and Diosdado Filipino. Of course there was the usual smattering of Americans—a Richard, Robert and Mike, each of them a geeky subgod among their rather odd professional class. I liked the programmers because they were good people. I'm sure some of them were freaks at night—Henry's man snatch was probably plastered in gay chat rooms across the internet and I'm sure Lili subbed out as a virtual dominatrix on vixensofthenight.com—but they were trying to write good code, doomed as it might have appeared, so you at least had to honor their effort.

My office was a windowless 6x6 shanty of a room in the darkest section of the floor. As I made my way there, my boss, a 30-something year old named Samantha, hollered as I passed by her office door. "HUGO! Get in here." Her voice was so dripping with quasi-maternal scorn that it made my skin itch.

I took a few steps backward and leaned into her office. "Yes, madam?"

"What did you say to Mark Stannage?" She pointed to her computer monitor. "Read this."

I scanned the text of an anguished email from the sales manager in Boston, from which I managed to extract a few phrases of agonized coherence: *"if the strategic objective of Screaming is the elimination of its sales force...[yadda yadda]...software features that we in the field have developed over the years by breaking our butts with clients...[blah blah blah]...those of us with families...* It was more than enough whimpering pathos for one Friday afternoon. It went on *ad nauseum*, written obviously with great pains and brutal angry breaths over late hours of the night in Beantown.

"Oh for Christ's sake," I said. "Just delete it."

"What is your problem? Why are you telling people we're getting rid of our sales team?"

"I never said any such thing."

"Look at this," she jammed her finger into her monitor and read out loud: "'*Hugo Storm'* –that's you— *'Hugo Storm said that the combination of online download capabilities and the right marketing approach could flatten the distribution stream and obliterate the need for regional field sales.'*" She looked at me with a chilling glance and repeated: *"Hugo Storm said—."*

"I couldn't possibly have worded it that way," I interrupted. "Besides, what I said to him was a hypothetical rambling ...an armchair analysis. It's speculative, to a degree, but based on emerging realities of the marketplace. Flatten the layers: that's the world we live in, Samantha. Take out the middleman. Put everything on a server and hire somebody to make sure it doesn't crash. Who needs a sales force? Think about it. That's what this revolution is all about, isn't it?"

* * *

Back at home that night, I'd finished my dinner and was having a decaf mocha when Cal, my roommate, walked into the kitchen.

"Jesus Christ," I said, "who are you?" I looked at him and realized that I couldn't remember the last time I actually saw him. The most we'd shared recently was a random hello at night through closed hallway doors.

"What's up, man?" Cal got a coffee cup from the cupboard and went to the coffee maker. He dumped sugar into a Giants mug then reached for the pot.

"I haven't seen you in weeks," I told him. "I mean physically seen your face."

He stood at the counter pouring some coffee. "Who sees anybody anymore?" he said. "I've been working my nuts off."

"Still dating what's-her-name?"

He nodded his head lackadaisically. "I'm actually supposed to pick her up fifteen minutes ago. She's gonna be *pissed*."

"Where you going?"

"Dinner. Guess what else, dude."

"What?"

Cal pulled an envelope out of his back pants pocket. "Vested!" He came over the table and sat down beside me, flapping the envelope between his fingers. "Check it out, dude, fifteen-hundred options I exercised at 16 bucks a share. We closed at $40-something today. That's over twenty-five thousand bucks. And it's all vested, baby. *Pu-u-u-u-r-r-r-re* profit." He slapped the envelope against his palm. "Sniff the green!"

"Oh my God." I had to wipe the drool from the side of my mouth with my spoon. "They just gave it to you?"

"I earned it, man. Any one of us over there could head down to the Valley and make a mint off some internet play, so they know they have to keep us close. Profit sharing has morphed into profit grabbing and Calvin McAllister is at the front of the pack."

I told him I could use some of that action.

"Are you still wasting your life over there at Superior?" he asked.

"Screaming."

"Yeah whatever. What're they paying you?"

I told him.

"A year? Get out of there, man. Unless you like them dry fucking you like that, go get something else or tell 'em to double your money. There's tons of opportunity out there, you just gotta snake it out. You could make a killing. You're the biggest talker I know. Get yourself into an internet firm—a real one, not that dumpy pony you're riding on now. I'm serious, dude, move on."

* * *

Early on a Monday morning. On the 4th floor of 580 California Street. I raised my Mango Madness juice bottle and tapped its plastic edge against Angela's biodegradable, soy-based coffee cup.

"Cheers," I said to my beloved best friend as we stood in her new cube, toasting her promotion to Director of Technical

Development. Even in a flat hierarchy like Celia Green's Thrive.com, there were some rank privileges to getting promoted, in her case a cube with a view.

"Thank you thank you." She laid her palms flat atop her new desktop and grinned wildly. "I am *so* excited."

"Well done," I said. I was feeling distinctly jealous, even though I was glad for her. More importantly, I was optimistic about what it could mean for getting me out of my Screaming hellhole. There was plenty of opportunity those days. Cal had gotten a bite of it. Angela was getting more of it. It was becoming a painful realization: my peers were starting to rake in the dough while there I was still separating the wheat from the chaff.

*   *   *

Several days passed and my roommate's admonition rumbled around inside my head alongside my fully sprouted disenchantment, a previously intangible bit of silence which at last had found its voice. What it screamed was, *I need more money!* Having just finished my taxes, I knew that with compensation plus bonus I was making barely 50K. It was almost a livable wage in San Francisco at the end of the 20th century. Livable, but not very luxe. All one had to do was go to a place like South Park to be reminded of that.

South Park was the heart of SF's multimedia gulch, about a block and a half from my office. The park was an oval oasis of green grass and wrought iron benches, fine restaurants and emerging private real estate, hidden in a secret block within the grim grid alleyways South of Market. The park used to be full of crack addicts and homeless but in recent years it had been transformed into something with a much more gentrified flavor. At lunchtime in decent weather the park was filled with people brown-bagging their meal or eating carry-out. The lines spilling out of the expensive cafes on the perimeter of the park were filled with casually dressed people who were self-consciously stylish, chatty, luminous, engaged and, it would appear, well paid. Contrast that with my current, lowly self at the time: how a young man of such imagination and inner resources could have sunk into such petty drudgery was a mystery to me. Even the pigeons twittering along the grass muttered rude sentiments underneath their breath:

Low wager.
Lump.

Whipped boy.
Wage slave.
Nonads...

"Bitch, where have you been?" Geoffrey sat down on the bench beside me. He was the information architect in our company—an IA Engineer in the language of the day—and he knew everything about web software that mattered. He wore severe, heavy-framed eyeglasses that rested like window panes across his face. His clothes were requisitely black and fashionable and they all but screamed *I am an overemployed internet junkie working in the fabulous multimedia gulch; I have a pair of chihuahuas, three boyfriends, and such a perfect abundance of urban starkness in my Mission District loft it would make Mies van der Rohe cream his jeans.*

"I have been ringing your pager for half an hour," Geoffrey scolded. He took a massive sandwich out of a paper bag and gently tore at the white paper binding it together.

"Sorry," I said. "I turn it off when I'm eating."

"And where is your cell phone?"

I patted the outside of my jacket pockets and discovered they were empty. "Um. Back at the office?"

"You are the most irresponsible salesman I have ever seen. Which one of your peers leaves his office in this day and age without his cell phone? Now reach in this bag and take out your device."

I stuck my hand into the paper bag he'd brought. Resting on the bottom was my cell phone.

"It was sittin' on the men's room sink, Hugo Stormtrooper. Now put it in your pocket where it belongs. It must've rang fifteen times while I was taking care of business."

"Yeah, yeah." I checked the missed calls list as Geoffrey bit into his sandwich. "Only Samantha," I told him.

He shook his head and chewed. After he managed to choke down the bite he looked at me with a flurry of disbelief dancing across his eyelids. "That one—" he said. " *'Help me find Hugo!'*," she says to me as I'm walking out of the boys' room. Just like that: on a rampage. *'Help me find Hugo!'* So I say to her, 'I'll help you find the word *please*, and once we find that then *maybe* we can talk about finding out where Hugo is at.'"

Geoffrey was at least six-foot-two. His aura shimmered with all the wonderfully gaudy unsubtlety of Las Vegas. He was thin and usually wore tight black jeans and a blousy button down shirt. He swiveled as he walked. He wore a minimum of five silver rings on his hands because four was not a good number in numerology and also because symmetry, having two on each hand, was as a concept dead. You didn't mess with him. It was dusk one evening and I'd just started working at Screaming. Geoffrey and I were walking together, chatting amicably on our way out of the office. An extended-cab pickup truck with monster tires was in the slow line of cars slogging toward the onramp to the Bay Bridge. "*Faggot!*" someone called out from the dark interior as we crossed the street in front of the truck. "God damn right, you right-wing bricklayer," Geoffrey hollered back. Then he looked at me and stated boldly: "We spent the Reagan decade clawing that word out of the hands of the religious right and now we own it. Fuck him if he thinks it hurts."

Geoffrey took another bite of his sandwich and rolled his eyes. He uncapped a bottle of iced tea. He drank back a big swallow then decreed of Samantha, "She's got the grace of a pig at a trough. What's she on the warpath for now?"

"Who knows."

"I thought maybe she's seen webViper," he said.

"What do you mean?"

"You know *exactly* what I mean, Hugo da Storm. I've seen you chatting up the developers and looking at their code. That system is a class-A mess. You know it, they know it, nobody in management wants to admit they know it, but we all know they know it. I've grown tired of trying to make them see they need to start listening to me and make some changes. When that mess goes available to paying customers there is going to be some serious butt-kicking and finger-pointing. Unfortunately a lot of it is gonna come landing back on this fine black ass of mine, no matter how many times I try to warn them."

"The customers are going to hate it," I said. "Off the record, of course."

Geoffrey wagged his finger at me. "Nuh-uh. You better start saying something *on* the record. You're out there selling this mess, pushing the web version down their throats. When they don't start biting and you can't even get close to your sales targets you better be hoping you have some serious CYA insurance. If you don't cover it now…mh-mh. Your ass will be grass and the both of us, along with that Salinas weed-sucking technical lead, will be living in a cardboard condominium alongside the bus station."-

I slurped up some lo mein noodles I'd bought at *China-a-Go-Go*. I nodded slowly in acknowledgment as Geoffrey's words joined in on the cacophonous whirl inside my head. Were we really in that bad of a shape? Was Screaming as poised for failure as I feared, and as Geoffrey had unequivocally declared, or was my perception clouded by my sense that I was sorely underpaid? Originally I was going to go see Samantha after lunch and demand a raise, but with that sort of endorsement I wasn't even sure I should stick around.

Geoffrey interrupted my thoughts: "By the way, you going out with that delicious dish of yours this weekend?"

"Angela?" I asked.

"Mh-hm."

"We'll see."

"That girl is fine," he said, "just *fine*."

* * *

Back at the office I passed by Samantha's door and she hollered out: "Hugo!"

I stopped in my tracks.

"Come in here," she said.

"Good," I told her, taking an unanticipated cue, "there's something I want to talk about." The short walk back to the office had convinced me to tell her to give me a raise or else I was leaving. (What was there to lose?)

Before I could start she said, "We're going public."

I was speechless.

"I've been instructed to tell you," she said in her standard patronizing tone, "explicitly and in completely unambiguous terms that you are to keep your mouth *shut* about the company and webViper for the next ninety days. Not a single word, you understand?" She emphasized her next words with unambiguous cruelty: "When you feel the temptation to open your mouth, stifle it."

"We're going public?" I said. The phrase itself was like a dose of glittery magic going off inside my brain. It shut down my sense of direction and clouded my thoughts with too many wondrous things—and I mean *thing* things: cars, clothes, dinner out (if I could ever get away from that software plantation), a new TV, sound system, CD library...

"The email's in your inbox," she mentioned. "Stan just sent it out. But I wanted to track you down before you went around shooting your mouth off."

"How considerate."

"And when I say nothing, I mean nothing," she repeated. "No backseat speculations to other sales people, no false promotions when you're on client calls—you understand?"

"No more talking it up?"

"No."

"What happens when a client asks me about webViper?"

"You say that Screaming is going public and we're in our SEC-mandated quiet period. It's on track but you really can't say anything else. They'll understand."

"That sounds pretty goddam easy," I said.

"Yeah, we'll see. Now what did you want to talk about?"

"I forgot," I lied.

Since late in '97, the prior year, there had been pre-IPO chatter buzz in our office and we even had a mention in *Wired* magazine suggesting that our CFO was sniffing around for a willing investment bank. It all sounded like a crock of shit, given our company's über un-webness. But this was a world of new economics and rule-breaking. So from that perspective anything was possible, no matter how improbable it may have sounded. Sure enough, after I sat down at my desk there was an email from Stan, Screaming's President, acknowledging that a stock option plan had been put in place for all Screaming staff, details of which would be forthcoming, and that an investment bank had been hired to manage Screaming's initial public offering, which was scheduled for July 16th.

Only 3 months away.

I sat there and stared at my computer screen in disbelief. *I...P...O...*At last I was gonna be *in* the money. No more taking the bus. I had a BMW 3 series with my name on it and I would even be able to afford to rent a garage.

Of course I wasn't sure how it all worked. I knew we'd be NASDAQ-listed, which if you were a tech company was the only decent piece of real estate to put your corporate house on. Beyond that, they gave you some options, a bucketful of stocks; surely there'd be cash to go along with it and—and—I had no idea what else.

"Treasure—," explained Geoffrey with a vaguely patronizing tone as he stood at the entrance to my hovel. "You don't *have* to exercise but you *should*." He had come over to continue our lunch conversation but of course the conversation had shifted since we'd both seen Stan's email. (The first thing out of his mouth had been, "I assume you heard—.") We delved into the IPO and he opined, "We'll probably open around $20 a share and it's nowhere but upwards from there. Trust me. Exercise your options as soon as you get them and then cash out after the vesting freeze. Opt in low and get out high," he said. "If you can."

The news caused a tingling sensation inside me. "How many shares do you think we'll get?"

* * *

At the end of that memorable day I left the office a little bit later than usual. I had finished my list of calls then sat at my desk, lost to all time as my thoughts got bundled up in speculation about our incoming windfall. It was solidly dark when I finally went outside. From the corner of the alleyway I stood looking up at the twinkling lights in the headquarters of Ascend, the revolutionaries still up there whipping out code and visual stimulation, connecting the world into itself, folding societies in upon one another, melding boundaries and dissolving borders. Filled with orgiastic bliss over our own pending IPO, I gave a mental thumbs-up to the busy hive next door and then hopped on my familiar unfavorite, the 30 Stockton, toward home.

* * *

"No kidding," exclaimed Angela. "Hugo, that's fantastic."

"Calls for a drink, don't you think?"

"I'd love to but I have to work tonight."

"We still have to celebrate your promotion," I reminded.

"How about this weekend?"

"Saturday?"

"Hmm..." she hesitated. "Let's try Friday."

* * *

By the jittery end of IPO announcement week I'd had time to process my desires and line up all my wishes. The anticipation kept me up some nights calculating how I would spend my chunk of change once it was vested. When my brain grew tired of analysis, I closed my eyes and counted shares instead of sheep.

There was a nagging aspect to my newfound, impending fortune, though. I mentioned it to Angela that Friday night. We were in the Tenderloin sharing bowls of mild curry and garlic naan.

"Everything comes at a price," she said.

"Small consolation."

"Well, what do you want me to say, Hugo? I can't change your reality."

"I know that…What I'm asking is, what do you think I should do?"

"What does your gut tell you?"

"It says run like hell because no matter how many options I get I still have to work for Screaming doing exactly what I'm sick of doing right now."

"We-e-e-llll," she cast her eyes down as she went for a piece of lamb. "I'm not so sure about that. You've been selling shrink-wrap up until now. When you release ViperWeb—"

"WebViper."

"—your sales pitch has to change, doesn't it? I mean, you're not just selling shrink-wrap anymore, you're selling a hosted application. That's a totally different tactic."

"Bottom line: I'm still doing sales for Screaming. Still working for that horrible woman and those two pleated khaki losers who run the place."

Angela looked perplexed. She dabbed her bread into thick, pungent sauce. "I've never seen you so worked up. You like the work, don't like the company, you want the money—."

"But one more year? I can't bear the thought of going in for one more week. Who knows what opportunities I'm missing out on?"

"Maybe the money's worth sticking around. I mean, if you're changing your approach and you've got a new product line—a year flies by, Hugo. Before you know it, you'll be vested and you can leave."

"Cursed money."

"Don't let it blind you."

"It's not. Well, all right it is. But for the first time, it's like—I don't know, it's like—"

"Well-deserved compensation?"

I took a slug of Indian beer. "War reparations."

She rolled her eyes. "You know, for a straight boy you are such a drama queen."

After dinner we left the restaurant and ambled over to the bus stop. We stood waiting to wedge ourselves in among the crowd of 60-something year-olds, roving teenagers and the quasi-homeless. The hordes took their time loading onto the front of the bus so Angela and I did what we usually did when overcome with impatience: we darted to the back door and got in.

"No back door!" hollered the bus driver.

"FastPass." Angela yelled. We waved our monthly passes over our heads.

Oh, but soon, I was thinking to myself, as the scent of an overripe and underwashed welfare scion wafted through the back of the bus...*soon will come the options. I will sell my stocks and buy my Beemer and finally I'll be able to afford to take a taxi whenever I don't want to drive.*

Cal was eating a TV dinner in the front room of our boxcar flat when I got home. At the same time he had his laptop open and was checking email, tapping out messages in between bites of food. "Guess what, dude," he said. "I had an interview today."

"Cool. With who?"

"Company down in Cupertino."

"Yeah?"

He stopped what he was doing and looked at me. "It's killer, dude. Eighty thousand base salary. Options. Sign-on bonus of 15,000 shares. IPO in September."

"Serious?"

"Dude, if I get this I am *in* the money." He clenched his fist.

* * *

The next few work days came and went, each one indistinguishable from the next. We were in our IPO quiet period and the CEO and a marketing consultant were trying to work out the kinks of how we were going to promote WebViper. None of our clients were interested in the distributed version of the app because they were all waiting around to see what was going to happen with the web version, which meant I was stuck in my office all day dredging up bogus phone opportunities and farting around with my sales presentation. For the next few weeks I had more of the same to look forward to, day after day, stuck, a few unbearable heartbeats away from the Mock Princess of Sales: Samantha: dean emeritus of nothing special. A *moyenne* of talent. Humorless ruse. A shrew.

She had an Associates Degree in Business from an East Bay junior college and a BA in Art History from San Diego State. How she lucked into her sales job at Screaming might have been a mystery if it weren't for the fact that the guys who ran the company were your standard ass-breathing, penis-thinking men for whom the women of the world existed in order that they might bestow upon them their endowments (fictional or not) up until the point at which the women became enamored of them (for some god unknown reason) or threw down the *"Marry me or else"* card. Now before you jump all over my case for suggesting that Samantha was a mindless pair of breasts sitting behind a desk, realize that in college she displayed no real ambition. Her weekends were spent doing community deeds through her Simi Valley church—sorting through donated clothes for a women's shelter or reading the Bible in English to migrant workers in the fields. She did these things without objection and with a smile on her face because she felt it gave her life a bit of purpose. She hadn't exactly chosen a degree with tons of opportunity behind it. She'd chosen Art History because it was fun: looking at pretty paintings all day, thinking about art…Truth was, the only thing Samantha showed real ambition for was learning how to take tequila shots from between her tits.

She moved to the Bay Area after college and tried to find a place in the art scene. Instead, she ended up in a stint as sales secretary for some other firm. For a while she studied to get her real estate license but dropped out of night school when it became obvious that the California real estate market was in the toilet for an unforeseeable period of time. Somehow she found out about Screaming and submitted her resume. Marv, the CFO, felt Screaming needed a more experienced sales associate until Stan, the CEO, told him to interview Samantha in person. And from there, I imagine, her life went from innocuous to momentarily fantastic to utterly nauseating.

Marv was the CFO and he looked like a beet-red pickle. He was about five-eight, ovate when he stood up and squashed like a pear when he sat down. His face was textured like a sea cucumber and his grey eyes never simply looked at you, they could only stare at you with a mind numbing glaze of confusion and indifference. He was married, a poorly skilled socialite and a bit of a loser, a puffy white man of relative privilege telling lies to women on the internet while his wife lay asleep in bed.

Stan, the CEO, wasn't as physically repulsive—by some standards he was probably decent looking. He was, however, the snake that greased the hole from which men like his CFO emerged. He had a deceptively harmless Marin look to him, wearing high-waisted khakis or jeans and a dress shirt, looking always as if he'd just stepped off a houseboat in Sausalito. He was well over six feet tall, which meant his superiority complex had a head start over most of us. He was prone to fits of rage and thought nothing of flinging staplers, coffee cups or anything with a little bit of heft across the room when his tenuous serenity was disrupted by troubles at home or there at the office.

We had a company outing every summer in Tilden Park, in the hills of the East Bay, to play softball, barbecue, drink too much and drive home across the bridge at peril. About a month after I was hired, I was at my first company outing getting a beer when I overheard Pickle and Pete (as I liked to refer to them) murmuring and chortling underneath a tree near the food tent.

"I'd like to give her a tittie fuck she'd never forget," said Stan, his tongue dangling from his mouth and laughter snorting out through his nose. I looked around and saw Samantha in the near distance, seated at a picnic bench and wearing a long-sleeve Giants jersey that fit her like a glove.

No doubt Samantha had to work hard for her money, prove herself day in and day out, and put up with unknown volumes of shit from Pickle and Pete. Whether it was the work or the world around her, something had turned her mean. And because I was the only sales rep in the office—(our outside sales reps worked out of a remote office in San Jose)—as well as her closest neighbor and her direct report, I was on the receiving end of her shit more so than everyone else.

"Hugo!" her grating voice ground through the glass of her office door and grabbed me by the hairs on the back of my neck.

I opened her door and wedged myself between the door and the jamb. With great annoyance I confronted her: "What?"

"Sit."

"For what?"

"Shut the door and sit down, please." I knew there was trouble if she was using the word *please*. It must have taken her half the morning to choke down her pride enough to say it. She licked her plastic saccharine painted lips and lifted her hands from the top of a large white envelope with green trim. "The options packages are in."

"What does that mean?" I said.

"It means we're going over your options for the public company. Before we start, I've been instructed to tell you that options packages are like compensation packages. Other staff members' packages may be different than yours, so you should treat what we go over as confidentially as you do your regular compensation."

"In other words, don't tell anyone how big mine is."

"Stifle it." She lifted the flap on the envelope and slid out a small sheaf of papers. "This is your copy," she said, handing them over to me with absolutely no emotion. She proceeded to walk through the papers—the language, the disclaimers, my biographical information, the dates, the conditions, blah blah blah—pointing to each item with the tip of her red pen.

"Get to the good part," I told her.

We flipped over to the second page where, up near the top, was the magic. "This," she said, tapping at the small bold font, "is the number of options you're being offered."

I looked at the number and got all giddy, then I looked at the number again. I snatched the red pen from her fingers and counted the number of digits. I tapped off the numbers and read them aloud, certain there must have been a mistake: "Five-zero-zero." I looked at her in disbelief. "Five hundred shares?"

Samantha flipped around the papers as if she had no idea what they said. She nodded, turned the papers back around in front of me. "Yes, five hundred."

"Are you kidding me?"

"What? They're priced at fifteen a share. If we IPO at twenty, that's seventy-five hundred dollars right off the bat. For nothing."

For nothing? That was the wrongest use of that expression I'd ever heard in my life. "That's a pitiful contribution to the future of my well-being after having invested three years of my life in this place," I said. I knew full well she must have had some say in determining the final amount, and I was certain this shakedown was either payback or plain malevolence.

"In addition," she said, her breath filled with great waves of consolation, " you'll get a 5% raise in your base pay starting the month after the IPO date."

"Five percent? How generous." I calculated quickly that that was a whopping two hundred bucks before taxes. "Is the rest of the sales force getting this shafted?"

"I can't tell you what other people are getting, Hugo."

"Surely you know."

"Of course I do."

"Is this even commensurate with the other reps?"

"I'm not at liberty to discuss it."

"Why not?"

"Because it's confidential."

"Do you think what they're giving me is fair?"

"It's not up to me to know what's fair or not. There are a lot of complicated considerations that go into options offers."

"What consideration?" I picked up the papers and flapped them between us. "There was obviously *no* consideration gone into this. None, zero. That's one less zero than this lousy offer. Five hundred isn't even a rounding error!"

Then she flung me her typical brush-off: "If you have problems with what you're being offered, take it up with Marv or Stan." That was how she dealt with everything: Pickle or Pete, Pickle or Pete. Pass it off to Pickle or Pete.

"This is pathetic," I told her. I tossed her red pen onto the desk and grabbed the envelope. "Pathetic!"

What had started as a tranquil, nothing much of a day instantly decayed into a maelstrom of vileness and greed.

I stormed out of Samantha's office and went directly over to confront the Pickle.

Marv sat there slurping on the end of an expensive ink pen as I stared at him from a chair on the opposite side of his overwhelmed desk.

"Well, Storm," he blathered, "there's a lot of calculation that went into these things. The investors have a say and the investment banks chime in. There are only so many shares the SEC will allow us to allot for existing employees without incurring excessive expense—not just for us but for you, as well. You don't want to pay a lot of tax on these shares, do you? We think we worked out an equitable deal for everyone. No pun intended: equitable deal...equities...get it?" He drew the back of his hand across his pinkish-white lips. "If you have a problem with the distribution you need to bring it up with Stan. If you're not worried about taking a dictionary upside the head then I'd say, go for it."

I called Angela from my office in despair and said I needed to see her. It was three o'clock. She indicated that her day was barely halfway over and she only had a few minutes to spare. So I left my office and hopped on a 15 to the Financial District. The bus jolted its way across Market Street and I cursed Screaming Software under my breath all the way to the main entrance of 580 California.

"What's wrong?" she asked. I could see that her increased responsibilities had started dragging her down a little bit, giving her a rushed appearance. She did her best to appear attentive. I told her about the stock option shafting I'd just gotten and she gave me a hug. "I'm sorry," she said. "That sucks." She turned as if to leave.

"Don't you want to hear more?" I asked.

"I have to get back to work, Hugo. We'll have a beer this weekend."

* * *

Back at the apartment, I stood in the kitchen talking with Cal. "You got it?" I said to him. My stomach dropped toward my nads and my saliva turned to dust. "They offered you the job?"

"Hell yeah. They recognize talent. And these days, boom, there's no time to waste. Good talent doesn't wait around."

"Well done," I said, turning rigid with envy. "When do you start?"

"That's the problem, man." He looked at me apologetically. "They want me to start next Friday. They don't have a San Francisco office. It's Cupertino or nothing. There's no way I'm doing that commute, so I gotta move out."

"Serious?"

"Yeah, dude, sorry. Look, this is short notice so I'll pay through the end of next month. That'll give you a good five weeks to get somebody in here. Or if you hustle yourself right you can probably afford it on your own. You started looking for something yet?"

"Uh, yeah," I lied. "Not very hard yet, but I've got feelers out there." My brain started brimming with ponderances and possibilities, not all of them pleasant or good. What if I couldn't rent his room? How could I pay the rent on a lousy two hundred dollar a month raise? Worse, San Francisco was full of freaks and flakes. What horrors from the side show of humanity was I going to have to wade through before finding someone I could live with?

"When are you physically moving down there?" I asked him.

"Soon as I can. I told them I need a couple days to get settled."

"You found a place?"

He shook his head no. "I bailed from StarTech this morning. I'm going down south first thing to find something."

"Well done," I said. And although the pot of jealousy was simmering dangerously on high, I was glad for Cal. "I mean it." Then I threw in the requisite plea: "Hey, d'you think—?"

He cut me off. "I know what you're gonna ask, but no. These are hardcore engineers, man, and they've got a tier one biz dev team. There's no place for you down there. Sorry."

-3-

THE FINE ART OF SEDUCTION

Not long after, on a grey Saturday morning in April, in his superb condominium atop a shoulder of Nob Hill, Stuart Piers looked out from the comfort of his bed and could scarcely make out the jagged landscape of the Financial District. The entire city was slumbering in a bath of fog.

He stretched his arm out and picked up his cell phone: nine o'clock. *Christ.* The gravity keeping him in bed was strong and yet in spite of the late hour he felt no urge to resist it. He flicked a few blonde-ish strands of hair from the mattress—after turning 40 he had started to shed—and then tapped out a text: *"Angelita – gr8 to see u. free 4 lunch?"* He set the phone down and rolled back toward the center of the bed. Lying there was Carlos, a tall, sinewy Latino, an artist, who was sound asleep on his side. The young man from LA was sleeping facing the wall. On the slender muscle of his exposed back was a large tattoo of Our Lady of Guadalupe. Stuart gently slid the sheets up over Carlos' shoulder to avoid having the Virgin Mary staring at him. He slipped an arm around the artist's waist and lowered his hand to the place where resided a more solicitous tattoo, an inked *XXX,* just above his crotch.

They had met two nights before, a Thursday, at the apartment of Manny and George, owners of a Latin American art gallery where Carlos' recent etchings were on display. Manny and George lived in a two bedroom flat above their Hayes Valley gallery. Stuart had known Manny for years and had reluctantly inherited the brusque partner, George, as a consequence of that friendship. They had invited him to dinner under the pretense of getting caught up and to introduce him to someone that Manny thought Stuart would find, *"ehh..."* he stumbled suspiciously for a word, *"interesante."* The three of them were in the kitchen: Manny, George and Stuart. The *interesante* one, Carlos, was in the shower down the hall washing off airplane stench. The other dinner guests, a younger couple who were acquaintances of George and regular clients of the gallery, hadn't arrived yet.

"Is this a setup?" Stuart asked as Manny prepared dinner and George opened a bottle of wine.

"A setup?" George replied. "Heavens no. We figured you haven't had time to go trawling the Central Valley for a boyfriend, so we thought we'd save you some time."

Manny shook his head in embarrassment.

"Besides," George added morosely, "our Carlos has a lover in the Mission."

"Ex-," insisted Manny.

"We'll see."

"Oh please. He hasn't mentioned Quique in ages." Manny looked at Stuart: "*Orale pues.* He's a very good artist."

"But he's not at all your type," quipped George. "He speaks English *and* he has a green card."

Soon after, Carlos entered the kitchen. "Hey," he said. He went straight for the refrigerator and pulled out a Diet Coke.

"*Carlitos,*" Manny told him, "*tenemos un invitado.*"

"*Ya ya.*" Carlos went over to the butcher block table where Stuart was standing. "Hi there." He held out a large, slender hand, smiled and said politely, "Carlos."

At dinner Stuart sat on a long side of the table next to his friend Manny. To his right, at one end of the table, was the artist. At the other end was George, who liked to eye his candy all throughout a meal. Across from Stuart and Manny sat Peter and Paul. They were a mousy and unintriguing couple: two bland pieces of white toast in otherwise smart outfits from *agnès b.* They looked fairly alike: they were the same height, wore short haircuts tamed aggressively with hair products; clearly a pair of club boys turned working married gym whores. They had hardly a word of anything interesting to say beyond chronicling their sexploits in the Mediterranean while on vacation or recounting the excretionary idiosyncrasies of their twin Jack Russel terriers. Stuart tried to engage them in conversation but considered the effort futile. Mostly they just sat there, nibbled on their supper and chuckled at all the right times. It was easy to imagine they got invited to parties simply so that the host could fill up a room.

"So you live in LA," Stuart said to the artist.

"Riverside," he nodded.

"How long have you been in the US?" asked one of the Peter and Pauls.

"'Scuse me?" said Carlos.

Manny wagged a hand to try and deflect the conversation.

"I'm a US citizen, *perra,*" said Carlos defensively. "I was born in LA."

Manny added quickly: "The family moved from Boyle Heights to Riverside when Carlos was…how old were you, *chico*?"

"Eleven," said Carlos.

"Eleven."

"My old man worked in a packing factory—you know, where they pack oranges and stuff. You been to Safeway, you've seen his handiwork."

An uncomfortable silence deflated the meal until Stuart, refocusing the table's attention, smiled enticingly at Carlos and asked, "You get up here often?"

By the end of dinner, after George had had his fill of wine and the two narcissistic lovers and the forgone conclusion that they would never be anything more than window dressing in his dining room and a kiss on the cheek in the hall—the same more or less for Carlos, although the relationship with that one, laced as it was with unrequited desire, was also woven with the strings of finance; and after Manny had politely served everyone to their fulfillment and steered the night out of treacherous waters and endured his husband with a well-aged indifference and grinned as he caught glimpses of Carlos' eyes staring engagingly at Stuart; and after Stuart had let his leg drift up against Carlos' and felt the warmth and tingle of reciprocation; and after Carlos had weaned himself of the urge to knock Peter (or was it Paul) across the face and let his attentions fall to the well-dressed businessman to his left instead; after all this, and a homemade Santa Rosa plum tart, Peter and Paul rose and announced they had to leave. "We have to walk the dogs," said Peter, giving Manny a hug. "Lucifer will tear up the place if we're not home by ten."

Said George: "Call me when you get sick of those creatures. We have a *wonderful* recipe for *birría.*"

Stuart took the boys' departure as a convenient cue to head out. He stood and picked up his dessert plate.

"No, no—," protested Manny. "Leave it there. I'll get it."

"As you insist." He put the plate down. Standing behind Manny's chair, he patted his friend on the chest, said goodnight and kissed him on the top of his head. He looked over at Carlos, who was still seated at the table. "Can I give you a ride anywhere?"

Carlos stood up. "Sure."

"You're going out?" Manny asked the 25 year-old.

"Yeah, why not. The show's hung. I got nothing to do."

"Where are you headed?"

Carlos shrugged. "The Mission?"

George's chair screeched atop the hardwood floor as he stood up. "We'll have to send a rescue party to drag Stuart out of there."

Stuart approached him and smirked. "You overestimate the extent of my addiction."

"And you underestimate the power of other people's observations."

Stuart patted George on the shoulder. "Always the gracious hostess."

As he headed out of the dining room, the young artist gave his hosts each a kiss on the cheek and said, "See you later." He went down the hall and grabbed his wallet and a lightweight jacket from the guest bedroom, then left the apartment with Stuart.

The trees that lined that block of Hayes Street were lit year-round with small white Christmas lights, and a thin fog danced around the illuminated bulbs. On the way to Stuart's car, he and Carlos talked briefly about their lives, the typical get-acquainted stuff: Stuart owns a tech contracting firm, lives on Nob Hill; Carlos has been sketching and drawing since he was six; he turned to etching as a medium a couple years ago after taking a class in bookmaking. He recently bought a small press for his garage; family lives here, family lives there...

They got into Stuart's car. "Mercedes—" Carlos remarked with a slight lifting of his eyebrows. "Nice." He rubbed the wood on the center panel and laid his hands on the cool leather of the seat. He leaned over toward the driver side. "Not bad, *guero*. Not really my type, but...nice."

"Yeah?"

"*Sí, guero, sí.*"

Stuart started the car and headed down Gough toward Market Street. "George tells me you have a boyfriend in the Mission."

"You mean Quique? Hell no. That Quique shit was over *long* ago."

"Sorry to hear it."

"Don't be. He started doing crystal meth in LA and I told his sorry ass that was *it. No mas!* So he moves up here and starts sending me emails and calling me: *Baby, I miss you. Ya ya ya.* You know, I tell him, you want to kill yourself go for it. But don't drag my life into your sorry shit like that."

"I gather you haven't told Manny and George?"

"Hell no. They're like my mother. They'd freak if I told them Quique was a user."

Stuart turned onto Valencia Street, a slick shadowy avenue that ran the length of the Mission district. Streetlights arched out over the street and rained sprays of bright mist onto passing cars. At the stoplight with 16th Street he looked at Carlos: "Want to get a drink?"

"Sure," answered the artist. "How about El Rio. I'm guessing you know where that is."

"Yes, I know where that is." The artist's hairline was ragged and a few hairs poked out from around his ear. Stuart's hand moved effortlessly toward Carlos' face and he caressed the hairs back into place. "Unless—."

* * *

The sun was rising above the bay and it pierced through the side window of my kitchen. Unable to sleep, I had dragged myself in there for a glass of water about twenty minutes earlier. Nauseous, and with a tingling in my fingertips, I pressed my palms to my face and tried rubbing the hangover out of my eyes.

Ordinarily the view from the kitchen was a superb swath of San Francisco's finest—its heavily populated hills with rooftops, apartment houses and church spires filling the urban vale along Columbus Avenue. On this Friday, though, it was my window of shame, with a thousand households full of people sitting about, all looking through their windows down into mine, snickering at my anemic "prize" for being salesman of the millennium at the company of the year. I'd been shafted by that goddam Screaming place. In retaliation I went down to Grant & Green, the local dive bar where Angela and I played pool, and had eight or nine conciliatory beers. Angela stopped in on her way home from work and had a gin and tonic alongside me. When finished she sucked the pulp out of the lime wedge and dropped the rind into her glass.

"You're hammered," she declared. She stood up and asked if she should walk me home.

I declined, telling her, *"iss ony du box."*

"Cut him off," she told Liv, the bartender, a husky girl with long black hair, tattoos and a chest of fire.

"Will do, princess."

Angela leaned in and gave me a kiss on the cheek. "Nowhere to go but up," she whispered in my ear. Then she disappeared into the night.

I lifted my head and looked up at Liv—guardian, Athena, biker dyke—. *"I thi- ah gonna thro up."*

My morning regret was of course as much psychological as it was physiological. I looked out over the populated hills of the City searchingly. From within the one small cluster of brain cells that wasn't dehydrated beyond functionality, Angela's reminder gurgled to the surface: "Nowhere but up…"

* * *

Up on one of those hills on the horizon of my urban view, where privileged high-rise apartment buildings jutted up into the sky, the same sun that was oppressing me was beaming into the windows of Stuart Piers' bedroom like a revelation. A low tonal beeping went off beside his bed. It was Friday, the day of Carlos' gallery show, the morning after their meeting. Stuart turned off the alarm on his cell phone and got up to take a leak. When he came back into the bedroom he was wrapped in a thick, mocha-colored bathrobe. He approached the bed and yanked the sheets off Carlos' body as if he were ripping the skin off a banana. "Wake up, *artista.*"

"Ah, *guero*, it's cold! Gimme the sheets." Carlos rolled onto his back, covered his morning hard-on with his hands as he stared at the stocky blonde hovering over him.

Stuart covered Carlos up to the waist with the sheets. "I'm going to shower. There's coffee in the kitchen. Help yourself to a yogurt. No time for a real breakfast, though. I've got a meeting at 8:30. I'll drop you off at Manny and George's on my way to work."

Carlos rolled back over. "Ok, call me at noon and wake me up."

"No…" He leaned down and kissed Carlos' belly. "We leave in half an hour."

Carlos buried his face in the pillows, muttering, "I am so glad I don't work for you."

* * *

Standing on the sidewalk halfway down the block from Manny and George's building, Carlos leaned into the car through the passenger window. "See you at the opening tonight?" he said to Stuart.

"Of course."

"OK then." He winked and stepped away from the car.

"Hey—," Stuart said. He pointed in the direction of the upstairs apartment and shook his head. "Don't—."

"Oh no way, man. Not a chance. You crazy?"

* * *

"Hugo?"

"Speaking."

"Yes, I know it's you."

"What's up?"

"Wanna go out tonight?"

"No. I have a hangover."

"It's an art opening."

"And that should make me feel better?"

"You can have some hair of the dog there."

"What's it for?"

"What do you mean, what's it for? It's an art opening."

"I mean, who's the artist?"

"I don't know. Some guy from LA."

"It isn't one of those horrible child prodigies, is it?"

"No no, he's established. He does bookbinding and etchings and things. Just say yes."

"Why?"

"Because there's somebody there I want you to meet."

"Who?"

"His name is Stuart."

"What?"

"Stuart Piers. He's a friend."

"You're recruiting again."

"Stop it. Say you'll go."

"What time?"

"It starts at six."

"Is the booze free?"

"If it's not I'll buy you a drink."

"Fine. I'll go."

"Meet me at Montgomery Street Muni at quarter after six," she said.

"All right, all right."

"The entrance by the Galleria. You know, when you go down from Montgomery and Post there's that circular group of shops with the flower stand and the gym?"

"Yeah yeah yeah."

"Use that entrance. I'll be downstairs by the turnstiles."

"Fine."

"Quarter after six. Be on time."

"I will." I hung up the phone. *"Jesus Christ, take a pill."*

At quarter after six, already late, I was standing on the corner of 3rd and Bryant, bobbing on the balls of my feet, waiting for the bus. At eighteen after six the 45 arrived. I sat in my seat and fumed as the bus just sat there, the tedium of waiting doing a tap dance on my dehydrated brain. At twenty after six the bus started moving. At six twenty-six my cell phone rang. I was speed-stumbling the last block from the bus stop on Market Street to the entrance to the Muni underground. I fumbled the phone out of my front pants pocket. "I'm half a block away," I hollered, the fog and the traffic noise and the wind chasing me down the street. At six thirty-two I arrived at the Muni turnstiles in the Montgomery Street station and there was no sign of Angela anywhere amid the flurry of commuters. I wandered in broad-stepped circles and peered around ticket machines, surveyed the area near the shoe shine guy, glanced behind the old Chinese man twanging *Greensleeves* on a two-string mandolin. Nothing. I hit Angela on speed dial and called into my phone, "Where are you?"

An indecipherable static filled my ear.

"I'm right here," came her voice.

I turned around as Angela approached from behind. "I called to tell you I was running late," she said. "I got stuck in a meeting."

"Glad I rushed."

We ran our passes through the turnstile and descended to the platform.

"How are you feeling?" she asked.

"Glad this day is over."

The J Church stopped in the station and we boarded.

"So who is this Stuart person?" I asked as we sat down.

"He's a friend."

"Yes, we established that earlier."

"He owns a contracting firm that mostly does Y2K stuff right now. I'd love to work for him, except—contracting: not my thing. And mainframes—?"

"Is he hiring?"

"I don't know. That's not—. Oh." She put her hand on my knee consolingly. "I didn't even think about that, sorry."

"So remind me why I'm here."

"I want you to meet him, that's all. He's a great guy. Sort of my mentor."

"I see." Feeling somewhat slighted, I slunk down into the hard seat of the train and closed my eyes.

"Greetings, greetings," said a short, middle-aged Hispanic guy standing on the sidewalk. He was having a cigarette just outside the gallery door, wisps of errant smoke settling into the crevices in his face. "Welcome to *Chapultepec*. I'm Manny, one of the gallery owners."

"Hello, Manny, I'm Angela." She held out her hand. "*Mucho gusto.*"

"*Mucho gusto,*" he replied with a dash of delight.

Like a girl on a scavenger hunt she asked excitedly, "Do you know if Stuart Piers is here yet?"

"You know our Stuart?" Manny looked at her as though he should have known who this young girlish thing was.

"He's a friend."

"*Ay mi hija*, and I practically brought him into this world with my own hands."

"How fun," Angela grabbed the back of Manny's arm.

"He's just inside, *chica.*"

Angela smiled. "Thanks." She lunged inside the gallery on her quest, leaving me standing there with the Manny man who was eyeing me with disinterest.

"Enjoy," he said.

Inside, a short Latino kid in baggy jeans and a white muscle tank top was pouring wine from behind a makeshift bar. I went over and said, "How do."

"*Hola,*" he said, displaying a mouthful of big white teeth. "*¿Vino?*"

"Got any Jack Daniels?"

He shook his head no. "*Solo vino.*"

I pointed to the bottle of red wine in his left hand.

"*¿Tinto?*" he said.

"Uh, yeah. That one." I reached out and tapped the bottle of green-tinted glass with my fingertip so that he'd serve me the burgundy colored beverage and not the anemic piss water in the blush green bottle in his other hand.

"One glass of red," he said with a strong accent, "coming up." He poured a splash in a plastic cup.

"By the way," I queried, "*donde* is the *baño*?"

"The bathroom? Over there past the big crucifixion. You pass through that door and go to the stockroom and turn," he paused, "—left."

"Right," I replied, taking my cup. "Cheers."

The gallery was small enough to be intimate yet busy enough on that night to allow one to momentarily lose track of the person you came with. Having ignored for far too long the dump I'd had to take since before leaving work, I headed toward a doorway in the back corner, where a large, roughly cut wooden crucifix studded with nails and pictures hung on the wall. As I got closer I noticed that the nails were piercing a slew of family photographs—summer trips at a riverside, holiday dinners, birthdays with blindfolded children swinging at piñatas, hordes of people drinking dancing singing laughing crying hugging and otherwise posing full of emotion on their way through the mysteries of life. The mix of candid color Polaroids were hammered to the cross by thick steely nails, creating a disturbing personal Gethsemane. In the center, where the two pieces of wood were joined, there was a hazy picture of a young Hispanic girl wearing a pink confirmation dress and white gloves. The face should have been bright and angelic but instead it looked like she was queued up for the next available Inquisitor. A railroad tie was driven through her chest, binding her in agony to the two limbs of splintered wood.

"*Harsh.*" I shook my head.

Through the doorway was the stockroom. There, loosely wrapped Mexican crafts and paintings were laid in unstructured order, pile against pile, wherever there was available space. I turned a dark corner and nearly ran into two people standing locked at the hips and lips.

"Sorry," I said.

"No worries," said one of them, the shorter, stockier one. "Restroom?" he asked.

"Yes," I said.

"Through there." He tilted his head.

"Cool." I set my plastic cup down on a nearby shelf and squeezed around the two men. "As you were."

I finished my business and retrieved my wine, then wandered through the stockroom back into the gallery.

Behind one of the display walls I saw Angela hanging onto some guy in a suit. I squeezed through the looky-loo's and approached them, trying not to knock over clay figurines of skeletons dressed in Victorian evening wear. The guy Angela was getting intimate with was in his early 40s, I guessed—a couple inches shorter than me. He had blondish-grey hair and big arms. He was stocky, like the guy making out with the other guy in the stockroom. He was dressed in a light grey suit with an expensive looking dress shirt opened at the collar. Might've been silk. *In fact*—. He definitely had some cash: the shoes and belt matched and he was wearing an expensive watch. He had a big smile that he couldn't seem to let go of. Kind of like Angela's hand. The two of them stood there smiling, holding hands. It was so father-daughter, brother-sister quaint—.

"Hugo Hugo." Angela grabbed my hand and pulled me in. "This is Stuart," she said with delight in her eyes. "Stuart, this is my good friend Hugo." Yes—it *was* one of the guys I'd run into doing a standing lambada in the stockroom.

"Pleased to meet you. Officially," he said. He held out his hand.

"Likewise."

He crushed my hand with his grip. The pain was significant but, fortunately, brief. "Angela's told me a little bit about you," he said. "We should talk."

"I'm all ears."

He handed me a business card. "Shoot me an email and we'll set something up."

Angela inched her body ever closer to Stuart, wrapping herself up in all of his loveliness. "I am so glad you texted," she said nearly lustfully. She intertwined both her arms around one of his. "What have you been up to?"

It would take an idiot to misinterpret a social cue like that so I said *"Nice to meet you"* and told them I was going to wander around.

Which I did.

To my dismay.

I spent some time wandering around the gallery, looking at the pieces on the walls and flipping through canvases I found stored in the back. I can't say I was too keen on a lot of the art. The show consisted of small, black and white wood block prints with overt themes of illegal immigration and fiscal oppression: *Controversial Cross-Border Art* declared the flyers taped to the front window. It seemed well enough executed but the lack of color didn't do much for me; I preferred bigger, bolder oils and mixed media pieces that made you think in order to comprehend them, something less in-your-face than, say, the Gomez family crucifixion or migrants in chains. I liked my art to ease into my consciousness and seduce me, not lecture me on the politics of the state.

As I stood in front of a series of the artist's twelve-by-twelve inch prints, a large white man approached me and smiled. At least I think it was a smile. It had the look of indigestion written all over it but I was under the impression it was the closest thing to a smile that this stranger could muster.

"What do you think?" he asked.

"Not my cup of tea but they seem to be well executed."

"Interesting choice of words."

"I don't—have a feeling for black and white, is what I mean." I was feeling defensive and figured it had to be either (a) an autonomic reaction to the man's grotesque aural energy, (b) the residual hangover sluice in my stomach, or (c) some combination of all of the above.

"So you find them—interesting?"

"Um…I find them rhetorical."

"Like your outfit."

"Excuse me?" I said.

"Let me guess," said the *gordo*. "Square-toed shoes, blue jeans, and a polo shirt from Gap." He looked at me with gaseous derision. "You work South of Market. You're involved in some sort of internet venture. Live in a loft."

"No, Dionne Warwick," I said meanly, "I don't live in a loft."

The gargantua seemed enthralled. "Delicious—." He grinned and held out his hand. "I'm George. My partner and I own the gallery."

"And this is how you work up your clients?" I wouldn't shake his hand.

I felt someone approach from behind. A sturdy arm landed across my shoulders. It was Stuart. "Hitting on the straight boys, George? You should know better."

"We were discussing Carlos' art," said the grotesque one to my rescuer. Naturally, I was a nanosecond away from saving myself and didn't require any help from Mister Wonderful.

"Of course you were," said Stuart.

"Your friend thinks it's rhetorical," said the old queen.

Stuart stood between us, his wide shoulders keeping the man at a distance. "To a point," he said, turning his attention to me. "We have an entire economic sector in this state built on the backs of people who come here willing to do the work that nobody else will do for lousy wages and few benefits, and the same people that benefit most from these people's labors pass propositions like 186 that basically negate the value of their existence. So of course it's dogmatic."

"And—?" I said.

Stuart stared at me: "One man's rhetoric is another's harsh reality."

* * *

"Did you enjoy yourself?" Angela asked as we headed north in a cab up the hills of Franklin Street toward home.

"Not much," I replied.

"What do you think of Stuart?"

What did I think of Stuart?

"What do I think of Stuart?" I repeated.

I didn't know how to respond. Here was a man whose life would intersect mine like arrows over the coming years. A man who clearly had his shit together, didn't care what other people thought, probably could have bought and sold my family for three generations forwards and back. How was I supposed to know what I should think? All I knew was that I could sense something different about the man. I felt a blind commiseration between us, an almost paternal bond. It was otherworldly and strange: I'd barely spent an hour in his presence but I felt like I'd known him for years.

I cracked the window and lit a cigarette: "He seems decent enough."

* * *

My roommate, Cal, was well versed in the fine art of seduction and he gave me a piece of advice once: Don't ever sleep with a girl from a bar you like to hang out in. If you want to get laid, go to a bar you normally never go to. That way you don't have to worry about running into a one-night stand in *your* bar. Keep *your* bar pure and sexless. Unless the girl's from out of town. His wisdom was top of brain that night, pushing aside the sensory assault of the gallery event. After dinner with Angela at Franchino, a small Italian place on Columbus where the seafood pasta was good and the owner stood on the sidewalk luring people in with his conviviality, I parted ways with my beloved and headed a few blocks down Columbus to the Bubble Lounge, a place on the edge of the Financial District where I didn't normally go. In other words, it was not *my* bar. Bubble Lounge drew a decent crowd of employed, basically urban people. There were plenty of dolled-up husband shoppers and jocks from the Marina District; Saturday nights drew a lot of bridge and tunnel traffic; and there was a lot of new money people in there—tech sales guys, entrepreneurs–less the geeks than the ones who tied yokes around the necks of geeks and made them pull their sleds.

Sitting at the bar and taking my Stella slow, I started chatting up a girl from Fremont, a dark-featured white thing who had short bouncy hair and a cute body. She had some meat on her bones, like a real girl. (I can't abide those girls who starve themselves so that their limbs look like sticks.) Her name was Maureen.

"Well, Maureen Doreen, actually," she said.

"Serious?"

She nodded with a delicate hint of embarrassment. "My parents are freaks."

I was almost afraid to ask her what her last name was but I couldn't resist. After she told me I excused myself, went downstairs to the men's room and texted her entire name to myself and Angela because (a) I wanted to remember her name in the morning in case we got that far, and (b) regardless, I just *had* to share it with somebody else: Maureen Doreen Dispazio.

Rich, as the fat old queen in the gallery might say.

Back upstairs at the bar I asked her, "So what brings you out tonight?"

"Honestly?" she asked.

"Sure. What the hell."

She crossed her legs and reached for her drink. "I'm *really* horny."

The next morning, Saturday morning, my cell phone rings inside the pair of jeans lying on the living room floor. I can hear the faint tonal beeping from my bedroom. The rousing noise reminds me in an instant that I am not alone. The eyes open and the head turns slowly toward the other side of the bed. There, Maureen Doreen Dispazio starts to come to life. I debate whether to get out of bed and see who's calling. I question myself if I'm going to make nice and take her to breakfast or if I should claim to have alternate, pre-arranged plans.

The phone rings again punishingly. I get out of bed, peering past the boxes sitting on the floor in Cal's old bedroom as I pass. In the front of the flat, I fumble the phone out of my pants pocket. It's Angela.

"Hi," I say quietly.

"How are you?" she asks.

"Fine."

"Where'd you go last night?"

"Bubble Lounge."

"Did you have a good time?"

"Can we talk about that later?"

"Ohhhh….you have company."

"Yes."

"Is she nice?"

"Can we talk about that later?"

"Of course. Hey, the reason I called—but it seems you're busy—Stuart invited us to have lunch with him and Carlos, the artist from last night."

"Oh really."

"Do you wanna go?"

"Eh…" I hesitated. Here was a perfect opt-out opportunity to avoid the commitment I had lingering between my bed sheets. But the offer itself—. "Not sure."

"Is your company a breakfast thing?"

"I don't know."

"Call me after you figure it out."

I picked my jeans off the floor and put them on, then returned to the bedroom. Just as I got to the door I saw Maureen Doreen sitting on the edge of the bed, her naked back facing me, her tousled head of hair turning in my direction.

"I, um—." Maureen Doreen bent over and picked up her underwear. She slipped them on and then glanced around the room. "Would you mind grabbing my bra for me."

* * *

Maureen Doreen and I grabbed coffee and a bagel at Caffe Trieste then we parted ways into the sunshine. I called Angela as I headed to the gym. She was heading into the office to put in a few hours' work.

"How do you know if you're a good lay?" I asked her.

"You mean me or you?"

"In general," I said.

"I don't know, you just know. Why? Did your date say something?"

"Not much. After we left Trieste she said, *'That was fun. Thanks, Hugo. Maybe we'll hook up again sometime.'*"

"There you have it. If she's willing to do it again you must have been good."

"And—?"

"What more do you want? Oh, hey. Stuart said he sent me an invitation to a recruiting breakfast for some start-up. He thinks you should go. I'll forward it to you when I get to my desk."

"Cool."

"I gotta run," she said.

"Shoot pool tonight?"

"Uhh—can't. But I'll call you later and you can tell me all about Maureen Doreen."

I stood silent at a street corner waiting for the light to change. "Who?"

"So bad," she said. "You are so bad."

* * *

At work on Monday I sat in my office reading the invitation that Angela had forwarded from Stuart. Geoffrey was seated in the chair across my desk looking serious and grim.

"Just go," he said.

"Got nothing to lose, I suppose."

"If he's all that and more, then I'd take mister what's-his-name's recommendation and go. Come to think of it, maybe I should get my lovely self over there as well. What day is it?"

"This Saturday."

"This Saturday?" Geoffrey stood up. "Girl's got to get her resume together if it's this Saturday."

That Saturday morning I met Geoffrey at the base of Four Embarcadero, a tall slender office tower down by the waterfront. He was dressed in serious Danville drag—khakis, a white polo shirt and navy blazer. I had to look twice to make sure it was him.

"What the hell happened to you?" I said.

"I may be fabulous but I'm no fool. How do I look?"

"Like you're going to the country club."

"As opposed to serving drinks in it? This is a white bread, *play the game* kind of get-together, Hugo Storyteller. A black man's got to set aside his fabulousness sometimes and put on his corporate drag if he wants to get ahead." He lowered his voice and his entire demeanor shifted down an octave or two. "This is one of those occasions."

I told him he was freaking me out.

"Relax," he said in his corporate voice. He flattened the collar on his blazer. "Let's go."

In a large office suite on the 23rd floor there were about thirty other guys and girls milling around drinking coffee and wearing name badges. A handful of scouts from the company were wandering around the grey-blue carpeted room chatting up small groups of potential staffers, smiling with exaggerated grins that paired perfectly with their pressed white oxfords bearing indiscernible insignia.

"Very Stepford," Geoffrey whispered to me.

I had some coffee, ate a danish, picked melon off of Geoffrey's plate. Then I started navigating the room. The thing about sales is that it's all about people. You find a target, introduce yourself, discern from a couple sentences what their needs are, then you hone in on their angst and seduce them into believing you're their savior. It's very basic. This event was weird, though. Everyone pattered around the suite of rooms reciting a list of all the places they'd been working at. Geoffrey, who initially stood around looking pretty and waiting for someone to come talk to him—at least that's what I thought he was doing—eventually broke open and started working the room, telling his own stories of professional transience in the same manner of all the other job-hoppers and techno-elitists he was competing against. I snagged the ear of one of the pseudo-suits—a member of the executive team, those guys in khakis and white oxfords with matching insignia. He pulled over the Senior VP of Sales. We connected. I gave him my business card. He patted me on the shoulder, shook my hand.

"Make a love connection?" Geoffrey asked when we reconvened near a picture window overlooking the bay.

"Senior VP of Sales," I said.

"Well done."

At 9:00 there were opening remarks from a suit, who must have been one of the venture investors. He was a tenant in the impeccable office space, whose every window overlooked the Bay Bridge, Treasure Island and everything beyond. He welcomed us with verve and a simple, self-effacing gratitude that was clearly intended to ingratiate himself to us while calculating exactly how much return he could get on the equity of our aggregated sweat labor. Following that spoke the CEO, freshly hired away from another startup, himself dressed in the uniform of khakis and button down white oxford. He was full of energy and enthusiasm, glad to see so many talented people in one room. He was seemingly more excited about the "ripping" culture that his new company had to offer than anything else, including the product. At 9:30-ish came a 20 minute Powerpoint presentation, an endless slide show of "where we were", "where we're going", "what's in it for you?", "get on board…!" and all the rest of that pseudo-speak that saturated the IT world. The fraternity-like atmosphere of the recruiting event and the near carnal enthusiasm of the CEO left me almost laughing, although it seemed to me that we were quite possibly at the ticket gate to a potentially lucrative ride.

That afternoon Angela stopped by my flat. I was sitting on the front steps staring at the tip of the Transamerica pyramid spearing upwards over the roofs of what used to be brothels, card rooms and simple shacks of the working class. Those days, those simple shacks you could barely touch for half a million; and if you did you'd have to rip out the plumbing and redo all the electrical.

"Hey," she said.

"Hey."

"What's up?"

I shook my head. "Gutting yesteryear." I stood up from the stoop and kissed her on the cheek.

"How was your recruiting breakfast?" she asked.

"Freakish."

"How so?"

On the walk home that morning a morose and tingling sensation had overcome me, like the kind you get from watching surgery on television. There was a cheerleading aspect to the recruiting event that had turned me off and was initially easy enough to discount.

Beneath that, though, there was some intangible, lingering, subcutaneous weirdness that I couldn't express.

"Hugo?"

"I don't know. The only place I've ever worked at is Screaming and these people have been at four, five companies—a lot of these guys not much older than me. I'm talking to the SVP of Sales and he's like, 'Where else have you worked?' I said, 'Nowhere…well, Kragen Auto Parts. But talent's talent,' I tell him."

"I don't think you have anything to worry about. You're good at what you do."

"You think so?"

"Well—." She hesitated. "You know, I'm disinclined to tell you this, but I will." She sat down on the front steps beside me and put her hand on my knee. "Stuart made a couple calls. You know that Samantha woman you can't stand? She actually has some decent things to say about you."

"What's he doing calling her?"

"Hugo, this is what I've been trying to tell you. If Stuart hadn't introduced me to Celia—it seems like almost no time ago—I would never be where I am right now. Not this fast."

"I'm not so sure about that."

"Listen," she said. "Stuart's a helper. If he takes an interest in you, just go with it. He knows a *lot* of people."

"So why's he interested?"

"Who knows. Probably because he cares about me and he knows I care about you."

I stared her in the eyes. "I think it's freakish that he would make unsolicited calls about me when he barely knows me."

She wrapped her hands around my throat as if she wanted to throttle me. "You drive me crazy sometimes," she said. She squeezed my throat and a tickling chill ran down my spine. "Accept. Assistance. Graciously." She kept her hands around my throat for a moment before letting go. "I realize you grew up an emotional orphan, but at some point you have to *engage* the world. Realize that it doesn't look like one of your cutesy Hollywood films from the 1960's."

"I resent that."

"Then you need to grow up."

"I'm fully grown up."

"You act like a twelve year-old sometimes."

"I resent *that* even more."

"It's true, Hugo. Seriously." And then she railed against my casualness, my *lack of intent*, and worst of all (in her opinion) my keen ability to enjoy life without considering how every single moment fit into some master plan.

I had no master plan. Intentions yes, plan no. My objective was to make a living. Nothing else.

"Hugo," she said, "you have talent. But you leave it simmering on a back burner somewhere while you wait for somebody to come along and take advantage of it. I'm not saying that every second of the day you have to ask yourself whether or not what you're doing is getting you closer to your goals; it's okay to live for the moment sometimes. But you can't go through life *never* asking yourself what you want to do with your life."

"I know I'm not using my talent. That's why I'm trying to get out of Screaming."

"Well then don't get all freaked out because somebody's trying to help you. That's just—. I don't understand these contradictions of yours. You're a talker, Hugo. That's what you do. Go talk yourself up. Play the game. Jump from company to company, if that's what it takes. Just don't settle."

Easy for her to say: Honors undergrad. Masters degree. "Fine," I told her.

She rubbed my back briskly with the palm of her hand and then stood up. "Do you wanna shoot pool tonight?"

"Can't," I said.

"No?"

"Going out with Maureen Doreen."

"Wow, a second date!"

"Not so fast...nobody's bringing a U-Haul."

-4-

EXERCISING YOUR OPTIONS

HugoSF

I moved to San Francisco in August of 1994, a twenty year-old Gen Xer from the flat corners of New Jersey looking to get away from a life that was demonstrably unintriguing. Growing up, I'd acquired the same lack of knowledge about California that most everyone in our red neck of the woods had. After spending many wilted weekends watching Aunt Alice's choice of Hollywood-hewn movies, I had pieced together a perception of a land filled with tranquil hills and rolling coastline that spread out like the cytoplasm of a cell surrounding a dirty nucleus, with smog-choked freeways connecting isolated communities of glamour and excess. In my California, quiet little towns dotted the shore, separated from the sprawl by an invisible divide. There, happy unemployed people surfed by day and fooled around into the night, causing no real trouble and achieving that penultimate state of grace: a satisfactory, unencumbered existence.

On one of those almost ancient Jersey weekends ago, Alice and I were watching Steve McQueen race through the streets of San Francisco in *Bullit*. I must have been around eleven years old because we were still living in the farmhouse in Buckshutem. I asked her, "Where's San Francisco?"

"California," she replied.

"I know *that*. What part? LA?"

"Well, there's desert and redwoods then the beach. Somewhere near the redwoods or beach I suppose."

"Ever wanted to go there?" I asked.

"San Francisco? Lord no."

A car flew over the crest of a hill and landed with its suspension rocking.

"How come?"

"Full of hippies and whatnot."

"What about LA?"

"Hush."

We sat watching our film. It was a Storm family classic rainy afternoon: Daddy working in his garage outside while inside scenes of California seduced me from the TV, a better life beamed in from a distant and far more interesting land.

"I *would* like to put my foot in the sand over there one day," Alice said, breaking a bout of silence.

That sounded odd. Desire was not a word I normally associated with Alice, yet here she'd expressed one—out of character, it felt—an untold need suggesting the sedentary winding down of a life lived in medium-hard work and forgone opportunities.

"I'll take you," I said to her full of optimism and belief.

"You do that," she said, and we slipped back into silence.

In my fictional California, life was easy and free from all boredom. Surely it was hectic for those in the movie industry, going from TV interview to interview, posing for pictures, shooting, working up scripts, haggling over cost and all the rest of it. But for everyone else it was a staid and manageable existence. Traffic sucked—true—but only inside the choking confines of LA. Contrary to Alice's opinions, it wasn't just "prostitutes and people makin' pictures" who lived in my California. I wasn't sure what everyone else did for a living but I knew that in my rendition you lived in simple houses in quiet neighborhoods; you squeezed oranges fresh from the trees for breakfast; year-round you took a swim in the pool after work because the weather was always warm. It was unexciting just as life in New Jersey was unexciting, except it possessed an indefinable nth dimension which made it desirable and unbearably intriguing.

"There a beach in Frisco?" I asked Alice during a commercial. Somewhere in my mix of smoggy and seashored images was situated San Francisco. I couldn't quite place it geographically or even sentimentally.

"Beats me," she replied.

Dissatisfied with our communal lack of knowledge, at the end of *Bullit* I rummaged around the house and found a US atlas in the back pages of a dictionary. I turned to California and found it to be cut in two: north and south.

"Look at this," I told her. I flipped back and forth between the two sets of pages. "San Francisco's here, near Sacramento…and look at all that up there above it."

"That'd be the redwoods," she surmised.

"Mh-hm," I said.

"Show me Los Angeles."

I turned the page. "Right here," I pointed to a sprawling blue mass at the bottom of the map.

"I'll be." Alice got interested in the layout of the state and started pointing out landmarks. "Look there: San Diego. Uh-huh: Death Valley—hottest place on earth. Imagine this here is where the produce grows." With her finger meandering over the vastness of the lower portion of the state, she muttered: "Who knew..."

I turned back a few pages to the map of the whole US. The map spanned the fold of the book, with the heartland states sunk into the crease of the binding. "Look here," I told her upon my discovery. "Here's Frisco over here," I said. "And LA's down here." Stretching my fingers like the tines of a compass I grabbed the two cities between my fingers and moved my hand to the East Coast. "Now here's us—." I placed my fingers on the book, with my middle finger resting on the little nip of South Jersey that juts out the bottom of the state like an appendix hanging off the intestine. My thumb landed down south. "And here's Carolina."

"Bout the same distance," she said.

"Mh-hm."

Alice looked vaguely bemused, almost as if she realized she'd been misled by years of misinformation. "I'll be," she said. Then she got up from the sofa and went into the kitchen to fix us lunch.

When I was twelve my father sold our place to a land company out of Philly and the three of us moved to a housing development up by Millville, not far from the arsenic-tainted bowl of land that held the aqua brown waters of Union Lake. Our farm in Buckshutem had been one of a handful of small working farms in the area, tucked amid the woods like patches in a patternless quilt. Since we had almost eighteen acres, all of it cleared and close to Road 55, "they gave us a good price," claimed my father. All of a sudden we were living in a newly built, suburban faux farmhouse in Millville, with neighbors within spitting distance and sidewalks stitching the spontaneous neighborhood together. Daddy worked in a wood shop in Vineland, then later he got full into construction when the town started revamping High Street. Alice kept house—and a judicious eye on the girls that Daddy dated. I attended a real public school with different teachers for different subjects, unlike at the small school in Goshen where it was a one-for-all kind of deal. In a short time it seemed like I'd been there all my life and that Buckshutem, land of my miraculous emergence, was somebody else's memory.

We moved to Millville in early '86. It was cold, rainy. Generally a lousy time to pack up and move. But that was the way it worked out: there's no managing time, only dealing with it, Daddy would say. For weeks the new house was full of unopened boxes. Nearly every bit of everything unessential was in a state of disarray. Alice and I set about emptying a box here and there when we had time, sorting things out and creating what sometimes seemed more of a clotting mess than a clean-up.

Lakeside Middle School, where I switched to in the middle of sixth grade, was neat and mostly clean, astringent the way public schools are, with broad windows on all four sides that allowed you a view of the woodsy flatland outdoors.

One weekday, maybe a week or so after we had moved into the new house, the students at Lakeside Middle all gathered in their respective home rooms to watch the space shuttle Challenger take off. It was the first time that a non-astronaut civilian was flying into space. The teachers were all giddy with excitement because Christa McAuliffe, one of their professional own, was that regular person. When the thing blew up a minute after take-off and the exhaust trail of the spaceship diverged into multiple streams of billowing white smoke, the room became a sea of hushed "omigod's," and "lord's" and the occasional "Quiet! Quiet!" from our teacher.

Those of us that wanted, or that our parents permitted, came home early that day so we could be with our families during "this difficult time." The school buses came by after lunch. Aunt Alice had given her permission, so I came home with the taste of a ham and cheese sandwich and corn chips still lingering in my mouth. The ride home was quieter than most. Once in a while a couple of the kids would mumble "wow" and "can you believe", while from the mouths of the emotionally disenfranchised came the occasional twisted utterance, *"cool, can you imagine?.."* as they envisioned a hurl of fire ripping the spacecraft apart.

When I got home Alice was sitting on the sofa, a large box beside her, flaps agape. She was slowly unwrapping serving ware we never used or some such suches that were wrapped in newspaper. Her eyes were glued to the TV screen absorbing re-run after re-run of the spaceship blowing up, her hands moving languidly as she unraveled household treasures and set them on the coffee table in front of her.

"It's crazy," I said coming through the front door, "huh?"

"H-shshsh..." she answered back.

After middle school came four years at the prison-esque Millville High, which looked like a modern brick church, low to the ground and spread out across a plain of grass that had been carved into what was once woods. The classrooms had only two narrow windows at opposite ends of the wall so that you had to beg the geometry of the place to allow you to see a tree somewhere out beyond. Basically you spent your days trapped looking past hairy ovate objects in front of you, lilting ever so slightly as they did from side to side at random intervals, as you tried to focus on the ceaseless rambling of the institutional little figure standing at the front of the room tapping the chalkboard with the tip of something (wooden pointer, chalk stick or pen).

"Now class..."

Practically overnight I'd gone from the open air of the farm to a glass box to a cinderbrick quasi-cage, unaware, until much later in life, that the nature of our institutions is to drive people indoors, into constraints, away from the land, forcing us to repress our memories of clear lakes and blue sky in favor of commercial spending and dreams of economic panacea, allowing us to reach back to the elements that actually gave us everything only on weekends or on government-mandated breaks. (And remember: don't spend more than ten minutes at a time in the water; don't get any in your mouth; wash yourself thoroughly afterwards so you don't get sick.)

But who could place any of that into a larger context at the age of ten or even fifteen? Back before the world unfolded, which would happen for me post-puberty, post-high school, post-arriving in San Francisco, to tell the truth...back before all that, my version of the world consisted of the Millville school district and home. One was filled with the usual assortment of pricks and losers and boring average people, a standard percentage of young girls destined for lives in trailers, and a generation of teachers with annually deepening disappointment in their eyes. The other was a place to linger and fashion stories about your life when the simple truth yielded nothing much to look forward to. My time at Millville High passed with such a blurring haze of three-ring binders and banality that when I try to think through the days of absent learning—the passive presence, borderline participation, boredom, the lack of context—I feel like the memory is going to choke me. It's as if life had been a corpse laid out in textbooks—history, biology and current events—words and pictures you could run your eyes over but you could never really touch.

Back there, things just were. Like the shuttle blowing up. The rule was as perennial as the rhythms of the farm: plant, tend, harvest, rest, replant. The past was. Today is. The future would be. Real life happened to other people.

But I'm getting ahead of myself, wallowing in bit of melancholic, future past-perfect reflection, when all I really meant to do was explain how I ended up in San Francisco.

[Regroup. Breathe in. Sit down. Relax.]

My father didn't have money to send me to a four-year college, so we figured early on that I would go to junior college and get an Associate's Degree in something. Then if I could work somewhere and save up enough money, we might be able to borrow enough of the difference to get me into a university.

"To tell you the truth, son," he told me during dinner early in my sophomore year of high school, just as the notion of college was entering my brain, "I always figured you'd grow up on the farm and take it over. I never figured I'd have to send you to college."

"Well, we got rid of the farm five years ago," I said suggestively, not wanting to ask him directly how much money he got for the place or why he hadn't started thinking about college during the interim, because even though he was mostly a nice guy he tended to get angry when anybody questioned his decisions.

"I know, son," he said with a strenuous grip on his words. "They gave us a decent price but there ain't much left. I had to buy this place so we'd have somewhere to live. I set aside what I could."

"Enough said," I thought to myself. It was clear from my father's financial malaise that I was going to have to take matters into my own hands.

The next day I went immediately to the guidance counselor to come up with an alternate plan of action. There were two guidance counselors at our school: one for the boys, Mr Clancy, and one for the girls, Miss—. Mrs—. Frankly, I don't know what her name was.

Mr Clancy was one of those men who defy description because they are unintriguing and descriptionless. They are the shape of most middle-aged men in America who sit behind desks and once a month go bowling or every weekend during summer barbecue hamburgers and cheap steaks on the grill. They are the simple-attitude, firm faithful believing kind of amorphous beings who, from way up high, probably look the way ants do to us: all the same.

Mr Clancy was a nice enough guy. He had a family (I think). A handful of picture frames adorned the tin credenza beside his desk. I took the people in those frames to be his family, unless he'd simply kept the sample photos that had come with the frames when he bought them.

He was also a bit of a pervert, but only inasmuch as his sexual perversities stepped slightly outside the bounds of traditional norms of intergenital activity and government-sanctioned forms of exploratory handplay.

Mr Clancy wore a butt plug.

Not every day.

Only on special occasions: half days; holidays; the last day of every semester; the first day of spring...milestone days. Days of great grace and promise, days we all looked forward to—kids, faculty and staff alike. These were days that were meant to be happy. And Clancy took out—well, installed is probably a better word—a kind of insurance policy to ensure that happiness. It was a five inch long, arrow-shaped (but softly rounded) wedge of black rubber that rubbed against his prostate. The flat base at the end of it prevented it from slipping all the way into his anus, a contingency designed to avoid unflattering and compromising hospital visits.

As fate would have it, it was a half-day the day I went into Clancy's office to talk about my financial situation. There was a Friday teacher's conference, which meant I knew why Mr Clancy was smiling. It gave me a grotesque gladness to see that cheek-lifting grin across his face, to hear the perkiness in his voice as he indicated that he was there to help me however he could. "Truly," he said emphatically. "Sit, Hugo Thor—."

"Storm."

"Storm. That's right. We don't see enough of you in here, otherwise I would've got it right. But what of it? Sit, sit. What can I do for you?"

It was nice to see somebody feeling genuinely happy about his work and the day at hand.

So I sat and we began our discussion.

I told him my lamentable tale of how my father was booted from our farm by greedy and cheap developers. I recounted the tragic death of my mother during childbirth, the forlorn financial situation we were in with regard to my garnering a higher education, and how it seemed that I was destined for a life pumping toxins out of the sludge at the bottom of Union Lake.

As I talked Mr Clancy sat there, slightly hunched, wiggling in his chair from time to time, trying, I imagine, to shift things around down there enough to keep it interesting.

"So what do I do?" I asked him with a faintly pleading note.

He sprang upright so his back was perfectly straight. "Scholarships!" he declared.

"What?"

"How are your grades, Hugo Storm?"

"Mediocre."

"What's your GPA?"

"2.1"

"Sports?"

"I ride a bike."

"Clubs?"

"I'm too young."

"School clubs. School clubs. You know: chess, debate, drama, language—."

"Um, none of the above."

"Hmmm." He began to rock ever so gently in his chair—not at great angles, mind you, maybe a few degrees forward and back at the most. It seemed he was trying to relocate his center of gravity. "You have to get out from under this mantel of underachievement," he said with great paternal authority. "You have to do things. Join things. Take a sport. Edit the yearbook. Scholarships require rock solid grades and a long list of extracurricular activities."

"Seriously?"

"It's early enough in the year, there might be enough time for you to turn yourself around so you can get a scholarship somewhere. It helps that you don't have the money. That's good: it demonstrates financial need. If you can wait a year and start college later than everyone else, that'll give you time to show three solid years of good academics and robust extracurriculars on your applications. Schools love that." He leaned forward with a secret: "On top of that, it'll give you a year to save up some money to spend on the coeds," he said with a wink.

I left Mr Clancy's office, half in despair at the thought of all the work I had ahead of me but energized at the same time. I passed through the glass door of the administrative offices, turned down the hall and walked toward the school library. There I flipped through a thick softcover manual of all the universities in America. Unavoidable curiosity led me to the section marked California and with growing addiction I ran through the list of names: Stanford, Berkeley, Pepperdine, UC, California State...I read the descriptions of their student life, their academic programs, their requirements, location, campus, et al. Then I pulled out the book on scholarships and grants Mr Clancy had told me to look at. I studied the requirements, evaluated the amounts of available funding, the timelines and process and all the rest.

I left the library and walked with newfound resolve to my locker. The half-day had officially ended so the hallway was quiet, save a few whispering cheerleaders and a lingering pothead or two. I opened my locker and looked at the chaotic mess of books and notebooks, clothing and scraps of trash. I brought order to the disarray, straightened my books so they stood tall and in decreasing order of size next to the notebooks and binders, which I'd neatly stacked with their spines facing outward. I gathered the trash and carried it a few yards where I flung it into the trash can. I went back, pulled out my light jacket for the ride home and shut the locker firmly with emotional conviction.

"I'll do it," I told myself proudly.

And I did.

I joined as many clubs as I could manage; studied my ass off nights and all weekends long. For nearly three years I busted my butt applying myself. Then I did as Mr Clancy recommended. I waited until the spring after graduation to apply to college. I had finished not quite valedictorian (because of my earlier grades there was no way to bring my GPA up high enough) and was voted "Most Likely to Succeed" and "Biggest Turnaround" of my graduating class. I filled out every scholarship and grant application I could find. I created a 2-color glossy pamphlet of my achievements that I sent along with my college applications, whose fees I paid with money I earned tutoring freshmen in biology. (Bonnie Hedglin's father, who owned the Print-o-Mat, made the color photocopies for me.)

And then it happened. Three months later: *"Dear Mr. Storm. Congratulations. You have been accepted for admission to the*

University of California, Berkeley, on the basis of your outstanding record of achievement and your disadvantaged financial standing."
Four years, three-quarters scholarship.
(Only three-quarters?)
Unfucking believable...
Unfucking true.

"Hugo—?" My father seemed annoyed.
"What?" I said.
"You got any ideas? Things you want to say?"
"Fucker," is what I wanted to say. Instead: "No."
"You're just gonna have to start out in junior college then see what your options are from there."
Such was the reality of my life.
In that reality, I would not sign up for clubs. I would not take up sports. I did not excel in my classes. I wasn't able to study all weekends because—I don't know, there were movies to watch, friends to hang out with, video games to play. I was not accepted at Cal because I never actually applied.
Destiny, even less enticing than it used to be—a patch of well-fertilized soil and cowfeed—was looking like vocational school followed by a job at the Vineland Superfund site.

* * *

A week or so after the recruiting breakfast I went to with Geoffrey, I was sitting at my desk. The phone rang. I answered in a disinterested tone: "Screaming. Hugo."
"It's me." (Angela.) "Any word yet from the portal start-up?"
"Not interested. The interview went well but they're looking for someone with more outside sales experience."
"Sorry to hear that."
"What's up?" I asked.
"I have good news."
"I could use it."
"Remember I mentioned Dede, over in Client Relations and Engagement Management?"
"Yeah."
"Guess who's got headcount."
"Serious?"
"She's going to call you to set up an interview."

"No way!"

"Yes way."

"Sweet." A smile spread across my face and I started looking at my stifling dwelling of a den as though it were the dingy leftovers of a soon-to-be former life.

From the office next door came: "Hugo!" Like sandpaper, Samantha's voice scraped at the cartilage in my ears. I closed my eyes and visualized an impermeable force surrounding me. "Get in here!"

* * *

This is the path. It looks complicated but it's very quick.

Bonnie Hedglin, the girl whose father owned the Print-o-Mat in the strip mall in Vineland, had a cousin who had a cousin who went to school at San Francisco State. (Bonnie's also the girl I lost my virginity to, but that's a different story.) The cousin's cousin was studying film production and was doing a short documentary on Superfund clean-up sites to see how far clean-up had actually progressed in the last 10 or 15 years; she wanted, in her words, *"to articulate their legacy,"* whatever the hell that meant. She vaguely remembered there was a site in New Jersey, and when she looked up information in the library she came across the Vineland Chemical Company site. She knew she had a cousin who lived in New Jersey somewhere near an industrial plant. She thought it was in Vineland but wasn't sure. It turns out that that cousin actually lived in Trenton. But *she* had a cousin, Bonnie, who lived near Union Lake, which is where, in 1983, when I was nine years old and just learning to enjoy the sensation of clear cold lake water on my skin, the EPA declared the Union Lake area a Superfund site because of all the mercury and arsenic in the lake's silt. So cousin called cousin called Bonnie. California cousin came from San Francisco and stayed at Bonnie's house while shooting part of her documentary film. Since Bonnie and I were friends—we decided after our first few fluid exchanges that we were a sexual disaster in the making and should aim for friendship instead—I saw a lot of California cousin and even got to watch her shoot footage with people who lived in the community.

That was kind of cool.

At the time, I was attending Cumberland Community College, which sat about halfway between the Holly City of America (our beloved town of Millville) and the Dandelion Capital of the World (Vineland, the next town north). I give Mr Clancy, the school counselor, some mental grief because when I was in high school I didn't feel like he'd helped me understand that if I was going to get out of my financial rut and lackluster educational trajectory I was going to have to work my butt off. However, he did give me one good piece of advice which, by some inexplicable but fortunate circumstance I actually heeded: "Take some computer science classes," he said. "Oddly enough, it looks like you might have the aptitude. It's a huge opportunity. Trust me."

I enrolled in some basic computer science classes at Cumberland County—logic, software design, beginner programming. They were foreign languages, basically, but I did okay with them. Okay, mind you—not great.

I was over at Bonnie's one day and we were in the TV room with Susan, the California cousin. We'd just finished reviewing footage she'd taken for her documentary and were jabbering about unmemorable stuff. Then she asked what I was studying at Cumberland. I told her and she responded with a big girlish smile, "Ohhh, my roommate Angela is studying that, too."

Yes: my Angela.

In an unrelated segue into nascent friendship she declared, "You should come visit. San Francisco's wonderful. In fact—wait." She ran into the guest room and returned waving a video cassette. "I have footage of us in Golden Gate Park." She popped it into the VCR, hit Play, and my eyes became instantly engaged by that angelic beauty I had always envisioned, dreamed of, surmised in my heart and groin but had never actually laid eyes upon—except, as in this very moment, in moving pictures.

There she was on the screen:

My Angela.

My California.

I just knew I had to get myself to San Francisco.

* * *

I was sitting on the toilet in my apartment reading the latest edition of *Wired* magazine when the phone rang. The sun was cutting in through the gaps in the plastic blinds, casting slanted strands of light on a data table listing share prices for the WIRX, a non-tradable index of New Economy stocks being tracked by the magazine. Outside, the stock markets rumbled quietly like precursors to an earthquake as the City waded in October's warmth.

The phone rang again.

From the kitchen I could hear my new roommate, Teresa, opening and shutting cupboards and drawers as she called out to me, "Hugo…Where do you keep coffee filters?"

And again.

"Teresa!—phone," I hollered nicely.

"Hugo—?"

"Christ…" *Wired* had recently created the index and already the stocks it was tracking were up 30% over the NASDAQ and near 60% over the Dow. It was fucking incredible. "Hey Teresa, can you answer the phone, please? I THINK I LEFT IT ON MY NIGHTSTAND."

"No you didn't—." I heard her answer: "Hello?…Hi , it's Teresa. He's in the bathroom. Who's this?"

There were footsteps down the hardwood hall. "Oh hi," she said delightedly. Her footsteps stopped in front of the water closet where I was sitting.

"It's Angela," she said through the door.

"Tell her I'll call her back."

"She said it's important."

"Tell her, please, that I'm preoccupied."

"He's preoccupied." she said. Then: "Okay then, I'll tell him…Bye…Call her the minute you flush," she said through the closed door. "Her words, not mine."

A few minutes of completion later, I stepped briskly into the kitchen and raised my hands in alarm. "I'm really not comfortable talking to people while I'm on the john."

"Don't worry about it," she said. "If you have privacy issues I can respect that."

"I wouldn't call them issues."

"Next time I'll take a message."

"Thank you."

"Did you call her back?" Teresa asked.

"Not yet."

"So call her."

"I will."

And I did.

"It's me," I said, "what's up?"

"You overbooked Wendy and Sam. They can't do kindercare.com *and* ubiquinet at the same time."

"They're not."

"I have it right here in front of me. You requisitioned them for a start date of Oct 12th for ubiquinet. But kindercare doesn't finish until end of this month."

"Since when?"

"Since last week's planning meeting," she said. "Kindercare.com was extended by three weeks because of requirements changes. You were there."

[True, I was.]

"So they can't be ready to start ubiquinet tomorrow, which is what you have in your work order."

"Can we prolong the design phase?"

"Are you kidding me?"

"Well, then, drag in a couple developers off the street."

"I'm not doing that."

"Fine," I told her. "We can figure it out when I come in."

"When will that be?"

"Half hour or so."

"Hurry."

I wanted to remind her that I'd just gotten home nine hours ago, at 10pm—barely enough time to eat something, wind down, get some sleep, then get up, shower, take a sh—. Then I realized she herself was already at the office.

* * *

Susan, the videographer, Angela's roommate, was kind of cute. [Yes yes, context. Back to New Jersey. Slow inhalations. Recall...] She had this elusive quality that was very consciously feminine and yet...not quite girlish.

"My God, Hugo, get your head out of the sand," said Bonnie. She insisted it was all too obvious: two young women in the park, one of them, a bit commandeering, taking video of the other one in coquettish, playful poses and book reading. The combination of factors all but guaranteed that the budding videographer was gay, and it levied heavy suspicion on her subject. I had done some math but never came up with the equation: Susan + Angela = 1 happy household. Matter of fact, the housewives in Millville, with their asexual haircuts and K-Mart fashions, looked more like lesbians than either Susan or Angela did. Nevertheless, I was captivated. I would find a way to San Francisco.

* * *

About an hour later came the moment to reconcile development staffing for kindercare.com and ubiquinet.

"What are we going to do?" Angela asked as the flags of Bank of America, beyond the window and across the street, lay limp against their poles in the still air of October.

"Get another developer," I suggested.

"We don't have time to ramp somebody new up."

"Sure you do. Get Trini from over at Screaming. He could do ubiquinet with his eyes closed."

"Trini?"

"Totally. He's a CGI freak."

She sat quietly for a moment as she pondered her options. "We don't have time to bring somebody in. I have to get headcount from Celia, then jump through all the paperwork hoops... And if he gives two weeks notice at Screaming then we might as well wait until kindercare is done and just use Wendy and Sam."

"Why not bring him in as a contractor."

"That's a thought."

"Do you have a spare cube?"

"There are a couple."

"Problem solved."

"How quickly can you get him in here?"

"Two days."

* * *

As a liar and a kiss-ass my skills were an exquisite match for the role of Technical Sales Manager at Thrive.com. Truth is, I didn't manage anybody. Mostly what I did was go on sales calls along with the Business Development Manager (i.e., Sales), the Relationship Manager (more Sales), Engagement Manager (ensuring future Sales) and, if a potential project was big enough, any combination of the VPs of those same groups (bend them over and feed them Sales). It was the other guys' roles to impress upon our neophyte and bewildered business clients the essence of why we were different from other boutique firms in the City and how we were so much better equipped than the super-high-priced agencies from New York or Silicon Valley. Once the BD, RM and EM people warmed the clients up to this, the Engagement Manager and I tag-teamed to eke out as much information about the project as we could in order to maximize the project bill...I mean, ahem, assure sufficient staffing for the job. Basically, I was a cog of internet protocol machinery that ran on the constant steam of hype-bill-hype-bill-hype-bill-hype…

Of course, the question begs asking: *Was I qualified for what I was doing?* The answer: *Not really.* The handful of classes I'd taken at Cumberland Community College helped ground me in the nature of software development but those few introductory classes constituted the extent of my formal training. I had fully intended to keep studying once I got to San Francisco. However, once there I realized there were three overarching priorities in the City by the Bay: rent, rent and rent. Education and play, although important contributors to a well-rounded life, came at the expense of paying to have a solid roof over your head. At the onset I was mired in the classic newcomer struggle: figuring out my way around town; convincing someone—anyone—that I was (a) reliable enough to hire and (b) capable of doing something, the *what* of that capability notwithstanding. For money, at first, I bussed tables at the Zim's Diner on Van Ness and made coffee in a café by the Panhandle. With my Fast Pass I rode the train and bus lines throughout the City, exploring the vales and hidden stairways of a place that was so extremely unlike the stale homogeneity of Millville that I felt like I had stepped into the fast-moving frames of somebody's TV show. Eventually I enrolled at City College in a web design program, which was an entirely new academic strand. Money was tight. Food was funded using a clever combination of manipulating the float time afforded by credit cards and "forgetting" to pay the utility bill once every couple months. This fiscal juggling act was borne out of necessity, since the only other option was the one so many of us chose when we first arrived in this exquisite if eccentric state within a state: communal living.

When I arrived in San Francisco to live, Susan hooked me up with a group house in the Lower Haight / Duboce part of town. I spent my first nine months in the City in a flat that had five bedrooms, a kitchen, a water closet and a bathroom. The fact that the toilet was its own private room was strange at first, but I got used to it and actually started to appreciate the solitary confinement it afforded me for those activities. Every room except the kitchen had been turned into a sleeping space—front parlor, back parlor, dining room, even the cold ante room behind the kitchen—which meant that the kitchen, a rundown shack of a room in the back of the apartment, was the only communal living space. Not pretty. My room was originally the second parlor, which had been shut off from the front parlor untold tenancies ago with a purely perfunctory plywood wall wedged into the old molded frame and painted an off-white. The side wall had a window that overlooked a shaft in between the two narrow buildings. The flat was cheap and it served its purpose well. It was crowded yet reasonably civilized, smelly in a not-too-disgusting way, kind of on the dark side, and constantly filled with muffled nighttime sex noises, laughter and the low whining of contraband broadcast music. (Headphones were the house rule, but hard to use and dorky if you're getting laid.) The tenants were mostly wayward young stoners with multiple piercings and tattoos. Think white chicks with dreadlocks. Artistic nevergonnabes. Kids with unspectacular backgrounds and questionable ambition.

Wild-eyed by the radical change in scenery and demographics, I found stability and safety in the company of Angela, who kept an eye on me and nurtured our friendship. We had met through Susan, who, after my constant prodding, eventually relented and gave me Angela's phone number. We met for the first time at Café Flore on Market Street and spent a couple hours talking. Somewhat unexpectedly, there was a synchronicity, that serendipitous linkage that occurs when interpersonal planets align. Angela and Susan had indeed been lovers but they broke up shortly before I arrived in San Francisco, after Angela had returned from some sort of language program in Spain. The change of scenery over there had opened her eyes to the reality of all the things she felt and knew but which her subterranean conscience encouraged her to ignore. "When you leave a place," she told me, "you start to see that place more clearly." For her, the place of difficulty was Susan: not the person herself but the awkward marriage of their lives, their forced interdependencies, the incompatibilities and their urgencies. The truth is, the two women were fiercely independent, and while they thrived on love and companionship they were inundated by it all the same. Angela assumed a mantra while in Spain: "Peace." It became her goal and destination, and although it sounds ludicrously unlikely given the madness of the Great Internet Boom—interminable work days, the capitulation of free time and all the corresponding time sucks and business drivers—she more or less managed to achieve and sustain a semblance of peace. "Spain," she told me one night at dinner in her bachelorette apartment in North Beach, "taught me peace amid insanity. It didn't show me the way but it showed me the destination."

I found my sales job at Screaming Software through Angela...no surprise. She was able to convince a friend of hers who knew Samantha, the Sales Manager, to give me a chance. Sick of the strewn-clothing style of living that I had in the communal flat, I quit my part-time classes and went to work full-time at Screaming. I hooked up with my roommate Cal by pure chance. To get to Angela's flat in North Beach, I used to take the N Judah train from Duboce then connect to either the Mason Street cable car or one of the Chinatown buses at Union Square. On one of my trips over there, I came across a For Rent sign and a phone number in the front window of a first floor flat on upper Grant Avenue. It was around the corner about a block and a half from Angela's place, on the sleepy edge of the 20-hour-a-day verve of North Beach.

North Beach is a triangular wedge of old San Francisco in the northeastern part of the City. It begins where the Financial District ends and abuts Chinatown for a number of blocks. The boundary is abrupt and yet oddly seamless. Like all San Francisco neighborhoods it is a world unto itself and an integral part of the greater community. It is a place where the fundamentals still matter: a plate of heavy pasta, gossip among friends, dodging dogs in the park, local politics, music drifting down foglit alleyways. After the Beats spent the 50s warming seats in Caffe Trieste and brandishing their poetry in City Lights Bookstore, the youthful focal point of the City moved to the Haight, where the antagonistic 60s culminated in an illiquid Summer of Love. During the 70s the Financial District got a high-rise facelift and the Castro become the locus of gay excess and indulgence. AIDS rained heavily on that particular party during the 80s and, as a result of its hard hit and progressive stance, San Francisco became further entrenched in its *outré,* one-of-a-kind status. Come the 90s, and pushing 2000, a new revolution had begun.

Living in North Beach, I was within walking distance of the battlegrounds of the internet revolution, as the old money of the Financial District fended off the SOMA-driven threats of the New Age. North Beach was close enough to be convenient but also insular enough to keep itself intentionally out of touch with the New Reality.

After a few successful months at Thrive.com, my life was definitely looking up. 580 California Street, home of Thrive.com, was a New Gothic high-rise office building at the intersection of the Financial District, Nob Hill and Chinatown. It was a 20 minute walk door to door from my uphill apartment, down through the curious shops and practical spots along the narrow corridor of Grant Avenue, then half a dozen blocks along the eastern edge of Chinatown. There at the corner of Kearny and California Streets, the doors to the building where I used to stop to meet or drop off Angela were now the doors I went through on a daily basis to my work.

* * *

The day was bright and lively; the City shrugged off its morning chill and offered a midday filled with robin's egg blue skies and serene warmth from the sun. People abounded on the streets of the Financial District, converging on every eating establishment. Windows were opened wide to announce the arrival of Indian summer, our great dame's brief affair with short sleeves before the onslaught of the cold winter rains.

A vibration went off in my pants pocket as I crossed the base of vertiginous Pine Street. Behind me, the low wall surrounding the Bank of America was lined with people, legs dangling over the edge, eating their carry-out sandwiches.

"What's up?" I said into my phone.

It was Angela. "I should know better than to try and plan lunch," she said tersely. "Tell Stuart I'll be a few minutes late."

"Will do. Where are you?" I asked.

"Embarcadero," she replied. "I'll try to leave in a few minutes. I'll grab a cab."

Meanwhile, I met Stuart at the front door of Le Central, a relic of an Old Media establishment near the Chinatown gate. He crushed my hand with his powerful grip. "Good to see you again," he said warmly as he ushered me into the cramped space by the maitre d' stand. He was dressed in a custom-crafted dark blue suit with flawlessly starched white shirt and a ribbony patterned tie. Inside, lace café curtains hung in the front windows of the French-styled bistro. The Ladies who Lunch, as Stuart referred to the wealthy women scattered throughout the restaurant, lunched there professionally. They threw wedding showers there and planned fundraisers and funerals there. Every Friday at lunchtime our stylish mayor sat in his power broker's corner, his fedora resting on the ledge behind him. The waiters wore white shirts and black bow ties; their aprons hung strapped below their bulging guts. The two rooms were separated by a bar. Back and forth scurried the suited maitre d', gauging turnover and rubbing palms with the regulars.

"Angela's running late," I told Stuart.

75

"No worries."

"Dr. Piers," gushed the maitre d' as soon as he saw Stuart. He held out his hand and the two men greeted each other affectionately.

"So nice to see you," said the maitre d', a man of slender stature and pronounced facial features whose off-fitting suit made him look rumpled and a bit impoverished.

"How are you, Abrim?"

"Very well, sir. Very well. How many are we today?"

"There will be three of us."

Abrim turned to the guest book, remarking to himself aloud, "I thought that—. Ah yes, here you are." He made a check mark in the book and turned to us. "I thought I saw you were only two."

Abrim led us to our table, a banquette in the front window on the left-hand side of the restaurant. As we sat, he asked Stuart, "Whom should I be looking out for?"

"A lovely young woman named Angela."

"Very well."

After Abrim left us there ensued a momentarily awkward silence as I sat across the table from Stuart feeling like I had nothing to say. The strong scent of disposable wealth in the restaurant hovered like a heavy cologne. I felt suddenly small and insignificant. I was clearly in a place that was out of my league economically, historically, culturally and stylistically. It felt like an attack on the complacency of my existence—the countless millions of dollars held in account by the small swarm of ambitious, well-swathed and completely made-up individuals holding court at their own white linen conference tables.

So I said to him: "*Doctor* Piers?" It was the only thing I could think of to say.

"PhD," he replied.

"That's a little rather queer, isn't it?"

We had both nearly finished our salads and I was on my second iced tea refill. After swallowing a bit of bread I continued on with my tale: "…We ended up living with Aunt Alice in her double-wide near the shores of Union Lake. Eventually my father remarried and he and his wife moved to Florida, where he sells emergency trailers to the government."

"They have any children?" Stuart asked.

"A girl," I nodded. "She's five."

"So you have a sister." He seemed pleased.

76

"Guess so."

"What about your Aunt Alice?"

"Sneaker wave."

"Excuse me?"

It was sad. Alice had always wanted to see California, I told him. So my Daddy flew her out one spring. They were up around Point Reyes—near the Lighthouse—walking along the beach. Daddy sat down in the sand while Alice went walking along the water's edge. Then all of a sudden—bam!

Stuart's eyes flared.

"Knocked her down, pulled her out. "

He leaned back in his chair with a look of alarm.

"She didn't have time to scream, it happened so fast. All of a sudden all Daddy saw was an arm flailing in the surf and a hard purse floating on the waves."

"Good God, Hugo, how awful."

"I know."

"Am I interrupting?" came a voice beside us.

"There she is," announced Stuart, seemingly glad for the distraction. He stood up and kissed Angela on the cheek.

"I am *so* sorry," she said.

"Clients?" he asked.

"Clients," she nodded apologetically.

"Don't worry. Sit."

The maitre d' pulled out the table and Angela slid onto the banquette beside me.

"They pay the bills," Stuart said matter-of-factly.

"Yes." Angela sat down and patted me on the leg. "Albeit painfully."

By the time Stuart paid the bill it was after two o'clock. The stock markets had closed for the day. A newcomer in the neighborhood was a guy we called the Wandering Wire. He had recently started roaming the streets of the Financial District just after market close shouting out the financial highlights of the day. He passed outside the restaurant, his voice booming. "NASDAQ on the rebound: 1546, oh-eight. DOW breaks the 8! Bull's got a running start at eight-thousand-one and forty-seven fractions…"

Inside the restaurant, sitting next to me, Angela folded her napkin methodically and patted it down eagerly on the table in front of her. She clasped her hands as if she were in church and set them on top of the napkin. She leaned slightly in and looked at both of us: "I have great news," she said with a grin.

-5-

THE GILDED VALLEY ABOUNDS IN FRUIT

On Tuesday I went in to take a shit and when I came out of the bathroom it was March.

"Can you believe it?" I said to Angela, who was standing at the entrance of my cube looking unresponsive and unimpressed. "March 1999 and we haven't made any plans for New Years." She looked like she was already in a different century. Her eyes were glazed over and you could see the endless processing going on in her brain behind them, she desperately wanting to shut it off. "What's up with you?" I insisted.

"Nothing," she replied. "Come on, let's go."

"Where to?"

"Industry Standard."

I was stunned. "You got an invite?!" The rooftop parties at The Industry Standard were *the* place to be on Friday afternoons. It was the peak of digerati chic. Usually you had to get in line and wait but if you were patient you'd eventually get in. This week's party, though, was invitation only. It wasn't for the *hoi polloi*.

"Celia got us in."

In an instant I logged off of my computer. "It's good to be snuggles with a friend of the boss." I slung my courier pack over my shoulder and stood up. "Be my date?" I held out my hand.

"Behave. Celia's going."

The Internet leveled the playing field among everyone—at least that was the theory. Standing on the deck of the Industry Standard building at the corner of Battery and Pacific, the ambient buzz was intoxicating and real. The social air was ripe with the smell of equal economic opportunity. You could see it condensing like spittle in the smiles of nouveau rich hipsters sipping wine and swilling beer.

Angela and I got there around five. The place was hip-hop happening, all the more so because the sun was warm enough to offset the chill of the spring afternoon.

"Don't drink too much," Angela said.

"Yeah yeah."

"It's a party but you're here on business. Celia will take your nuts if you embarrass her."

"*Let it go*, newly appointed Vice-President of Client Delivery. You are way too uptight these days. Live it up a little. Can't you see?...the gilded valley *abounds* in fruit."

"Melissa," she said with a smile.

It was music to my ears. So much so it drowned out the ambient tunes and chatter at the auditory height of the party.

She had raffish dirty blonde hair that fell to her shoulders and was uncontrolled enough to make it look totally inviting, like it was begging to be messed up just a little bit more.

"We got our first round about five weeks ago and we're looking to have a beta version next month," she said eagerly.

"That's fast."

"Gotta be, you know."

"What's your role?" I asked her.

"Product marketing."

"Cool."

"By the way, we're looking for a new agency," she said. "The one the VC got us is lame."

"Really?"

"We need somebody who can build a really hot promo site."

I produced a business card from my wallet and presented it to her with the elegant maneuver of a sleight of hand. "Look no further."

* * *

"Give her info to Marty, in Sales."

"How come?"

"Because," Angela said firmly, playing every inch the role of a member of the management team, which she now officially was, "there are rules and there are roles. Obey one and stick to the other. You're not in front-line sales anymore; you need to turn your leads over to the sales team."

"Fine. I'll give her business card to Marty in the morning."

Angela looked at the remnant shellfish in my seafood pasta dish with a determined eye. "You going to eat that mussel?" Without waiting she dipped her soup spoon in my bowl.

As I rolled my eyes I caught a glimpse of Franco, owner of Franchino, coming from the front doorway toward the table. "Oh, no," Angela muttered under her breath. From day one Franco had mistaken us for lovers. We tried to correct him early on but ultimately gave up in the face of his firm Sicilian refusal to yield. *"Bellissima—"* exclaimed Franco.

Angela raised her left arm. Franco took her hand and kissed it gently. "Nice to see you, *regazza bella*," he said in his ebullient Italianesca.

"You too, Franco."

I couldn't help but grin.

The restaurant was equidistant between our office building and our respective apartments. I lived at 1659 Grant; Angela was just around the corner from me on Greenwich, below the steps heading up the side of Telegraph Hill. Whenever she and I grabbed dinner in the neighborhood together we'd almost always end up at Franchino.

"Come è tutto, amanti? Eh? How do you like a that a seafood pasta?" he asked me, his breath heavy with the aroma of cigarettes.

"Good," I told him, "it's very good."

"Quello è bello che è l'amore. Nice to see you two," he said, his voice tinted at the edges with reminiscence. He patted the top of Angela's hand and called over to his wife: *"Josefina—."* He let go of Angela's hand and picked up our empty bread basket, which he lifted into the air with operatic lament: *"Per favore..."*

* * *

"How's your roommate?" Angela asked.

"Fine," I said.

The night was chilly. Fog was rumbling in over the rooftops of the buildings. People whistled for taxis. Laughter, music and traffic drifted along the narrow upslope of Grant Avenue as Angela and I headed home after dinner.

"You slept with her yet?" Angela asked.

"Excuse me!" I looked at her with astonishment. "What was your quote back there: rules and roles? Immutable rule number one: never sleep with your roommate."

"Just checking."

We arrived at my door and Angela kept on going without stopping. "See you tomorrow."

"Yep."

"G'night—," her voice faded.

I watched her as she passed the next few houses under night's umbrella then turned onto Greenwich, where she disappeared beneath a whispering orange streetlight.

* * *

"Hi, Hugo."

"Hi, Dede."

Dede was my boss Laura's boss, and the one who was ultimately responsible for rescuing me from Screaming. This was our skip-level meeting. The objective was to keep channels of communication flowing throughout the company, particularly outside of the normal chain of command.

Dede and I were seated in one of the mini conference rooms scattered throughout the floor. They seated only a few people in a close grouping of low plush chairs packed into a small space with a half-frosted glass wall. The objective of the tiny room was to allow people to bond in small groups and to facilitate casual discussions without disrupting the cube farm that occupied the rest of the floor.

"Thanks for meeting during lunchtime," Dede said. The light shining in through the clear band of glass set the tips of her red hair afire, to my eternal distraction.

"No worries," I said, looking her in her blue eyes. "Thank *you*."

Dede was a no-nonsense redheaded woman. She was notoriously domestic—she'd bake chocolate chip cookies for all 60 of us in the company when she felt we needed a lift, and according to Angela she could make fruit pies from scratch. She had the soothing voice of a southern aristocrat and was a stickler for wishing people well on their birthdays. But if you fucked with her performance or let vendors walk all over you during a negotiation she'd take you down.

"Your numbers are good," she said matter-of-factly.

"Thank you," I replied. At this brief period in the history of the business world in America, it was good to be cool, i.e., new and innovative. But for Celia, our boss, cool was only good if there was cold hard cash to go along with it. All promises of greater things aside, cash was king, and everyone who worked for her—Dede, Angela, me and all the rest of us—knew it.

"Are you happy here?" Dede asked.

"Absolutely," I said. "I really like Thrive. It's a huge improvement over—," I hesitated, then said, "where I used to work." Being at Thrive.com was about as *in* the internet mix as you could get. There was nothing to be unhappy about.

"Well, we're glad to have you on board, Hugo. Is there anything you want to talk about? Feedback on Laura you need to share? Issues, problems, concerns?"

Truth is, I had a litany of petty complaints about the micromanaging ways of my manager, but Angela had always warned me to overlook the little stuff and focus on the larger landscape. So I simply said, "No."

"Good, good. New topic." She folded her hands on her lap. "Laura will talk to you more about this but I wanted to mention it to you first. As you know, our focus is on delivering the best we can for our clients. However, as we look at the overall engagement we're seeing missed opportunities to expand our client relationships." Dede explained that Celia believed there was a way to extract more revenue from existing clients and she wanted me to pilot a test program to boost project revenue. "Celia's convinced that you'll be able to see opportunities that are opaque to other members of the team," she said.

"So is this something you want me to do casually—?"

Dede shook her head. "Oh, no. It's part of your new job description. If you want it. "

I was pleasantly stunned into silence.

That would have been a Wednesday, because I know I ended up in the Long Room afterwards. In order to keep the clan happy and well-fed, at least one day a week, Celia had established a policy of ordering lunch for the whole staff on Wednesdays. Catering might be too strong of a word for baskets filled with sandwiches, bottled water and snacks (sugar, salt, and starchy sweet energy bars), but in any event it was a freebie. It was a congenial bribe proffered to a group of people who were dedicating our lives to designing and building web sites, developing online marketing strategies, negotiating alliances, performing marketing research, or whatever else our roles were within the business cult of Celia's personality. We didn't have the amenities of other companies we'd been hearing about—foosball, on-site massage, cappuccino makers, all-you-can-eat bagels and fruit in the mornings—but we had what Celia liked to call our "family meal" once a week.

Thrive.com occupied the entire 16th floor of 580 California Street and our weekly lunch was served in the Long conference room, which stretched along one of the walls and overlooked the new brick of a neighboring building. It was not to be confused with the Short conference room, which was a windowless cave with conference table and eight chairs located in between the server room, where the computer servers and network hub were maintained, or the Timeout room, where one could take a personal moment of silence or pump breast milk.

There in the Long room, the matriarch thrived at the head of her pseudo-egalitarian monarchy during Family Meal. "Eat," Celia would command before bursting into praise over recent accomplishments—"Hey, how about that Gomez award for Ameribank!" *(one of our clients)*; "Nice job landing lumberport.com, Hal" *(a lumber exchange based in Seattle that resold lumber overstock at discount prices)*. Every week was different. Praise, dished out in genuine sincerity, was always on the menu, but equally there were expressions of disappointment when appropriate: "Too bad we missed our dates for Petquest..." *(some sort of online pet trading software)*; "Let's get our arms around improving (...*XYZ...you name it)*"... For all the occasional fluffiness and hardcore delivery pressures at Thrive.com, the environment was monumentally more gratifying than at Screaming Software, back where hi-tech met *Great Expectations* in a somber haze of indentured servitude. Here at least was a company striving to be fast-forward and, as much as that condition can exist in the workplace, somewhat humanitarian.

Angela cornered me, literally, in the corner of the Long conference room after my meeting with Dede. "You better say yes," she said sternly, just before biting into a tuna fish sub.

"To what?"

Her cheek protruded with sandwich: "The promotion."

"How do you—?" I retracted the question while she was chewing. "Never mind. Stupid question."

"Talked to Laura yet?" she asked.

"No."

"You will shortly."

Just then Laura arrived. She was five-foot-two and had been a junior teen gymnastics star in high school and then a member of the all-regions amateurs during college. A firecracker of a young woman, she appeared beside us almost out of nowhere, as if having just landed a double somersault at the end of a running vault. "Hi Hugo!"

"Hi Laura."

"Hey Angela. *March Madness*!" Laura squealed. "How about it?" Then she let out a *whoop whoop* kind of noise.

"Gotta run," said Angela.

"I hear Dede talked to you—," Laura started.

I nodded.

"Great." After a brief chat with her we went back to her office where we talked details about the position. With some trepidation about having to actually manage the deliverables of other people, yet not really having the option to say no, I accepted the new job offer, which was made sweeter by a modest pay increase and a healthy incentives package.

* * *

"Howya doing, Hugo?" my favorite waitress asked. It was some months later, after my new position had fully slammed down on top of me.

I looked up from my laptop. "I am *in the weeds*, Sandy."

"Busy, huh?"

"Swamped. How are you?"

"I'm doing great. You want the usual?—US fusilli, no mushrooms?"

"Yes, please."

"And a glass of house red," she added knowingly. "Coming right up."

Sandy was a curvaceous, stocky, blond-haired sweetheart who made everyone who came into the US Restaurant feel like you'd been her friend or favorite relative since childhood. US Restaurant was for me the way Franchino was for Angela: when I felt like having a sit-down dinner in the neighborhood, that's where I headed. The place was nothing fancy: a dozen or so tables, a fading mural of a Mediterranean fishing scene on the wall, dark blue carpeting, and an open kitchen lining the long wall opposite the mural. The floor staff there consisted of Sandy, a busboy and a middle-aged Italian host/owner/manager who ran credit cards and pulled espresso. Sandy was the reason I ate there on a regular basis instead of at any of the countless other Italian places that lined Columbus Avenue. She was the way your sister or your mother ought to be, someone who knows exactly what you need—not just what you want, but how you want it: chattiness when you're in the mood for talking and quiet when you needed some quiet. She was real life, genuine fresh air and smiles, as opposed to the cold bottled oxygen found in most of the other restaurants in pre-millennial San Francisco.

The intensity of my new job as an Engagement Manager was mind-fucking numbing yet the money was seriously better. I was liking the extra cash and I was able, for the first time in life, to save some money. (Angela told me early on, and I heeded her: *"Pay yourself first: set aside as much cash as you can every month."*) With the leftovers I could do things like go out to eat and hit the clubs once in a while. Finally, after four years in the City, I felt like I was financially surviving instead of only struggling to get by.

"Glass of house chianti," Sandy announced as she set the cup of wine on the table in front of me. "What're you working on?"

"A presentation." Celia had told Laura to have me put together an overview of the new inside sales role I was playing and how it fit into the overall engagement model for Thrive.com. She was going to present it to a VC firm that she was working with as part of her plans to expand the business. It was very hush-hush, and the only reason I knew what she was doing with the material was because Angela had told me so.

"I know you told me before," Sandy asked, "but what is it you do?"

"I'm in internet sales."

"You sell stuff on the internet?"

"No, I help companies build internet sites."

"Oh, websites, that's right..."

"Yes, basically." It was a dialogue I had frequently, especially with my father and his wife over lukewarm, disinteresting holiday meals.

"That's cool," she said. "I'll leave you alone so you can get back to work."

Next morning I stood in the grey-beige carpeted hallway outside Celia's office in the northwest corner of the floor. Laura arrived while I was waiting by the closed door. We had spent yesterday afternoon going over the outline, rearranging topics, striking content and deciding which graphs to use. By the end of the previous night, after working on the final touches while eating dinner, I had become saturated with the topic and knew every word on every slide by heart. Still, here was Laura, like my little mother, standing at my side to guide and over-protect me with a cheerleader's tone of insufferable enthusiasm.

The office door slid open, pushed outward by Celia's own hand. We had barely sat down when Laura started in: "We took one last look at it this morning, Celia. I think it captures everything we talked about yesterday."

"Thank you, Laura." Celia seemed appreciative but slightly irritated. "Good morning, Hugo," she said to me with a more engaging tone than the one reserved for my pesky boss.

"Good morning," I responded.

Laura laid a printed copy of the presentation in front of Celia, then handed me one. "Now—," she started.

"Purpose?" Celia asked pointedly.

"Oh yes, right." Laura smiled and looked quickly at us both. "We're here to review the updates to the Enhanced Engagement Revenue portion of the presentation you're giving this afternoon, which Hugo and I put together."

Celia nodded, glanced at the cover page of the deck and then set the cover sheet aside, face down and perfectly aligned with the rest of the pages. "Hugo," she instructed, "begin."

I walked us through the half dozen or so slides. We made red-lined changes here and there, fixed an oversight or typo or two—. "*Oops!*" Laura would exclaim at each.

All in all Celia seemed pleased with the final product. "Thank you," she said to us both after we reached the end of the deck. "Very nice work."

"We'll get the *final* final to you ASAP with these changes," Laura said enthusiastically. Then as she and I walked down the hallway to our zone within the cube farm she grabbed the back of my arm and squeaked in her most enthusiastic backstage voice, "Nice job! That went really well, Hugo, don't you think?"

"Five-nine, five-nine, five-nine."

She giggled like a girly girlfriend. I told her I'd email her the updates and then I veered off into the men's room.

Trini was in there leaning up against the edge of the counter examining his face in the mirror. He turned his face sideways and back, scrunched his nose and forehead, and when he caught a glimpse of me he stood back and started chuckling an embarrassed chuckle.

"Everything ok, Trini man?"

"Yeah yeah," he nervously laughed some more. "I was uh—. Nothing, just looking at my face."

"It's still there."

"Does it look any different?"

"How do you mean?"

He smiled widely, stretching his cheeks and squinting his eyes. "I finished the Western Bank project and got moved over to luvyourface.com." He pulled a narrow white tube from his pocket and held it out for me to look at. "At the project kickoff the business owner gave me a bag of samples. Most of them are for my wife but he gave this one to me to try on myself."

"Fringe bene's," I noted. "Cool. What's it for?"

"Prevents wrinkles in your forehead. Supposedly it's like Botox in a tube. For men."

"Does it work?"

"I can't tell," he said. "What do you think?"

"You look the same to me."

"I don't think it works," he declared.

"How long you been using it?"

"One week."

"Nothing's going to work in a week."

"They said in one week I would start to notice the difference."

"So get your money back."

"It was free."

"Exactly."

Trini shook his head. "Snake oil," he muttered as he looked in the mirror once again. "Do you want it?"

I shook my head, "Hell no," then went over to take a leak. "What are you doing for lunch?"

"I am building the product catalogue template." he said. "I want to finish it by end of today."

"Got time for a quesadilla?"

"Wel-l...I could do a curry."

"*Eh*. Not in the mood."

"How about the Russian deli."

"Russian?"

"You know, the one on Pine. I love their corned beef sandwich with the pink sauce."

"Oh, Krivaar," I said. "Yeah yeah, sure." Krivaar, an Armenian deli a few doors down from the outdoor European cafes along Belden Alley, had excellent corned beef with Russian dressing (what Trini called the *pink sauce*) and a creamy dill potato salad served with a tangy, crunchy pickle, a perfect hearty lunch that was best eaten with someone else who enjoyed it equally so you could both slather on about how wonderful it all was.

I went back to my desk, brushed through emails quickly, made final edits to the presentation and sent it to Laura. I then headed out for a well-deserved lunch break with my friend.

I suppose you could call Trini my friend. I hadn't given the topic a whole lot of thought really, not until we were standing in line at Krivaar. There, separately wrapped trays of baklava and meatballs rested atop the counter. A fat bald Armenian man with purely perfunctory facial expressions and two younger gypsy women in headscarves managed an endless stream of lunchtime orders in the tiny, cramped space. As Trini and I hovered near the narrow drinks cooler by the entrance, trying to stay out of the way of the dense crowd while waiting for our order, I started seriously thinking about the topic of friends. It was spurred by a comment from Trini that a good friend of his from Pakistan, Sameem, was coming over to the states on an H1-B visa to work at one of the big chip makers in the Valley. The excitement in Trini's voice was vivid and real. I thought back to New Jersey and realized that if Bonnie came out to visit I would have liked that but I wouldn't be nearly as glad to see her as Trini was to see his college buddy. There just wasn't anybody from New Jersey that I really cared about. I certainly didn't keep in touch with any of the friends I had growing up, and Bonnie and I rarely communicated. That was just my reality.

Trini and I took our lunch and we sat on the wall in front of BofA, on a low portion where our feet could reach the sidewalk and provide leverage as we maneuvered the tall sandwiches into and out of our mouths.

"Good choice," I told him.

He nodded agreeably, his mouth full and a grin on his face.

"Question for you," I said to him at one point. "Do you have a lot of friends?"

"Over here? Not so much. I have my wife. And we have our Indian friends: the other couples who we met after we moved here. They have become our friends."

"No buddies?"

"You mean like Hajad? Not so much. My good friends are all still in Karachi."

* * *

"I don't have any friends," I bemoaned.

"What am I?" Angela asked, pacing the quasi-lit and thumping corridor.

"I don't have any *guy* friends."

"What about Dennis and Fred?"

"They're drinking buddies."

"You want something deeper?"

"Maybe."

"Then quit being such a dyke-mike."

"A what?"

"A guy who only hangs out with dykes. It's the much rarer, male equivalent of a fag hag."

"How could you say such a thing?"

"Because it's true. You spend all of your free time with me."

"No, I mean how could you call yourself a dyke?"

"Ha ha." Angela glanced around in frustration. "I thought you said there was a restroom back here."

"It's right there." I pointed to a dingy white door with a faint cut-out of a woman's figure on it.

"Good lord. From this I'm supposed to discern it's a women's bathroom? It looks like a mobius strip." She barged in and nearly collided with another girl coming out.

"Hi," said the girl with a smile. Then in a low monotone after seeing me: "Oh."

Oh indeed. That was the worst part about going out clubbing: the awkward *Oh*.

Her name was—.

"Lost my number, yeah?" she said.

Angela smirked as the door drifted shut behind her.

"I, uh—SIM card died."

She nodded knowingly. "Mh. No worries. I think I accidentally deleted yours."

We both knew we were lying.

I wouldn't call it a pattern. Neither was it the first awkward *Oh* of my life. There had been a few since my arrival in that foggy Gomorrah of a place.

Case in point: Jane.

Jane was a plain but smiley girl. When she donned a baseball cap she looked kind of like a boy. But when she took it off she was *all* girl.

I met Jane one day at SFMOMA, the wildly brickish modern art museum with a zebra-striped central core.

Stuart had a couple museum passes which he gave to Angela, which she in turn gave to me because even though we worked for the same small company she was actively climbing the corporate ladder whereas I, dreamily ambitious but in reality not all that driven, was inclined to put in the mandatory few extra hours each weekend that the job demanded but that was it. My body required an occasional weekend of unencumbrance, which meant no laundry, no chores or any other sort of drudgery.

"Either of you wanna go with me to the modern art museum?" I had asked my two pseudo-friends, the aforementioned drinking buddies who had befriended me at San Francisco State during my brief tenure there.

Dennis was a geeky Nordic-like gadget freak who lived in Chinatown and had a head like a satellite dish. "Eh no," he replied in a condescending midrange monotone, suggesting that (a) art galleries were for the intellectually under-developed or (b) a fear that he might have to surrender one of his electronic devices at the coat check.

Fred, the pussy-chasing Cow Hollow denizen who almost never got laid, replied: "Do I look like your girlfriend?"

So I went alone.

I took the elevator to the top floor, intending to work my way down through the exhibit floors. In a corner wedge of the top floor was sequestered a multimedia exhibit: a long colonnade of squat white walls with TVs and other apparatus projecting out from their surfaces. Wires danced around the ceiling, interconnecting the technical devices in a seemingly random mess. An alienating mass of TV and computer monitors on top of the pillars scrolled indecipherable text and imagery across their screens. An audible shimmer of electricity passed through the hanging wires and it frazzled the air of the lofty room, filling the space with a beehive-like din. Some cryptic nonsense on a placard on the wall dared to describe it: *Radiant Persephone: Strings of the Outerworld.*

"Great title, don't you think?" came a voice beside me.

I turned to my side and there stood a girl with bobbed blonde hair and a heavenly smile. "What does it mean?" I asked.

"Well…" she started coyly. She ran her finger down the several paragraphs of impenetrable ramblings. "*A child shorn from her mother…dragged into the underworld. The hissing strings—*" she looked down into the installation and then pointed upward—"*represent the cries of the mother in search of her child echoing down into the folds of the newly fissured earth. Life distorted. Dissonant. Intertwined with outbound whisperings from either the fields of Elysium or the folds of chaos*—your choice."

"What do you mean, *My choice?*"

"Well it doesn't say '*your choice*'. I said that. Apparently it's up to you to decide if this underworld is a heaven or a hell."

"I don't know about the exhibit," I said, feeling roundly obtuse, "but I'd have to lump that text into the latter category. That was the biggest jumble of—."

"I'm Jane," she interrupted, seemingly untainted by my ignorance.

"Hugo."

"I admire your perseverance."

"How's that?"

"Most people don't make it all the way up here," she said. "Or if they do, they poke their head around for two seconds and then leave. They're usually too wiped out for the esoteric installations."

"I see. Well, I actually just got here. I wanted to start from the top and work my way down."

"Oh, you're backwards. I love it." She pointed down the passageway. "Shall we?"

Jane was a library scientist. An indubiously puzzled look must have rendered across my face when she told me what she did for a living. "I work with taxonomies," she explained. "Classifications, information architecture…" She looked at me quizzically to see if I was comprehending her. Frankly, the phrase *library science* sounded like an oxymoron and I was stuck on that: was there actually a science behind stacking books?

"Yes, there is," she said as we were lying around on my bed. The indefatigable lure of desire had led us back to my place after roaming a couple floors of the museum then having lunch in its café. My roommate was out of town on one of her parent-funded, Taoist vegan retreats so Jane and I had the place to ourselves. We had finished having sex. We'd cleaned off and were relishing that mischievous sort of post-coital Saturday bliss. I was lying on my back and she was crouched naked on her knees next to me, looking down at my semi erection. "But let's talk about something other than your *clearly* erotic obsession with the Dewey decimal system," she said. A navy blue baseball cap was resting on top of a stack of *Wired* magazines by the bed. She leaned out of the bed to grab it. When she put it on her head it gave her the appearance of a midwestern tomboy. "I never met a guy who could get an erection so soon after sex." She looked pleased.

"Is that the new topic?"

"It may be…" She grinned and knelt over me, straddling my legs and resting her butt on my thighs. In a slow, mannered and expedient mode, she rubbed her crotch up and down my hardening penis without letting it get inside of her. "There's something slightly different about you, Hugo," she said.

"Because I can get a hard-on so quickly after sex?"

"No, not that."

"Good," I said. "Because this is unusual."

"There's something…receptive about you. Most guys are pretty uptight. They're all bound up in their *stuff*. They're monochromatic. You know what I mean?" (I didn't.) "I think of guys like paintings," she continued, "like canvas stretched out on a frame. Most guys have a base coat and then a single layer of painting, or two if they're lucky, and then they stop. With you I get the feeling that you're willing to be painted and repainted and repainted, so that whatever people see in you is compounded by these deep layers of other existence."

"Really."

"Mh-hm." She brushed the backs of her fingernails up my chest. "I suspect you're layerable."

"Layerable?"

She lifted her fingers and slid her hips backwards onto my thighs. She started gently rubbing my balls with her hand while reciting the definition: "*Layerable*: Receptive to allowing oneself to attain multiple layers of meaning through increasingly varied and liberating experiences."

Then to my horror she slid her middle finger down between my ass cheeks and started fondling my anus.

Angela was the only person on earth who knew about my encounter with the bunghole pestering library scientist. I informed her that Jane was cute and that we had had good sex, and that I was interested in her concept of layering although not willing to surrender to it to the extent that she wanted to layer me. I listened to her openly, after recovering from the initial shock of having my asshole titillated, as she expounded her theory that the reason so many men are fucked up is because they refuse to accept the fact that their assholes are erogenous zones. That was tolerable, as it was merely theory. It got freakish, though, when she told me that she used to have a boyfriend who liked her to fuck him with a strap-on dildo, and she was getting turned on thinking about doing it to me.

"Wow," Angela remarked, as if a subtle endorsement.

I did try to call Jane again. Once. To apologize for ending our afternoon so abruptly. If you subtracted everything good about her, there was probably almost nothing bad left over. Unfortunately the leftover was a nightmare I couldn't escape: I couldn't date a woman who literally wanted to fuck me. So I never called. Naturally, I ran into her in Whole Foods one night after work. I was at the chicken rotisserie go-round, a circular warming station where the browned aromatic corpses lay in plastic warming trays. As I worked my way around the counter looking for a dinner-sized chickenette for one, who should I run into but—. "Oh," I said. The awkward *Oh*. This time all mine. "Eh, hi." Jane smiled politely and proceeded to place a chicken in her shopping basket before walking away without saying a word.

"Are we done here?" Angela asked after she came out of the nightclub bathroom.

"Yes, she's gone."

"No, I mean are we *done* done?

"What do you mean, done?"

"I mean are we leaving?"

"It's barely nine o'clock." We walked out from the dim buzz of the service corridor into the purple blue-black haze of the club at Minna and 2nd, a blended realm of Financial District suit coats and baggy SoMA cords.

"I'm ready to go, but stay if you like."

"Why are you in such a rush?"

"I'm going biking this weekend and I need to go home and pack."

"Harley biking or Huffy biking?"

"Huffy," she said with slight annoyance. "I'm going mountain biking in Tennessee Valley."

"With who?"

"Somebody new. I'll tell you more on Monday."

"Ohh…so it's a weekender date."

"It could be a Saturday day through Sunday brunch kind of date, yes." She winked and added: "We'll see."

"Did Celia approve your time off?"

"I approved my time off. A girl's got to get some once in a while."

I wished her good luck.

"You, too." She gave me a quick kiss on the cheek. "By the way," she added, "and I'm not supposed to tell you this, but the VCs really liked the material you put together for Celia's presentation. Repeat a word of that to anyone and I'll kill you. Now go make some friends."

* * *

In Silicon Valley there were myriad characters of varying means and intellect but none that was as revered, feared, envied, loved or despised as much as the VC. The Venture Capitalist. They scoured the region for ideas and when they found what seemed like a good one they stuffed the underneath of it with cash as if it were kindling and set the whole thing on fire. They recruited a management team then took over the Board and stoked the flames to their ultimate end, which sometimes included walking away to let the fire burn out on its own.

I'm downstairs in Neiman's Market, in the first floor of our building, waiting on my mid-morning bagel one day when this middle-aged, fifties-ish guy—clearly a VC—is standing alone in the register line. He's well put together, in good shape, has a light healthy tan. His hair is silvery white with streaks of black leftover from his youth. He looks like a well-dressed skunk. He's wearing black tennis shoes, black denim jeans and a long-sleeved black v-neck sweater with a perfect hint of white t-shirt showing through the V just below his throat. He's blathering into the voicepiece of his cell phone which dangles from a cord that runs from a small plug of plastic implanted in his ear down to the clipped phone at his waist. He's trying to doctor up a cup of coffee, get his change and do business on the phone all at the same time.

At the other end of the spectrum, and at this particular moment sitting at a café table in the back of the narrow deli, is the Wannabe Capitalist, or WC. A stark and unfortunate creature, his ooze is a bit more deleterious than that of a real VC. At quick glance he may look like an old school VC: the clothes are more or less orderly, the age is about right; he's got the phone and the headset and carries a briefcase. But then as you observe him closely you realize that the shoes are cheap—probably the only decent pair he owns, bought during a clearance sale at the outlets. Scuffs and scars hide beneath the polish and the heels are in need of replacing. The faint stripe of brown in the slacks doesn't quite jive with the fleck in the sports coat. The dress shirt is from back in the day when that style of button-down was worn with ties; it wasn't made for today's dress-down-tieless-with-attitude kind of style. The cell phone is a low-end device: free with any one year plan. The tone of speech is borderline manic and slightly confused. Usually what is said is a lengthy babble of modern jargon with little substance, full of desperate promises. What the WC attempts to do is cash in on this, his latest, his probably last chance of making it big in a world that operates on layers of unspoken rules and connections, networks from which men like him are ultimately excluded. As a consequence, everything about the man is slightly off, slightly wanton, slightly sorry. Slightly lost. "If I, we—if we can just sell a thousand seats," he tells his companion, a good- but stupid-looking beefcake guy in a charcoal suit sitting across from him. "That's what it's called these days," he tells his sidekick. "It's seats, not units. Units are for widgets and gadgets and pens and stuff. Software's all about seats. If I can just sell—I mean, if we can sell a thousand seats at 250 bucks a pop, that's a quarter mil. We'll get an office space downtown and there'll be VC's clawing at the door." The hunka chunk of dumb looks like a model who was dragged out of a locker room and shoved into a suit that was one size too tight, given a script and put on display for the sole purpose of eliciting that all-important erotic loosening of the wallet and other body parts. The WC continues eagerly: "You can be national sales director, man. We'll make a killing…"

"How come *seats*?" asks Tarzan.

Back at the register, the VC says into his voice-piece in a very salesy tone, *"They're working insanely long hours. It's a selling point, you know? They're into the work more than some misguided addiction to the medium, if you know what I mean."* Julio, one of the counter help, hands the guy his change. The guy flips a nickel into the tip jar—*"That's money in the bank"*—and the rest goes into his pants pocket. He picks up the empty sugar canister and waves it at Julio. "Hey! More sugar." Then into the air: *"They got product. They got major upside potential. And if they're each pulling in 60, 70 hours a week they got time-to-market nailed. Hang on."*

Julio hands him a full sugar jar and the guy in black empties a load of it into his coffee. As he goes for a wooden stirrer his earpiece cord tangles around the Styrofoam coffee cup. The cup tilts and starts to topple. The VC grabs the cup before it hurtles over the edge, preserving his Prada sneakers but soaking his hand as the cup regurgitates half its contents. "Shit fucker!" he calls out. Coffee splashes all over the box of Clif Bars by the register. *"No, not you, I spilled my goddam coffee."* Steadying the cup he shakes his wet left hand at Julio and says, "Come on, man. Napkins, a cloth—do something."

Down my way, the cute hippie-esque white girl who recently started working the counter holds up a small white package and calls out: "Whole grain wheat-free bagel toasted dark, easy on the cream cheese?" She flings it into a paper bag with a *ssschlap.*

"Mine," I take it out of her hand, and smile at her. "Interesting morning down here."

"New age white slavery," she grins. "It's the new black."

I nod appreciatively and fumble for a graceful afterlude. "I—um—been meaning to introduce myself. I'm Hugo."

"Emily. You work upstairs?"

"16th floor."

"What do you do?"

"Technical sales."

"Internet?"

"Yep."

"What about you? Well, I mean—."

"You mean, why am I working here? I'm a songwriter," she says in a confessional tone. "Unfortunately nobody pays us to find our creative soul."

"I guess not."

"You into music?" she asks.

"Eh," I bob my head sideways. "Mainstream stuff, I guess."

"D'you club?"

"Once in a while."

"Like where?"

I mention a couple dance clubs I'd been to, the bars I usually went to with Dennis and Fred.

"No live music?"

"I saw Dave Matthews at Shoreline this year."

"Hmh." (That didn't seem to do much to improve my standing.)

Days later I'm downstairs in Neiman's waiting for my bagel and making nice eyes with Emily.

She looks at a short line of tickets hanging in front of her. "Hey, Hugo," she says to me, "this says light cream cheese. You sure you want lo-cal?"

"No no. Easy cream cheese—easy, not lite."

"Lite's disgusting."

"Seriously."

She smears the bagel, wraps it in a sheet of wax paper, slices it down the middle, wraps it once more and lifts it up. "Bag?"

"Sure."

She drops the bagel in a small white bag and hands it to me. "Kill a tree," she winks.

"Doing my best." I thank her and turn to leave. I stop. "Hey," as I turn around. "Is there anything going on in the music world this weekend?"

"I'm sure there is. You interested?"

"I thought it would be cool if we caught a show or something."

"Are you asking me out?"

A soft breeze of excitement wafts through me. "Yeah. What do you say?"

She hesitates. I think she's toying with me. Then she smiles: "Sure. I'll check around and see who's playing. Swing by later and we'll make plans."

And with that, it seemed, I had a real date. It had been a while. I could hardly call my hook ups with Maureen Doreen Dispazio dates; those were hook ups. There'd been a couple one-night stands thrown into the mix as well...

"You actually bother to classify all of this?" Angela asked.

We were at Grant & Green having some beers and shooting pool—which was even longer overdue than my having a real date.

"Yes," I said in my defense. "A date has longer-term potential; a hook up is—a hook up."

"You mean, just sex."

"Right."

"And that differs from a one-night stand how?"

"A hook up has intent. A one-night stand just happens."

"Do you define all this while you still have your clothes on, or do you wait until after the fact?"

"It depends. No two are the same. It's like clients, babe. They're all different."

"I don't get it."

"Oh, please," I said to her. "You never hooked up with someone?"

"According to your definitions? I don't know."

"You never slept with anybody just once?"

"Of course I have."

"And never talked to them again?"

She hesitated. "Once or twice."

"So that's a one night stand. Now, did you ever hook up with somebody knowing it was just a hook up for sex and it wasn't going to go anywhere beyond that?"

"Well, that's—this a grey area, Hugo. Unlike you"—(I felt her tone of voice sounded particularly condemning)— "when I sleep with someone I don't just do it for sexual reasons. There's usually a deeper bond involved. One night stands happen by accident, but they're still a way of connecting with other people emotionally."

"That so?"

Angela chalked up her cue. "Sex is a bond, Hugo. Sometimes it's weak and sometimes it's strong. Regardless, there's a bond when you 'hook up' with somebody, even if it is just a 'hook up'."

"If you say so. Now, would you please shoot."

Angela surveyed the table. "I would *so* hate to be a perpetually heterosexual woman," she said. She bent over the pool table and sank a ball. Then she smirked: "No offense."

* * *

That Saturday rolled around. I put in my four hours of project planning at the kitchen table during the morning to avoid falling behind in my work. By lunch time I was eagerly awaiting going out with Emily.

"What's with you?" asked my roommate, Teresa, as I paced around the kitchen foraging for something to subdue my stomach.

"I'm hungry. And I've got a date tonight."

"No way."

"Yes, believe it or not."

"With who?"

"A girl who works in the deli in my building. She's a songwriter."

"Cool. What does she write?"

"I don't know. Urban—folk, funky ballads or something. I haven't heard it."

"Where you taking her?"

"We're going to hear a band at Café du Nord."

"No dinner?"

"Yeah, a Thai place on Franklin and Geary."

"Nice...spicy."

"For real?"

"If it's real Thai, yeah. Hotter than hell."

"Oh crap." I didn't do hot; I always maintained that my taste buds were pure New Jersey vanilla. A little pepper in something was fine; once in a while a mild curry...I shoved the refrigerator door shut and declared with frustration, "There is *nothing* in here to eat."

"Have a rice cake."

"Gross, no."

"What do you mean, gross? Rice is a staple for billions of people throughout the world."

"Good for them. I need something with flavor."

"Do you realize that you would die of malnutrition if you had to spend a sustained period of time in a third world country?"

"I know. That's why I live in San Francisco. The food options are endless."

"Except in your kitchen."

"Corner market," I said to her proudly. "Frozen pizza. Meat-stuffed pockets."

"That is so disgusting."

"Hey it's food. Millions of Americans couldn't survive without frozen food."

"It certainly keeps those in the health care industry well-fed."

"She quipped in an editorial tone of voice—."

"Yes, I am being editorial." Teresa looked at me as if I didn't have a clue—a not uncommon interchange in this sometimes self-righteous city. "Look at the cycle, Hugo: big companies manufacture cheap processed food. Poor people buy it because it's cheap. It's also unhealthy. They eat more of it, the companies get bigger, and so do the people eating it. They contract diabetes and heart disease, which lands them in the hospital or under chronic care as their diet slowly starts killing them. The cost of health care goes up. The cost of insurance goes up. The big companies keep making money off of the poor while the ad agencies compel us all to be thin and drive expensive cars and be famous. Yet poor people can't afford nice cars, so they get frustrated and eat more cheap processed, sugar- and chemical-filled food to make them feel better. But they get fatter and don't feel any better; in fact, they start feeling worse. Big industry gets bigger. The stock market grows. Big people get bigger. Models get skinnier. No-talent barflies get richer and more famous by being skinnier and richer than everyone else. The working poor have no money to invest in the markets and they'll never be able to own a house because the cost of everything keeps growing exponentially because one-twentieth of the population—the ones who can afford fresh food—are getting richer and skinnier while the other ninety percent are suffocating from the inability to pull themselves out of the downward spiral of failure-based economics." Teresa threw up her hands. "Go eat your frozen pizza."

* * *

"Geez..." Emily looked exhausted by my recitation of the kitchen exchange. "She makes a valid point, but it's just a frozen pizza for Christ's sake. Clearly she's never had to barter her health because of hunger."

"What do you mean?"

"I mean, she's probably never had to buy a ninety-nine cent burrito out of desperation."

"No, definitely not." Teresa was one of those people who always seemed to have money. At twenty-two, in college part-time, working part-time, there was always sufficient amounts of everything: rice cakes, party money, weekends off. There was never an excess, but courtesy of the mystery missal she received by snail mail every month from her parents, there was never a shortage either.

"Some of the most enduring liberals," Emily declared, "are spoiled suburbanites who can't comprehend the living conditions of the people they hold up as their suffering heroes. They've never had to experience being without." She tweezed a shrimp out of the soup bowl with two of her fingers and bit the pink body off. "How did you find her?"

"Craigslist," I said.

"Wow. Roommate roulette."

"You're lucky you live alone."

"Tell me about it." Emily went quiet, pondering the large bowl of soup sitting between us. "You know, it's like a pond," she said conclusively. Then she looked up at me.

"What is?"

"The soup. It's like you live on one side of the pond and I live on the other, and the more we talk the smaller the pond grows—the easier it is to reach our hands across the pond—like this." She had me lift one of my hands and leave it there. She very slowly moved her fingertips across the orange Formica table toward my hand, which hovered above the half-full broth of coconut milk, lemon grass and chicken. "Shrinking...shrinking...," she intoned as her fingers inched closer. She touched her fingertips to mine then she turned her palm face up and latched our fingers. "The distance diminishes," she said softly, holding on. "The wide gulf has been reduced to the familiar size of a soup bowl built for two. Bodies meet..."

I was starting to think she was a freak, yet her hand was warm and encouraging.

"I hope you like the music tonight, Hugo Storm."

"I'm sure I will."

* * *

"How was your date?" Angela asked.

"Good."

"Just good?"

"Nah, it was nice."

"Is nice better than good?"

"I don't know," I said. "They're the same thing. We had a good date."

Angela grinned, knowing full well she was rattling my cage.

"How about you?" I asked.

"Tamara's hot."

"You're back early. I didn't expect to see you until tomorrow.

"She had a public gathering to go to."

"Did you fuck her?" I asked.

"Excuse me."

"Did you," I begged correction, "make love?"

"Yes, we did."

"Was it good?"

"It was great."

"First time, *whoo this chick is wild* kind of great, or *oh yeah this girl's the one* kind of great?"

"Hmm…a little of both."

My nipples were getting firm thinking about her thinking back on her weekend sex with—. "Tamara?" I repeated wrongly, as in *tomorra*.

"Tamara," she said, "it rhymes with camera."

I flipped open the pink section of the Sunday paper. "Tamara which rhymes with camera. Did you make her come?"

"I am *so* not going to discuss that with you, Hugo Storm."

* * *

On that first Monday morning after Thai food and a show at Café du Nord, Emily made my bagel for me at Neiman's. I thanked her for a fun time on Saturday and she replied, "I had a good time, too." It was basically the same exchange we had late Saturday night (early Sunday morning) as we stood at the doorway to her four-story brick apartment building on Leavenworth Street and said goodnight. Then, we both agreed we'd had a good time. We both expressed interest in doing something together again. I kissed her on the lips briefly and gently. It was a polite kiss, filled with the warmth of genuine appeal but restrained in its intent. Then she went upstairs and I went home to my own bed to jack off and relieve the tension. On that Monday, the sense of obligation was strong as I took the paper-wrapped bagel from her hand.

"Is this awkward?" she asked.

"Not at all," I replied, truthfully. "You wanna do something this week?"

"Yeah, let's. I have a couple things going on this weekend, so maybe Thursday or Friday."

* * *

"Office romance," Angela declared ominously as we rode up the elevator.

"It's fine."

"For now," she warned.

"What does that mean?"

"What happens if things go south? What are you going to do then, find a new deli?"

* * *

Round about that same day or so, as the obligations of work consumed me and the only thing I really looked forward to was my second date with Emily, I found myself being stared at unforgivingly by Glynnis Hoffmeister over the tops of her black cat eye glasses (fashionable again after five decades for some God unknown reason). Glynnis was the Usability and Human Factors Manager at Thrive.com, my own private demon tormenting my own private domain. She might have been attractive had she not dressed like a dowdy librarian from the 1950s. She was only in her early 30s and probably, beneath the costumery, fairly pretty. Sad though it was, it seemed that the stylishly dressed, sexy businesswomen of the 1980s had evaporated or gone AWOL into the suburbs, and in their place arrived a dowdy set of also-intelligent young women who dressed, oddly enough, to reinforce their geeky stylishness and social chafe. Her bland decoration notwithstanding, I disliked Glynnis as a person and she disliked me even more. She was mean and unapologetic. She effused intellectual arrogance. She didn't know how to smile. Everything was measurable or a statistic, even human emotion. She loved her work but performed it to such an excess that she was unbearable to work with. I seethed whenever I knew I had to stop by her cube and talk to her or, worse, had to subject my clients to participating in one of her usability and capability studies: U&C, as she called it.

"Did you send me a virus?" she leered, leaning up on the toes of her witchy-poo shoes so she could see over the wall of her cube as I passed down the hallway.

"I sent you a Word file with my comments on the U&C for superthrift.com," I replied.

"It was infected with a virus."

"No it wasn't, because it worked fine on my laptop."

"It crashed my PC."

"So reboot," I said.

"Haven't you ever heard of antivirus software?"

"Glynnis, it wasn't me. So *let it go...*"

"I'm not going to let it go, Hugo. Why don't you be accountable for a change. You hosed my PC because of your technical ineptitude, do you realize that? I don't know how you manage to work with our clients."

"Must be my impeccable charm."

She lowered herself and said pointedly: "You are such an ass."

"True," I replied, turning the corner. I stood in the entryway to her cube. "Now, is there a reason you're on my calendar at 6:00 in the evening?"

"Sit," she said.

It was the most painful word in her vocabulary, the one dreaded by all who heard it.

I obediently sat.

Glynnis proceeded to sort through a stack of neatly labeled folders and then pulled one out that had one of my client's names on it in perfectly stenciled black letters. "Look at this." She extracted a slim report from inside and handed it to me. "Look at these results." She began to recite a litany of *mal* praise for a customization I'd worked on with a shopping cart vendor: "Facility: low. Intuitiveness: low. Procedural flow: poor. Help content: none. Accessibility: none..." She adjusted her glasses and shook the papers in my face. "Did you listen to anything I told you before you started this ridiculous bastardization?"

"They were in a hurry," I told her. "We built exactly what they asked for. They got what they wanted and they wanted what they got. Period. End of sentence."

"It's a piece of crap."

"That is true."

"It's unusable."

"That is probably also true."

"Have you even gone online to try it?"

"Uh, no. It was a hundred thousand bucks: in out boom done. And who cares. Their business model sucks. Their organization sucks. They got five million in seed money last August but they'll never get a second round because their burn rate is 125k a week and their product, their organization, their engineering...it all sucks. They're basically on life support. Believe me, they'll be gone in two months and this beautiful—bastardization, as you call it—will be forgotten."

"You don't get it, Hugo, do you?"

"Yeah I do. The work is done and they paid their bill."

"You can't just put crap out there."

"Yes you can and sometimes you have to. This was one of those times. Now let me ask you a question. Did we pay for the U&C out of our own pockets or did we charge it back to the client?"

"I don't know. But if—."

"Right. You don't know who pays for the work you do. So focus on your studies and your results. And don't schedule me at 6:00 in the evening to berate me with heuristics. This is my *quiet* time."

* * *

My second date with Emily was great. It was filled with all the effortless, non-mechanical interchanges that characterize early dates of people who are destined to spend some time together. I took her to dinner at a busy neighborhood restaurant on upper Polk and we spoke about anything that came to mind; there didn't seem to be a need to impress each other. Somehow just *being* seemed sufficient. It was all very get-acquainted kind of chatter—that slow harmless and interesting peeling away. She talked about her hippie parents in Santa Cruz; I told her about my uninspiring father and sensible, selfless Aunt Alice. We lifted some of the veils that guarded our souls without revealing too much. Outside of the noisy restaurant, after dinner, we walked past the bars and restaurants full of other people like ourselves—well, more like me; Emily indicated that upper Polk wasn't really her *scene*. "Sorry, it's a stupid word but my parents ingrained it into my brain when I was growing up." Nevertheless, she liked the food and said she appreciated the foray into (her word) normalcy. On the walk back to my car I held her hand and told her I found her interesting.

She stopped. "Uh-oh. *Interesting?*"

"No," I insisted, "that's good."

She looked at me and smiled. "Okay then, Hugo, I guess I find you interesting, too."

Back then, before I owned any emotional courage, while my mind was busy devising endless possible romantic outcomes to guard against what could only be called a hesitancy to commit, my deepest fear in life was not ending up alone. I feared women like Glynnis. What if, after an endless series of futile forays into attempting to attract women of simple tastes, strong affection, gentle hearts and practical shoes, I ended up having to barter my soul and share a bed with an arctic rock like Glynnis? I couldn't fathom it. I would acquire a tolerance for men if Glynnis was the only alternative, although frankly I knew there was no way I was joining the tonsil choir.

"Hugo?"

I let out a startled yelp. It was Glynnis, standing at the entry to my cube.

"Did I startle you?" It was obviously a trick question.

"Somewhat," I said. Glynnis had let down her hair and it wasn't alluring, it was, on the contrary, frightening. Her entire head was frizzed out like a witch's. All she had to do was smudge her eye liner, let her lips dry out, and wake up in my bed the next morning and my nightmare would have been complete.

"Do you have a few minutes?"

"Yes, but I have to leave at seven o'clock sharp. I have a doctor's appointment."

"Psychiatrist?" she inquired.

"Chemical castration."

She sat down in the spare chair in my cube with an armload of papers. "You're lucky I don't keep a journal of all the derogatory things you say around here."

"I know," I told her sarcastically. "I might get fired for *derogatory* harassment."

She glared at me with contempt but it didn't register in her eyes like a real emotion. It was more like a ray gun of meanness emitted effortlessly from a mechanical robot. "The ice you stand on," she said, "personally, professionally, and from the standpoint of basic human dignity, is dangerously thin, Hugo Storm."

"Point taken. Now what can I do for you?" Of course what I wanted to say is, *"Come closer. Don't be afraid of the light. It's only human warmth. You might melt a little bit but it won't kill you."*

* * *

"So *that's* Glynnis," Emily exclaimed. I was reciting the drudgeries of my encounters with my Thrive.com nemesis and when I described the human factors expert to her she knew exactly who I was talking about: "The one who always has a pen tucked in her hair? Oh my God. Onion bagel, margarine only, no cream cheese. She's a *witch*! I don't know how somebody can let themselves be so unhappy."

(I didn't either.)

* * *

One work afternoon in late spring, Angela and I were having lunch at the Chinese restaurant on the corner of California and Grant. It's the one that all the German tour buses stopped at. The food was surprisingly ok and affordable. You sat upstairs on the second floor and were surrounded by glass on two sides, offering a good view through Chinatown and down into the Financial District.

"We still haven't made plans for New Years yet," I lamented. "Time's running out."

"Better hurry up," she said disinterestedly. "This is a big one."

"What do you want to do?"

"I don't know, Hugo. I can't think past this week."

"Let's do something together. Unless you're doing something with your new wife."

"Possibly."

"Are you in love?"

"Please," she said dismissively, "it's only been three months."

"So what would be a good thing to do? Hotel party—? Tahoe—?"

"I don't know. Let's talk about it later. Please. I really can't think about it right now."

"Fine," I muttered. "Hot sauce, please."

She'd been hogging the glass jar filled with pulverized red chiles in a red-tinted oil. Looking somewhat stunned, she slid the jar my way. "This is *very* unlike you."

"I know." I dabbed a few timid drops on my chicken and snow peas. "Emily's had an influence on me."

"Careful," she said mockingly. "Don't overdo it."

We hadn't gone out to lunch together in ages. Now that I was working with Angela in the same company we saw more of each other in passing and less in time spent together. Our friendship seemed to be slipping. In fairness, though, we'd both been heads-down, working non-stop. I was tied up on multiple projects and had a headset talking noise into my ear nine hours a day while trying to oversee the work of teams of people and trying to schedule an occasional date with Emily. Angela was busy managing the entire development staff and navigating the newness of her relationship with Tamara, at whose Berkeley apartment she spent successively more nights. Our beer and pool outings at Grant & Green became fewer than ever and even further in between. There was no notion of *normal* or *consistent* outside of the bleary cycle of work-sleep-work.

"So what's up with this All-Hands Meeting?" I asked her at the Chinese restaurant. There was a staff meeting scheduled for 4pm that afternoon in the auditorium on the second floor. *Mandatory.*

Angela bobbled her head from side to side, chewing down a piece of kung pao. "If you tell anyone I'll kill you." She wiped her mouth with a napkin. "No, I take it back. I'll cut off your testicles, put them in a jar and auction them off on eBay. Along with a video of the actual castration."

"Sweet."

She looked around at the neighboring tables to see if there was anyone who looked suspiciously industry-like, then she confided to me: "Celia's selling Thrive.com."

"What?!"

Celia had built Thrive.com after vectoring off from a joint venture with her former business partner, Stuart Piers. Years before they had had a consulting practice that specialized in business process development. It was part Six Sigma and part Japanese influence with a bit of ISO certification thrown in. They worked together for almost six years before strategic and other differences finally ruptured their relationship. They either sold or dissolved the business—it wasn't clear—and moved on in separate directions. Celia founded Thrive, a marketing consultancy, to which she appended ".com" at the onset of the internet boom, shifting emphasis from traditional marketing to building online presence and promotional web sites. She located her company at 580 California Street in order to be close to corporate clients and to give her New Economy company a bit of Old World flair. Meanwhile, Stuart established The Swarthmore Group, a company that placed computer programmers and other professionals on a temporary basis for large corporate technology projects. Both were succeeding enviably.

"It's being positioned as a merger," Angela said, "but it's really a buyout."

"Who's she selling to?"

"I can't tell you."

"Come on."

"I really—. Well. If I tell you, you can not, can NOT repeat a word of it before Celia makes the announcement. Do you understand me?"

"Yes." I wasn't going to tell anyone; I just wanted to know. I liked knowing something other people didn't know. It gave me a sense of power.

"goFORTH," Angela said.

"No."

"Yes."

There were a handful of big agencies back then. goFORTH was one of them, with offices throughout the US: New York, Chicago, LA, Miami, Seattle, Houston. They had a decent shop in Silicon Valley but surprisingly no presence in San Francisco, so they were buying Thrive.com to strengthen their Bay Area position.

"What does that mean for us?" I asked her.

She shrugged her shoulders. "We still have jobs obviously; there's plenty of work. Culturally, I don't know how it's going to be. I assume we'll have to work harder to stand out. But I hear the options package is going to be strong."

(Cha-ching.)

I swore myself to secrecy about the merger. Angela paid the check. We walked the precipitous block down to our office building. To my litany of questions—*When will it take effect? Will I keep my same job? Are we going to stay in 580? Who are we going to report to?*—Angela responded with a distant, consistent, "I don't know, I don't know, I don't know..."

The staff of Thrive.com convened at four o'clock in the afternoon in the second floor auditorium, all muttering with curiosity amongst ourselves. I knew why we were there, though. But as I thought about it, a tiny fire of deceit quickly grew in my brain: how long had Angela known this merger information? Why did she wait until the very last minute to tell me, AND swear me to silence when the very same information was clearly going to be announced mere hours later? She winked as she walked past me to take her seat in the front row alongside Celia's other favorite managers. When the staff had all assembled Celia stood up in front of the room and announced with very little introductory comment that we were being merged with goFORTH "to strengthen our ability to deliver top-of-the-line brand experiences to a broader base of local and national clients."

Eh?

The room was stunned into silence and then a scattered gasp or two turned into a half-hundred hushed conversations muttered between neighbors. The transition to this "superb opportunity for each and every one of us," Celia instructed us loudly over all the voices, was scheduled to be completed over the next couple weeks. Our employment with goFORTH, though, would officially take effect on the coming Monday.

I looked at Trini, who was sitting next to me. "Monday?" We stared at each other in disbelief.

In an instant a familiar discomfort shot through me. I pulled my hand to my face, covered my mouth and breathed slowly into my hands. With my eyes closed and the soundtrack of the sea playing willfully in my brain, I strained to hold onto my breath.

3 PARALLELISMS

Parallelism # 1: Courting Emily

When the shock of transitioning from a small 60-person agency to a huge, national firm with over 4,000 people settled in—one never really recovers, one simply has to adapt—it became clear that life had taken an upside leftways turn. goFORTH was a high-flying start-up comprised of a vast pool of internet amoebas vying for attention while market capitalist power-masters asserted their superiority in conflicting directions. goFORTH had a client base ten times the size of Thrive.com's. They had deep investment capital pockets and were trading well on the NASDAQ. They had a can-do attitude which permeated their culture, at the heart of which was a near-obsessive emphasis on building up their client list at all costs. To me it resembled what I imagined our old Screaming neighbor Ascend was like (ironically they were now a rival), although goFORTH was on a serious overdose of steroids. In addition to the size issue, Thrive.com had been merged into goFORTH along with a couple other small agencies that had been gobbled up at the same time. The three merged entities, aliens to one another as well as to our adoptive parent, were thrown together into one space to become, instamatically, the San Francisco tentacle of the goFORTH octopus. Also gone was the central Financial District. With goFORTH it was back to South of Market. The sales and marketing group of the firm occupied half a floor in a newish office building at 222 Main, in a more 'uptown' portion of SOMA known as Rincon Hill, further from the gritty multimedia gulch and closer to the soft touristy and high-rise edge of the Embarcadero.

A new company also meant a new boss, which meant a new set of somebody else's priorities to suck up to as we all tried to figure out how to get things done in a bigger and more fractured organization. The guy I was working for was named George. He was a talented and self-aggrandizing sales manager who had a way of transforming dubious statistics and anecdotes into such fictitious tapestries of remarkability and allure that even I was impressed. He was a bit of a high-water panted near-relic, though, a pre-manopausal 50-something who could easily manipulate other men of his age into buying his wares and services regardless of the certainty of their need—the true hallmark of talent. He had a good five years of peak performance left in him, I figured. Pushing burnout, it was worth fearing him for the time being. George wore good clothes, probably expensive stuff he bought at Bloomingdale's, though he wore them poorly. He combed his hair in a conservative, Sacramento government style: boorishly parted on one side, cleanly raked with a fine tooth comb during every trip into the men's room. He was sort of an odd combination of mainstream and exception. His pants were a true oddity. His dress slacks always sat a little too high on his waist. When he wore a sports coat you couldn't really notice it but when he wandered the floor without a jacket or stood up to present in the conference room you couldn't help *but* notice it. He might've had strange body proportions hidden underneath his clothes; who knew. The consensus, however, drunkenly discussed at more than one happy hour outing, was that he was just a dork. A super-efficient salesman but a dork; icon of an era. One can imagine him on the Santa Cruz sand, a twelve-year old child at the beach, shirtless for the very first time in public, his Seventh Day Adventist mother berating him for the sinfulness of his appearance: "Georgie, why for heaven's sake, pull those shorts up above your belly button. It's bad enough you've taken off your shirt; at least for the sake of heaven cover up your navel." Turning away she would roll her eyes and add, guilt-ridden and ashamed for allowing her husband to endorse such a venture: "What a grotesque display."

Whereas at Thrive.com there was a grand total of 60 people, at goFORTH there were almost 60 people in the Marketing & Business Development group alone. I was part of the nascent San Francisco team, led by Georgie High Pants. In the transition to the new company I lost the majority of my direct selling duties and all aspects of engagement management. (I did not cry for the loss of the latter). The principals who were doing the direct selling had come from other offices with established client bases. There were three of them: one woman and two men—a shark, a closer and an ingénue. In that order. My business card said *Hugo Storm, Sr. Manager, Business Development*, but the title was nothing more than a glamorific for *Sales Secretary*. My job was to help the team prepare proposals and paperwork and to facilitate the initiation of new project work with the Delivery team. It was a bit of a demotion job-wise but the money was decent and there was nowhere to go, potentially, but up.

Meanwhile, Laura, my peppy former boss at Thrive.com, was moved to the Delivery group as part of the merger. She retained her Directorship and nurtured a near-orgiastic thrill at the infinite possibilities that lay ahead of her in this much larger, more aggressive land of burgeoning opportunity. Her boundless enthusiasm was endearing at first but would eventually turn her into a *persona non grata*, that annoying little pest you had to disinvite from every possible meeting so you wouldn't have to suffer her shrill exuberance over every micro enhancement to the HTML standard. Fortunately my interactions with her were minimal: I colluded with her team members to expedite delivery while she interrupted to point out my grammar mistakes every once in a while. At the same time, Angela and her newly expanded development team, Trini included, had been vectored off to an entirely different building, a large postmodern industrial space a few blocks west which had been designed for the engineering and creative teams and was built using dump trucks full of New Economy money. The physical distance between us, although not geographically great, enhanced the sense of estrangement I'd been feeling from her ever since the announcement of the merger of goFORTH and Thrive. Truth is, I was angry at her. She had withheld.

"Oh please," she said one day after I confronted her. "Do you think I liked not being able to say anything? It was driving me crazy."

"But you're my friend."

"And friendship and business are like this." She turned the backs of her hands toward each other. "They shouldn't mix."

Whatever anger I harbored toward Angela over news of the sale of Thrive.com was at least offset by strange new feelings of wonderfulness around Emily. I liked Emily. She had told me up front that she didn't want to go too fast, which was fine with me. "I like my freedom," she said. "I like dating. I don't want to get tied up soon." I agreed with her wholeheartedly.

Soon after the Thrive/goFORTH merger, Emily quit her job at Neiman's deli. The morning hours were becoming unbearable; sometimes she would stay up all night before going to work instead of trying to suffer through a shift on only a few taunting hours of sleep. Fairly quickly after that she found a job doing part-time merchandising at a head shop in the Haight and she started hostessing nights at an

Ethiopian restaurant in the Lower Haight. With our conflicting schedules we didn't see much of each other, which, in retrospect, was the secret behind our limited success as a couple. Things were fine. She had her freedoms and her refusal to commit, and she wore these things on a string around her neck like amulets. She harbored her allure in the folds of the long gypsy dresses and the loose gauzy pants she wore; it leapt into the wind as she strode the grimy streets of the Lower Haight, alighting from the tips of her wavy hair as she lured inexperienced men like me who were hypnotized by her motion. The woven belt around her waist kept us tethered together gently, and although it felt as if the connection could erode into dust in an instant, the tenuousness felt less like a peril and more like a loose bond of safety. With Emily, things simply were. And that was good enough.

Sex came late. It wasn't until our fourth or fifth date that I ever saw Emily out of pants or one of her long skirts. It was then when deliberate touch became permitted, when it replaced the incidental meeting of clothed bodies, which had been the extent of our physical relationship up until then. We were sitting on cushions on the floor eating Chinese carry-out at the low square coffee table in the middle of her studio apartment. Candles were lit and there was lounge music playing in the background. We sat at a right angle to each other and she grinned every time she introduced a question.

"Do you like your job?" she asked.

I told her it was ok. It was sort of lateral demotion but I was back in sales, which is where I belonged.

"So you like selling things."

"Yes. It's tactical and it's instinctive." For me selling was like seduction: you learned how to size somebody up quickly, figure out what turned them on, and then you went for it. You probed for their soft spots, their weak points, their feelings of inadequacy or desire, then you wove what you had to offer into a story that made them believe you could fulfill their needs.

Emily turned contemplative. She leaned back against the edge of the bed behind her and stared up at the peeling corners of the off-white ceiling. She then sat back at the table and stuck her chopsticks into the container of rice. "I know what you're saying: selling is seduction. But it almost wants to be reflexive, and that's—." She picked up a clump of rice. "I have trouble thinking of sex as a sales pitch."

The remnant scraps of dinner turned cold in their white boxes and our discussion turned toward society—me with my middling unstructured arguments, she with her brief rants that broke like howls against the walls of urban sidewalks before quickly disappearing back into the morass of noise and voices out beyond the window. Tired of talk, Emily pulled a case out from underneath her bed. Inside was a wooden, xylophone-like instrument that had nine or ten long, harp-like strings. "This is a *guqin*," she explained. "It's a traditional Chinese instrument. Can I play you something?"

"S-sure."

She turned off the stereo with a remote control that was resting on the table. "I'm into hybridization: urban sounds, unusual instrumentation...My music is different." Against the back wall stood a synthesizer with an abbreviated piano keyboard and a flat, deep casing covered with sliding guides. "I have to keep the volume down in here." She pointed upstairs: "Music haters." She made some adjustments to the synthesizer and a mid-ranged bleeping noise emanated from it quietly. She looked at me and smiled, then knelt down in a clear area of the floor. She closed her eyes and waited for the digitized harmony to send her brain into a trance. Once into the groove of the beat she began plucking at the strings of the *guqin*. It was the worst noise I'd ever heard in my life: like the steely brakes of a cable car choking hold on the cable that runs underground.

After a few minutes, she pushed aside the *guqin* and turned off the steady beat from the synthesizer. "Well?" came the dreaded question.

"It's very different."

"Exactly." She seemed pleased. "The idea is to invert the notion of what's beautiful."

Mission supremely accomplished.

"Don't get me wrong," she added, "I like beautiful music. As a songwriter I'm amazed by people's ability to create great songs. But somebody has to reflect the noises of life. We're living in a completely inverted, noisy, fucked up society. Everything can't be moving and pretty all the time, don't you think?"

I thought it was a rhetorical question so I sat there waiting for her to continue.

"Hugo?" She put the *guqin* in its case and pushed it back under the bed.

"O-oh—. I guess so."-

"Look at the internet boom: it's ridiculous. The stock markets are going through the roof. The media all claim that Old Money and tradition are under attack. But it's all a crock of shit. Nothing is being usurped. There is no revolution. If anything, greed is more entrenched than ever and the drudgery of making a living has only increased. Even worse, for those of us on the fringes, our once admirable if pitiable lives are compounded with shame because of our so-called lack of ambition." Her voice turned sharp with ridicule: "Not everyone wants to be an internet millionaire."

It was impossible to formulate a rebuttal so I asked if she wanted me to go to the store and pick up another six-pack.

"Stay here," she said. "We don't need any more beer." Resting against the edge of the bed, she pulled her knees up toward her chest. "You think I'm a freak, don't you?"

"No," I swore, and I was being honest—although part of me was starting to think that she and my roommate should form some sort of social commentary tag team. The hem of her loose cotton pants lifted up and revealed the tail end of a tattoo that meandered up her calf. "What's that?" I asked, as my attention turned abruptly toward the ink on her leg. Slowly I neared a finger. She lifted the fabric to reveal the long tattoo of a snake. "Wild—," I said.

"You like it?"

"Yeah." It was a thrill for me. I'd never gone out with a girl who had a tattoo like that. Usually they were innocuous bits of body art: hearts or Celtic crosses tattooed on a discreet crook in the back or on a shoulder blade; mini-piercings in the eyebrow or nose...But nothing like this. Here was a genuine, poodle-eating python twisted around the lower half of her leg. "Can I touch it?"

"Sure."

I knelt in front of her and traced the path of the snake with my finger, following the winding route toward the bend of her knee. I caressed the delicate muscle of her exposed calf with my hands and then leaned in and kissed her.

"Are *you* a freak?" she asked as she pulled me down on top of her.

"A New Jersey freak or a San Francisco freak?"

She laughed from her prone position. "I'm sure you're no San Francisco freak." Then she took in a long slow breath; exhaled. She smiled: "You know, I think it's about time—."

* * *

When I was sixteen I lost my virginity to my Bonnie Hedglin, back in New Jersey. Bonnie had big brown hair that bounced around her shoulders in broad discombobulated curls. We had been friends since middle school. We had classes together and spent a lot of time together socially but that was it. Always platonic. Until—.

"*Well*—?" pressured Bonnie as sophomore year came to a close and the lust of early summer descended on the Jersey hinterlands. "*What's it gonna be, boy?*"

Bonnie had gone from girl to grownup after 7th grade, around the time I started masturbating. I was hooked on the poster girls back then—all the hot bathing-suited babes. For boys, at least when you're still a virgin, there is a disconnect between jacking off and having sex. Sex is a sort of construct at that point—a social concept, or strange imagined possibility like *Star Wars*. Jacking off, though, was pure reality. The fact that the two could be synthesized, that the sensations of jacking off could be transmogrified into some sort of physical coupling with another human being, required a catalytic conversion inside the brain. For me, that switch took place during sophomore year. Christmas Eve, fresh out of church and hanging around in my room out of boredom, who should pop into my mind as soon as my dick popped out of my pants: Bonnie. At first I was mortified: how could I have lascivious thoughts about my friend? Was imagining penetrating her as much of a transgression as trying to spy on her in the girls' locker room after field hockey practice back in 8th grade? Would I ever be able to look her in the face again if I had an orgasm while fantasizing about her? There was a JC Penney insert from the Sunday paper shoved in amid the junk strewn across my desk. I flipped through it to try and get Bonnie out of my mind. It didn't work. It only led me to ponder what color underwear she wore and to conjure up the various means by which I would remove it.

"*Well*—," I replied to her proposition, hesitating from within some irrational state of ambivalence, surprised and yet excited that she wanted to have sex it with me as well. "*Sure*," I said.

So one Friday night in early summer after sophomore year, Bonnie and I drove out of Millville listening to Springsteen on the cassette player in Bonnie's mother's car. The shadowy two-lane streets that curved through the nowhere's land of Cumberland County were dotted with rural houses on either side, their lights emerging in loose clusters at distant intervals. This was the New Jersey that I simultaneously loved and wished I could wean myself of: the expansive, endless, thick stretches of woods that trapped you in at night yet in daytime opened up in magical spots to reveal sudden fields of corn or brisk, private lakes.

Bonnie turned the music up loud. "I love *Candy's Room*," she said of the song filling the car. "It's fucking brilliant!" she hollered as she accelerated.

We drove twenty minutes past Mauricetown down toward the river.

On the south end of town, well before the bridge, there was an old barn that had been converted into an Antiques Mall where folks from neighboring counties came to sell crap from their basements and attics. Set off of Highway 47 just a bit, there was a gravel parking lot in the back where you could park and not be seen. "This is it," she announced as she turned the car into the lot. She parked, turned the car lights off and then opened the windows to let the pale breeze in to dispel any amorous humidity. A dim light shone from the front of the old barn, giving off just enough hazy grey light for us to be able to see as we clambered over the bucket seats into the back.

"This is kind of cheap," Bonnie said deliciously. "Back seat, middle of nowhere…"

"It isn't cheap," I teased, "it's free."

"Ha ha," she said, loosening the back strap of her bra. "Now come on, Hugo, get romantic."

* * *

The lights from Leavenworth Street cast the silhouette of tree branches against the curtains covering Emily's apartment window. Where she lived, Leavenworth Street was lined with leafy green trees that grew up anxiously against the facades of the brick apartment houses. They were planted there on the sidewalks in uncomfortable closeness and the branches stretched achingly out over the street in search of breathing room. Emily's window was cracked open to let in the warm autumn air. Along with it came the constant din of automobile traffic heading up Russian Hill, punctuated by the noise of shrill voices, junkies, shopping carts and other droning foot traffic. It was as comforting and full of life as it was annoying.

Emily got out of bed and went over to her music rack. She pulled a CD from one of the shelves. "I've been doing some research because of you," she said.

"Oh yeah?"

She slipped a CD in the player and brought the remote control back with her to bed. "In honor of the New Jersey freak—." She got back under the covers and kissed me. She clicked a few buttons on the remote. "I've been listening to some vintage Bruce Springsteen." She clicked again. "This one is hot."

Candy's Room.

I went delirious.

* * *

"This won't be any zipper fuck," Bonnie announced. "I know you're a virgin, so I'm going to guide you along. You're not going to stick it in for a minute and then be done with it."

She pulled the t-shirt off of my chest and cooed, "Mmm, nice." At sixteen I had an okay body—nothing particularly outstanding, it was just average. If you spent any time down at the Jersey shore at all, which we did on occasion, you became keenly aware of your position on the anatomical scale. Mine resided somewhere around average. There was no *'wow'* factor to my physique, a fact that Bonnie gratefully seemed able to overlook. She, on the other hand, had a nice body—curves and softness, all of it a formidable lure.

"It's ok to touch me," she said aggressively.

* * *

The intensity of making love in Emily's room blended with the recall of Bonnie and me when, on a night not unlike that one, a piece of my youthful longing melted into beloved female warmth.

* * *

Either Bonnie pushed away or I pulled out of her. Sweating and panting, I could barely hold off.

"Wait," she cried, "I'm close." She rubbed herself feverishly and then cried out, "Ah!"

She writhed in delight and I thought she was going to spontaneously combust.

"Ah!" she cried again.

I couldn't hold off any longer. I grunted. I came on her stomach and hit one of her breasts.

"Wow!" she gasped, sweating, her breathing heavy. "Ah! Nice." She closed her eyes and squeezed my waist. "Fucking nice."

* * *

Emily blew out the candles on the stereo and turned out the bathroom light. Back beneath the covers of her bed she twined her legs around mine. "Nice."

* * *

True as it was of New Jersey, true it was for San Francisco: by day, life was tangible and real. At night, though, most of life became a mystery. Night was the carrier of loneliness, and no matter how closely you were intertwined with somebody in bed, night held you captive to all the stories that had been left untold in your life, waking dreams of things that never were.

For me, those untold stories revolved around my mother: What would she think of Emily? What would she have said if she found out I lost my virginity to Bonnie Hedglin behind the antiques barn? What kind of clothes would she wear these days? What would her hair look like? What would she smell like? Would she be a woman that wore a perennial smile or frown? Would she still be living in the farmhouse in Buckshutem with my father now, their shoes clomping on the wooden stairs coming down from the bedrooms as the aroma of coffee and bacon filled the sky and years of chatter about the same old things turned them weary—the difficulty of making a living off the land; things that were falling apart in the house; untenable things happening to undeserving people? Would she lay a hand on my back at night before bed and kiss me, or would she simply whisper good night and then disappear as she turned out the light? I drifted to sleep knowing that what lay beyond the night was anybody's guess, and everything that came before was unknowable. What was clear, however, was that my life seemed to have completed a full rotation.

Parallelism # 2: Taming Tamara

"She actually said to you, *'Religion is a dark energy'*?" Angela wedged herself into the mass of bodies on the bus.

"Mh-hm." I leaned against her as my courier bag indecently assaulted strangers with each jolt of the bus.

"Does she randomly say these things or was there an actual context?"

"The former." At least that was the impression I was getting: opinions were held; they were proffered; they were dropped. In Emily's defense, though, there *was* context for her religion as dark energy remark. We had been talking about different kinds of music and she brought up at one point how the Catholic Church thought in the Middle Ages that music was dangerous because the melodies could cause the devil to possess you, which is why they originally only chanted in church. Then later on, when they realized that music could be used to bring people into Mass, they started writing religious music specifically for religious rituals: "Manipulation for financial gain."

"I see," remarked Angela as she clung to the overhead rail. "And she told you all this before or after you...got busy?"

"Before."

"Nothing like a little religious foreplay to set the mood." Our morning bodies jostled backed and forth against other morning bodies on the crowded 41 headed downtown. Angela strained to get a glimpse of her cell phone. "She sounds like an interesting woman."

"She is."

"When are you going to stop hoarding her presence so I can meet her?"

"As soon as I get to meet your Tamara."

* * *

In the valley of low-hanging fruit one had to grab whatever success lay within reach, be it the quick technological win, the short sale, the big brand account, the demon's apple. Deeper, prudent notions of fundamental rightness fell victim to the short-sighted axe of time-to-market, which dictated that speed was king. This was the guiding principle for the work we did at goFORTH. For me it meant doing everything I could to ensure that we closed sales quickly. For Angela it meant driving her programming teams to the point of exhaustion. To some extent it was also a guiding principle behind personal relationships during that time of distinctly limited personal time.

One fine foggy day in June, our schedules coincided such that Angela and I were able to ride the bus home together. She had emailed me earlier in the day to ask if I wanted to have dinner: *"Tamara's going to meet us."* Of course I accepted—anything to return us to some variation of normalcy, and be able to finally to meet the infamous one. We caught the bus around 7:00 in the evening. The bus traveled through the Financial District and the onboard crowd grew as pods of working drones piled on at each stop. We sat and I kept on rambling, Angela scanning emails stored on her laptop, flagging some for action or drafting rapid replies to others, her arms scrunched up beside her and the screen tilted to minimize the view from peering eyes. I continued my perambulation on the skewed ethics of sex in an age of immediacy. The same was true of relationships, I suggested: expediency for the purpose of short-term gains: sex without commitment or promise. Dating was like being listed on the NASDAQ.

"That's a startlingly utilitarian viewpoint," she remarked. "A woman isn't a piece of fruit on a tree."

"No, but is there anything *other* than utilitarian dating these days? Who has time for a relationship?"

"You have to make time, Hugo."

"Whatever."

We soon sat down to dinner at Franchino, where, during the minestrone course, she asked, "So are you in love with Emily?"

"God no. Don't even go down that road."

"Relax, it was just a question." She looked at me from across the table with disgruntlement on her face. It was a familiar, annoying, and therefore reassuring look. In a classic Angela non-sequitur, she declared: "I don't know why you order seafood pasta when you don't eat the seafood."

"I do," I said defensively.

"Look at these clams." She retrieved the white-shelled creatures with her spoon and carried them over to her plate.

"Clams are for seagulls," I said.

She shook her head.

It was true. At the seashore, if you found a clam stranded ashore there were two options: one, you could throw it back into the ocean; or two, you could crack it into pieces, tear the stringy fibers apart and toss the shell into the air until it attracted the attention of nearby seagulls. The scent of slimy innards would inevitably bring droves of them. Whichever bird got lucky, it would grab the shell in its beak and take off into the sand dunes for a private feast. Sometimes the horde would dive-bomb you and your small cache of broken clam parts. Like a scene from *The Birds* they would descend on you in a torrent, chomping and squawking menacingly, tearing at your flesh, the least of which you could do was flee the scene before they picked you apart like winged piranhas.

"*Bellissima…*" A familiar masculine paunch appeared tableside in a snug, striped dress shirt.

Angela grinned. "Hi Franco."

"Your boyfriend doesn't finish his food again, uh?" Franco looked at me. "What's a matter? You don't like the seafood pasta?"

"I love the seafood pasta, I just don't like clams."

"Clams are good for you."

"Clams are for seagulls."

Franco motioned to his daughter to come clear our table. "You want a tiramisu now," he asked Angela, "or you want to wait a for your number three to show up?"

"We'll wait," she said.

"*Prego.*"

Angela wielded her spoon in my direction: "So? When do I get to meet her?"

"Well. Now that I'm finally meeting Tamara—."

"My God. Is *everything* with you a transaction?"

Tamara Lewis was an activist and social worker who lived in Berkeley in a rented apartment near campus. A Berkeley graduate, she felt compelled to stay close to her *alma mater* for reasons of intellectual security and for the professional connections it offered. She worked for a non-profit women's health organization that provided health care to the East Bay's uninsured women. She was also active in the anti-female circumcision movement and she poured additional time and energy into AIDS prevention for women of color. A decade prior, in her 20s, she was a whistle-blowing, lay down in the street, arrest-resisting member of ACT UP, then a militant anti-AIDS group. Driven by the death of her brother, whose terrible passing cast torrents of light on the complacency of her upbringing, she adopted a life of social struggle, immersing herself fully in the waters of engagement, committing herself to rendering difficult truths from other people's denials. Unlike a vast percentage of Americans, Tamara didn't live for days off; she lived for her work. For her, the two were indistinguishable. They were equal parts joy and strain, and each day she awoke with the same mission: to lessen the suffering of those around her by holding the greater forces of society accountable for the consequences of their actions or indifference. However, given that life was a round-the-clock event and anger was a force that was difficult to silence, Tamara immersed herself in her work continuously, and as a consequence found it difficult to escape the continual churn.

Per Angela: "She's in constant motion."

Tamara, wearing dress pants, white shirt and a basic navy blue blazer, arrived in a breeze of urgency and fatigue. "Hi, honey." She leaned down and kissed Angela on the lips. She introduced herself to me and we shook hands. She wasn't what I expected. Not that I was entirely sure what I expected. I think if you had said to me at that point in my life that I'd be having dessert with a die-hard lesbian political activist, I would have expected to see a short-haired woman with a gun-runner's torso and stressed out vocal chords wearing a set of blue jeans and suspenders. Instead there showed up a professional woman—not quite pinstripes financial, more of the non-profit attorney sort. Her hair hung down to her shoulders and was curled up slightly at the ends. Ironically, my own counter-cultural girlfriend, Emily, looked more like my vision of an activist than the businesswoman who'd just sat down across from me.

"Did you eat?" Angela asked her dotingly.

Tamara nodded. "We had pizza during the Board meeting."

"Mm, yum. Well, dessert is on the way." She turned around. "Franco—," she called softly.

"*Si, bellissima?*" He approached the table. "Ah. *Buena sera,*" he welcomed Tamara. "Can I get you something to eat? You want a food? A cappuccino?"

"No, nothing thanks."

"We'll take the tiramisu," said Angela.

"I bring it a for you now."

"Thank you," Angela smiled.

Franco returned shortly with a spongy block of tiramisu layered with cream and dusted with chocolate. He looked me in the eye as he set the plate down in center of the table. With a glance and tilt of his head he asked the question of the two women. I nodded my head yes. He raised his eyebrows with a tinge of disappointment but ultimately, one presumes, gladness. "Enjoy."

"*Grazie*," Angela said.

"*Prego, prego.*" Then he went outside and lit himself a contemplative cigarette.

* * *

Angela and Tamara awoke on a Sunday morning and saw nothing but blue sky and ocean from their weekend bed. Contrasted with the day before, in which fog had smothered the Sonoma coast and whispers of moisture dripped from the sky all afternoon, this Sunday promised to be sunny and glorious. Yesterday they had sequestered themselves indoors, playing Scrabble and watching *Indochine*; they even took an afternoon nap. On this exquisite sunny Sunday, day after their day of rest, they would walk along the beach south of Jenner, the Pacific waves whipping high, the sand cool, and from a distance watch sea lions sprawled out along a sandy stretch where the Russian River met the sea. They would lunch in Duncan Mills and wander through the train museum for all of the ten minutes which that activity required. In the evening they would drive to a waterfront restaurant in Bodega Bay that Stuart had recommended and have dinner before returning to his weekend house on a bluff, which he had granted the two women so they could spend a weekend alone, far away from the populations that made constant demands on their lives.

"You doing ok?" Angela asked. She stood at the kitchen counter pouring the morning's coffee.

Tamara was sitting on a stool staring out at the sea. It spread out in front of her as far as she could see. The reverberations of waves crashing against a colony of offshore rocks were carried along sound waves as moisture from whitecaps glistened along strands of sunlight. Sitting there silently, Tamara discerned that deep in the sea there was a constant pattern of chaos underscoring the rhythm: the rage of the formative graces that gave birth to easy, lapping waves could just as easily render tsunamis.

"It's difficult," she acknowledged of the anniversary of her older brother's death. Chronologically he was brother number two, but from the standpoint of importance and affection he was family member number one; more so than her parents, the simple but comfortable Lutherans; more so than her elder brother, the unaffectionate and greedy one; more so than her younger sister, who, after the tears subsided, would alienate them all upon becoming an evangelical Christian. Ten years ago to the day, Tamara sat in a hospice room sensing the life flowing out of her brother's limbs, watching as liquid from the IV seeped from his skin into puddles beneath his arms. She held his hand and watched as the morphine shut down whatever was still working inside him until a few final breaths snatched away the last filaments of his life. Her parents sat motionless on the other side of the bed, her father's face pale and unreachable, her mother's pink and sagging with tears. Her sister sat rigid in an arm chair against the wall while the elder brother stood within easy reach of the doorway and a well-timed escape. Afterwards, Tamara observed in her elder brother's obsession with his own affairs, in her younger sister's fear and in her parents' overwhelming sense of helplessness and lingering shame the same forces that she believed held society down generation after generation. In her rage against her family's submission she moved out of the house and took up activism against all of the issues that were deemed inappropriate for polite dinner conversation or, in her own case, had taken away her only true friend.

Angela and Tamara both knew that it was risky going away for the weekend on such an anniversary. As disinclined as Tamara was to taking time off—she preferred to work through her pains, as if that would erase them—she went to Bodega with Angela because she knew it was the right thing to do. She recognized the patterns of her own behavior, knew that when it came to herself and her needs and her feelings, when she claimed she was dealing with something she was more often than not actually avoiding it, stirring motion and distraction around her like the storm of water swirling around the outcropping of rocks she sat staring at. On the anniversary every year she allowed herself to confront the loss of her brother only briefly. In mid-morning, around the same hour that he died, she would put flowers on his grave then spend some time alone. Sometimes she would go for a walk through the redwood groves in Golden Gate Park, find a bench and cry. Sometimes it was a quiet lunch. But as soon as the private mourning was done the very busy Tamara re-emerged, and the pain that led her to her current practice was boxed away for another 364 days.

Angela stared at the silhouette in front of her and then approached. "You know, hon, nothing's off-limits. Anything you need to say—."

Tamara nodded appreciatively.

Angela handed her a coffee mug and sat down on a stool beside her. They sat quietly sharing their view of the Pacific. Angela knew and appreciated the value of this sort of silence. She understood that sometimes silence was a medicine. Silence had been used for many means when she was growing up. Usually, though, the menace of silence was scraped from the hard edge of words wielded during her parents' fights at dinner, which were a defining element of their marriage. After arguments with his wife, Angela's father would retreat into the silence of his den at the back of the house where he would pretend to read or pretend to pay attention to the TV, all the while letting the hard granules of the argument dissolve into an immaterial dust—that was his way of letting it go. Invariably, when he returned to the kitchen or whichever scene of discontent, his wife, after having let her anger simmer and grow in silence as she cleaned the dishes, hemmed clothes, prepared Angela's lunch bag for school, or whatever the chore, would erupt once more like a volcano and then, having spent herself with the final words of the fight, collapse into an armchair and return to silence or wrap herself in tears. That there was love underscoring those frequent rounds of strife, and the idea that two people so vitally different could be so vitally in love was difficult for young Angela to assimilate, especially as the night deepened and its corresponding mysteries blanketed her world in confusion. From the silence of her bed, when it seemed the house had finally returned to safety, she would say a tiny prayer that in the morning everything would be forgotten. She would ask for help from the unknown forces that she believed surrounded her and guarded her, imploring that when she got older they would never let her get involved in a relationship like her parents'.

Angela rested a hand on Tamara's leg. "You okay, hon?" she whispered again.

Tamara shook her head no and the tears flowed readily and abundantly down her cheeks.

And there, in a Bodega weekend house, where the passage of time made itself evident in the bits of rust forming in cabinet hinges, in the musty seaside scent of the rugs and in spreading cracks along the wooden deck, Angela forced a smile through her own evolving tears and wrapped her arms around her girlfriend.

Parallelism # 3: Remembering Ramon

Stuart Piers approached the front window of a small white taxi and asked the driver, "*¿Cuanto por el centro?*" The *taxista* gave him a price and Stuart nodded agreeably; it seemed a reasonable fare from the airport to the center of town. He climbed into the back seat and asked the driver to take him to a decently priced hotel—nothing extravagant, nothing too shabby. Specifically, he needed to be located close to the center of town, near to where his friend Ramon lived.

They settled on a peso range for the lodging and the *taxista* drove out of the airport onto a dark, fast-moving highway. The brassy swing of a *cumbia* tune swirled throughout the decorated taxi, its fraying undercarriage rattling like off-beat percussion as a strand of fringed balls danced along the inside of the windshield. Stuart's gaze remained fixed out the window on the star-saturated sky as they drove toward central Hermosillo, capital city of the desert state of Sonora.

The *taxista* told Stuart his Spanish was good and asked him where he studied.

Stuart grinned: "All over."

The trip to Mexico was a spontaneous one. He hadn't seen Ramon since the boy returned to Hermosillo for his father's funeral. He was supposed to be back in the States already, but after a failed and frightening attempt to cross the border near Tecate, Ramon had resolved to stay where he was—for a while at least. And since one of Stuart's client projects fell through it seemed an opportune time to get out of town.

Earlier in the day he had gone to the doorway of his business partner Celia's office and told her, "I'm going to Mexico."

She looked up at him with a blank expression. "Excuse me?"

"I'm going to see Ramon."

Celia may have rolled her eyes, or maybe she simply lowered her head toward her work while still looking at Stuart, thus giving the impression that she was bemused and perhaps disturbed that the good-looking, well-educated man standing in her doorway was off to visit a 20-something year-old migrant worker in Mexico. "Are you shitting me?"

"No."

"Where are you staying?"

"I don't know." In Stuart's mind you didn't plan; it was Mexico, after all. All you had to do was make sure you had a plane ticket there and back. This was before the advent of cell phones so he reassured his partner: "I'll call you with the phone number when I get there, in case anything comes up."

"When are you leaving?"

"This afternoon."

The taxi passed through Plaza Zaragoza, the town's central square, which was bordered by various colonial-era government buildings and the *Catedral de Nuestra Señora de la Asunción*, its white façade and sturdy spires illuminated in the night. The layout was the standard arrangement, indistinguishable from so many other Mexican towns yet somehow, as with the rest of them, stamped with a flavor uniquely its own. In the center of the plaza a bandstand was lit up for the evening and countless people milled about, absorbing the relief of evening's shade after a day of searing heat. A block off the plaza the *taxista* turned down a narrow street. He stopped halfway on the sidewalk in front of a small, shabby hotel, which seemed to be sweating off the remainder of the day. He told Stuart to wait there. He then got out and rapped his key ring on the metal gate that cordoned off the courtyard of the hotel. "*¡Hóla, buenas tardes!*" he hollered into the interior space. A woman on the brink of middle age came out of a room just off the courtyard. "*¿Hay alguna habitacion libre?*" the *taxista* asked her.

"*Nada mas una,*" she replied, wiping her hands on a dish towel.

No longer a *señorita*, having willed away her youth with marriage and round-the-clock responsibilities, as a *señora* she still possessed a beautiful head of straight black hair and the remnants of a once-alluring figure. Time was her keeper now. She unlocked the gate. She propped it open with her elbow and pointed inside. The only available room, she informed them, was the front room, there on the first floor, just in front of the gate.

Stuart got out of the taxi and pulled his small suitcase off the seat. He opened the door to the hotel room and looked into the drab compartment. The toilet and shower were in the far corner on the other side of the bed, separated only by a plastic curtain. There was water on the floor and towels were tossed onto a single wooden chair, which offered the only seating in the room. There was a passable piece of furniture that supported an old TV with rabbit ear antennas. Above it, a narrow sliding window with bars sat high and fronted the street. The bed looked perfectly perfunctory, although it had recently been used and remained unmade.

"*Acaba de irse una pareja,*" she explained. She would clean up the place from its recent tenants and get fresh towels if Stuart wanted it.

"*¿Cuanto vale?*"

"*Cuatro cientos por noche.*"

He shrugged, feeling a sense of adventure overruling his ordinary demands for comfort. For $40 he could walk easily to the *zócalo* for dinner and come back and get a decent night's sleep. In the morning he would scout for a new hotel before connecting with Ramon. "*Bueno, ya lo compro.*" Stuart paid the *taxista* and thanked him. As the *taxista* drove away, the woman locked the gate behind them and Stuart followed her into the drab courtyard. She told him to wait by a stand of potted geraniums while she cleaned the room.

All night long *taxistas* pulled up to the front of the hotel in search of a room. They parked and got out of their cars then rattled the gate next to Stuart's room and hollered into the interior courtyard, "*¡Hola buenas noches! ¿Tiene cuartos?*" Stuart stirred in his bed with each loud rapping and clanking of the *taxistas*. He buried his head under the thin pillows and when he awoke around nine o'clock the next morning he was exhausted from lack of sleep.

After breakfast at a café by the plaza he called Ramon from a public telephone. A woman answered, presumably Ramon's mother. Stuart asked to speak with him. "*No te cuelgas.*" She set the phone down and her voice echoed through a few small rooms on the other end of the phone: "*¡Ramon!*" Stuart could hear a young man's voice in the background followed by footsteps. "*¿Bueno?*" he said excitedly into the receiver.

They had first met at the Brave Bull, the oldest and one of the very few gay clubs in California's Central Valley. Stuart was 33; Ramon was 21. A big burgundy-red building slapped down next to a convenience store, the Brave Bull was an anachronism of place and cultures, defiant in its existence among the condescending white Republicanism of the land and the overlay of strong Hispanic Catholicism. It was a persistent reminder that the Americas are a land of numerous flavors, not all of which are to everyone's liking.

There were two young men sitting on the edge of a pickup truck bed smoking cigarettes when Stuart pulled into the gravel parking lot that night. As Stuart locked his car, the boy on the right said to his friend in a loud voice obviously intended for Stuart's ear: *"Ay guapissimo."* He whistled lasciviously and called out, *!Hola papí! ¿Tiene amigo?"*

"No chico, estoy solo," Stuart told them as he approached their truck.

The one who was doing the talking hopped down from the edge of the truck and flicked his cigarette onto the gravel. *"Perfecto."* He was the older of the two, lankier, and his face brimmed with sexual loneliness and desire. *"Es happy hour—dos por uno."* He put a slender arm around Stuart's waist. "Two for one, *papichulo.*"

Stuart grinned then turned his gaze toward the boy who was sitting quietly on the tailgate of the truck. He had a round angelic face, descended from centuries of native people and mixed with the diluting blood of the Spaniards. Everything about him seethed with preternatural seduction as a sky full of stars glittered above the California heartland.

He hopped down off of the truck.

His name was Ramon. He was a sturdy young man whose quiet demeanor belied the complicated heritage of his condition. Ramon was an emblem of generations of men who had come to the United States in order to find something unavailable to them in their homelands; and yet instead of angry rebellion they offered a capitulatory peace. Ramon had been in the States since he was 15, living first in Arizona and then moving to California and the Central Valley, where he traveled the mid-section of the state harvesting produce and doing construction work in order to take care of himself and send money back to his parents in Hermosillo. He knew hard work. He knew loneliness. He knew isolation and he knew how to make himself invisible. He believed that people followed the path God led them on, the way *Jesucristo* was led down the path of the Stations of the Cross. He believed that God could just as easily put a good looking *guero* in his path one night as he could cause the rain to fall unceasingly, making it difficult to find work in the following days. In Ramon's eyes all things were equal: God gives; man responds.

He approached Stuart. He lifted his eyes and said, *"Hablas bien, papí. Wha's* your name?"

Inside the bar they drank a few beers and each had a shot of tequila. They spoke in a clumsy Spanglish mix until they switched over entirely to Spanish. Leaving the friend behind, they spent the night at the EconoLodge on the highway and the next morning went their separate ways: Stuart back to his exclusive condominium in the City, Ramon to his migrant housing near an almond orchard. Months later, worn from the physical strain of his work and wary of a future filled with dodging agricultural machinery like the one that had caught his shirt sleeve at an artichoke farm near Salinas and without the intervention of a worker named Tio would have taken off his arm, Ramon moved to the city of Oakland and found a job bussing tables. The bayside restaurant where he worked had a view of the San Francisco skyline and was only a forty minute walk and bus ride from the downtown apartment he shared with an effeminate boy called Miguelita.

Some further months later, on one of his ceaseless missions to satisfy his irrevocable longing, Stuart went to the Bench and Bar, a gay club in rundown, downtown Oakland. The music was surging with a salsa beat and the bar was packed with men of all measure. Stuart moved throughout the bar with insistent ease, drinking in random whiffs of cologne and filling his nostrils with pheromones. At one point, as he stood at the end of the bar ordering a beer, he scanned the crowd of faces and, against the loud backdrop of the sound system, the moving lights and blustery bilingual chatter, he could hear his mother's disappointed voice: *I wish you would find someone your own age*, or *Does this one speak English?* or some other uncharitable expression—a mother's ceaseless lamentations lain at the feet of her son's inexplicable desires. Just then he felt a finger tapping him on the shoulder blade. He turned his head and looked.

"*Hola, papí.*" Ramon greeted him with a cautious smile. " *¿Me recuerdas?*"

In Hermosillo, Stuart sat on a bench beside the bandstand in Plaza Zaragoza waiting for Ramon to arrive. The spires of the cathedral just beyond rose into the bright blue sky like the tiered heights of a wedding cake, at their tips an elaborate pointed construction, at the base a mass of intimidating ecumenical imperialism. Eleven o'clock approached, and with it the rising heat of the day. The plaza was fairly quiet except for the racing of Stuart's mind and the thumping of his heart in his chest. Ramon arrived draped in smiles and the two of them embraced. He kissed Stuart quickly on the lips as they walked down a dilapidated and isolated road in the center of town. "Oh my God, *papí*," he exclaimed, intertwining his arms around one of Stuart's, nearly pulling him down with excitement. "I can't believe you're here!"

They went to a new hotel room that Stuart had rented with a view of the eastern hills. Laughing as he flopped himself down on the double bed, Ramon teased Stuart for having spent his first night in what was essentially a brothel. "I can't believe he drove you to *El Arroyo*."

"Maybe he thought I wanted to find a pretty girl in the plaza and take her back with me."

"Oh no…!"

"No," Stuart grinned. "Not as long as I have this handsome thing underneath me." He stretched himself out atop Ramon. "Do you like the hotel, baby?"

Ramon grabbed hold of Stuart with passion: "*Ay, papito*, I don't care about the hotel. I am so happy you're here. This is like a miracle for me."

The following morning, while Ramon went to the house he shared with his mother to pack a backpack of toiletries and clothes, Stuart rented a small car from an agency on one of the main streets near *el centro*. The two of them then drove west through the mountainous desert to the Bay of San Carlos, on the coast just above the fishing town of Guaymas, where they spent the better part of a week under a palapa in the sand.

"You know something, *papi*?" said Ramon one afternoon. They were having lunch looking out over the Sea of Cortez.

"What?"

"My mother would love to come to a place like this. She has never been to a place like this. *I* have never been to a place like this."

"Maybe we should have brought her."

"Ha. She would love you for that. She would never understand, but she would love you for bringing her."

"What wouldn't she understand?"

"This." He waved a hand to indicate the two of them. "She would wonder why we were going to a resort with a rich *guero*. Well, she would know but she would never ask. She would go and say more prayers and be nice to you when you were in the same room, but in the back of her mind she would be sad and in her room she would cry secret tears and she would pretend that it didn't exist."

"And when she came to our room and saw that only one bed was unmade—."

"*Ay, papí*, she would *darse vueltas*." He whirled his hand like a centrifuge and chuckled. "She thinks I am with friends. For this week your name is Servando."

"Gladly."

Under the table, Ramon gently pinched Stuart's Achilles heel with two of his sandy toes and told him, "I love you, *papí*. You have no idea. Can I call this our honeymoon? Do you mind?"

"No, I don't mind."

"For me this is our honeymoon because I will never have a real honeymoon in a place like this. Never. I'm just a poor *bracero*. I know people look and they probably snarl like dumb dogs or look at us with embarrassment like my *mamita*, but I don't care."

"Nobody's looking."

"No, *papí*, you don't pay attention. When they welcome us they only welcome you, did you notice?"

"No."

"See. A rich *guero* doesn't have to pay attention. But a poor *indio* like me—. When we come to the hotel they say *Bienvenido*, meaning *you* are welcome. If they say *Bienvenidos* that's for both of us. But they say *Bienvenido* because they know you won't notice the difference and they know I will. For them I have no place here because I'm dark, and it's better to send the *indios* up north to work than to serve them *mariscos* at the seaside. If I wasn't with you they wouldn't let me inside this place."

Leaving the US to return to Mexico after his father died had put at risk everything Ramon had crafted in the way of a life back in the US. It was well-stated among undocumented immigrants that the US was a *carcel de oro*, or golden prison. In the US you could earn money; send money home; live in the place and obey its rules—drive the speed limit, avoid trouble, work hard—and survive under better economic conditions than you could ever dream of having back home. But as a place for crafting a life, so much of which depended upon the proximity of family, *el norte* fell dismally short for many. "When you are poor, everything has a price, *papí*," Ramon had said on more than one occasion. "In *el carcel* you can receive only visitors and you can't always choose your friends."

He had done well enough for himself, though, in Oakland. He had steady work and he shared a small two-room apartment with Miguelita, who was extremely fond of him. He told Stuart he slept on the sofa, although whenever Stuart came over Miguelita would stay at a friend's—"She has many friends," Ramon said of his roommate—and let the two of them have the bed. Ramon knew his way around the bedroom with such ease that Stuart simply assumed that he and Miguelita were lovers. It never occurred to him to ask, and on the night Ramon found out that his father had died and as he announced his plans to leave the States—he would give up his job, ride a bus for three days, bury his father properly, tend to his mother for a while and then cross the border back—Stuart and Miguelita sat on the sofa, one on each side of Ramon, and Miguelita's flowing tears spoke all about the relationship that Stuart needed to know.

Now that Ramon had spent over a year back in Hermosillo, working wherever he could doing whatever he could for a few pesos a day while watching his mother transition into loneliness, he was ready to return to California. He loved his mother and he didn't want to leave her, but he needed to get back. Foreign a place as it was, after so many years on his own there, California had become his new reality; Mexico, in particular Hermosillo, seemed like somebody else's dream.

Ramon and Stuart were lying in their bed at the hotel on the Bay of San Carlos late into their trip. It was afternoon and the doors to the balcony were open. The blue sky blended directly into the sea as a slow-moving breeze lured the sheer drapes of the room into a soft flowing dance. Ramon lay looking at Stuart's back as the rich *guero* lay looking out onto the sky. "But *papí*," Ramon insisted, "the *coyote* I am talking to is reputable. He brought relatives of my friend Tio last year. He's been a *pollero* for many years. Tio would only recommend somebody he trusted." On Ramon's last attempt he had been picked up by the Border Patrol just across the border at Tecate and then processed—"searched, shackled, photographed and shuttled"—along with a group of men back to the Mexican side of the border. He didn't want to risk the same this time. Still, Stuart didn't like that Ramon was thinking about paying someone to smuggle him back into the States. "He will take care of everything," urged Ramon. "He will give me a bus ticket from Hermosillo to Naco, where we will spend the night with our group, and then very early in the morning we will cross the border on foot and be picked up by a truck on the American side. It's very simple, *papí*. And it's so much easier than last time. I talk to many people and they all say it's getting harder and harder to get across. The *coyote* will be good for me."

Stuart rolled over and faced Ramon. He stroked the thick hair around the boy's ear, brushing the hairs into place as if they each were strands of a difficult story that needed taming. He then gently traced the curve of Ramon's black eyebrows and leaned forward and kissed him. "How much does he want?"

"Fifteen thousand pesos."

"And he guarantees you'll get across?"

"What do you mean?"

"I mean, if he fails the first time, will he bring you again the next time without a fee?"

"No, *papí*, there is no more next time. We will make it across, and this time I am staying for good."

* * *

Memory is a long and meandering road, like that which stretches from the busy populated hills of San Francisco to the barren internal solitude of the Central Valley. Stuart was making the long two hour drive from San Francisco to the Brave Bull one Saturday evening. After a beleaguering period of abstinence he was heeding his friend Manny's advice: "Well, *caballero*," Manny had said over the phone, "since I only have poor artists to introduce you to, and you turn your nose up at the ones who are professionals, then you might as well go out and find yourself a bit of forbidden fruit." So Stuart headed east with the glittering lights of the city fading in the rearview mirror as he passed through the long suburban corridor of the 580 freeway out to where it faded into the darkness of the Central Valley. As he drove, memories of Ramon flooded his mind. At moments the valley resembled the Sonoran desert surrounding Ramon's hometown, a vast flat plain with a city and hills far behind him. The loneliness and quiet of the night reminded him, as well, of the long agony of the Arizona desert—that deleterious place, locus of an implacable guilt.

Before leaving Ramon in Hermosillo, Stuart gave him fifteen thousand pesos to pay the *coyote*. He also gave him a hundred US dollars for emergency. He made sure Ramon had his phone number on a piece of paper tucked into his wallet—"Call me when you get across. And call me again when you get to California."

"*Sí, papí, sí.*" Ramon hugged him. *"Te quiero mucho. Mucho mucho."*

They left Naco at night, a group of fourteen, twelve Mexicans accompanied by a young couple from Guatemala, led by a man in his forties who wore dark brown denim and a cowboy hat. Even in moonlight the man's face looked dark and it was lined with crevices carved by the desert heat. He led the group to an unsecured crossing spot at the border, where he urged them to hurry as he softly spoke commands into a handheld radio. As promised, they were met a few hundred yards up the road by a small delivery van. The driver, a jittery young kid who, from the looks of it, was probably a petty drug dealer as well, shuttled the group into the back of the van and locked the door.

The drop-off point was to be in Benson, Arizona. Those who had paid the minimum would be left there. Those who paid more—depending on what they'd paid—would be taken as far as Phoenix. Ramon's fee would get him to Tucson, where he planned to pick up an interstate bus to return to the Bay Area. As the van jostled along the long Arizona road, light from the sunrise crept into the cramped space through a small ventilation window on the side. Whenever he thought too much about the confines of the space—fourteen people sitting close, their thighs pressed together as anticipation and excitement grew—Ramon had trouble breathing. It was just the eagerness to get out of the van, he told himself, as the air turned incrementally denser. He closed his eyes and he thought of the hotel on the Bay of San Carlos and the languid blue sea and the iridescent sky. He pictured Stuart at his desk and Miguelita in her bed, both of them awaiting a phone call, all three of them anxious for Ramon's journey to end. In less than an hour they would arrive in Benson, an older man in the van kept reminding the group; the most difficult stretch was over. Ramon leaned the back of his head against the aluminum wall and silently repeated the reminder: "*menos que una hora, menos que una hora, menos que—*." Suddenly there was loud popping sound, like a small explosion outside the van, and the driver's corner of the vehicle lurched downward. The shrieking of the metal wheel dragging at high speed along the pavement echoed deafeningly throughout the back of the jostling van. The van came to a rest and the engine was shut off. The group of 14 sat wedged toward one corner for a few moments, breathing heavily in wonderment and concern. The rising sun undid the final straps of darkness and after what seemed too long a time to be left in that condition they started rapping on the wall of the cabin to get the driver's attention as the heat inside the cabin grew to a stifling level. The Guatemalan woman, tears forming in her eyes, urged, "*¡Vamanos!*" She reached for the door only to discover that there were no handles. In a panic, some of the occupants started banging against the walls of the van while shouting, their unanswered calls turning quickly into obscenities and breathless pleas. Two of the men, fighting weariness, kicked against the doors but they couldn't break them open. Ramon closed his eyes and told himself to stay calm. The group of 14 continued that way, rapping, kicking, calling, praying. As the temperature and tempers inside the van surged, Ramon sat rocking with his knees against his chest and told himself that whatever the outcome—whether they set themselves free or got arrested by *la migra* or, as would be the sad case that morning, forgave whatever obligations they had remaining in life and surrendered everything right then and there despite their stubbornest efforts—whatever the outcome, he knew that something better had to lay ahead.

* * *

As thoughts of Ramon surged into Stuart's memory on the long drive into Modesto, he did what he normally did in those moments of recall: he closed all the windows, turned the radio up loud and yelled at the top of his lungs. Once the rage of recall and his voice were spent, he turned the radio back down, lowered the windows, reminded himself where he was and what year it was, and he let the memory of Ramon—along with its wonders, adversities, terror and shame—get sucked out the window and flee into the night.

-7-

DAY OF (REAWAKENING) THE DEAD

The winter holidays in San Francisco officially began on Halloween. From there it was a two-month splurge of festivity. Work barely slowed down, though—imperceptibly if at all—which left inhabitants exhausted from all the activity come January. By Halloween 1999 the City was in full party mode. In the internet industry, which dominated the media, anticipation was high for the first real, huge online Christmas shopping season. 1998 had been a minor season, and in this, the last holiday season of the century, everyone expected to see brick and mortar outlets languish as their cyberspace counterparts overtook them. All of our goFORTH clients were good to go, or at least getting there: we'd built countless ecommerce systems that allowed people throughout the country to order almost any conceivable necessity or indulgence online.

Halloween fell on an inconvenient Sunday that year. Inconvenient for Celia Green. No stranger to needing to be first at everything, Celia wanted to be the first among her peers to give a party during the millennial holiday season. She decided she would host a Day of the Dead party. Normally the Day of the Dead is celebrated two days after Halloween. But Day of the Dead fell on a Tuesday that year and Tuesdays were not good party days so Celia pushed her celebration ahead to the Saturday night before Halloween.

Celia lived in an elegant upstairs flat in a wood-shingled, two-unit building she had recently bought in Presidio Heights. The house represented a portion of the gains of her most recent business transaction, the selling of Thrive.com to the growing monolith of goFORTH. In one deft and seemingly transparent move she had lured the giant to her bedroom door, gently parted the folds of the handsome kimono she wore to disguise herself, and then seduced the giant into bestowing upon her large amounts of cash and unrestricted stock in exchange for the contents of her dominion.

Emily and I arrived in Celia's neighborhood around eight o'clock along with our escorts, Angela and Tamara. They had picked us up at my place and we drove over together in Tamara's tiny car. With Emily and I snugly shoved into the back seat, I couldn't escape the feeling of being a child being driven to the prom by his parents. Tamara, who had only met Emily once, looked at us in the rear view mirror. "How long have you two been going out now?" she asked.

"A few months," I said.

"Five," Emily corrected.

"When's the wedding?" Tamara winked, inciting terror.

We eventually found parking a few chilly blocks away and walked briskly to Celia's house amid the winter light. I watched as Angela and Tamara ascended the entry stairs ahead of us. At the top of the steps Angela stood out beautifully, looking as luminous beneath the overhead porch light as the adjacent window full of candles. She touched her fingertips to her girlfriend's as if to say, *Well, here we go...*

I took the hand of my own—girlfriend? We hadn't committed to being anything specific, although I guess for all practical purposes we were boyfriend-girlfriend. (I only ever introduced her by saying, "This is Emily" and she, "This is Hugo.") Nevertheless, we were coming into a perilous time of the year. Halloween was the beginning of Christmas, which meant impending obligations in the way of romance: one can't sit in front of a holiday fireplace with the girl you're going out with and pretend you're in the Burger Barn having lunch. Those fireside kisses, no matter how strenuously the girl invokes the artistic privilege of non-commitment, can instantly transform into delusions of cohabitation and children and in-laws. Next thing, you're expected to fork over six months salary for a ring she can show off to her friends. The delusions or dreams turn into an awkwardly bended knee; tuxedo rentals and dress shops; an excess of planning and project management; drugstore pregnancy tests; frantic discussions and so-called delight; weepy sentimental calls home to the parents. In a few years' time arrives a monotony so overwhelming and all-consuming, like a toxic fog pouring over Twin Peaks, that you begin to suffocate from underneath the onslaught of your very own life.

"You ok?" Emily asked as she pulled me upstairs.

"Just thinking."

I was warm underneath the open collar of my dress shirt. I tried to blame it on the residual angst of the claustrophobic ride in the back seat of Tamara's two-door midget car. I endeavored to believe it was due to the wall of heat emanating from the mass of bodies and the inescapable orgy of flaming candles in the room. I denied that it had anything to do with my fear of commitment.

"Well—?" asked Emily.

"Well what?"

"Well for starters," she said, "I'm wondering if we're going to stand here all night or if we're going to actually go inside."

Celia's flat was decorated in a warm, appealing style. The living areas had thick, comfortable seating set upon rich Persian carpets. There were nods to modernity in the art and lighting fixtures, those assets being perfect accomplices for the mood of contemporary elegance she sought to portray and the *nouveau* wealth she artfully sought to conceal.

"I always wondered how the other half lives," Emily remarked as we stood inside the front door.

It was a large flat with a full living room, full dining room, modest-sized kitchen, three bedrooms and two and a half baths. All of the rooms shimmered in elegant light from the many arrangements of candles of all sorts and sizes, which caretakers would keep burning throughout the night. Throughout the living and dining rooms multi-colored banners of *papel picado* were strung about, draped on long strings affixed to walls and framing doorways. The tissue-like paper squares contained cut-out images of skeletons at rest, skeletons at feast, skeletons at celebration, tombstones, and a selection of intricate, non-specific patterns cut into the tissue paper like lace. They might have clashed with the décor of the place had it not been for Celia's eerily efficient talent for creating illusions. The party wasn't meant to celebrate the dead in the true manner of Latin Americans; it was merely a borrowed costume with which to adorn her new home and celebrate her good fortune, as well as give a celebratory nod to the end of the 20th century. An added bonus was the fact that the NASDAQ had surpassed 3,000 points on Wednesday and closed above the 3,100 mark on Friday, making for a resoundingly festive mood among the many guests filling the public rooms.

Behind the kitchen there was a pantry which held a bar sink, wine cooler and cupboards for storage. A long granite counter served as a staging site for all the party necessities. Three Hispanic women in long peasant dresses and embroidered shirts came and went from the room, using its contents to restock ice buckets and plates of hors d'oeuvres—*tamalitos*, roasted vegetables and other *tapas*-like creations. Theirs was a slow but steady stream of activity, seemingly random on the surface but underneath it had a deep, rhythmic structure.

Stuart and his new boyfriend Alejandro, a Mexican guy in cowboy boots and hat, arrived after we did. We said our *hellos* to them and then we all dispersed as conversations went off on tangents.

At one point Alejandro left Stuart in the living room and went to talk with the women working in the pantry. Celia approached Stuart, who was sitting alone on a sofa, and sat down beside him: "I see you brought your own help."

"That's a deeply callous remark."

"I'm just teasing," she insisted. "What's his name again?"

"Alejandro."

She repeated the name, drawing it out with exaggerated inflection.

He told her she could call him Alex: "If it's easier on your wicked tongue."

"Where'd you meet him?"

"In a bar."

"Fabulous. What does he do?"

"He drives a forklift."

"Are you shitting me?"

Stuart looked at her sternly. "Are you drunk?"

"No, I'm not drunk." She lowered her voice: "Why in God's name are you dating a man who drives a forklift?"

"Did you look at him?"

"Beauty fades, my dear."

"He happens to be a very genuine soul. I don't care what he does for a living."

"Really?" She didn't believe it.

"You know, Celia, when my mother dies you can audition for the role. In the meantime, give it a rest."

"Oh, please," she said mockingly. "I've known you for how long, and you've always been an inconsistent lover. Your taste changes with the wind. I think you choose all these people simply because you know the relationship will never go anywhere."

"What do you mean, *these* people?"

She drew a wide semi-circle with her arm. "All of these people. The United Nations of race and gender that you've dated over the last fifteen years. There isn't one of them you could have had a real, sustaining relationship with."

"You think."

"Oh I'm right, Stuart, and you know it."

"I think there's something deeper than that."

"I think you're full of shit," she told him in a whisper.

Stuart stood up. He squeezed Celia's shoulder as he walked away: "You would know."

Chaotic systems tend toward order so it was inevitable that Angela and I, our dates sequestered in a corner somewhere interrogating each another on topics of art and society, would be drawn again to where Stuart was. We encountered him in the back of the kitchen talking with a man who looked like a literature professor, neatly dressed and his eyes reflecting a mind in perpetual contemplation.

"There you are," Stuart said to us. "I was afraid you'd left."

"We thought the same about you," Angela said. "Where's Alex?"

Stuart pointed toward the pantry.

"You put him to work?"

"Of course not. One of the women is from the Poncitlán, not far from him." Changing topic he took her hand. "Do you—?" he started. Then he addressed the man to his left: "Jorge, you remember Angela. And this is her friend, Hugo."

"Nice to see you," said Dr Salazar.

"You've met before," Stuart told her.

"I—" Angela hesitated.

"The language school in Seville," prompted Stuart.

"I believe we danced together in Barrio Santa Cruz," said the professor.

"We did," Angela remarked delightedly as she extended her hand. "It's so good to see you, Dr Salazar." She looked over at Stuart, who grinned. She then smiled like an ingénue disrobed and took a sip of her gin and tonic. "My god," she added, "that seems like ages ago."

I inserted myself into their reunion: "Ehh…summer of '94 by any chance?"

In the Barrio Santa Cruz, the old Jewish quarter of Seville, down south where it is hotter than every other part of Spain, the streets are narrow and winding, framed by a dozen centuries of conflated history. In summer, even at nighttime, the heat escapes from your body only in weak traces as the stone walls of the barrio themselves seem to drip with sweat. There in the medieval quarter it is easy to get lost. All the more so if you've been drinking decanter after decanter of chilled wine, watching flamenco, dancing with friends, and all the while embracing the life of the moment while fighting off an unforgiving longing. In the very early hours of one morning, Stuart's fine leather shoes stepped out of a bar onto cobblestone. Wrapped in his right arm was the left arm of Angela Green, a recent graduate from his home town of San Francisco and a fellow student at the Seville Language School's accelerated summer program.

"That was the most fun I've ever had in my life," Angela said to her newfound companion, a well-dressed American with an invasively alluring aura and beautiful arms. They had gotten acquainted in the common rooms of the school but didn't have any classes together: Stuart's Spanish was advanced and Angela was merely a beginner. On this night, amid the carefree jostle of new acquaintances, they had immediately become close.

In the Barrio Santa Cruz it is difficult to tell north from south and east from west. If the streets were not so narrow you might be able to see above the rooftops to locate the tall spire of *La Giralda* and guide yourself home accordingly. But there is no such guidepost. Nor are there tourist maps designed for intoxicated visitors. Stuart and Angela laughed as they wandered the streets of the *barrio* looking for a way out. Angela's arm remained locked in Stuart's. She rested her palm on his forearm, stroking the hair on the thick of its muscle. He in turn savored the sensation of her breast and hip brushing elegantly against him. Eventually they stumbled upon a small road that led them to the great cathedral situated on the perimeter of the old Judaic quarter. Once in its shadow Stuart let out a sigh of relief and bent over as if he were winded. "I never thought we'd get out of there," he said, pulling himself upright. "It was like a maze. I wonder how long we were lost."

Angela laughed. She was delirious with delight and drunk on white sangria.

"You know," Stuart said. "I don't often do this—." He put his arm around her waist. He leaned in and kissed her on the lips.

"I won't tell anyone," she said after their mouths parted.

Stuart looked up at the ancient cathedral. "This is a good sign."

"The church?"

"It means we're close to home," he explained.

"Oh that—yes."

"Tell me again where your apartment is," he asked her.

Angela shook her head. "I'm following you."

* * *

"You slept with him?!" I couldn't believe my ears. Or my eyes. The picture that was forming in the forefront of my brain was a torment.

"Just that one time," Angela said. She and I were at that point alone in the back of the dining room in Celia's house.

"How in—? Why—? I, I—."

"For heaven's sake, Hugo," she said. "You know me."

"Yeah, but—with him?!"

"Obviously you weren't listening. We were a little drunk. We were having a wonderful night..."

I was stymied. "I got all that. But I don't tie one on with the guys and then go home and have sword fights with them."

Stuart returned from his trip to the pantry. "Where's Dr Salazar?"

"I guess he didn't want to reminisce with us," Angela said. "No, no, kidding. He's in the living room rounding up his wife. They have another party to go to."

I asked Angela if Dr Salazar's wife knew that she danced with her husband in Seville.

Angela glared at me. "What kind of question is that?"

"Something up?" asked Stuart.

Angela looked at him and then looked at me. Her lips were pursed in annoyance. "I don't know why it's such a big deal," she insisted.

Stuart, obliviously: "That you danced with Jorge?"

"No, Stuart. I mean—." She wagged her finger to indicate the two of them.

"Oh..." he said plainly. He tilted his head as he looked at me: "You didn't know?'

"No," I said angrily.

"That was quite a month," he said.

"A month?"

"The course was one month long," Angela said coddlingly. "Stuart and I—we were only together that one night."

153

"In *that* way," he said.

"Yes, in that way," she repeated. "We were almost never separated after that but it was purely platonic."

"Well—," Stuart seemed ambiguous on the point. He kissed Angela on her cheek. "In any event, this one saved my life."

"Likewise." Angela looked at me as if an explanation might right things: "I had decided that when I got back to San Francisco I had to break up with Susan. I just couldn't get it out of my mind until I met Stuart and we started hanging out together. Of course that was nothing compared with Ramon—."

Stuart lifted his hand. "Nope. Don't—."

For what seemed an interminable interlude Angela stood there staring at Stuart, the two of them communicating telepathically, seemingly channeling pain and forgiveness and other indiscernible energies.

"Who's Ramon?" I asked.

Angela shook her head.

"She can tell you later," Stuart said. "I'm having too nice a time to reawaken the dead." A pained look came over his face, which he pretended to erase with a grin. "If you'll excuse me, I'm going to take my forklift driver home and do all sorts of *un*-Catholic things with him."

* * *

"Did you guys have a good time?" Angela asked from the front seat.

"I can't believe you slept with him," I said from the back.

"Hugo," she said, "let it go."

"But he's a fag. He's a houseboy-loving, bona fide butt-munching queer."

Tamara veered into a driveway and slammed on the brakes. "Get out," she said. She shifted the car into Park and yanked up the parking brake with aggression. She turned around in her seat and told me pointedly, "You don't talk like that in my car!"

Angela laid her hand on top of Tamara's. Emily leaned her head against the window.

"What?!" I said.

She glared at me. "*You*—do not get to talk like that in my presence."

I stewed silently for a moment. "I'm just playing around. It was only a comment. Jesus Christ, everyone knows he's as gay as can be. Don't I have a right to be amazed that a guy who's clearly, immutably queer hops in bed with a—a—with Angela?"

"He's not a bunghole-munching whatever you called him. You don't get to use that language, Hugo Storm," she said accusingly. "Not you."

"Honey…" Angela whispered.

She turned to Angela: "No. He can say whatever he wants to at home but he's not going to do it *my* car, in *my* space!"

Angela turned around formidably: "Apologize, Hugo."

"For what?"

Emily backhanded me on the thigh.

"Apologize," Angela demanded.

"Fine," I said. "I apologize. Now drive me home."

Tamara turned around one last time and barked at me, "Did your mother teach you no fucking manners?"

-8-

OH, MILLENNIA

Emily and I woke up late the next day. We both had morning breath that could peel paint. She rolled out of my bed muttering regrettably, *"Brain cells* of the dead." From the doorway to the hall: "Do you have any aspirin?"

We eventually, after showers and toast, wandered down the hill to Mama's, on Washington Square, for breakfast.

"I like Tamara," she said blandly as we stood outside the restaurant waiting for a table.

"You what?"

"Granted, she jumped on your ass kind of strong. "

"You think?"

"Did you know she had a brother who died of AIDS?"

"No," I said. "Did she bother to remember I don't have a mother?"

"Still, Hugo, you don't call somebody a faggot."

"I called Stuart a fag. There's a difference."

"Hardly."

As a friend I'd been wronged by Angela not telling me up front that Stuart was more than just her mentor. She had plenty of opportunities to tell me they slept together, but, as I complained to Emily, "She withheld. She obfuscated."

"She *what?*"

"She obfuscated."

"That's a ridiculous word. Don't use ridiculous words. My God. It's bad enough you're in love with her. Don't turn it into a drama by using ridiculous words."

"I'm not in love with her."

"Whatever." We shuffled along the sidewalk. "You know, she doesn't owe you anything. Getting to know people is an unfolding."

"Is that so?"

We eventually got a table at Mama's and were rummaging through the Sunday paper while feeding our hangovers. Emily had possession of the Pink section and was perusing art happenings for the week. I was scanning the Business section, which was thick with advertisements from venture firms, investment banks, Tiffany & Co, business class airlines and all kinds of other purveyors of business extravagance and calculated desire. The tone of the business news, as with most of the journalism having to do with the internet boom surrounding us, was of intimidation and awe. Those of us who had little were inspired to attain more. Daily we bore witness to high-priced mergers and acquisitions like plates of passing pastries heaped high and dripping with the sweet fiscal taunt of desire. To read the admirable news of someone who had just flipped his company for tens of millions when the ink on his business plan was barely dry was always accompanied by a sense of sting because for many of us, most of us really, the real goods—access to low strike values, early IPOs, fat paper parachutes—always seemed just out of reach.

"Check this out," I said to Emily. I had to read it out loud to believe it. *"Internet consulting giant goFORTH is in merger talks with Hartmann-Holley. Gartner Group analysts report that the two industry leaders are in private talks discussing a possible merger. The combined company would merge goFORTH's web development and implementation practice with Hartmann-Holley's strategic internet consulting expertise, creating the largest single provider in the nascent internet services industry."*

"Is that good?" Emily asked.

"It's huge. I don't know if it's good or not." Quite simply I was stunned. It was as if my life was in a perpetual state of astonishment those days. There was nothing stable to hold onto, nowhere safe to sit and breathe in the fresh air of calm. We were living in a state of hyperextension where everything real was more and more like a shell game of trying to keep up. "This is first I heard about it."

"What do you expect?" she said. She was unmoved by news of my company's proposed merger, except that it raised her sense of global disenchantment a further notch. "Do you really think they're going to tell you ahead of time? You're cheap labor."

"I am not."

"Are you making a hundred thousand dollars a year?"

"No."

"There you have it. Capitalism relies on a steady flow of cheap, expendable labor, Hugo, and not just in the lettuce fields. Hate to say it, but that's us, babe: ex-pen-da-ble."

"No," I had to disagree. "We have more job requisitions at work than we can fill. There isn't *enough* labor out there."

"For now."

"Don't say that."

"Get real, Hugo. Nothing lasts forever."

"Wait and see," I told her.

"Whatever."

There you have it. She'd said it again, full of pious authority. Much as I liked Emily, her purposely retaliatory use of that word really pissed me off. If you said something she disagreed with, whether on the basis of fact or merely her own conjecture, she would lacerate your opinions with that sharp-edged word of hers as if to say, *I'm right; don't you doubt it.* But she was wrong about the internet industry, and as an artist existing on the fray she didn't realize how little she knew about it. Granted there was more hype than market fundamentals driving many of the stock prices, but as Geoffrey, the information architect at Screaming Software, once explained to me, the World Wide Web was a chaotic system in which all the players interacted in seemingly random disorder, each one seeking out places of refuge or familiarity—one's favorite search engine, news sites, a gaming domain. At the structural heart of this chaotic system was the internet, its massive clusters of web servers throughout the world routing traffic through massive pipes and funneling it through insatiable nodes. "Now," Geoffrey had professed, "the internet is a strange attractor, Hugo the Hurricane. A strange attractor is a place of return or of focus, a locus shifting in all its facets and dimensions as chaotic systems whirl around it. I myself am a strange attractor: strange in that I don't abide by the standard rules of physics, an attractor in that I attract. Yet I am neither stationary nor random. I am a beacon of stability and persistence and the forces surrounding me can not help but be drawn in by my mathematical appeal." With a flourishing wave of the hand he added, "I meld with the arrow of time."

Analogous to the web, Geoffrey insisted, was geography. Places like Silicon Valley, San Francisco, Research Triangle and Boston were nodes of the greater intellectual system that brought the internet to the world. The geographic locations were levels in a recursive hierarchy whose structure was replicated from the minutest physical molecule all the way into the unquantifiable dominions of outer space. These clusters of daring, intellect and even foolishness were powerful attractors, luring countless people like myself into their domain. However, like the nation-state empires of old, the internet was just the latest in a string of empires, Geoffrey stated cautiously. One had to wonder, he insisted, when our current locus of attraction died and another took our place, what would become of us? Where would history leave us—in what condition? Would we be huddled in some arid hole or picturesque ruin, retracing our steps to glory and the pitiable missteps that had led to our downfall? Or, on the contrary, was our reign as interminable as the internet pundits all claimed? If, after we bridged the year 2000 and all things remained the same and life was still good and our worlds hadn't collapsed in upon themselves, would we in the internet industry continue to reign supreme?

It seemed so.

It seemed fairly certain: Life was determinate and we were living out our necessary destiny.

"You think?" said Emily dryly, not looking up from her newspaper.

"Yes. That's what I believe." Of course, for me there were only two strange attractors at that particular moment: Emily, who sat across from me reading the arts and entertainment section of the paper as if it were the holy grail, and the mild throbbing in my brain stem from whichever tequila shot it was that did me in at Celia's Day of the Dead party.

* * *

"How come ya didn't bring her?" my Daddy asked. He sat opposite me at the round oak dining table in the kitchen of his home by Turkey Lake, outside of Orlando. His face was tanned and he sat with his forearms crossed on the table in front of him, within reach of his ever-present Tampa Bay Buccaneers coffee mug.

"We'd a loved to meet her," added Polly, his wife, topping off Daddy's coffee. Polly was a nice enough woman with a professional bowler's figure and short dirty blonde hair with random wisps of grey hiding in it. She and my Daddy had dated for a few years prior to my leaving New Jersey and decided to get hitched and move south right after that. They had a kid together, a red-headed girl they called Trisha. Technically she was my half-sister but she felt more like a stranger. "They're your *family*," Daddy tried to convince me. I'd been down to

Florida to see them all only a few times since moving to San Francisco. It had been a couple years since I'd been back, and with the Year 2000 coming up it seemed important to steal a few days away from work and spend that Thanksgiving with them. Especially since I wouldn't be able to make it back for Christmas and there was no way in hell I was going to spend the biggest New Years of my life in Orlando.

I told the two of them again (like I'd said on the phone) that Emily couldn't make the trip with me because (1) she didn't have any money, and (2) I wasn't about to bring a girl to meet them anytime soon. The last thing I had on my mind was getting married, and normally if you brought a girl home to meet your father on Thanksgiving she was going to think you were thinking about whether or not you wanted to marry her. With Emily, though, I couldn't be sure. Whatever I did, I didn't want to scare her off.

"You must like her," Polly declared.

"Mh-hm." I opened up my laptop to show them pictures of the two of us.

"Ooh, that's nice," Polly cooed over interspersed city scenes and shots of the bay with one or both of us in the foreground.

On one close-up of Emily Daddy asked, "What's that?"

"Em's tattoo," I said.

"Lordy that's big," noted Polly. "That a snake?"

"Mh-hm."

Daddy raised his thick eyebrows dubiously. "She a good girl?" he asked.

"Hell yeah," I told him.

"With tattoos?"

"Just that one—plus a sylph on her shoulder."

"A what?"

"Triangle inside a circle. A sylph's a spirit that lives in the air and forms the clouds. They communicate with God."

"You mean angels," said Polly.

"What does she do?" Daddy asked.

"She's kind of a musician."

"A musician?"

"Mh-hm," I nodded.

"How do you spell that siff-thing?" Polly had gone over to the refrigerator and was standing beside it with a pencil in her hand.

"S-y-l-p-h."

"Have to look it up," she said, scribbling the word down on the grocery list affixed to the refrigerator with a magnetic binder clip.

"Careful what you get yourself into, boy," Daddy said to me. "She into devil worship and all that mess?"

"Hello, no."

Polly came back to the table. "She a Christian?"

After pictures were finished my father went out to do some work, leaving me at home with Polly, who was waiting for the little girl to get home from school. Polly poured me a tall mug of chilled apple cider and we went out back and sat on the screened-in porch, which overlooked the other screened-in porches that lined the back side of the tightly spaced single family homes along Brockton Heights Boulevard (no boulevard at all, if you asked me; nothing more than a bland two-lane street lined with immature trees). "It was hard on your Daddy," she said as we talked about them leaving New Jersey and moving down to Florida. We had some variation of this same conversation the last time I visited. "You gotta remember, he lost everything 'cept you: the love of his life, his farm, his faith—all his dreams died the day your momma died. And then he gave it all up and started over again. That takes a lot." She stared admiringly at the small tiled patio between us and the road.

"What about you?" I asked her. "Aren't you the love of his life?"

Polly shook her head. "I'm just somebody he loves. And somebody who loves him like crazy. I'll never be your momma—not for him or you; that was then. The past doesn't torment me, though—neither mine nor nobody else's." That seemed a radical viewpoint for someone who grew up in the swamps around Chokoloskee Bay with mosquitoes biting at her skin at night and snakes and baby alligators slithering through the muddy waters on the floor of the house anytime a storm passed through. In August of 1969, when Polly was 17 and still living in the swamp, Hurricane Camille tore through the Gulf of Mexico, slamming Mississippi with all its force. The storm missed Florida's Gulf coast down where Polly and her family lived but it sent enough wind and rain to flood the low-lying swamplands and knock a tree down onto the back side their church's congregation house. The day after landfall, once the rains subsided, everyone in the Ten Thousand Islands vicinity headed off to church to give thanks that the hurricane, the worst in 35 years, had only grazed them. They converged on the First Chokoloskee Church of Our Lord

Jesus Christ damp and slightly dazed, where the minister stood wearing a white robe in front of the broken tree that had flattened the back end of the ramshackle church. The altar opened up into a tangle of branches and a matted grey sky. Dampness from the leaves dripped onto the altar upon which the preacher stood. "Jesus!" he shouted, "is who saved you. Jesus! is the one who protected you." He turned around with a flourish and pointed at the fallen tree: "But it was Satan!" he declared, "who felled the tree. Jesus, overworked by constant miracles—overworked from having to atone on a daily basis for your wicked sins—caught the tree and kept if from felling this holy place. Jesus! sent the hurricane westward instead of landing directly on our parish. You! owe your thanks and sorrow to Jesus." (Never mind what the folks in the next parish were feeling about Jesus for sending the storm their direction.) He invoked the name of Jesus at least 64 times and warned that a plague of locusts would be followed by a rain of toads from the sky and "no matter the depth of sincerity of your so-claimed apology before the eyes of God, it was He that was gonna decide—He and his almighty Son, Jesus Christ—whether your soul would ascend into the glorious peace of Heaven or if the maggots of Satan's wolves would devour your skin for the rest of all eternity in Hell."

(Frankly, that sort of shit would have tormented me all the way to the grave.)

Polly added simply: "Jesus gives you a path to follow and you can follow it with dignity and faith or you can curse with the devil and fight the Lord all the way."

"Amen." I said. I sipped my cider and raised my eyebrows in best imitation of my doubting father, grateful that he and Alice had only ever dragged me to church on holidays.

"You go to church in San Fran?" she asked.

"No," I said flatly.

"How come?"

"Why bother."

"You know, your daddy didn't go to church when I first met him. Back then he was sad, sad…He had nothin' to look forward to; no faith; no optimism. Course he had you, and you were everything to him. But there was still a hole that your momma'd left in his heart. Even after all that time. I brought Jesus back in to fill that hole, and now look at him." She stopped talking to let an airplane pass overhead. When the noise subsided she added: "We go to church every Sunday. His family's growin'. He's workin'. He has friends."

"Praise Jesus," I said, trying to sound sincere.

It was true: with Polly, Daddy was a man unlike the one I grew up with in New Jersey. Back then he was subdued and almost apologetic to most people in his everyday life. With me he always seemed distracted. When he'd ask me, "How's your day, son?" it didn't matter what my answer was: his response was limited to a pale vocabulary that marked his voice with disinterest: *Mh-hm; Don't they got people to help with that?; Customers are always a pain in the ass*...useless non-conversational crap like that. He was less a father than parent to me, which was odd, given our circumstance: you would've thought we'd be closer. If it weren't for Alice keeping an eye on me and being there to listen to me talk, who knows where I might have ended up.

("Rest her soul," said Polly, as she did at any mention of Alice's name.)

Frankly, and I couldn't find a polite way to say this to Polly, but I'm not so sure it was Jesus that converted my father from a lonely man to a family one. More likely it was a fundamentalist Christian girl from the swamps who moved to New Jersey after losing her home to Hurricane Andrew in 1989 and gave him a daughter. Of course, if it *was* Jesus he's got either a 137 bowling handicap or pig tails.

Speaking of...the latter of the Lord's possible incarnations ran through the front door hollering gleefully *"Mommy, Mommy!"*

"Out here, sugar," Polly called.

The little girl dropped her backpack onto the kitchen floor with a thud and scurried onto the back porch with some sort of artwork flapping in her hand.

"It's a turkey, Mommy," she said proudly as she held out the construction paper creation.

"For me?" her mother asked.

The little girl nodded, beaming with delight.

"Thank you, baby, it's beautiful." Polly gave her a kiss on the forehead and then asked her if she recognized the person sitting next to her. The little girl shook her head no bashfully. (The last time I was there Trisha was only four years old, so I wouldn't have been surprised.) "Why, it's your brother," Polly said with astonishment. She looked at me and seemed almost embarrassed: "Of course she remembers you; she's just being clever." She took Trisha by the shoulders and turned her to face me. "Say hello to your brother."

Trisha bowed her scraggly red-haired head and lifted her eyes to look up at me. "Hi, Darryl," she said softly.

* * *

"Darryl?" Emily laughed. It was like a jab delivered through the static of my cell phone. Then: "Sorry. It's just....Hugo, Darryl. They're very different."

"It's my *given* name."

* * *

At Thanksgiving dinner there were just the four of us. Polly had made her standard Thanksgiving fare: a frozen turkey with built-in pop-up thermometer, stuffing in a box, instant mashed potatoes, round slices of canned cranberry jelly and frozen peas. There was no wine, only sparking apple cider, the likes of which I could only tolerate in small doses, otherwise it gave me the runs. "Remind me again why we can't have wine?" I asked.

"We don't drink alcohol in this house," Polly replied matter-of-factly. "The Lord wants us to abstain."

"What do you mean, the Lord?" I liked Polly as a person but I found her addiction to religious doctrine excessive and contradictory, so I felt it compulsory to agitate on the topic once in a while.

"Alcohol is the devil's nectar," she declared.

"You're kidding me," I said incredulously. That was a phrase I'd never heard out of her lips before. "When Jesus invited five thousand people over for fish he served them wine, and there was nothing wrong with that."

"That was a different time," she said.

"It's glorified as a miracle for crying out loud. You mean it's ok for Jesus to sot the people of Israel but I can't have a little red wine on Thanksgiving?"

"I would appreciate it if you could respect our traditions, that's all."

"I do. I'm just trying to understand them."

"Darryl," my Daddy interjected firmly, "listen to your stepmomma."

"I'm just having a discussion," I told him. "You sanctify someone for turning water into wine and then declare that alcohol is the devil's work....Well—?!"

"That weren't wine," my little half-sister spoke up, "that were his blood."

Okey-doke.

After a quick Biblical correction lesson, the topic shifted to less volatile terrain: the life of Dwight and Polly and Patricia there in the semi-urban, pre-planned suburbs of the Turkey Lake development: routines, neighbors, the latest golf course or driving range. He was my Daddy and I loved him for that. But it seemed clear that his life and mine had diverged so widely since we both left New Jersey that he was becoming as unfamiliar as the teetotaler and her miraculous birth child there at the table.

Over pumpkin pie and ice cream we managed a civilized segue onto my life in the internet industry: "Ooh, right there in the thick of it," is how Polly put it.

"You got benefits?" Daddy asked.

"They're pretty good," I said.

"You got medical insurance?"

"Yep."

"Can't be without that," he said.

"Yeah, it's covered. Get this, we even have a dry cleaning service that picks up our laundry and delivers it back to the office."

"So you can work longer hours," Polly said insightfully. "Doesn't sound like a benefit to me."

I told them I was willing to make the trade-off of time for convenience.

"They pay you overtime?" Daddy asked.

"Nope. Salary and bonus."

Polly shook her head dolefully and my father added, "You can't be all work, boy."

"It's all right," I said. "That's just the way it is."

"Sounds like they're taking advantage."

"Pop, I got eighteen-hundred shares of stock when the last company I worked for got bought out. That's over thirty-five thousand bucks."

"Lordy! They just gave it to you?" Daddy asked.

"Mh-hm."

"Cash?"

I shook my head no. "Stock."

"What's stock?" Trisha asked, drawing a river of molten ice cream on her plate with her pinky.

"It's like money," I said, then I told them I had exercised my goFORTH options just a week ago, and those stocks that I got for $20 each were trading at $56 now.

"I'll be," remarked Polly.

"They're worth a hundred thousand dollars."

All eyes lit up around the table.

Naturally that wasn't the end of the story. (Nothing stayed the same for very long back then.) I conveyed to my family that the company I worked for, goFORTH, was going to merge with another big internet services company, Hartmann-Holley. The merger was going to happen at the start of the new year and the new company would be renamed in January. For every share of stock that we owned in goFORTH we'd get .85 shares of the new combined company stock. From what I'd heard our old stock was going away. (*"It's a buy-out,"* Angela informed me via email.) The new stock would basically track the Hartmann-Holley stock. Even though my total number of shares was diluted, Hartmann-Holley was trading higher than goFORTH, so I was actually making *more* money off of the merger.

"Not sure I follow," my Daddy offered, "but sounds like you got a good thing goin'."

A good thing indeed. If someone had told me that within a year of leaving Screaming Software I'd be shopping for a loft South of Market I would have told them they were crazy. Crazy or not, at the age of 25 I was poised to buy my own place. Mortgage rates were low and you could get a loan with as little as 5% or in some cases 0% down.

"Now's the time," encouraged Angela. "Tamara and I are looking, too." (This was before she ended up on my shit list for not telling me she had slept with Stuart Piers. But I nevertheless clung to her opinions.) At the time it was sage advice. Real estate was appreciating all over the Bay Area. Property wasn't cheap but the money to pay for it was. I'd actually started researching places before I went to Florida for Thanksgiving. There were a bunch of new loft buildings being built South of Market, and the more I struggled with parking in North Beach and the leaky windows during cold weather, the idea of being in new construction, with a garage, close to work, sounded quantifiably appealing. There were any number of lofts priced between 300,000 and half a million dollars. Despite my insistence that I could never afford a half-million dollar property, Angela encouraged me to see a mortgage broker and get pre-qualified: "You might as well know how much house you can afford. With a pre-approval you're ready to go the moment you find something you like."

To my surprise, I qualified. With the NASDAQ riding high, my paltry but hundred percent vested quantity of shares of Screaming stock were trading at $55. They were worth a surprising $27,000 plus change—not bad at all. If I sold those, I calculated, I could make the down payment on a $450,000 place then finance the remaining 95% and still have about $5,000 left over for furniture. The goFORTH stock, unfortunately, I couldn't touch until it vested.

"Amazing, isn't it?" I said to Emily in early December.

"You know how I feel about private property," she said, suggesting disapproval.

"Somebody's gotta own it. Besides, I need to diversify: I have stocks. I need real estate. As populations grow, land becomes more valuable. Everybody needs a place to live."

"People could stop having children."

* * *

A brisk wet wind whipped down through the Tenderloin as Emily and I made our way to Ruby Skye, a nightclub in the small theatre district that abutted Union Square. Christmas was lingering around the corner, with all the high-end stores, the St Francis Hotel and the plaza itself lit up and decked out in green garlands and glittering trees and wreaths. The countdown to the end of this new beginning—new millennium, new mode of global work and commerce—was in full swing. Online sales, predicted to quadruple over the prior year, were ratcheting up. Clearly, we believed, the New Economy forces that had been driving the stock markets precipitously upwards marked the death knell for bricks and mortar. Granted, plenty of people still swarmed to stores on Black Friday for the start of the Christmas shopping rush. But for relatives who lived far away, for clients or friends they weren't going to see during the season, and as a food for laziness or cure for agoraphobia, there was the internet: go online, buy it, and let somebody else mess with wrapping, packaging and shipping it. This was a storm surge change we were experiencing. This was life and commerce tilted on their axes. You couldn't *see* it the way you could see physical crowds descending on San Francisco's central shopping district, but buzzing quietly in the background were thousands of web servers processing millions of orders across the continent. Many of those transactions were through websites I'd had a hand in developing, be it securing the contract or managing the implementation itself. I was proud of my virtual accomplishments. In time we'd see what the retail sales numbers revealed: we'd see how well our online domain was actually dismantling the old order. In the meantime, Emily and I were going dancing.

"Congratulations, baby." She squeezed my hand as we passed underneath a theatre marquee. I had just that day opened escrow on a place down off of Folsom Street, a good sized loft with a small media room in the back, a full bath and bed upstairs in the mezzanine, a parking space in a garage and a view of—well, it was right on a bus line but there were four restaurants and a pool hall within a block, so it didn't have to have a view. Didn't matter. In thirty days it would be mine. Emily grinned. "Momma's gonna buy you a drink."

There was a line at Ruby Skye but it was moving. In less than half an hour we went from back of the line to the velvet entry ropes, where Emily insisted on paying the cover charge. When the bouncer wasn't looking she popped an X tablet onto my tongue and then kissed me. Inside, the club was happening. It used to be a movie theater but by then it was a church of music and light and dance for youth. Emily bought us each a shot of *añejo*, which we washed down with Stella Artois. "Cheers," she said, uncharacteristically bubbly and bright. "To the soon-to-be homeowner capitalist!"

* * *

Almost imperceptibly, Christmas came and went. Like an extended night at a dance club, the holiday whirled by in a swirl of multi-colored lights and cacophonous glitz, a quickly forgotten disruption layered onto something altogether different. Back in New Jersey Christmas morning had been a mellow affair: Daddy, Alice and I would gather in the living room and exchange our simple presents. Since we'd gone to church the night before, we had most of the day to do nothing. Alice would fix a big breakfast and Daddy and I would watch a game. Some of our Millville neighbors would come by and bring us a basket of baked goods or jarred something or other. Daddy and Alice and I would sit down with them and politely chit-chat, and eventually one of them would admire the Christmas brooch that Alice wore every year pinned to her woolen dress over her heart: it was a swirl of sharp metal holly leaves and a cluster of red glass berries, the whole thing not much bigger than a silver dollar. No doubt they found our family arrangement odd, and they'd invariably ask Daddy if he was dating anyone—not that it was any of their business, they'd exclaim, but you knew in their hearts they felt sorry for the guy. Some of them would look consolingly down on me, inviting me into their sorrow, which I didn't bother to share. There was one, Mrs Palton, who would always dip her head to the side just before leaving, bunch up her lips in sadness as though she were talking to a dog tied to a lamppost outside the market, and then press a gloved hand against my cheek. It was always the same soft leather glove and I could recall its stitches tickling my face well beyond the day when she died of a stroke while riding a Greyhound bus to Minneapolis to visit her great-granddaughter one summer. After visitors we'd drive an hour to my Aunt Lois', my Daddy's younger sister, where I was forced to hang out with her trio of nasty children. They were snide little shits who called me a hick just because they happened to live in a three-story house with a swimming pool while I was the freak who, they liked to remind me, was born upside down in a farmhouse—"just like a retard." To ease my evident pain, Alice would give me sips of her beer while we sat in shared boredom and contempt as my cousins ran throughout the carpeted rooms showing off their Christmas presents. At some point Polly came into the slow-moving picture of my Daddy's life and insinuated herself into our Christmas ritual. With her around there was a lot of church-going in the weeks leading up to the holiday and a lot of thanking Jesus at nearly every gathering and at every meal. It got so much that Alice started listening to public radio in the kitchen in order to have a polite way out whenever Polly started in on her Jesus stuff: "Sh-h," she'd tell the strange Floridian, then point to the radio on top of the fridge, "I wanna hear this interview."

Emily spent Christmas Eve 1999 with her parents in Santa Cruz then drove up in the morning to spend Christmas Day with me. I made some spaghetti and we sat in my kitchen drinking Stella and watching the City vibrate in the cold sunlight. We didn't exchange any gifts because we had agreed at the start of the holidays that Christmas was about being together. That and Emily felt uncomfortable exchanging gifts when there such an income disparity between us. How, then, Christmas differed from any other day wasn't clear. Why she had made a special trip up to see me wasn't clear either—unless she simply wanted to get out of a mandatory family visit. In any event, the holiday seemed a fair metaphor for our relationship: the very light hand that was painting our relationship painted our lack of embrace of that high holy day of worship and commerce. Having no Christmas presents to exchange—before Emily got there I'd opened the trio of small packages sent by my Daddy and his family while having coffee in the kitchen—and she not being into football in any way, shape or form, we headed out for a walk.

One of the amazing things about San Francisco, among its array of attributes, some of them sequestered in posterity, some of them spiraling outward into the future, is its walkability. Back in New Jersey you could walk and walk and never arrive anywhere except to a string of uninspired air-conditioned shops or a gas station. In San Francisco you could walk for twenty minutes and pass through three different worlds. The temperature was never much colder than the chilliest days of autumn back East, which on rainless days like that last Christmas of the century made meandering along the city's undulating avenues a near-perfect pleasure.

Like many parts of the city, North Beach was filled with old, low-rise buildings that each housed two or maybe a few different flats. This being my last holiday season in North Beach—in about a month I'd be moving south of Market Street to SOMA, land of work and ownership—I succumbed to a bit of melancholy at leaving the place. Place is like a mother, and that neighborhood where I had landed, North Beach, sometimes felt like a replacement for my absent mother's presence. The narrow streets of North Beach hummed with stories you could never know. The residences were built of plaster over lath and each looked different from its neighbor without ever feeling like strangers. They had endured the occasional shaking of the ground over the years and they'd persisted throughout all the transitions of dubious men. Here and there, bay windows bowed from years of weathering, yet despite being worn they seemed relentless. They begged you to pay attention and try to discern their history, to save them from the dust of forgetfulness, to hold up their sagging frames with your breath.

I took Emily's hand as we cut through Washington Square, a grassy block fronting the Saints Peter and Paul cathedral. The park was filled with people and their dogs, homeless with their shopping carts parked beneath the trees, old Italians sitting on some of the benches, old Chinese on others. A mediocre guitarist fumbled with the strings of his guitar by the playground as the sound of organ hymns and dreary voices seeped out from the prominent church. As on that walk, although at the time I'd have been hard pressed to admit it, sometimes if felt like Emily and I were walking apart even in our togetherness, even as our hands were clasped and our footsteps headed in the same direction. Clearly we had some differences: Emily liked searingly hot, spicy food and she yearned to talk about the dangerous influence of social forces; I was happy sitting around simulating reality in computer games like The Sims eating a bag of plain, lightly salted potato chips. (Actually, I'd been doing pretty well with a Sim character I named Mister Smith until, in an ironic act of wish-fulfillment, he spent so much time sleeping that he never cleaned his guinea pig's dirty cage and he died of a filth-borne virus.) In the Sims you lived, you worked, you ate, you slept, you died. You didn't have to really win at anything. My relationship with Emily was like that: we had no targets to meet, no destinations to arrive at, no specific obligations other than living. Our relationship simply was.

After a beer and a plate of fries at the Bohemian Cigar Store, we ambled along Columbus Avenue, the principal thoroughfare that stretches from Fisherman's Wharf to the Financial District, where its terminus at Montgomery Street was marked by an iconic pyramid. I loved that one block of Columbus above the park, with its big shrubby trees that lined the sidewalks and stretched along the narrow median. We crossed Columbus onto Stockton, a market street, into the heart of Chinatown. Most of the shops were closed for the holiday, their fronts cordoned off with graffiti'd rollup doors. Emily and I zigzagged through the quiet neighborhood, strolling down otherworldly alleys and cross-streets. We cut back over to Grant Avenue, which was merely dusted with curious tourists instead of being slathered in them as usual. A block further lay Kearny, the least interesting of the three Chinatown arteries, and we headed in that direction, still slightly hungry, toward a place that Emily liked to eat at.

One sip of tea, a couple bites of kung pao shrimp, and the next thing I knew I was back at work on Monday morning to work the remaining few days of the century. The goFORTH / Hartmann-Holley merger was going to take effect January 5th. As of that date we would be one company of twice the size, numbering around 9,000 people. Due to the short timing of the merger and the vast size of the two companies, full integration wasn't expected to happen for at least six or seven months. However, there was a wider spectrum of services we'd be offering effective the beginning of the year and our office was planning to pick up a couple reps from Hartmann-Holley, so the volume of work required in advance of the merger was going through the roof. Already in discussion with our new partners, we began running along the muddy trail toward unification, tugging each other along in semi-blindness and with a rootless sense of urgency. As a result of the planned merger, our share price had dipped about ten percent, knocking it down from its high of near $90. Some market analysts felt that the company wouldn't be able to shed its bloat. This added to the mild sense of dysphoria that accompanied news of the union—no great way to end the year. We were reassured through constant emails from on high, however, that the share price would regain its momentum after the first of the year and that when it came to servicing clients, size *did* matter. MORE BIGGER BETTER NEW was the merger mantra. For all the effort they expended in convincing us of the rightness of the merger, the slogan might as well have been tattooed on our forearms so we were never without it. It was pumped out at regular intervals by the internal communications department and emblazoned on banners and coffee mugs along with the two company logos, which when put together sounded kind of ridiculous: Hartmann-Holley | goFORTH. Ridiculous, that is, until we heard our new name.

* * *

The week between Christmas and New Year's had a resoundingly wintry look and feel. The sky was heavy and chilled, painted as if God had put away his bright acrylics from summer and gotten out his somber watercolors and brushed thick grey bands across the sky. With his brush still wet he dipped a corner in red—just a droplet—and swirled the tip to create a soft airy pink. *Now,* God says, like a public television artist with curly hair and a voice so calm it's practically a sedative, *I've dabbed a little pink on my brush and we're going to take the brush and just 'wisp, wisp, wisp' a few strands of pink into the grey clouds. Mix it in ever so slightly, like this. See how we have a hint of blue in the background and now we've added our touch of pink: now it's not so gloomy.* Being God, he had brushed away the morning fog that had gathered like thick cumulus clouds on top of the bay to reveal the wanton and yet still beautiful sky. I could scarcely see it from our Main Street sales office, though: adjacent office buildings interrupted the view on all four sides. It was only when I headed out for lunch that I fully got a glimpse.

"Grey day," said a familiar sounding voice from behind me as I stood in line for a sandwich at Working Girls, my favorite grey weather deli, on Mission Street.

I cocked my head around and was surprised to see Stuart standing there. "Hey." Then again, "Oh, hey. What are you doing here?"

"Getting lunch."

"You work nearby?" I asked.

"I do," he said. "And you?"

"Right upstairs. Well," I pointed upward into the corner of the deli. "Over there. 222 Main."

"Who knew. We're in 200 Beale. 8th floor. You know, from my office I actually have a direct line of sight to your front door."

"No kidding."

"Funny," he remarked. "I've probably seen you come and go countless times, not even realizing it was you."

"I'll wave from now on. Just in case." I might have been still annoyed with him for having slept with Angela; it wasn't clear. I was more surprised than anything at seeing him, and surprise has a way of momentarily silencing all other recall, especially when your mind is clouded with work and a million other things.

"You and Emily coming Friday night?" he asked.

I had to pause for a second. Then: "Yes. Yes."

"You sure?"

"Absolutely. I—almost forgot Saturday was New Year's Day. Work has been insane."

"I'll bet."

"It's like I know and I don't know at the same time," I told him. "You know what I mean?"

He nodded presciently.

I told him that what I really wanted was to drop everything and try to enjoy the build-up to the New Year, to somehow mark the end of the millennium as the final days fell around us. I didn't want to work until the very end, pop a cork and then head back to work the next day as if nothing had happened.

"You're up." He pointed toward the counter.

As Stuart and I stood against the wall waiting for our sandwiches to be made he added, "I hear you. Personally, though, I'd rather be in the middle of it all then sitting around doing nothing."

"I suppose." I asked him what his company was doing to get ready for the transition: "You have people on call this weekend?"

"We set up a hotline and we have developers on call for all of our clients. As of this morning all systems are set to go."

Stuart and I left Working Girls to go back and eat our lunch at our respective desks. He patted my arm again. "See you guys Friday."

The last four days of that final week of the millennium were a haze of mad last minute rushing to get our projections for 2000 turned in and close out our sales performance and other metrics for 1999. Then, on the final day, Friday December 31, 1999, we did nothing of any use except watch replays of the fireworks from around the globe on a TV set in the communal kitchen as New Year's Day arrived in the South Pacific, then Asia and then Europe. Beginning mid-morning, the 11th floor of 222 Main was filled with the voices of people reciting "See you next century" as they slipped out of the office before the official 1pm close of business. (Over in Angela's building there were lengthy geeky discussions about whether 2000 or 2001 was the actual beginning of the century, whereas we in the sales and marketing division had made our decision and it was final.)

My cell phone rang as I was shutting down for the day. It was Angela calling to tell me that Stuart was having an impromptu pre-New Years party at Le Central, his antiquated Old Economy restaurant fave on Bush Street.

"Well, of sorts…" Angela shouted.

"What do you mean 'of sorts'?"

"It's not an official party," she hollered. I had difficulty hearing her through the din emanating from the bar out onto the street, where she stood amid chatter and hollers from all around. The markets had just closed and in the Financial District the sky was raining calendar pages and cheers. It was an annual tradition among brokers and other financial workers to rip their day-at-a-glance calendars from their housings and toss the sheets out open windows, creating a ticker tape sort of rain from on high. In the midst of it all I could hear the Wandering Wire broadcasting the final close from nearby: *"Oh, Millennia…! DOW seduces the dame at eleven and a half. NASDAQ comes home after four, for the third day in a row: Four thousand, sixty-nine and 31 grains of salt. Oh Millennia, Oh Millennia…How sweet the sound!"*

"Just come! We're having drinks."

I did. With a hybrid sense of gutteral thrill and mental circuitry overload, I left the office building and headed up Market Street. I veered off at the See's candy store wedged into the corner arrowhead of

Market and Bush and headed into the urban thicket. The sidewalks were littered with slips of paper and every few paces another one fluttered from a window ledge where it had gotten temporarily caught. People abounded on the sidewalks and the streets heading for the Bay Bridge were clogged with cars heading noisily home.

Angela and Stuart were in the bar side of Le Central with a small clique of other people, taking up one of the curved booths in the back, hidden somewhat securely from the rest of the crowd that had jammed into the place. This was no formal sit and greet sort of thing. It was a typical Le Central gathering, full of tailored sports coats, fine shoes, clinking glasses and women of all ages for whom the cocktail party had started generations ago. People lounged in the circular booths effortlessly, standing or sitting at will and rubbing their way up to the bar or back to the bathrooms with ease and seduction, rather unlike the typical middle class ball busters and bra bandits I tended to hang out with.

Angela and Stuart were seated in the center of the booth like host and hostess. There were three other Marina-looking types sitting with them: two good looking and clearly self-sufficient girls and some guy in a suit. Stuart introduced me to everyone and we all said hello and we shook hands and I had no idea who they were or what their affiliations with him were. Angela had been drawn into the mix because she and Stuart (as established) were close. The others, I surmised, were either rich family friends or business compatriots. I squeezed in next to one of the pretty young women, who looked like a French movie starlet and smelled like a flower blossom. I had to position myself on half of my ass while resting my leg in the aisle. It was physically uncomfortable and the noise level was so high I could barely focus on any of the three different conversations taking place at the table, much less the interference coming from the standing brood beside us. I did manage to discern that Angela was heading to Berkeley after she finished her drink: "Tamara and I are having dinner with some friends before we head back into the City for Stuart's party." I also learned that despite the fact that he was throwing a huge party that night, Stuart had already gone to the gym and met the caterers at his place so they could get the food in the refrigerator. He had bought the champagne months before to avoid getting price gouged and had picked up wine a few weeks before the Christmas rush. There was a staff of four coming at five—or five coming at four; who knew—to finish setting up for the party. The housekeeper was there making sure everything was in place. As it was, there wasn't much he had to do except, in the words of the already-sloppy male acquaintance, "Get the party started!"

Giggles and Candy and Biff—I have no idea what their real names were—all raised their glasses on Stuart's lead and Angela grinned like a princess. I had to grab somebody's glass of water because I didn't have a drink, which caused Giggles to lament, "Ohhh...." Then she jabbed Biff on his upper arm with three fingers and said, "Get him a drink, baby." And I responded, as we all had our glasses in the air: "I'll get one, don't worry." At the same time, Candy leaned into me insistently, "You can't toast with water!" Yet the toast carried on despite me raising a glass of somebody else's water: "Happy New Year!" we all called out. There was a clatter of clanking glasses and a quick burst of convivial cheers. Sipping was accompanied by a brief silence—at our table—and then the fifteen different topics of conversation resumed.

* * *

If I thought Celia's flat over in Presidio Heights was nice, I was totally unprepared for Stuart's place on Nob Hill. From the outside it looked decent enough; nothing extravagant. It sat on the steep northern edge of Mason Street, about a quarter of the way down on a corner of one of those distinct and classically hidden San Francisco alleyways. It looked like there could have been ten or twelve units in the five-story, pseudo-classical, renovated building. As it turns out there were only four. The first floor consisted of a small lobby and a garage; the rest of the floors were comprised of one large unit on each.

There was a man who looked like a football player in a black suit and trench coat standing at the main door when I arrived for the New Years party. "Good evening, sir," he said. (Did I actually look like I belonged there?) "Your name?"

"Hugo Storm."

He scanned his handheld and tapped the screen. "Welcome." He pointed to the elevator just inside the enclosed courtyard. "Top floor."

"Thanks, boss. By the way, my girlfriend's coming later."

"Emily?"

"Uh—yes."

The elevator buttons in Stuart's building read L, 1, 2, 3, and PH—just enough silliness (a penthouse in a 4 story building?) to keep it from being truly pretentious. Normally you had to have a card key to make the elevator work but for that night it had been programmed to allow anyone to go up to Stuart's apartment. When you arrived, the doors opened onto a small foyer, which opened onto a big living room with a striking view of the Financial District.

"Wow!" I said with distraction to a guy standing in the foyer. "What a view."

"Thanks," he said.

It was Stuart. It took me a second to recognize him. He was wearing a tuxedo and had a few overcoats draped over his arm. "Wow. Aren't you all dressed up," I told him.

"Only happens once in a century, this one."

"True," I said. I looked down at his shiny shoes and glistening cufflinks. I felt kind of slovenly in my jeans and navy blazer but that was all I had in the fancy clothes department. I had a black suit that I'd worn to Aunt Alice's funeral but I wasn't going to wear that. It only would've made me think of Alice and start missing her. She used to talk about making it until the year 2000; she wanted her life to span the centuries.

"I'm glad you made it," Stuart said. "Where's Emily?"

"Working. She gets off around ten then she'll be over."

"Fantastic."

Just then a kid who looked like a model, dressed in black and with his long hair slicked back, came into the foyer. "Sorry, sir," he said to Stuart. "I got bogged down in fur." He lifted the coats from Stuart's arm and headed back into the apartment.

Stuart brushed off his sleeve and let me know that *hors d'oeuvres* were being served all evening. "Don't fill up, though, because there's roast pork at midnight."

Sounded good to me.

"If you need anything," he added, "ask one of the boys in black."

"Thanks, I will."

He smiled and squeezed my shoulder. The pain was only mildly excruciating; perhaps I was getting used to it. "It's hard for me to spend time with everyone at these parties," he warned, "so enjoy yourself. Go mingle. It's a good crowd; very mixed. If any of the guys try to hit on you, tell them you're with me." He winked. Then sensing my alarm: "Relax. I'm kidding." He patted me on the back. "Come find me when Emily gets here."

"Will do."

Stuart's place was fuck-you-in-the-ass rich. There wasn't a thing out of place or faultily considered, neither a shadow from a light nor a statue nor a picture frame on the mahogany bookshelves that lined the living room wall. The seating was arranged to take advantage of the incredible close-up view of the downtown skyscrapers with a peek-a-boo view of the bay. There was a long hall lined in dark wood that led past a thoroughly masculine dining room and gourmet kitchen to two picture-perfect bedrooms and a paneled den.

Emily arrived about an hour later. "Isn't this shit amazing?" I said to her as I led her through the apartment.

"Don't get a hard-on," she said. "This place was built on the backs of people like us."

"Oh, quit being such a communist." We snuck past Stuart's heavy four poster bed and went into his opulent, modernist master bathroom. "You want something to aspire to? Screw music, screw poetry. This—," I waved my arm around the bathroom, with its recessed bathtub, a glass-enclosed shower stall, double vanity and sequestered toilet. The toilet was partially enclosed by frosted glass so you couldn't be seen if you were sitting down. I coveted that toilet. "*This* is worth aspiring to."

Emily looked at me like she'd just eaten a squirrel. She turned around and walked out of the bathroom muttering something like, "You've got to be joking..."

* * *

Midnight came. The room erupted in cheers. Emily and I kissed. Angela and I kissed. Tamara and I shook hands. Simultaneous sets of fireworks burst above the Financial District and countless others shot up from around the bay. Stuart came over and wished us all a Happy New Year then kissed Angela on the mouth for what seemed an inappropriate duration. I looked at Emily and raised my eyebrows as if to say, *What the f—?* In their defense she mouthed the words *No tongue.*

Celia, our former boss, was at the party as well. She came over and wished us all a Happy New Year then she grabbed hold of Stuart around the waist and hugged him as he kissed her, too, on the lips. "Sorry your Mexican cowboy isn't here to celebrate with you," she said to him when their lips had parted. "Too bad he had to spend the weekend with his *familia*." In between the false sincerity of her lines you could hear a tone of desperation and envy, as though she were offering herself to Stuart as a consolation prize. The aforementioned Angela and Tamara had brought luggage with them to the party. They were going to spend the night in the exquisite guest room to avoid having to cross the bridge in a car along with all the drunks on the road. "How thoughtful," Celia said to Stuart upon hearing that. "You'll have company after all."

Boys in black came around with champagne. Roast pork was set out on large platters with tortillas and salsas and some sort of toasted, sliced bananas on the side. "They're called *tostones*," Stuart said. "It's fried plantain."

There was pastry. There were cakes.

We began the new century with gluttony and sate, and at some point, before the sun rose, we went to our beds—to whichever bed—to sleep off the excitement and ease our way into a wondrous, new and unpredictable day.

-9-

GONE SOUTH

Date: January 1, 2000.
Time: Circa 11am.
Location: bed.
Me: "Do you feel any different?"
She: "No."
"Did any planes crash or banks fail?"
"Not that I'm aware of."
"I guess we survived it."
"Happy Saturday, then." Emily rolled back over and covered her head with a pillow.

* * *

In the early days of the new year, once the champagne news coverage had flattened and Y2K fears failed to manifest, media stories started breaking about what a disaster the online Christmas shopping season had been. Sales numbers were admirable but the fulfillment aspect—the part where people actually received what they ordered—was abysmal. Huge percentages of goods failed to be shipped in time for Christmas. Countless orders lingered at online retailers whose pickers, packers and shippers were overwhelmed by the unanticipated volume and underwhelmed by the back-end disorder that prevented them from processing orders in a timely manner. More often than not, the internet front-end of the shopping sites were all perfectly digitized while in the stockrooms there was a sea surge of unmanageable paper and manual processes.

The mixed mess that was the first big internet Christmas season left a black eye on ecommerce retailers and on agencies like goFORTH that built their shopping web sites for them. Accusations flew that all the agencies had done was create pretty facades for online stores while ignoring computational black holes in the back office. For some it was further fodder to feed their insistence that the internet was neither the great equalizer nor the revolutionary force that its deluded proponents claimed it to be. They'd bring up inflated stock valuations and point an accusatory finger at our shabby work and ludicrous ideas. Their opinions flared in the op-ed sections of business journals and newspapers as we took cover under protective rebuttals published in our own trade publications. Talking to ourselves, we reassured ourselves that we were learning this new commerce mode—all of us: client, agency and consumers alike. We allowed ourselves to be rattled for a moment or two as the markets took away some of the sweet punch they'd rewarded our industry with at year-end, but we remained convinced that we were on the right track. The stock markets would once again surge forward in the early months of 2000, with the NASDAQ pushing closer and closer to its magical 5,000 mark by Spring.

Given that I worked for one of the largest internet ventures around, it was no surprise that a disproportionate number of the negative articles made mention of my employer. E-MERGE, as we were now embarrassingly called, was being bounced around in both the press and on the NASDAQ. During the month of January our stock price dropped from its peak of $89 a share down to the mid $60s and hovered there, bobbing up and down, with analysts and pundits all pointing a continual finger at the merger as the cause for its faltering valuation. Georgie High Pants, my boss, gave any number of pep talks folded into our weekly sales meetings. These, coupled with the barrage of positive spin coming out of the main office (wherever that officially was) told us outright that the drop in share price was to be expected after a merger of such magnitude. The Kool-Aid that flowed into our company trough was the relentless merger mantra: MORE BIGGER BETTER NEW.

A few days out from closing escrow on my new place, I got a call from the real estate agent who was handling my purchase of the loft on Langton Street. He was tall and annoyingly good looking. His name was Rick. He lived in the Marina and he had a well-baked, jockish body that suggested he spent all of his free time in the gym. He hustled himself in the real estate market and appeared to be doing well. He reminded me of me—not his mercurial, entrepreneurial, high-end porn star appeal. More it was a sense of him being me if I weren't entirely me. Me if I were somebody I could be, as opposed to the me that I presently was.

"If that makes any sense."

"No it doesn't," Emily said boorishly as we waited in the sales office on Langton Street waiting for Rick. That his name rhymed with dick was no coincidence. In addition to his Marina Boy perfection he had a pricky bossiness about him which I once might have aspired to, a sense of *This is the way things are; you may not like it but you'll appreciate it once this all is over.* It was a ruthless sort of condescension that he exuded well. He held the reins. It seemed a flattering attribute at first—like a good haircut—but after a very short time interacting with him I realized he was just a prick. He had been referred to me by the agent who was selling the lofts and so he was an inheritance as opposed to an act of willful selection. *"Collusion,"* Emily had cautioned back at the beginning.

Rick wanted me to drop off a post-dated cashier's check so everything would be lined up when I went in to sign the final escrow papers at end of the week.

"Curious," Emily remarked distrustfully when I asked her to go with me.

Rick strode into the office in a rush. "Dude! Great to see you!" He ushered us into a small white windowless room. Emily and I sat down. Rick dumped a stack of papers on the round white table. He dragged a chair from the corner of the room and quickly sat down across from me. He flipped the papers around so I could see them. "Let's sign."

"Isn't it early?"

"Nah."

"I thought—."

"Dude. If this escrow doesn't go through then my mother's a butt pirate." He glanced at Emily. "Seriously." Then back at me. "Did you bring the check?"

I retrieved the cashier's check from my jacket pocket and set it gingerly upon the table. Sensing my uncertainty, he told me to, "Relax. The lender signs off in a day or two. It's going to go through. Trust me. I'm going to Tahoe this weekend so I wanna get this turned over to the broker before I leave."

"What about the keys?" Emily interjected.

"Saturday. As planned. Escrow closes Friday then gets recorded. On Saturday you can pick up the keys here at the office." He handed me a pen. I stared at the mound of papers, various of which were tabbed with different colored flags where I'd be signing and where Emily would witness.

"Here we go."

* * *

"So much for ceremony," Emily remarked as we left the building. We walked down the block and stopped. We stood looking up at my soon-to-be new home. The loft was one of six in a row, a rowhouse essentially, with a cement façade and industrial detailing. Each loft was the same: there was a front door on street level with a two-story window through which you could see the living area and sleeping loft upstairs. Emily looked upwards. "You gonna charge admission?"

"What do you mean?"

"I didn't realize you could see right into the bedroom from the street."

The loft had a small room in the back, behind the kitchen on the way to the door to the service hall. I'd planned to put my TV and music in there. "I'm not sleeping back in the media room," I told her.

"Then you better invest in some curtains."

* * *

During the interim days between signing the loan papers and getting the keys, I was filled with a sense of endless possibility. Yes, the transition to home ownership had been more clinical than I'd expected. Yes, I was going to have to sell the rest of my Screaming stock to furnish the place. Yes, I'd lost nearly thirty thousand dollars of value in my goFORTH stocks because of the merger. Still, despite those unpredictabilities and the aggregate of those unplanned and yet somehow ordinary and necessary ventures, I remained filled with a belief that anything was still achievable.

"Welcome to the lifecycle," Stuart grinned. In order to celebrate my new state of home ownership he bought me lunch at Sweet Joanna's, a deli near our offices. "A caution, though," he added. "You've bought into a speculative market."

"What are you saying?"

"Only that I think you've done well with your purchase. I'm also sounding a note of caution."

* * *

Some numbers you remember in life. For me, 1-2-1 is one of them. On January 21st I picked up the keys to my first home: 121 Langton Street, Unit #4. As I walked through the front door with the key in hand—my hand—I was overcome by a sense of amazement and thrill, as well as a very subtle, softly acknowledgeable bit of sadness. I didn't much believe in fairy tales but I was as susceptible as anyone else to pondering notions of *what if*. In my *what if* scenario I wondered what it would be like if my mother had been standing beside me as I unlocked the front door to the loft. I wanted to try and feel what my mother would have thought of me: twenty-five years old, a kid with no particular skills or extensive education, now a homeowner. Somehow I had to discern her pleasure or pride, to divorce it from her worries about the grimy neighborhood, the high cost, etc. and carry the positive feelings with me as I led her around the open plan of the first floor then up the metal circular stairs to the sleeping loft, walk-in closet and bathroom. I only occasionally used to do it, and at that time it seemed a relevant effort: I tried to picture what she would have looked like—what kind of clothes she might have worn; how she would have done her hair; what expressions of delight and excitement she might draw on her face as we rode the cable cars up Nob Hill later that day. Not knowing the answers, save having an impression of her dressed in flowers and hazily lit as if in an old photograph, I came to the conclusion that she would, in all regards, have been pleased.

"Guess where I am, Pop." I'd called my Daddy to let him know the news. "In my new place."

"Get out," he said. "So you got it?"

"Sure did." I wandered the open space of the first floor, my voice echoing off the cement walls and tall ceiling.

"I'm proud of you, boy."

"Thanks."

"You gonna be able to manage the mortgage without a roommate?"

"Yep," I said. My monthly payment was about two thousand dollars a month but I was making enough at E-MERGE to cover it. With taxes and insurance, though, I joked to my father that that kind of outlay was going to force me to learn to cook.

"You can get yourself a girl for that," he said with all seriousness. "You still seeing that Emily?"

"Yes, sir."

"She gonna be living with you?"

"No sir, not a chance."

"What's *not a chance*?" Emily asked after I hung up the phone. She was moving through the living room taking long strides, her feet spread a few feet apart with each step.

"Nothing," I lied.

Emily stopped mid-floor. "Mh." She was making rough measurements of the space so she could help me pick out furniture. Crossing to the other end she announced, "Living room's about sixteen by twenty." This sort of open living was distinctly urban and new, unlike the traditional flat I had in North Beach, and it attached itself to me the moment I saw the place. Emily glanced around: "I guess that'd be living *and* dining room, actually." From the front door she walked the length of the wall that stretched all the way back to the media room in the back. "This is a big-ass wall," she announced, coming back to my side. She pointed at the fifteen foot tall expanse of barren white space that framed the left-hand side of the unit. "You could put some gorgeous artwork up here. It's screaming for a Basquiat or something ultra modern like that."

"What's a Basquiat?"

She wrapped her arm around my waist. "That's why I like you, Hugo Storm. You're like an open staff, nine lines of musical opportunity just waiting to be composed upon."

"I'll take that as a compliment."

She stepped away to get a look at the large wall from the other side of the living area. "Basquiat was a New York street painter who died of a drug overdose," she explained. "His work is definitely not pretty but it's powerful."

"And I should cover my walls with his ugly art?"

Emily clapped her hands in appreciation. "Absolutely. Right there!" She drew a frame in the air with her hands to envision it. "His big pieces probably go for around a hundred thousand."

"Ha! You're out of your mind. How much money do you think I have?"

"I don't know, baby. You just bought a half million dollar loft. I guess you have a lot."

"Reality check," I warned as I went over to the kitchen. It was a narrow u-shaped space that offered a perfect spot for bar stools on the other side. I pulled a scrap receipt out of my wallet and a pen from my courier pack. I wrote down a number and carried the slip of paper over to her. "This," I informed her, "is the decorating budget."

"What?!"

"That's what I can afford to spend."

"You can't decorate an entire apartment on two thousand dollars."

"Why not?"

"Far be it from me to encourage you to go out and spend money on *stuff*—. But talk about reality checks, Hugo. Do you have any idea how much a decent sofa costs?"

"No."

"Of course not. You've never bought furniture before."

"I bought a bedroom set."

"At the Salvation Army."

"Yeah—."

"You can't bring all that crap from your apartment over here. It'll look like a cheap dorm room."

"What am I supposed to do?"

"Shop."

"You—?," I pointed at her confoundedly, "want me—?," I pointed at myself, "to go out and buy a house full of furniture from some overseas sweatshop where twelve year olds are bound to upholstery machines for their entire youth?"

"Hardly," she said cursively. "The good stuff is made in North Carolina."

* * *

"Well of course it was expensive," Angela said one afternoon as she stood in the living space of my loft. "Everything has a price." She knew. She and Tamara had started looking for something in Berkeley to buy together. She had officially given notice on her apartment in the City and was moving wholesale to the other side of the bay, confident that the two of them would be able to wend their way through the frustrating reality of multiple offers and buyer competition that was a hallmark of home shopping in the tree-lined village she was exchanging San Francisco for. "You figure out what something's worth to you and that's that. What the market will bear…" She wandered past the kitchen into the media room in the back. Coming back out, nodding—impressed, I assumed—she asked when the housewarming was going to take place.

"Not sure. You bringing Mrs. Green?"

"Tamara? We'll see."

"Am I still on her shit list?"

"Well—." Angela pondered a polite response. "She hasn't quite warmed up to you yet. Although I admit the two of you got along well at New Years."

"I thought so."

"Give it time." She leaned in and hugged me. As she pulled away she remarked, looking over my shoulder, "That's a really big wall."

* * *

In the gallery of one Walter Edict, on the uppermost floor of an elegant, early 20th century mansion in Union Square that had been converted into high-ceilinged art galleries and small office rentals, I stood in front of a canvas that was 84 inches wide and five feet tall.

"What is it?" I asked Mr Edict.

"A birth."

"Of what?"

He shrugged. "The planets. A nation. Maybe a cow."

"Indeed."

"The artist wants you to come away with the sense of having witnessed the birth of something. What that specific something is is entirely up to you."

"I see. Does he have anything that *doesn't* look like an abortion?"

* * *

In the gallery of one Miriam Howe there were some tear sheets of copies of posters of Matisse and Chagall in fanciful overwrought frames of faux-gilded wood.

"They're called lithographs," said Ms Howe.

"I see. How much for this one?" I pointed to a small piece with floating angels and stars against a royal blue sky and cartoon rooftops.

"Eighteen thousand," she replied. "They are only going to appreciate over time."

"Indeed." I declined to remind her that I'd seen at least three other galleries within the vicinity that were hawking companion pieces culled from the same plethora of poster books that had been dumped onto the market all at once. "I'll give you four hundred dollars."

* * *

In the gallery of one Halter & Claire I saw an exquisite pile of rocks just inside the entrance.

* * *

The Ace hardware store on 4th Street was jammed into the first floor and basement of a vertiginous, claustrophobia-inducing relic that might have survived the Big One back in 1906. I asked a red-vested clerk nearing retirement where I might find some paint.

"House paint or spray paint?"

"Mmh. Either."

"Only reason I ask," he explained, "is because we keep the spray paint locked up so the kids don't steal it. If you want it, I have to get the key from the front. Somehow I came to work without my key chain. Well—," he continued, as though I might have been interested or concerned or otherwise engaged in his pseudo-psychotic monologue, which I wasn't. "I got my house keys, but the cabinet keys I keep 'em on a separate ring because there's a lot of them and it's too much to carry if I'm just going to the market or somewhere, you know." I nodded and tried to shake his madness from my head.

He led me down a steep and narrow flight of stairs. The downstairs ceiling was low like a tomb and the air stank of must and sawdust and the metallic brine of screws and nails.

"What color you want?"

"I don't know yet."

"Well if you want custom colors we can mix it at the counter. Just bring the color sample over to Barry there and he'll take care of it."

"Thanks," I said.

"There's brushes over here," he continued as he shuffled a few feet down the cramped aisle. "And if you need drop cloths or anything—."

"I'll be fine," I said. "Fine fine fine, thanks."

With a bobbing nod of his loosely connected head he departed.

* * *

"What the hell is that?" Emily's tone of voice was derogatory.

"I call it *The surge of the emerging phallus encapsulated by a river of dreams.*"

"It's hideous."

"I thought you'd appreciate my attempt to find my creative voice."

"I appreciate the effort, but this is just *wrong*." (This from a woman who creates homicide with a treble clef.) "Number one, it's poorly executed. And number two, it doesn't fit. You've got this super contemporary, quasi-elegant motif going, and then there's this pedestrian *mess* all over the wall. Look at the scale of it. It's ridiculous."

"But you said the wall needed something big."

"Big and *wonderful*. Not big and hideous. What a fucking *mess*."

* * *

Once the work of filling up the spaces of the loft with furniture and *stuff* was done; once my foray into self-expression had been painted over thoroughly so there wasn't left a trace; once Emily had drained my liquid assets and convinced me to ratchet up my debt a little further ("It's a *great* wall unit"), I started enjoying home ownership. Buying a home was a leap of faith. Like anything else into which you put your time, your money and your effort, a home was an investment. And in some ways it was also a gamble. A home was a deeply held belief and a promise to yourself that there was some certainty in life. Some persistence. Home was place and place was mother and mother was a concept which at one point had been breath and flesh and had now been transmuted into drywall and cement and expense. And faith.

* * *

"You like it?" I asked Stuart as I showed him around the now fully-furnished space.

He nodded favorably. "Well done."

* * *

Into every presumptive aspiration, however, there eventually creeps that sordid detail called reality.

Angela emailed me on April Fool's Day 2000, mere months after I moved in: *Done your taxes yet?*

Not yet. Why?

Instantly my desk phone rang.

"What's up?" I asked her.

"Brace yourself."

"Why?"

"Did you exercise your goFORTH options last year?"

"Yeah of course. Why?"

"Those were non-qualified stock options."

"Meaning—?"

"They're taxed like regular income."

"So?"

"The spread between the price of the option and the market value at the time you exercised them is taxable income."

"Try it in English."

"Look at your W2."

"I don't have it here." I kept my tax stuff in a box until I was ready to file. I never did my taxes until the last minute. I usually owed very little if anything, so I couldn't justify filing early.

"You better look at the one from goFORTH. You're in for a shock."

I rushed home that evening and pulled my manila tax folder out from the box of financial paperwork I kept in the closet. I tore open the W2 statement from goFORTH. In Box 12 there was an amount of $72,500 and next to it a code V: *income from exercise of non-statutory stock options*. It was just as Angela had warned. I owed income tax on an additional seventy-two thousand, five hundred dollars; and not a penny of taxes had been taken out of it.

I crouched on the floor with my back against the wall. My chest constricted and I began breathing anxiously through my lips. With each exhalation I expelled more air than my lungs could consume on re-inhalation, and the light beneath my eyelids fluttered warbly grey with flashing lights as a buzzing sound rose to a deafening pitch in the channels of my ears.

*　*　*

"Fuck," said Emily as we sat at the Thai restaurant up the street from the loft. She'd worked the day shift that day. Although she'd planned to spend the night at her place, she came over after I called her in my distress. I ordered my food mild. I was already so sick to my stomach I could barely eat; the slightest heat would have melted a hole in my stomach lining.

"How much do you owe?" she asked.

"Combined state and federal, probably around twenty-five thousand bucks."

"Fuck. When's your appointment with the tax guy?"

"Monday."

"Fuck."

* * *

Wilfred Baumgartner's office occupied a drab corner on the 9th floor of an old office building on Market Street. The lobby outside his door was painted a slightly sickening fuchsia with blended burgundy and green carpeting striving unsuccessfully for a note of glamour. In deference to all the renovations and new building activities over the years, buildings like his—remnants from the old, post-war, pre-70's resurgent San Francisco—remained squarely on their footings of neglect. Baumgartner's building existed along a forgotten stretch of Market Street up where ambling tourists who'd strayed too far became intermixed with strippers and drugged out denizens of the single room occupancy hotels. There were several rooms in Mr Baumgartner's office suite, each one of them secured by an old wooden door. The various occupants of those offices kept their doors open to draw in some light. The rooms hummed with the running of clunky desktop computers and the high-speed tip-tap of fingers manipulating adding machines and keyboards.

"You're lucky Stuart Piers is a client of mine," Mr Baumgartner said with searing precision. On either end of his desk rested two incredibly tall stacks of folders, neatly arranged but ominous. "Today's April 12th," he remarked.

"Yes sir. I'm extremely fortunate that Stuart Piers is a friend of ours both."

Mr Baumgartner reached a hand across his desk. "What have you got?"

I presented him with my manila folder, which held a few envelopes and the paperwork surrounding my stock options.

"That's it?"

"I'm fairly uncomplicated. I have my escrow papers in my bag if you need them."

"You bought a house?"

"In January."

"Did you pay anything in December?"

"Five hundred dollar security deposit."

He shook his head. "Don't bother." He opened the folder and extracted my W2 from its envelope, a slim piece of disposable ink and tree pulp which represented a week's worth of nearly immeasurable angst. Added to that angst was some unnerving bouncing in the stock markets that had been going on lately. Ever since the NASDAQ hit its magical 5,000 marker in March all of the stock markets had been wobbling up and down with more volatility than they'd seen in some time. Shortly before I left work to head to Mr Baumgartner's accounting office that Monday, the markets had closed for the day and the NASDAQ had fallen 250 points, giving up in one startling session all that it had gained in the prior week. Georgie High Pants passed by my cube as I was leaving for Mr Baumgartners'. I made mention of the market bleeding and he threw a dismissive hand into the air: "Stabilization point. Automated trading fucked everything up back at 5,000. The market's just trying to get back in synch with itself. There's nothing to worry about."

"Do you own a car?" Mr Baumgartner asked.

I nodded yes.

"How much is it worth?"

"I just bought it." I'd been warned by Rick, the real estate agent, not to go out and buy any big ticket items during escrow, so I waited a few weeks after getting the loft to finally buy my BMW.

"Cash?"

"Five year loan."

"How much savings do you have?"

"A few months' living expenses."

"Any stock?"

"Just that goFORTH-Hartman-Holley-E-MERGE…whatever it is."

"Anything liquid?"

"Isn't that?"

He shook his head with indifference. "These are staggered two-year options. They don't begin vesting for another 8 months." He looked down again and scanned the numbers on the various sheets of paper. "Where are the proceeds from this?" He held up the sell record for my Screaming stock.

I hesitated. "In the house."

His eyebrows lifted gently. "It's all gone, I presume?"

"The cash?"

"Yes."

"Yes," he repeated. "Yes, of course." He gathered the papers back together, neating up their edges and re-inserting everything thoughtfully back into the manila envelope. He slid it back toward me. "Eight hundred dollars."

"That's all I owe?"

"No," he said plainly. "That's my fee. We can get you set up in our client roster, file your return, and establish a payment schedule with the IRS."

"How much do I owe?"

"What was the number you told me?" he asked.

I repeated what I'd told him in my panicked phone call a few days prior, an amount which was equivalent to four months' salary.

He nodded. "About right."

My heart sank and I shut my eyes.

After the demoralizing visit to the accountant's office, I took the street level F-train back to the office. I wanted to see the City from above ground. I wanted to be among people amid the open air with an opportunity to escape if I needed to; I didn't want to be stuck in a tunnel, susceptible, ensnared. Palpitations from my heart beating heavily echoed in my chest as the car jostled along Market Street. A familiar heaviness crept into my lungs and a nervous tingling began to consume my nose and throat. I gripped the overhead rail and watched the throngs outside the window blend into one. I closed my eyes and relaxed my shoulders and tried to let the rattling of the street car become my breath.

Two days later, on the afternoon on Friday April 14th, Year 2000, people rushed around the Financial District filing tax extensions, ranting over their exorbitant tax burdens and queuing up in festering lines at the post office to file packets of paper and blood money as news media jostled for position on street corners to chronicle a day in which all things financial had abruptly gone south. After a week of slow bleeding the NASDAQ was headed for a further drop of 350 points for the day. Practically everyone throughout our E-MERGE offices had had financial web sites open on their computers all throughout the week. They had spent every moment from the moment they arrived on Friday morning hitting *Refresh* on their keyboards as they watched the markets tumble. By midday the tickers had turned into a sea of red. By end of day, end of week, the NASDAQ had suffered a precipitous and unrecoverable 25% loss. In a short series of elusive breaths, a trillion dollars of worth and value had evaporated. At market close on Friday we just stood there, thinking, staring unremittingly, and in some cases muttering aloud, "Fuck me."

* * *

I lay beside Emily in bed the next morning contemplating the short strands of her hair, all askew on one side from the pressure of sleep. From the fibers of her hair and the pores of my arms emanated the faint odor of coriander and fenugreek, a residual perfume lingering from the previous night's Indian dinner. I had taken her to the place in the Tenderloin that Angela and I used to go before she started spending all of her nights at Tamara's. It was a somber dinner, marked by a sort of palpable grieving not just at our table but in the ashen expressions of people passing along the angularly lit street outside. The faces of my working class compatriots reflected an angst that I could see mirrored in my own eyes as I stared at them through the plate glass window. In contrast, the eyes of the poor and homeless passing by seemed indifferent, almost content in a burned-out, unaffected way. Lucky, I even at one point brazenly thought. "A crashing stock market can be a painful equalizer," I remarked.

"True," Emily said. "The only thing that keeps us out of the gutter is the curb."

If the markets were really only comprised of people, I pondered that Saturday morning as I lay in bed stroking Emily's hair, and if people are comprised of thoughts and needs like desires and greed, then aren't the markets—themselves, by extension, living things—as susceptible to those detrimental urges as they are to the lure of superficial beauty? Don't the markets swing in the same way our moods do? Do we drive them down by our doubt and despair? And is it only our false optimism and deceits that keep them moving upward? Surely what we'd been witnessing up until the previous week was the beauty of the financial markets at work—the burly, confident forces of human nature creating something powerful out of absolutely nothing. (Money is just a construct, after all. If I have two rocks, one shiny and blue and the other one drab and grey, and I claim that the blue one has value because it is beautiful whereas the grey one is worth nothing because it's not, I am assigning value arbitrarily, the same way value is ascribed to something like gold and gemstones. And if I print a batch of paper and stamp my insignia on it as well as a number and declare that it's worth one four-course meal at the Chutney Indian restaurant, mango lassi included, how different is that from a government printing currency and declaring that ten of these things will get you one of these other?)

"What are you thinking?" Emily whispered into the air.

"I'm not sure."

"You worried?"
"Of course."

* * *

There are insufficient metaphors to capture the essence of the ensuing few months. It was like riding a roller coaster when you knew one of the tracks was loose: maybe you'd make it; maybe you wouldn't. At E-MERGE, clients started dropping like flies as additional funding rounds went unfunded by the same venture capitalists who had driven the valuation of companies with ridiculous premises like Bonez (a faux currency) and NetParamedic (get a defibrillator delivered with your pizza) first into the stratosphere and then into an early grave. These lesser components of the index, and all strata of our clients, fell deservedly ill and ultimately died of fiscal starvation.

Summer brought the NASDAQ a temporary reprieve in the form of modestly bolstered stock prices: the index had snuck up to around 4,000—by and large a reasonable sign of health. But faith had already begun slipping and our latest round of optimism was short-lived. The IT industry had been suffering from an epidemic of self-consumption and all the emerging indicators suggested it would be terminal for the vast majority of those involved. As a company whose seams were shredding, we at E-MERGE held our collective breath and pumped ourselves full of whatever mantras we could contrive to keep ourselves believing that the company would survive. But by November 2000 the end of the party loomed. It was clear that our company's financial roller coaster was going to collapse. By Halloween our stock price was a whopping $3.19. I know the dollar figure precisely because that's the day I sold my remaining 830 shares. What had been worth over $40,000 just six months beforehand would at that point barely cover one mortgage payment. With funereal solemnity, I slipped a copy of the sell order into my manila folders labeled 'Taxes' and with my fingers crossed I transferred the proceeds into my savings account.

* * *

December 2000.
"Thanks for letting me come over," I said to Stuart as he shook my hand. I'd invited myself over to his office on an auspiciously awful day with the hopes that he'd have some sage words to offer, some comfort to render, some perspective with which to bolster my waning, nearly lost confidence.

He walked over to his window and looked out. "Grim?"

"Like a firing squad," I said. I joined him by the window and looked across Spear Street. You could see through the alleyway between the buildings and past the plaza to our main doors, just as he had once said. Stretched along Main Street beside our building was a line of yellow taxi cabs waiting curbside.

"How many people are being let go?" he asked.

"About forty from our building. Nearly a hundred in Tech."

"Ouch."

"Yep."

"But you're ok for now?"

"Shockingly, yes. My boss said that anybody who wasn't called in by noon was safe."

"That's a good sign," he said.

"You think?" I asked him.

"You don't have a pink slip and a taxi voucher."

* * *

Grim was the mood at E-MERGE all throughout the holidays and into the first quarter of 2001. Surprisingly we had hung on throughout the winter without significant attrition. There had been issued all sorts of pep talks and emailed memos from management trying to assure us that the company would persevere despite the challenges we faced. Even though our client base was evaporating and the landscape of opportunity had changed, we would, they insisted, find a way to adapt. The chatter had a net effect of zero, though, since it was pretty clear to all involved that the stock option conversion that took place at the end of 2000 had signaled the death knell: any company that retracts its twenty and thirty dollar options and re-issues them for ninety cents is simply bargaining for a little more time.

One might wonder where Angela was in all of this—why and how she'd managed to keep such a low profile. If the facts be known, then the facts are these: having a keenly prescient awareness of things about her, Angela quit her job at E-MERGE during the stock market freefall of Autumn 2000, prior to the first round of layoffs. She had spent the summer networking and landed a senior manager's role at a telecom company: "Not very exciting," she said, "but it'll pay the rent." From her perspective E-MERGE was a dying duck riddled with NASDAQ shrapnel, not a super-fat phoenix that would rise, slimmed and agile, from the pile of its own ashes (i.e., the smell of burnt stock options). It was the opposite of where I believed things were trending.

I maintained, if through nothing more than foolishness, that E-MERGE would shed its excess and emerge a more efficient and capable machine that would be able to stay afloat and possibly even thrive in the flailing marketplace.

On March 12, 2001, however, the patient officially died. The NASDAQ closed beneath 2,000. It would take one last gasp during the next market session trying to resurrect itself. It would teeter over the edge of 2,000, only to ultimately retreat in collapse, shorn of its earthly glory, stripped of all future possibilities. E-MERGE shares closed that day at forty-nine cents. Days later I was reading *The Industry Standard* (which at that point should have been called *The Idiot Stranded*). In it a writer was imploring the implausible, that it wasn't too late to make it as a net zillionaire despite the plain carnage littering the streets of the Multimedia Gulch, San Francisco, Silicon Valley and Wall Street. *The Economist*, reporting on the same timeframe, came out and officially declared the internet boom a bust.

A few days later I called Emily from my office phone. "Can you come get me," I said to her.

"Well, I'm—," she started.

"That wasn't a question! Come pick me up!"

"A-all right," she stammered. "Where are you?"

"I'm at the office. Where are you?"

"Still at your place. I was just about to get in the shower."

"Get my car and come pick me up," I insisted.

"Fine," she said. "What time?"

"Now!"

It had been pretty clear that morning that something was amiss. There was an all-hands meeting being held at ten o'clock. *Mandatory.* We descended on the auditorium, about two hundred of us, the remainder of the San Francisco workforce. One of the SVP's made a cursory announcement about the sorry state of affairs of the company. He concluded his message with the highly anticipated and equally dreaded, "As a result, we are having to take some drastic measures to keep the organization viable." The head of Human Resources then took the podium and announced that she was going to read a list of fourteen names. "After I call the names, will you fourteen please stand up." I was seated next to Trini and we looked at each other anxiously. The HR woman read the list of names aloud—neither mine nor Trini's was among them—and at the conclusion she said, "Those of you whose names I called, please leave the auditorium. If I did *not* call your name, please remain in the auditorium until the conclusion of the presentation." That remainder, a solid 90% of the San Francisco office, was informed that our employment with E-MERGE was being terminated effective immediately. The HR woman indicated that there were flyers available that summarized our rights as terminated employees; the flyer included a list of frequently asked questions and relevant phone numbers, as well a secure link to information on the E-MERGE.com employee extranet. She regretted that the announcement had to be made *en masse*, but "given the large number of employees affected, it was not logistically feasible to inform everyone on an individual basis." Further, as was policy, we were to gather our personal belongings and leave the premises immediately upon the conclusion of the meeting. We would be paid through the remainder of the day but would not—in fact, could not, as our network access had been rescinded—be asked to perform any work or be allowed to send out any emails.

There was a low wall outside of our office building that was suitable for sitting on. I hung out by the wall waiting for Emily to pick me up. Those of us who were waiting for our rides, or were bewildered enough that we didn't know what to do next, sat on the wall with our white moving boxes of personal goods at our feet. There were no taxis for this round of layoffs; we were left to our own means. It was difficult to look at each other without feeling a sense of shame or despair, and more than a few people shed tears. We hugged each other and could scarcely say a word aside from *Sucks, eh?...Fucking unreal...Keep in touch.*

As I milled around in front of the wall pacing and smoking, Trini approached, a white box extended from his arms.

"Well, my friend—," he said. And that was all he could say. A slight tear formed in each of his eyes. He shrugged and choked up.

"We'll be all right." I put my hand on his shoulder and gently squeezed.

We stood that way for a moment or two. Finally Trini set his box on the ground and said weepily, "My wife is pregnant, Hugo."

"I didn't know that."

He shook his head. "I just had a bad feeling about all of this. I didn't want to say anything. I am so worried now."

"You'll be ok," I told him, not entirely sure I believed it myself.

"This is terrible." He sat down on the edge of the wall. Anger came over him and he kicked his white box: "This is all a big SHIT."

Eventually Emily arrived, driving my car. My Montego Blue exterior, Saddle Brown leather interior, 3 Series coupe with 6 CD changer and electric everything. Ahh...thing I'd always longed for. Car of my dreams and exultant expression of my simple but not entirely meager existence. The day I bought that car I felt the long undulating road of opportunity beneath the wheels as I drove it out of the dealership. After I parked it in the secure, covered garage in the back of my building and traced its contour with my hand as I left it alone for the first time in the concrete warren, I couldn't help but be overcome by a sense of pride and accomplishment. So what if it was material goods, as Emily remarked with a sneer (followed by a bit of delight upon riding in it for the first time). For me the car and the loft were a *fait accompli*. No matter that I didn't drive the car to work: I only sat at my desk as I was merely a sales secretary. No matter that I went on occasional sales calls in somebody else's car. I. Yes I, Hugo Storm, owned a 3 Series.

Emily lowered the passenger window and waved tepidly.

I looked at the car's beautiful dark blue profile resting against the curb where there lingered ahead of it only one or two spouses in cars awaiting other booted E-MERGEnt serfs and all I saw was a dream tarnished. (Not to mention a heady car payment and insurance.)

Fuck me, I thought.

"You wanna drive?" Emily called out through the window.

"No." I opened the door and tossed my white box, filled with pictures of my loft and my new car and me and Emily, my tchotchkes and mouse pads and stress squeegees—all of that crap, which once decorated a cubicle desk that signified a mundane yet somehow regal personal geography. It landed on the back seat with an unceremonious thunk. I got in and slammed the door shut—for which I apologized to the car—and lifted my hand in sadness to Trini.

"Drive—," I told her urgently. "Please."

* * *

"What now?" Emily asked after she got out of the shower.

"I don't know." I was angry. I was in shock. I didn't know what I was feeling. Each sentiment was fleeting and furious and wound back in upon the others, a chaotic compilation playing out in waves that twisted my interior into knots. "I can't fucking BELIEVE IT." I slammed the kitchen counter with the palms of my hands. "What in the hell am I going to do?!"

And then, as the vast realm of everything I believed I believed in went swirling around inside my head, persistence and possibility gave way to a kitchen counter that vibrated underneath my fingertips. Emily opened a drawer beside me to retrieve a bottle opener to uncap another beer. Her rustling of the kitchen tools sounded as deafeningly loud as a squad of mechanics hurling tools onto a repair shop's floor. And when she pinched herself with the bottle opener and cried out in pain, instead of a yelp I heard the high pitched wail of sirens. As the bottle slipped out of her hands, the cap went flying and the bottle bounced around with the crackle of thunder; droplets of foam exploded into the air as pale ale flooded the counter in front of me like an ocean. The scent drew me immediately back to remembrances of sneaking beers in the sand beneath the Wildwood boardwalk with Bonnie Hedglin and friends when we were in high school—there and then those moments consumed by a sense of eternal, protective permanence. Then, as if by some retractable umbilical cord, my memory was yanked abruptly inland and the scent of musky green summer filled my nostrils with its choking humidity. A rising chorus of cicadas chattered unceasingly in my brain as footsteps traveled in desyncopation down a flight of hardwood stairs behind my eyes, dragging a metal cart in between them, and then suddenly the entire room, the entire loft, started to turn. I found myself breathless and wondering if I was alone and where I was and then, in an instant, I felt my knees disappear and everything went silent and dark.

-10-

FAREWELL THE LOVELY

After a couple months of unemployment I was starting to lose my mind. There were only so many Craigslist job ads you could respond to and never hear back from; so many episodes of *This Old House* to watch in order to distract yourself; so many phantom business opportunities you could conjure and attempt to set down on paper (unsuccessfully) before you began to understand what Emily meant by "the curb." The only thing that keeps us out of the gutter, she had said, was a treadable but treacherously shallow curb lined with financial havoc, drug use, psychosis—any one of which I felt susceptible to after having been laid off by E-MERGE. Beyond the pure financial angst of the situation, the sensation of being unemployable was disturbing; it felt like a social malignancy. Having been burned by the optimism of the boom I didn't want to turn into a pessimistic lout, but after the recent, steady stream of ego deflation and dismissal it was hard to avoid believing that the past few years of *do anything, be anything* had been a hoax perpetrated at the expense of people like me.

Whereas Emily only warned about the curb, I at least had my father to reassure me that I could avoid slipping off its edge. He advised me before I moved to San Francisco to keep aware of that. One benefit of living to middle age, he had said, is that you can see into the past. It's then you realize there are things in life you can control—those thing being the choices you make. "Then there's things like your Momma's passing, which you have no say in whatsoever: leaves you helpless as the clouds. That's why you gotta make choices you believe in. They're the only thing that give you comfort as you grow up." His admonition served as a sort of benediction, a blessing for my journey as we drove the two hours it took to get from the house in Millville to the airport near Philadelphia on the day I left New Jersey and moved to California. We had a Ford Ranger at the time: two doors with a backseat and a covered hatch. One of my suitcases, a full-on hard shell

Tourister, was all the way in the back; the other rested on the back seat beside Aunt Alice, who had her left arm resting on top of it. I was seated up front beside my Daddy, in my lap an old green backpack I'd been hanging onto since forever. The two suitcases could fall out of the cargo hold of the plane for all I cared: everything in them was replaceable. The life that mattered existed in the green carry-on backpack: in it were my plane ticket, address book, a few old photos of Ma and Pop and Alice, music CD's that made a difference, and a tour book of San Francisco that Alice had given me as a going-away present.

"Quite an adventure," Alice called out as we crossed a tall rusted bridge heading south of the city. A thick gush of summer heat blew in through the open windows. "Remember Henry Fonda in *The Grapes of Wrath*?"

"Yeah," I leaned around and told her, "except I'm not driving in some old heap across the country."

"Only just across the Delaware River," laughed my Daddy.

I stayed turned around in my seat staring at Alice. She stared me back in the eye and then winked, then turned to look out the window. She sat there bouncing in her seat, jostled by the bad springs of the truck, helpless as the clouds. She looked happy and sad at the same time, her lifelong suppression simmering as it always did beneath a face that rarely revealed much. Alice was mother, grandmother and aunt all rolled into one. I looked at her and focused on the adventure of things, trying hard to avoid the difficult feeling of leaving her. Didn't matter, I tried to tell myself; she and Daddy were bedrock. There was no need worrying about them; they'd always be around.

"What are your thoughts, ma'am?" I hollered through the wind at Alice.

She looked back at me and gave a sort of smile: "I'm thinking you're gonna survive just fine in California, boy. You got a brain in your head and it works."

"You think?"

"Keep your guard up and you'll be fine," she said. "I ain't worried."

It was precisely the sort of innocently planted mantra of faith that I found myself reciting as I stood in my San Francisco kitchen with no job and no prospects, contemplating three decades of mortgage payments ahead of me, holding the keys to my brand new car payment, calculating in my mind how few dollars I had left in my bank account and how long they would carry me until I had to sell the large Chin Wu painting on the wall or sublet my place and squat in Emily's studio over in Polk Gulch.

I'd been emailing everyone I knew, an entire cadre of new world revolutionaries who, like myself, had failed to read the right books. I asked them to keep their kindred fool in mind if they came across any job leads I'd be good for, and I promised to do the same. Each one of them represented a tiny glimmer of possibility, some third degree chance of connectivity, despite the fact that most of them were jobless as well. Nevertheless I kept pinging them, hoping I would find something before I had to break down and tell my father I'd been laid off. I felt ashamed that I was out of work and I didn't want him to find out. I'd lied to him once already: we spoke pretty frequently and twice he'd asked how work was; I said it was still rocky at the company but my position was hanging on, even though I'd already been laid off. I felt terrible for lying. At times it felt like I'd left New Jersey out of selfishness and foolishness, and with the layoffs and the bust I'd just been given my sad reward for taking those arrogant chances. Each generation, it seems, falls into California's alluring trap. Each heads west chasing some hidden promise and when things go south we're left figuring out if we're going to keep pushing on or if we're going to pack what's left of our pride and our belongings and retreat. Guilt was an unavoidable monster as well. No matter the greater forces at play, there lingered a sensation that I had a role in my situation: that I had unmade my proverbial bed and climbed into it willingly, and after the fast, delicious, consummating act I alone was solely responsible for the outcome, regardless of how many others had been rolling around in the lusty bed alongside me.

"They let you go?" my Daddy said with a bit of shock after I finally mustered the courage to call and tell him.

"Me and 99% of the company."

"I'll be…What're you gonna do now?"

"I don't know, Pop. I'll find another job. The bad IT companies all went to hell in a hoopskirt but there are still some decent ones left."

"IT?" he interrupted. "What's IT?"

"Information technology, Pop." I swore I was sick of telling him what it stood for. "Serious, how many times have I told you that?"

"You think you can find something?"

"Think? I don't get to think about it. My mortgage is two thousand dollars a month."

"Get out."

"Plus insurance and taxes...Taxes are another five hundred a month almost."

"Lord have mercy." I could hear him cover the mouthpiece of the phone and call to his wife: "Polly, you can't imagine how much our boy pays each month just for his apartment." He uncovered the phone: "How big is your place?" he asked.

"One-bedroom plus."

"One bedroom," he tells her, the mouthpiece covered again. "Twenty-five hundred a month."

"Plus insurance and utilities," I tell him.

"Plus insurance and utilities."

I heard Polly go *whoo-wee* like a cowgirl. Then: "Tell 'im he should move to Orlando where the weather's nice and he can find a decent, *affordable* place to live."

"Not anymore," Daddy argued.

"Well, Dwight, it ain't as expensive as California."

"Suppose so." Then he spoke to me: "You hear all that, boy?"

"I'm not moving to Florida, Pop."

"Sure about that?"

"When Jesus himself, and not some cheap imitation, reincarnates and walks across Turkey Lake then maybe I'll consider it."

"Now boy-y-y..." he said chidingly, his voice rising. Then he laughed a little bit and told me to keep him posted, and reminded me that if I needed anything he was there.

"Who was that?" Emily asked after I hung up.

"My Daddy."

"Oh." Then: "Why do you call him your Daddy?"

"What do you mean?"

"I always wondered why you refer to your father as your Daddy."

"Because that's who he is. Does it bother you?"

"No, I was just wondering."

"If you have to ask *why* somebody does something," I said getting agitated, "then obviously you think there's something weird about it."

"No, it's kind of cute in a strange way; that's all."

"Well, he *is* my Daddy. You want me to call him something different?"

"No, Hugo. Jesus, back off."

"I realize that maybe a guy in his twenties usually doesn't call his Daddy Daddy—."

"Jesus Christ, Hugo, chill. Take a pill. (As you love to say.)" She wrapped a scarf around her neck and announced brusquely, "I'm going to work. Psycho."

"Need a ride?"

"From you? No thanks." She grabbed her keys and stuffed them in her purse. "You need to find a job."

"No kidding."

As she headed for the door she announced, "By the way, I'm staying at my place tonight."

That stung. Not that she was sleeping at her place—we had an agreement that we could spend the night in whoever's place we wanted. "Fine," I told her. What hurt was to be scolded and then abandoned. "*Think of me...*" I sang furtively as she passed through the doorway.

"Good night, Hugo."

"Make money," I called as she closed the door. I dragged my hands through my hair. "Because I'm fucking broke..."

* * *

"You are?" Trini said with alarm.

"Well not entirely," I confessed, taking a drag off a cigarette as I spoke to him on the phone outside my place. "But if I don't find something soon, and I mean *soon*, I'm fucked. I have no income, Trini."

"You don't have any savings?"

"I have about six weeks' worth and that's it. If I'm not working by the end of this month I am screwed. Have you heard of anything? Do you know anybody? I've put my resume on every job board out there."

My friend from Karachi made a choking noise: "Ackh. Job boards. The black holes of cyberspace. Why not go to work for a venture capitalist. They are the only ones with money left."

"And do what?"

"I don't know. I am trying to come up with ideas for you."

"There's nothing where you are?"

"Here? Oh my. If you think Screaming Software was bad, this place is like a Bihari sweatshop. I only took this consulting job because it was recommended by a friend of a friend. What a mistake. At least it's money. I am still looking almost every day for something different,

I hate it so much." He took a breath. "What about your rich friend with the consulting agency?"

"Swarthmore Group?"

"Yes yes, the one with the fancy penthouse you told me about."

"I already called him. They do mainframes, Trini. I don't know anything about mainframes."

"Maybe he needs someone to sell his services."

"No, he doesn't. I already asked."

"That's too bad. You are very good. You could sell a Punjab bricks."

* * *

Any other relationship, any other two people, and perhaps it would have been more noticeable that this was an anniversary lunch. Two years prior Emily and I had gone on our first date, back when she was working at Neiman's deli, she the night-prowling bagel maker who somehow managed to get up early and slather schmear for office dwellers. After a few months of those incongruous hours of work and life (she told me that sometimes she would stay up all night, it was easier than trying to get only two hours sleep), she quit and found herself a job seating people, serving honey wine and clearing dishes in Pagume, an Ethiopian restaurant on lower Haight Street. That stretch of the street sits topographically lower than the infamous Haight Street, hence its *Lower* Haight attribute. Upper Haight—Haight Street proper—is like a little Disneyland of weed and white Rastafarians. It's Main Street for the Haight-Ashbury, a semi-autonomous neighborhood (like most of San Francisco's neighborhoods) where grandchildren of hippie baby boomers try to keep the revolution alive. Dressed in rags and sporting dreadlocks, they gather in hooka shops and lounges pontificating less on the deceits of the State than on the blissful state of elemental truth and beauty that marijuana and ecstasy have convinced them underscores their lives. They bathe in Patchouli as if to resurrect the scent and sentiment of forty years past. They live in their own peculiar isolation, and in some cases squalor, although most of the squatter dens were replaced by expensive housing before I ever moved to the City. For those more interested in moving forward in time there is the Lower Haight, a rough melded neighborhood of low to middling incomes, progressive hipsters and the occasional gunfight. Emily, akin as she was to any neighborhood—symbol or representative of some specific place—the Lower Haight was her domain. The neighborhood embodied her and she embodied it. We were, therefore, a contrast. How we had persevered for two years was starting to become unclear. Maybe it was because we hadn't spend a great deal of time together: we ordinarily only saw each other in bed or on her nights off. We went out when we could—usually after her work, which meant that Friday and Saturday nights often rolled into Saturday and Sunday mornings, creating the notion of an endless party and obviating any sense of normalcy. As I look back on the relationship it was clear that we connected: there was just enough conservative tendency in her to be lured by my whitebread tendencies, and there was the right amount of danger and irresponsibility within her to draw me toward the edge, like star matter on an event horizon, without letting myself get fully sucked in. However, after I got laid off we began seeing each other relentlessly, unavoidably, and that was when things began to fall apart. Our moods around each other started to shift. Instead of an enjoyment, she became the one I turned to in frustration or bewilderment as I struggled to scratch a sense of pride back into my shapeless ego. In exchange I became the sounding board for her increasingly visceral attacks on the sad state of American social and economic affairs, her tirades aggravated by a notion of blame epitomized by her recurring phrase—*"When normal people like you get sucked into it..."*—which all but offered me up as the poster child for our nation's failures.

"How's the pasta?" I asked her as we sat at the dining table we rarely used.

"Fine," she responded blandly, her voice filled with the same distraction that she'd been harboring for days on end. She had wanted to go out to a restaurant for our anniversary. She thought it reflected a lack of confidence on my part that I wasn't willing to spend the money. "Just charge it," she'd said. "It's *one* lunch. It's not like you'll never be able to pay it back." When I responded that I didn't like having debt, and that for the couple years before I bought the house I never had *any* debt (Angela had taught me to pay off my credit cards every month), she reacted as though I'd accused her of being the cause of my financial difficulties. I tried to assure her that she wasn't, to which she responded with her standard jab: "Whatever."

After lunch, Emily went upstairs to shower.

After rinsing off the dishes, I went upstairs. I got undressed and joined her in the shower.

"You're horny," she said matter-of-factly as she squeezed water from her hair.

"No."

She looked down. "Well, you look horny."

"I just want to be close."

"I'm not having sex with you." She stepped back from the showerhead and squeezed her way around me. "I'm going to be late for work."

I hadn't intended to disrupt her schedule. Wasn't looking for anything more than to recover a sense of affection which had gotten misdirected of late, and which hadn't, I was hoping to convince myself, been irrevocably lost.

She stepped out of the shower and then leaned her head in around the curtain. "Will you drive me?"

Later, as we drove through Civic Center, the pensive silence that had filled the car with a sense of shared isolation was lifted as Emily spoke up: "Don't take this wrong, Hugo."

"Take what?"

"I feel like I'm spending too much time at your place."

"What do you mean?"

"I feel like we're living together."

"So."

"You bought the place more than a year ago and I've barely seen my apartment since."

"Hardly."

"Well, you know what I mean."

"No I don't."

"I mean I'm spending too much time at your place. Seriously, I feel like I live there sometimes."

"That's fine. We have an agreement."

"I know."

"If you want to spend more time at your place, that's fine."

"I know."

"So what's there to take wrong?" I asked.

She sat silently and stared at people ambling freely along the streets of Hayes Valley as we headed in to the Western Addition. "I don't know."

Emily spent that night at her place. She spent further, subsequent nights at her place. She spent so many nights at her place that I lost track of how many nights we were apart. It was a manageable distance at first—a relief, in some ways. I could walk around the loft at whatever hour and in whatever condition I wanted without disruption or commentary. The constant feedback mechanism that was my girlfriend was gratefully absent and at first I relished the quiet. We spoke occasionally—brief check-ins initiated by me, answered obligingly by her—but as time progressed our main mode of communication became a series of shallow text messages that we used to identify our physical locations or offer curtailed wishes that the other would have a good night, on occasion footnoted by me with what must have sounded slightly pathetic: *c u soon?* In time the grateful absence turned into a void, and it did so more quickly than I would have imagined. I began missing Emily. I missed having someone around. With no ready body beside me, no voice to respond to my own, no one to listen to or counterpoint my arguments, I began to feel the slogging weight of isolation descend upon Langton Street.

Days or possibly weeks later, thanks to perseverance and heady dose of luck, I received a phone call as I sat at the kitchen counter paying bills and watching my savings account balance dwindle before my eyes. It was Stuart.

"Working yet?" he asked.

"No."

"How does this sound: Four months. Onsite in the Financial District. Project coordinator for a utilities company. It's less than what you were making at E-MERGE but it's more than you're making now."

"Um—."

"They need someone right away."

"Yeah?"

"Potentially as early as tomorrow. I'll hook you up with Carol and get you processed if you're interested."

"What's a project coordinator?"

"Does it matter?"

* * *

In my contract job at the power company I was basically a serf. I was making a survivable wage, even with the pay cut, but I was still a serf. My day consisted of tallying and reporting. Dallying and describing. I was hired to record progress on the myriad facets of an infrastructure project that was nearing completion (at least according to somebody's skewed perceptions). As I would learn through casual gossip, the coordinator whom I replaced quit so she could move back East with her fiancé four months before the project ended, the timing being orchestrated specifically to come across as a snub to the management team. I was hired to assume her responsibilities as well as play the role of sycophant yes-boy for a horrible project manager named Sarah.

Sarah the Project Manager was one of those gifted no-talents whose only skill was in navigating the political waters of promotion and self-preservation. Work-wise, she didn't know what she was doing. She didn't care if a project path was in jeopardy; in her mind it was better to sugarcoat, to simply give everything a "green status. If you make it yellow," she said once with comic authority, "then everyone will start asking questions. It just turns into noise, and we have too much work to do to deal with a bunch of questions. Everything will work itself out, and if not, James [her Vice President and a fellow graduate of the school of unctuous self-promotion] will take care of it. We just have to make it look like we did what we we're supposed to." She was a timeless sort of ilk and I couldn't stand her. About every other day I had to remind myself that it was only a four month contract; after that I would move on, she would persist, and somehow in the midst of all that I would continue paying my bills and the city of San Francisco would still manage to keep its lights on.

Added to this dearth of professional fulfillment was the absence of Emily. Our separation had extended well beyond the start of my contract, and those two egregious pains merged into one sufferable but disappointing state of existence. I emailed Emily. I phoned her. I texted. She responded less and less frequently and in successively terser messages, claiming she was busy or that she needed time to herself. I went by the Ethiopian restaurant a few times, only to be shushed out of the place by her insistence that, "I can't talk about this here, Hugo. I'm working…" And then would loom in front of me the owner of the place, a slender but menacing looking African man in an open-collared shirt with wide lapels and a crazy pattern. Emily promised we would talk if I didn't come by the restaurant anymore bothering her. I obliged but I continued texting her in order to remind her that I wasn't going to simply evaporate off the planet's surface no matter how infrequently she cared to acknowledge my existence.

Then one afternoon I got an unexpected text: *"Dinner tonite?"*

I went straight from work to meet her at the Thai restaurant down the street from my place. They had a table for two that sat by itself in a quiet corner by the front door. I had called the restaurant ahead of time and asked them to reserve it; I figured she and I could use a quiet place to talk. I'm sure the wait staff thought I was going to ask Emily to marry me, or something ludicrous like that. The host smiled when we came in and grinned the whole time as if he knew a secret. The waitress and busboys came and went with the same knowing grin each time they visited the table, although I imagine toward the end our interaction they were dying to know why every slight scrap of joy had been sucked out of the air between us. It must have clearly gone down as the worst proposal of marriage in the history of Basil Thai Restaurant.

I was lonely, I told Emily over *larb gai*. I missed her.

Then out of nowhere, shortly after the main dishes were brought out, as we tried to formulate a civilized meal from within the bulky discomfort of silence, she said, "I'm moving to Mexico."

"Excuse me?"

"Well I'm not *moving* moving. I'm keeping my apartment. Might sublet it, depending."

"What about—?" And one could have finished the questions with a dozen different things. What about us? What about me? What about the last two years? What about making a living? (Dumb question, for her, as she could earn two nickels and stretch them out as if they were ten.) What about the status quo? What about living without expectations or obligations? What about, God forbid, the future?

"I have to get out of here," she said, searching not so much for an explanation but for a concise assessment, a neat package to drop at my doorway, finite and full. "The atmosphere in this city is stifling."

"When are you going?"

"In a few days."

"For how long?"

"I don't know."

"You don't know?" (As if I had asked what she was wearing to work tomorrow.)

"No."

"Weeks? Months?"

"Hugo, I don't know. I just need to get a way for a while."

Shell shocked, I said, "So where does that leave us?"

"Well." She looked as though she was thinking but I could tell what was coming had been well rehearsed. "When I go to Mexico," she said, "I need to be free."

"Free of what?"

"Everything."

"Including me?"

She nodded slightly.

I looked her in the eye. "So you're dumping me."

She hesitated. "I need to leave without any bonds, Hugo. Yes. Let's end it."

I set down my utensils. "Why?"

"Because."

"Because you feel like it? Because it sounds like a good idea? Why?"

"I'm sorry, Hugo. It's not y——."

"Bullshit."

"We're a bad mix."

"According to *who?*"

She wadded up her napkin and put it beside her plate. "After a while you'll realize it."

I flagged down the waitress and demanded the check.

"You want this to go?" the waitress asked.

"No, just the check." Who wanted the remnants of a meal like that? I looked back at Emily. "Well?"

"We process life differently, Hugo."

"That isn't necessarily a bad thing."

"No, but it's not working for me right now."

"What about me?"

She shrugged, suggesting remorse. "I can't live my life for your feelings. I need to take care of myself."

The waitress approached and set the check down gingerly between us. I grabbed it, looked at the total, and threw down some cash.

"And so that's it?" I asked Emily incredulously.

She reached down and raised her fabric purse onto her lap. She slipped a hand inside and retrieved a key, which she set on the butcher block paper atop the table then slid definitively toward me. "Hugo, I'm sorry. Truly."

As I stood up I grabbed the house key and shoved it in my jacket pocket. "What about your stuff? You have a dresser full of clothes—"

"I already got it. I picked it up while you were at work. I got the stuff in the bathroom, too. Anything else just toss."

So much for reconciliation. I embarrassed myself just thinking about it—embarrassed that such a thought could have consumed my work day with such meager optimism in the hours after she'd texted me. That such a thought could even have crossed my mind as I pondered the options for the outcome of the evening on the bus ride to the restaurant. That I believed there was the slightest chance of having her back in bed beside me come morning; that familiarity might revisit my place, transformed and renewed. "This is stupid, you know. This is you being impetuous and noncommittal—."

"I'm taking care of me."

"Exactly."

Outside, the summer fog blew down Folsom Street in a cold wet current. "Need a ride?" I asked her angrily on the sidewalk.

"No, thank you," she replied. Nothing more. No embrace. Just a cold, self-absorbing air. "I'll take the bus."

"Enjoy Mexico."

We stood for an awkward second or two and then Emily said, "Bye, Hugo." She scurried across the street toward the bus stop as I began my solitary walk of shame back home.

* * *

We take our places, one by one, standing in line waiting for a cup of coffee, a subway ticket or ham on rye. We stand, shoulder to shoulder, in anonymous and anxiety-ridden elevators, praying to God that the thing won't get stuck or, worse, snap a cable and go hurtling down to the parking garage—how tragic, your last eight seconds in life wedged among a group of screaming drones, recalcitrant only in the face of certain death, when their refusal matters the least.

"Do you agree?"

"Completely."

"You weren't listening, were you, Hugo?"

"Sorry," I said to Sarah, the project manager. She had called me out at the conference room table, around which sat eight or ten vaguely familiar peers (my *clients*, as the account manager instructed me to think of them). Some of them had chuckled at my embarrassment, and in addition to those of us in the room there were a handful of people on the conference call line. I seethed on the inside. Sarah had asked if I agreed with one of her stated lies—if I agreed a certain item should be closed from the issues list as being satisfactorily resolved, despite the fact that I knew closing it was far from appropriate given that it was nowhere close to being resolved. Correction: the imminent, easily packaged issue was fully resolved but the underlying, more fundamental issue that lingered in the background was a massive elephant that remained untouched and would so because—*We don't want make a fuss*. But that was the sort of project it was: count how many line items had been opened and shut; measure the stack of documentation as an indication of progress. (At one horrific juncture James the Vice President said to me: "Look at all of these documents. We're doing an awful lot of work." I kid you fucking not; he actually said that.) Sarah had seen I wasn't paying attention during the meeting; I was lost in contemplation and angry over Emily's abrupt departure. Worse, for Sarah, I was rubber stamping her every thought with a simple "yep, yep, yep..." She was the type that needed constant ego stroking and not just a bland acquiescence from her underlings. She wanted me to speak up on occasion, in front of other people, and commend her for her astute command of team dynamics. She had said as much to me in her office one day: "I just need you to stick up for me once in a while. Let people know how good I am. If we stick together we can be a great team." (Again, IKYFN.) Since I wasn't interested in playing her little game that day—my insides were doubled over in sadness—she called me out and she nailed me. So no, I wasn't sorry for not paying attention; not in the least. But I rubbed my nose in her ass a little bit toward the end of the meeting and we ended on a high note.

* * *

Near the end of my contract, some forgettable stretch of time after Emily dumped me and went to hang out in Mexico, beyond the shaming in the conference room, and well past the point at which I'd gotten re-accustomed to living with only myself, I received an email from Stuart Piers inviting me to dinner. My new, supernatural state of panic and the shorn confidence of those difficult days made me wonder if the invite was a cover for him to tell me that I sucked as a consultant, even in the remedial role of project coordinator, and that this contract was likely going to be my last.

I called him back, hesitant. Mentioned that it wasn't the best time. Told him Emily and I had had it.

"All the more reason—."

* * *

The ambient light of the restaurant had a woodsy, rusty, brick-orange tone to it. Bacchanal was a powerhouse place for well-heeled South of Marketers. It was way out of my affordability range so luckily Stuart was buying.

"How are you faring?" he asked as we stood at the hostess stand waiting to be seated.

"I'm all right," I told him.

"How's that easily bruised man-ego of yours?"

"You mean Emily?" For over a month I'd been wallowing in a tub of life that was half empty: no girlfriend; soon to have no job; feeling tenuousness about the next emotional pursuit—the inverse of how I usually perceived things. But being in Stuart's presence suggested that the time for mourning was done. He had that effect. I reiterated that I was doing well, despite what I felt on the inside. Intellectually I knew that time would reverse things: life would grab my hand and keep pulling me forward; the sting of Emily's abandonment would eventually recede and I would probably come to the same conclusion about us that she had. And some day, one day, there would be someone to replace her. Meantime, it still hurt.

"Sucks getting dumped, doesn't it," he said.

"Like you would know."

"Ha." He put his hand on the back of my shoulder and gently pushed as the hostess led us into the dining room.

* * *

"Like the wine?" Stuart asked.

"It's great." I thanked him again for inviting me out: "This is just what I needed."

"It's the least I could do. You helped save an account." Evidently the relationship between James the VP and Stuart's consulting firm had strayed into perilous straits around the time of my predecessor's abrupt departure. "She was a difficult personality," Stuart explained. "Good. Bright. Talented but difficult. I think we were all glad to some degree, but ultimately disappointed, when she left."

"Farewell the lovely," I said.

"Yep. Between you and me, *our friend*—(Stuart would never refer to his clients by name out in public)—is a mess, but he brings me a lot of business. Being able to slip you into the role, and the fact that you're doing such a great job, helped him forget the Meghan debacle somewhat. So I thank you for that."

"No," I told him. "Thank *you*. Seriously."

"And what's better is our friend no longer *personally* blames me for the whole thing."

"Did he really?"

Stuart nodded his head. "Persecution complex. He's a train wreck. But he's one of the few people with budget so we love him."

Stuart and I had a nice dinner. A long, leisurely, lazy dinner. Some might call it hedonism: one starter course followed another, which was followed by a main course which was paired with a bottle of wine that was thick and filled with a seemingly bottomless flow of gossamer crimson liquid that washed down the cocktails that had initiated the meal. Stuart had perfected the art of lingering with a purpose.

"This is nice," he said at one juncture, as if reading my mind. "I feel a sense of ease I haven't had in a while."

"Yeah?"

He hesitated and went uncharacteristically quiet. His silence may have been pensiveness; it may have been the earlier Manhattan; maybe it was a dance between the two. Then he smiled and lifted his wine glass: "To the dumped."

I lifted my glass dubiously. "How's that?"

He tapped the round-bellied body of his glass against mine. "Alejandro couldn't stand this place."

"Couldn't?"

"He thought it was pretentious."

"He dumped you?"

Stuart nodded. "A few days ago."

"What happened?"

"What happened is, we weren't a good match. He thought I was trying to buy his affection; thought I didn't love him; thought I just wanted a Latino trophy to loll around whenever it was convenient."

"And—?"

Stuart shrugged. "Sometimes I think Celia's right. I get into these relationships knowing they'll never work out."

"Mom says that?"

"Mom?"

"That's what we used to call Celia behind her back."

Stuart nearly choked with laughter. "She'll have a fit when she hears that!" He coughed into his napkin. "Oh my God, I can't wait to tell her." He laughed again. "*Mom...*"

Stuart's laughter was infectious and I started to chuckle. It was a rare moment for us. Different. I'd always lived largely impressed by him. I admired him, and when I was around him I existed slightly in fear of him. He was Stuart the Impenetrable, but when he started laughing about Celia he suddenly turned into a human being.

"Sorry about Alex," I said after he quieted down.

"Eh." Stuart drank. "Onward."

During dessert, the discussion topics turned familial. Stuart started talking about his patriarchical, driven father and his formidable society mother who still lived in the family's condominium apartment at the top of Nob Hill. In exchange he probed my relationship with my father and surveyed my kinship with Aunt Alice from what seemed an admiring or even enviable perspective, with both of us coming to the conclusion that I'd had an amenable growing up—all things considered.

"Yeah, Alice was a godsend," I said. "If she hadn't been there to take care of me after Ma died, who knows how I would've ended up."

Stuart looked at me with a puzzled look on his face. "*After?*"

"Well—. As a kid." In an instant the room inverted and I realized I was about to be had.

"You said after."

"Well yeah. After she died I was a kid, right? *When* I was a kid—."

"N-no." Stuart held up a finger to halt me. "I thought…"

* * *

So.

* * *

My name is Hugo Storm.

I am a liar.

Not a malicious liar. Not a fabricator of deeply fraudulent schemes designed to better my station in life at the expense of others. No, I am a simple liar. A mere *fabricant*.

And as I said to Stuart that night: I have a confession to make.

The truth about my mother is this—and this, unlike my many other harmless little petty falsehoods, I swear to God is the truth:

In the middle of summer, right before I was about to turn eight, before third grade, my Daddy took me outside after dinner. "Darryl, come on," he said as Aunt Alice clanked away cleaning the dishes. He took me by the hand and led me out to the porch.

"Where we going?" I asked.

He led me down the steps and over to where a swing hung from a lone tree that stood beside the porch. The dusky air was warm and in the fading light the fireflies started to flicker. Daddy lifted me onto the swing, then knelt and grabbed onto the ropes on either side of me.

"You know your momma's been away for a while?" he said.

"Uh-huh."

"Boy, your momma's very sick."

"But she'll be better," I said.

My father laid his hands on my knees and gently, cautiously shook his head no. He knelt there quietly for a moment then finally he spoke again. "She's gonna go back to God."

"Ma's gonna die?"

"Yes, boy."

"How come?"

"I don't know, boy, that's just the way it is. It's up to the Lord. But he's gonna take her back and he'll take care of her and she'll keep an eye on us from then on. And we'll all be fine, won't we?"

"You say so."

He pressed the heel of his hand against his forehead. Taking it away, he told me, "Tomorrow she'll be home from the hospital. She don't feel good so she needs her rest, you hear?"

"Yes, sir."

He stood up and gave the swing a gentle push.

"The three of us—you, me, your Aunt Alice—we're gonna take care of your momma while she's here, won't we?"

"Yes, sir."

"That's a good boy," he said looking down on me. "You're Daddy's good boy."

According to Aunt Alice, who clarified things years later, that was in late July, a bad time of year for a person to get sick on a farmstead. My father was busy with the tedium of detasseling, unable to pay much of anyone to help him, and to have his wife dying of leukemia at the same time just about wrung him out.

Had I been older I might have noticed that something was wrong with Ma. No doubt the mood of the house changed after they realized she was sick. I must have sensed it, even if I didn't know it for fact, because whenever I think back on the time before she died all I can conjure is a sense of strangeness. Almost a blankness of slate, or a jumble written on a chalkboard. There was the occasional coughing, the complaints about fatigue, Ma pushing scraps of food around on her plate at dinner sometimes. Alice told me there had been medical appointments during my school hours that I wasn't aware of; any lapses or downturns in Ma's health were explained away through stories: "She's been working too hard, caught a bug that's goin' round...". Whatever. It wasn't until Ma went into the hospital the last time that Daddy ever told me she was really sick. Before that she'd only been "not feeling so good."

For the first few days after Ma came back from the hospital she could barely move around the house on her own. She was skinny as a rail and wore a scarf to hide the straggling filaments of hair that sprouted out from underneath. They'd done a few intensive rounds of chemotherapy at the hospital – all that we could afford – but then they couldn't do anything more.

After a while, back at home, Daddy had to carry Ma if she wanted to go anywhere in the house. For my birthday he carried her down to the living room and propped her up on the sofa with pillows against her back. For presents I'd gotten a dark green, military-like backpack to carry my school stuff in and a Hot Wheels lunchbox to go with it. Ma was partly sitting up but kind of tilted over to one side. She gave me a smile as I leaned up from my spot on the floor and kissed her on the cheek. "Thanks, Ma. Thanks, Daddy," I told them.

"Alice picked out the backpack," Ma whispered.

Dutifully I walked over to Alice, who was sitting in her chair beside the TV stand. "Thank you, ma'am."

"Welcome, boy," she said with a sliver of sadness in her voice.

After that Ma spent all her time in bed, with Aunt Alice acting as her nurse. She didn't eat much. Mostly Alice went in there and fed her Jell-O or ground up meat and soup. She'd change Ma's sheets, give her medicines, and wipe her down with warm cloths.

"I help?" I'd ask upon seeing Alice heading toward Ma's room.

"Nah, you go shuck peas or scrape the lunch dishes," she'd tell me. My chores were relegated to the scraps of work leftover from Alice's tiresome day. All the real work of helping Ma I spied through the bedroom door, which Alice kept cracked a little whenever she went in to care for her.

"Daddy says for me to help," I finally protested one day. I was standing defiantly in the hallway in front of Ma's door.

"You help by husking the corn."

"Let'm in," I heard Ma say weakly.

"For what?" insisted Alice.

"Let'm in."

I went over to Ma. Her eyes had deep colored lines underneath them, her cheeks were sucked in. There was a grey towel wrapped around her head to capture sweat and a busy patterned scarf tied over that trying to make her look pretty.

All she said, repeatedly, was "My boy." She slipped her hand out from underneath the bed sheet and laid it on top of mine. She looked like a ghost and could barely speak: "My boy..."

It seemed like months that she was there at the house, wasting away in the room that was intended to one day be my little brother or sister's. In reality, as Alice recounted, it was barely two weeks. Soon after my birthday, Daddy carried Ma downstairs and laid her on the living room sofa. Alice had lain a clean sheet and a couple towels beneath her. At the arm of the sofa she'd set a couple soft pillows to prop Ma up a little bit. Ma was lying there, her head tilted, facing out at the room, her eyes once in a while turning toward the door so she could get a glimpse of life coming and going through the front of the house. She was hooked up to a metal pole which had a clear plastic bag filled with clear liquid hanging from it. A tube went from the bag into a hard syringe taped into the crook of her arm. She was breathing heavy and slow and her mouth was wide open, as if she wasn't able to catch the air. Her lips were dry and the only language that came out of her lips was grunts.

Each day since Ma came home, Daddy would call Dr Bing and talk to him about her condition. Bing was a friend of Daddy's, about the same age. He was the doctor who delivered me at the hospital in Goshen when I was born. He's the one who had brought the IV pole and clear bag of liquid when Ma came home from the hospital. "Morphine," he explained, "to help with your Momma's pain." This particular day, when Daddy called Dr Bing he seemed all out of sorts, silent yet with a Noreasterner of a storm brewing inside him. Later on that morning Dr Bing arrived, moving solemnly from his car in through the front door. He went over to Ma and checked the IV connection to her arm and then knelt down beside the sofa.

"Hello, Janie, it's Bing," he said softly into her ear.

Ma's eyes scanned the space around her. They landed briefly on Dr Bing then turned back up to face the ceiling. They fell shut again as Ma tried to mutter something from her throat.

Daddy looked down at Dr Bing. "What'd she say?"

Bing shook his head: "Don't know. Her tongue's swollen." He

laid the tips of his fingers on the side of Ma's throat. She gasped and her eyes flung wide open and she started panting. Then her breathing stopped entirely and the room fell silent until she started breathing again. Ma's eyes shifted toward Bing. Seeing him, she closed them again as if comforted and resumed her slow act of consent.

Ma died a few hours later. It seemed like an eternity in between. She lay there on the brown plaid sofa, life eking out life as her breathing grew raspier and shallower until eventually it stopped altogether. She gasped two times. All eyes in the room remained transfixed. Daddy knelt down crying, holding Ma's hand. Alice pressed a dish towel to her face to catch her tears. Dr Bing laid his fingers again on Ma's pulse and looked at his friend with difficulty. Ma exhaled one last time, pushing the last gasp of life out from her as I stood by the front door, alone, my chest so constricted with fear and a sudden loneliness that I could hardly breathe.

* * *

I hadn't ever told anyone. Had I thought about it, I certainly wouldn't have chosen a high-end South of Market restaurant filled with people to do it in.

"When I was a kid," I told Stuart, he who had filled the air between us with a sense of familiarity and comfort, "I always thought that maybe if I had been different—. Helped my father more on the farm. Paid my mother more attention. I even thought—well, how stupid is this. The day I was born, Ma went into labor at the house in Buckshutem. They were all sitting around the living room when Ma's water broke. Daddy called Dr Bing right away. Bing told him there was nothing to worry about; he'd be by (Daddy wanted him to deliver me there in the house to avoid hospital bills). Well. No sooner had they started watching Richard Nixon leaving the White House on TV when I started coming out feet first. 'Mighta had the umbilical wrapped around your neck,' Alice told me. 'What a ruckus, boy, you can't imagine. Scared to death every one of us.' Luckily Bing was there at the house. He did what he could to keep me from coming out. Then he and Daddy rushed Ma to the hospital where a surgeon did a c-section to get me out." The noise of all those years ago rushed back and filled my head. I got heavy in my breath. My forehead started to ache. "When I was younger," I confessed, "I used to think that if I'd been born normally then maybe my Ma never would have died. Figured if my Daddy didn't have to pay for the c-section there would have been money to get

Ma more chemo. Thought we might have been able to get her better. Told myself maybe Ma would have never left me."

And then the tears came forth unexpectedly and they were gushers. I'm sure I turned our table into a spectacle but I couldn't control it. I shoved my napkin against my eyes and I cried. I'd never felt a pain like that, a hurt so deep from a lie held so long.

In what seemed like no time at all, Stuart was leading me out the front door of the restaurant, his arm wrapped around my shoulder. Once outside, he pulled me close to him as I continued to press the wine-stained napkin against my face. "I'm sorry," I whimpered as we waited for the valet to retrieve the car. Stuart wrapped his arms around me and pulled me to his chest. "Cry it out," he told me. "Cry it all out." His grip was strong and reassuring. It felt like something that had been missing all those years. Needing nothing more than to be held, I let myself meld into his embrace. Soon my crying calmed into slow deep breaths and for the first time in my life I felt like I could finally breathe.

MY NAME IS DARRYL STORM

At first they left Janie Storm on the sofa with her face uncovered, sullen, departed. After a while they decided she ought to be moved to bed until the ambulance arrived to take her to the funeral home. Alice went ahead of Dr Bing and Darryl's father to straighten the sheets and make the room presentable. The men then carried Janie up the stairs and laid her in bed. Alice wrapped a pretty dress on Janie and brushed her hair while Dwight sat on the edge of the bed feeling the warmth go slowly out of his wife's legs. Then they all went downstairs to wait.

During the wait Darryl, not yet called by the name Hugo, wasn't able to sit still; he didn't harbor the same sense of grown-up tiredness and loss that the adults in the room shared. He was agitated by the belief that his mother was still just sleeping in her room and in time would stir back to life. Against Dwight and Alice's wishes he went up to Janie's bedside and touched her face and tried to hold her hand but there was no response.

"Ma?" he whispered. "Ma."

After the ambulance finally arrived, two drivers in white went upstairs and put Janie on a stretcher. They covered her body and face with a white sheet, strapped her onto the stretcher and carried her down the stairs. Darryl stood nearby, capturing every moment, storing and recording the clanking of the stretcher, the wheezing turn of the wheels across the living room floor and the anxious clicking noise it made on the rocky driveway. His father leaned down and kissed Darryl on the top of his head and said, "Back in a while, boy." Aunt Alice rested her hands on Darryl's shoulders as they watched the two men climb into Dr Bing's Chevy Nova and follow the ambulance down the drive. With the vehicles kicking up summer dust, Darryl broke away from Alice and started running down the driveway after the two vehicles. Once they hit Buckshutem Road and turned north, their acceleration increased and they were gone. Darryl stopped in his tracks and fell to the ground. Crying and doused in dirt, he lay on the ground shouting for the men to stop. Alice shuffled down the driveway and caught up with him. She knelt down, pulling him into her lap. "Easy boy," she said, trying to console him. "Take it easy." Young Darryl started hyperventilating as he fought to stand up. "Breathe in, boy," said Alice, trying not to lose hold of him. "Relax!" She grabbed his shoulders and pulled him in. "Siddown, boy. Take a breath…slow…That's right. It'll all be—."

* * *

When Tamara and I arrived at Hugo's loft I wasn't sure what to expect. Stuart had texted me while we were having dinner at Rivoli. It's a cute place down the street from us in Berkeley. Warm and homey but still kind of elegant, it's filled with professors and neighborhood regulars, a mix of creative and talented people, a lot of comfortable middle-classers with decent jobs. The back wall is all glass and it overlooks a kind of classically pretty northern California garden. There's a huge manicured tulip tree in the middle that when it blooms in January is just spectacular. Each night a procession of animals come by to feed on dry cat food that the owners leave out beneath a stone bench under the tree: first a cat, then a possum, then a raccoon – they come in sequence after the other one has gone, as if they have their own pre-arranged seating times. Tamara and I were lingering over herbal tea and a fig tart while we watched the raccoon methodically nibble away at some kibble while he kept an eye on his surroundings. Tamara had been working hard to get a grant renewed for one of the non-profits she sits on the Board of and they had just found out that day that they got the renewal. So part of the reason we were out was to celebrate; the other part was simply to have a quiet night together. As for me, work was going fine and it felt relatively stable. It was busy, but it was a good busy; it wasn't the hectic, never able to get caught up kind of work I'd been doing with Celia and then again at that awful big agency where Hugo and I worked. (I was *so* glad to get out of there.) It was one of those nights when everything was ok and you felt like life was tucking you in under the covers and giving you a kiss on the forehead. Everyone should have nights in their life when they feel like that. Anyway, as we're eating dessert we both heard my phone vibrating in my purse. I wouldn't dare see who it was, though. We had a rule: when in Rivoli, one's cell phone was unanswerable. It took me ages to convince Tamara that she could turn hers off without incurring any sort of penalty from life, and so she eventually she learned to keep it turned off when we went out to eat in certain restaurants. I, on the other hand, was allowed to keep mine on vibrate because, quite frankly, I wasn't addicted to my cell phone the way the rest of humanity was. It was easy enough for me to ignore it.

"Gonna check and see who it is?" Tamara asked. I knew she was toying with me.

"No."

"Might be important."

I leaned in and whispered, "Yes, maybe somebody was in an accident. What if they only have an hour to live, and if I ignore it then I'll miss seeing them before they die."

"That's right. You'll spend the rest of your days wracked with guilt because you enjoyed a fig tart instead of answering your cell phone."

"Exactly," I said.

We smiled.

Tamara was learning.

We eventually left the restaurant and went outside, where Tamara ran into a colleague who worked at the university. The two women started talking on the sidewalk, there in the unreliable warmth of summer. A veil of fog was creeping in from the bay and soon would be rolling over us. I stepped to the curb and checked my phone. *Can u come to SF? Hugo needs u.* Worried, I called Stuart. I was afraid something had happened to Hugo; worried he'd gotten hurt; worried – who knows what. When I got him on the phone, Stuart said Hugo was ok but he was upset. He needed, in Stuart's words, "someone a little more motherly than I am."

When we got to the loft Stuart answered the door, which surprised me in a way. As did his condition. "My word," I said to him. I couldn't believe my eyes. "Have you been crying?" I put a hand on his flushed cheek and held it there. "Or have you been drinking?"

"Both."

"I'm not sure I'm *glad* I missed that dinner or if I wish I'd been there instead."

I went over to Hugo, who was lying face down on the sofa, his head resting on a pillow. I sat down next to him and rubbed his back. "You ok?"

He seemed worn out. Still he mumbled encouragingly, "Mh-hm."

"Wanna tell me what's wrong?"

He shook his head no and so I looked over at Stuart, who shrugged his big shoulders and mouthed the words: *Talk to him.*

"Hugo—."

Hugo let out a wailing groan into the pillow and then flipped himself onto his back. He looked at me, his boyish eyes still possessed of their usual stirring self.

"What's wrong?" I asked.

"I told him not to text you but he wouldn't listen."

"Who, Stuart? Of course he's not going to listen to you."

"Look, I'm fine. Really. I just—. My life is one big fraudulent mess; that's all. I'm fine. You didn't have to come over."

"Oh, that's it?" I called over to Tamara, "Come on, honey, it's nothing. We can go. Hugo's life is a fraud, that's all." I pinched Hugo on his arm. "What are you talking about? Huh? What's the matter with you?"

I don't know if Hugo ever described himself but he's about five-foot-ten, on the slender side of average. He has dark hair that's sort of wavy, almost but not quite curly at the ends. He'll never be a romantic lead but he's cute. His cuteness permeates, even to this day. I think back then he used to believe he was defective somehow – not good enough or I don't know what. In talking about himself once he told me, in what I thought was uncharacteristically revealing for him, "If I had to sum up the kind of guy I think I am, it's this: Jersey girls fantasize about falling in love with lifeguards down at the seashore but by the time summer ends they end up with guys like me."

I know why some people used to get the wrong impression about Hugo. He doesn't come across as taking things seriously. He makes up little stories (even now, though not nearly to the same degree) and it's never always clear when he's telling you the truth or when he's pulling your leg. I think that sort of – juvenile – approach is what mischaracterizes him. Truth is, Hugo is very conscientious. He's a hard worker. And to his further credit, he's adaptable. That's probably his distinguishing characteristic: adaptability. I've always admired that; always been a little bit jealous of how well he shifts from one life setting to the next. Granted, getting him to the front door can be a test; but once there he doesn't linger, he barges right through. Me, I feel like my constant mission in life is to find quiet – peace, tranquility, an uninterrupted ease. (Foolish, I know.) That's my constant struggle, and I think the more you struggle to find something the more elusive it becomes; it certainly makes it harder to adapt. Unfortunately for Hugo, being adaptable isn't something that people readily appreciate when they're trying to pigeonhole you into a category. (We love our categories. We think we're nothing if we're not categorizable. We get uncomfortable when people or events don't fit neatly into our safe and familiar little boxes. Clearly – sadly – the trend seems to be deepening: true individuality is dying. It's getting sucked out of the American psyche through all sorts of willful surrender. So much so that I worry we'll one day all end up living in *Logan's Run*.)

I asked Hugo if he was upset because of Emily.

He shook his head no.

I asked him if he was upset about work.

Again he shook his head no.

"Then could you possibly tell me what the two of you have been crying about?"

He raised his arm and pointed at Stuart. "He started it."

I sincerely doubted that. I rested my hand against the back of the sofa and leaned over him, attempting to channel a sort of imposed understanding between us. "Really," I said.

I heard Tamara quietly ask Hugo if he minded if she went back and watched the news. It was a rhetorical question – we're talking Tamara – and before Hugo replied *"Sure"* she was already past the kitchen.

Stuart came over and sat down in the black leather Barcelona chair near from the sofa. I said to him, "So it's your fault?"

"Absolutely."

Hugo shoved a pillow on top of his face and groaned again. He removed the pillow and looked at me with what I call his yielding face. It's a strange little combination of him giving in and yet trying to seem insistent, as though he thinks he's in charge. "Of course he didn't start it," he said.

"Then why—?"

"Because," he said. "You know that I—, I—."

"That your reality is loosely based on fiction? Yes, I'm well aware of it."

Hugo peered around me and stared at Stuart, as if asking permission.

"It's past due," Stuart told him.

"Fine." Hugo looked up at me. "I lied to you. Big time."

* * *

About six months after Janie Storm died, the Dwight Storm residence received a call from the elementary school in Buckshutem. As with most household calls, that one was answered by Aunt Alice, who was in the kitchen, which is where she spent most of the afternoons of her adult life. She listened to the person who was speaking on the other end of the phone. She responded with a continual "*Mh-hm, mh-hm, mh-hm...*" When they were finished she hung the phone back in its cradle on the wall. On the stove was simmering a stock pot with a mostly meatless chicken carcass floating in water along with two bay leaves. Alice looked at the stack of carrots and celery that were resting in a colander in the sink along with a mound of yellow onions. She debated for a moment whether to continue on and string the celery, peel the carrots and onions, chop them all and put them in the stock, or if she should halt the work and deal with the latest of these troubling interruptions. With a grimace of resolution she gave the vegetables a quick splash of water and turned off the fire on the stove. She pulled off her apron and tossed it over the back of one of the chairs. She walked out to the front room and from the coat closet she removed a warm jacket and buttoned herself up before heading outside to the barn.

"You there, Dwight?" Alice called, peeling apart the heavy barn doors. She didn't like the barn. Ever since she went out looking for Darryl one summer and instead found a nest of garter snakes she avoided the place like religion. She crept past the tractor and headed toward a fluorescent light that emanated from a shanty workroom in the far corner.

"Back here," Dwight hollered.

"Nephew—," said Alice as she stood in the frame of the door. She peered cautiously around her feet and at the visible corners and underneath Dwight's workbench. "The boy's school called again."

"More stories?"

Alice shook her head no.

"Then what?"

"Beating on the Brammer boy. "

"Hurt him?"

"Scared him is all."

"Jesus Christ." Dwight set down the metal file he was using to sharpen a set of threshing blades. "They want him to come home?"

"Yep."

"How many times now?"

"Boy needs help, Dwight."

"I know that, Alice. What kind of help am I gonna give him?"

"Can take him to see a psychiatrist."

"I'm not taking him to any psychiatrist."

"What about church?"

"The boy doesn't need religion."

"I don't mean *go* to church, but he can talk to a pastor is all I'm saying."

"Why, so they can pray? Prayer didn't save his momma."

"I know that, Dwight, but maybe he can give the boy some advice."

"The boy misses his momma, Alice. What kind of advice is a preacher going to give him? That he shouldn't miss her? That he's just gotta accept that the Lord took her because that's what the Lord does?"

"Principal says—."

"I don't care what the principal says! What the boy needs is a dose of reality and some discipline."

"Boy's got more reality than he can deal with, Dwight."

They stood at odds, united at least in their unknowing about what to do with the eight year old, who'd been making up and spreading lavish stories about where his mother had gone: on a cruise she won on a radio game show; to take pictures of a volcano that exploded out West; to visit wealthy relatives in Florida... On that particular day Darryl had gotten into a tangle with Bobby Brammer, a scrawny little kid who made up for his runted unhappiness by being spiteful. Bobby had once clipped a chunk of Lucy Bevan's hair with scissors during art class because he'd heard on the news that scientists would soon be able to figure out all sorts of things about who you were from strands of your hair, and he told the girl he was going to send the batch of hair he had just carved out of the back of her head to a national science center and they were going to determine that Lucy Bevan was a retard and a stuck up little—and then he used the s--- word and the entire room, after having already been shocked by the swift dexterity of his scissors, erupted into chaos as the boy was forcibly dragged out by the assistant principal with one arm around his waist and the other covering his obscenity-spewing mouth.

Darryl had gotten into it with Bobby Brammer because the boy insisted in front a group of kids on the playground during recess that Darryl's mother wasn't on a vacation at all. He claimed she ran away because no mother would want "an f'd up kid like you for a son." So

Darryl grabbed the boy, who was a good three or four inches shorter than him and many pounds lighter. He gripped one of his arms and grabbed the waist of the boy's pants with his other hand and he pulled him out from the playground onto the parking lot. Darryl yanked his own belt off and looped it through the back of Bobby Brammer's and then around the metal bumper of a nearby pickup truck. The nasty little kid was kicking and fighting him as other kids drifted out to the parking lot to see what was going on. Darryl managed to strap the boy to the bumper and then he told him he was going to get in the truck and drive off, dragging the kid behind him.

"I told him I was going to smear him down a five mile stretch of Highway 55."

Bobby hollered at Darryl that he was too short to drive a truck and besides he was too stupid and a retard. Try as he did, though, he couldn't undo the belt because he was hanging nearly upside down, and the more he squirmed the more impossible it was to right himself.

"He deserved it," Hugo said. "Know what happened next? I got in the cab of the truck and I started banging around and rattling the gearshift and yelling at him through the window that I found the keys and was gonna drive off right then and there. He kept on yelling and yelling and I'm yelling back at him to just wait, I was gonna take off any second. And then all of a sudden some other car nearby turns on its engine and he screams SO loud—."

Hugo let out a quick laugh. Then he smirked. Then his face went kind of sour. "Stupid little redneck."

* * *

"Guess I'll go get him," Dwight said.

"No," replied Alice. "You stay here and finish what you're doing. I'll go get him."

Alice went back inside. She returned briefly to the kitchen and finished her vegetable prep work and put all of the broth ingredients on low heat on the stove. She left the lid slightly ajar and picked up the keys from the kitchen table and went outside again. She climbed into Dwight's pickup truck and rolled the window down partway. "Check the water every half hour to make sure it don't boil away," she said.

"Then what?"

"If it's low, add some more."

"How much?"

She pinched her fingers. "A couple inches from the top."

"You gonna be long?"

"Gonna take the boy for a drive. Try and clear the air."

She drove off down the dusty driveway and rolled the window up and turned the heater on, watching Dwight in the rear view mirror as he stood idly and troubled in his silence beneath the tree near the front porch. "Good luck," he muttered to himself.

Soon after, Darryl sat silently and unrepentantly on the passenger side of the truck bench, acting as though he'd done nothing wrong. "Where we headed, ma'am?" he asked his aunt.

Aunt Alice was driving the opposite direction of their house. "Going to Mount Pleasant."

"What are we going all the way down there for?"

"To see your momma."

"What for?" Darryl said angrily.

Alice didn't respond.

After a duration of silence, as the heater blew lukewarm air into the cab and the back-end of the pickup bed rattled with every inconsistency in the road, Darryl spoke up: "Better stay off the highway."

Alice didn't have a driver's permit. She ordinarily restricted her jaunts in the pickup truck to back roads and short distances. The cops in Millville would never pull her over or cite her, even though they knew she didn't have a license; frankly, they didn't care. But with the s.o.b.'s on the Garden State Police force, with their radar guns and bad attitudes, she avoided the highways more devoutly than she did the family's barn. "I know that, boy," she told him.

They took the County Road into Mauricetown and passed through the center of town. At a stop sign, as Alice was shifting the gear into second, the transmission made a scraping noise, like a metal structure grinding and about to snap. Alice swore out loud and punched the clutch with her foot and managed to get the gear into place.

"Grind the gears and Daddy'll be p.o.'d," Darryl said.

"Not nearly as p.o.'d as he'd a been if you hurt that Brammer boy."

"He mad at me?"

Alice waited to respond. Ever since Janie died, Alice found herself measuring her words to Darryl carefully. She didn't want to harm the boy any more than he'd already been harmed. Didn't want to say the wrong thing. Sometimes she thought so much about how she should or shouldn't say something to him that when she finally went to open her mouth she wasn't sure if she'd already said what was on her mind or if she'd only actually thought it.

"Your Daddy's not mad at you, boy," Alice finally said. "He's disappointed."

"What's the difference?"

"Mad is when you done something out of meanness. Disappointed is when you done it because you're hurt."

"I ain't hurt."

"Talk proper."

"Huh?"

"I'm *not* hurt," Alice corrected.

"Just talking like you and Daddy."

"That doesn't mean it's right. Speak like you're supposed to."

"Fine," Darryl said drolly. "*I am not hurt.*"

"You wanna make a living in the bigger world you gotta act like the bigger world, not like a turtle trapper from the salt marsh."

"Yes, ma'am."

"You gotta make your momma proud and stop giving your Daddy a difficult time."

"I'm not."

"You tied a boy to a truck."

"I wasn't going to drive it."

"You scared the Jesus out of him."

"He's a jerk."

"Doesn't matter."

"He's mean."

"Doesn't matter."

"Calls everyone a retard."

"Best medicine is to avoid him."

"Hard to do that, ma'am."

"Gotta try."

"God takes people like Ma away but leaves jerks like him around." Darryl looked out the window. "Isn't fair."

"No, boy, it ain't. God ain't fair. That's why you gotta make your own way."

* * *

I have to admit, I was kind of hurt when Hugo told me what had really happened to his mother. All along I'd known him as a guy who grew up with no mother—without any hint of who she was, of never having even been held by her. But then to find out that she died when he was eight years old was just astonishing. I felt badly that he felt he to had lie about it, whatever the reason. ("Clearly couldn't cope," Tamara would blandly remark.) More difficult was the fact that he couldn't share the real story with me. We've always been close and we've never had any secrets. (Well, now. Wait, I guess. I stand corrected: Stuart and me…All right then, who's the liar now.) Anyway. By the time Hugo finished telling me everything, Tamara had fallen asleep in the media room and Stuart looked like he was eager to get home and change into his pajamas. He asked if we wanted to spend the night in his guest room and I declined, reminding him that by the time we found street parking up in his neighborhood at that hour of night Tamara and I could easily be across the bridge and home in our own bed.

After Stuart left, I sat quietly and sort of sadly beside Hugo. There were times when I used to try and understand our relationship, especially those times when he was annoying me and it seemed like we were destined for a rocky dissolution. I would struggle to make sense of why it was we connected; how on earth had we achieved such a bond? That sort of analysis can be a dead-end, though; clearly the *why* doesn't matter that much. What happened to me on that night, though, is that a familiar and unpleasant emotion reared up inside of me: I grew up in a screaming household. My parents fought all the time. There was constant tension, disagreement, tears and yelling. When they were fighting it was terrible; but when they weren't fighting it was as if they were perfectly happy together. In love. Best friends. They were one huge walking contradiction, so I was completely confused by their relationship and I hated that. They were good to me and loved and always supported me, but I've always had this underlying anger toward them because they just *made no sense*. And there again, in Hugo's loft that night, I was feeling about him the same way I felt about my parents: my heart went out to him but at the same time I was angry. He was like a little brother to me. He had obfuscated. He had withheld.

* * *

In the Our Lady of Angels Cemetery, hidden away on a rural road in a back corner of Mount Pleasant, New Jersey, where there existed little of anything save the faint chalk of salt in the air and pine needles strewn amid fallen leaves in varying stages of decomposition, Alice stood before a small white headstone with a grudging eight year old boy at her side. She wore a floral dress over thick beige stockings and topped it with what was essentially a snow parka. "Go on," she said, and released the boy's hand.

The boy stepped forward. "Ma, it's me. Darryl Storm."

"She knows your name, boy."

Hugo turned his head slightly and glared at his aunt. "You told me to tell her who it was..."

* * *

It was getting late at Hugo's loft. I asked him if he wanted Tamara and me to stay.

"No, I'm fine," he said. "You should go."

"You sure?"

"What, am I no longer trustworthy? Yes, go. Go. Go. I'm sure."

"All right, then." I went into Hugo's small media room in the back and gently shook Tamara, who woke up with a jolt. "It's all right, hon," I told her.

"Oh my God," she said, fumbling into a sitting position. "I was having the weirdest dreams."

When we came out into the living room, Hugo was standing near his front door beneath the large piece of art that hung gracefully on the tall white wall. "Nice painting," I said, then gave him a hug. He looked ready to sleep, his eyes drooping and pink. He and Tamara said goodnight but didn't touch. She walked out the door ahead of me, and as she did Hugo said quietly, "Sorry."

"For what?"

"For being a liar. And keeping you here so late."

"It's barely one o'clock," I told him. "Don't apologize."

"Am I a bad friend?"

"You're a good friend."

"You don't hate me?"

"Of course not."

I gave him a kiss on the cheek.

"Thank you for coming," he said.

"You're welcome. Now go to bed."

As the door shut behind me I said a little prayer that he'd be safe in his thoughts, safe in his life, ever adaptive and always himself. Whatever residual anger I carried out the door I knew would devolve at first into a temporary sense of weirdness and then quickly into the realm of the forgiven until it was ultimately, effortlessly forgotten. It may not be a formula that agrees with everyone, but it works for me. We all have choices to make in life and I couldn't begrudge Hugo his. I didn't like that he never told me the truth about his mother, but I didn't live inside his head; I didn't share his experiences. The important thing was to remove my feelings from the equation and just try to be supportive.

"He has a picture in his bedroom of a young woman holding an infant," I mentioned to Tamara as we drove the grimy SOMA streets toward the onramp to the bridge. "He always said it was his mother's sister, but I'd bet money it's actually his mom."

"I wouldn't be surprised," she said sleepily, almost disinterestedly.

"I just can't fathom—."

Tamara reclined the seat as far back as it would go. "I'm tired, hon," she interrupted. "Are you ok to drive?"

"I-I'm fine." In all honesty I was taken aback. I wasn't going to start a fight late at night, but I was annoyed. Tamara didn't like Hugo. That was just the way things were. It was an unforgiving conviction, one of a handful of hers, that we would have to deal with over time. I only wish she could have let it go for one night, though, and tried to be understanding.

Once suspended over the bay, where tankers lay dormant like mechanical toys in the middle of a make-believe lake, I looked across the long glistening bridgeway over to the East Bay, staring through the clear night at hillsides dappled with lights that blended into the sky to meet the stars. I looked at Tamara reclining and decided to simply leave life on simmer for a while longer. Just like my father, I would keep my mouth shut.

* * *

"See out there?" Alice said to Darryl in the cemetery. She had just released him from a hug and stood up. She'd thanked him for being a good boy and apologizing to his mother for his behavior. She'd praised him for promising to set a good example and for aiming to make his mother proud. She retook his hand in hers, which this time he didn't resist. "See out there the trees and the clouds?" she said to him.

"Yes, ma'am."

"Well—" she started to say, and then she stopped herself. *This is what I believe,* she thought: *If people are flowers then our bodies are annuals: they live for a season of life and then die, leaving behind the seed for subsequent generations scattered across the floor. Our souls, on the other hand, are perennial: they bloom and re-bloom over and over until one day they, too, after having fulfilled their God-given journey, having completed their cycles of work and growth, surrender themselves in gladness and merge indistinguishable back into the flow.* Alice spoke aloud: "I used to ask God for His forgiveness for not loving Him through church, boy. Not any more."

"That so?"

"I ask him to see that raising a momma's boy and caring for his Daddy is my way of giving thanks and doing right in this life. Only thing a church glorifies is the man in the pulpit, boy."

"Think so?"

Alice nodded her head gently. "Hear the birds rustling?"

"Mh-hm."

"Smell the broken leaves?"

"Mh-hm."

"Feel the grass under your feet?"

"Yes, ma'am."

"Gonna tell you to do something, boy, but don't ask me to explain it."

"Okay."

Alice looked straight down at Darryl. "Lift your arms and close your eyes."

Darryl closed his eyes and raised his arms toward the sky.

"Feel the breeze on your face, boy?"

Darryl nodded yes.

"Feel the way the wind wraps around you like a sea of arms?"

Darryl nodded yes.

Alice closed her eyes, breathing in the scent of the lost familiar. "There's your momma, boy. Always with you."

* * *

Once back home, Tamara and I tucked ourselves into bed and gave each other a kiss goodnight. She fell back asleep immediately and I lay there with three decades of ponderings rattling around in my head. Like the bright lights of the San Francisco city skyline – like the few burning lights of memory from the Jewish quarter in Seville late one summer years ago, opposite the lights of a riverside fiesta shutting down in view of a rented apartment bedroom window – the noisy stars in my head on the night of Hugo's breakdown shone a mental path back to Stuart Piers. After Stuart left the loft, I made Hugo tell me why he'd been crying. Reluctantly – I guess he thought it was privileged information – he said he had asked Stuart about "that Mexican kid", meaning Ramon, and Stuart told him what happened. Hugo related the story back to me in his standard, rapid-fire, executive summary style and my heart scraped bottom for the second time that night.

The truth about Stuart and Ramon is this. I promised Stuart fidelity – I promised him silence – but I think this is important. The night in Seville where I got to know Stuart, to really know him (*okay, intimately* know him), I was just amazed by him. He was so good looking and obviously well-off. He was smart and his aura was so – this sounds very hippie but it's true – he was such a fascinating blend of male and female energy that I couldn't *not* sleep with him. Then when I woke up in the morning and I saw him staring out over the Rio Guadalquivir fighting back tears I started to wonder if it had been the white sangria doing all of my thinking the night before. I asked Stuart if he was okay and he said it was a complicated story. It was Saturday, I reminded him, and we didn't have any classes. Besides, we'd planned to spend the day together anyway (drunken though the promises might have been). I showered and then I got dressed in a pair of his drawstring pajama bottoms and a t-shirt. I sat on the bed beside him and listened as he relayed the whole story about Ramon, including the part – and this is what I didn't have the heart to tell Hugo, the part that I was afraid Stuart had omitted – that Stuart never actually paid for the *coyote*. He had told Ramon he thought it was a waste of money; he'd more likely get ripped off and be abandoned on the Mexican side of the border with even less than what he started out with. "Hordes of people come across every day," Stuart said to me, as though he was trying to convince himself. "He had done it before without any help. Granted he got picked up the second time, but—." So with Stuart unwilling to give him the money, Ramon, in the story that Miguelita later related, called his roommate/lover/whatever she was and asked if he could borrow five hundred dollars. Miguelita managed to come up with the money and she wired it to him in Mexico. Ramon used that to hire a lesser *coyote*, some unknown and unreliable *pollero* that he'd heard of second- or third-hand, not the more reliable one that his friend Tio knew. "*That!*" Miguelita shouted accusingly over the phone to Stuart when he called to tell him that Ramon had died, "was *your* fault! If it wasn't for you my Ramon would still be alive!" Suffocating in guilt,

Stuart told me that he had to tell someone the truth but he swore that, after telling me, he was never going to tell another living soul the truth about the *coyote*. The only way he could survive going forward was to lie about it, to completely re-remember it, otherwise the thought of what he'd done – well, what he hadn't done – would have killed him. So it was with sadness, at least with regard to Ramon, that I learned unequivocally on the night of Hugo's breakdown that Stuart Piers was a man of his word.

Naturally, as I lay in bed thinking of all of this – of Spain, Stuart, Hugo – it got me thinking of Susan, my soon-to-be ex during that time. Susan and I were a train wreck. With the benefit of distance I discovered to my personal horror that the reason our relationship was so bad is because I was trying to relive my parents' marriage with her. I was the quiet, pensive, *let-it-go* one like my father; she was the living gas-powered blow torch that was my mother. I looked over at Tamara with a bit of wonder and uncertainty and I asked myself the dangerously obvious question—.

This much I know: change comes with an awakening. From a willingness to learn. And what I've learned over the years is that we all have our dark places—our brusque fathers, absent mothers, contrived appearances, less than healthy relationships...whatever the affliction. Like Stuart; like Hugo; like me, there are countless people who build their lives dreaming away or trying to avoid these dark places. We claim they don't have any influence. We tell ourselves stories, believe whatever it is we want to believe, each one of us denying and defying, wandering along in search of some secret bliss. Much as he'd like to deny it, that's what Hugo was doing every time he told a fib about his mother. Or Alice. Or whoever. And because I do the same exact avoiding-life-kind-of-thing sometimes, I feel compelled to say that my name, too, is Darryl Storm. Many of us are Darryl Storm. We are all of us Hugo – his co-conspirators, his family and friends. However, unlike Hugo, who is smarter than a lot of people realize, we often fail to remember that truth is read *between* the lines.

Just between the lies.

-12-

A Brief Touchdown in Paradise

When I think of all the things I'm not...
I don't give a shit.
I don't mean that in a disrespectful way. I'm not trying to be an
insolent little prick.

The Hiring Manager stared at me. He had a rectangular face
with square black glasses and a short reddish moustache, trimmed
perfectly on the horizontal like a sunburnt hedge. He tilted his head at
45 degrees, as if that would give him a more accurate vantage point
from which to assess my strangeness. Contempt coursed throughout the
synapses in my brain with expediency and frequency as I sat through
that interview, yet another in a string of dead-end pursuits. It was a time
of an unending supply of labor coupled with exasperatingly little
demand. I believed, therefore, that crassness had its place in the
zeitgeist of emotion, narrow and unhealthy an approach as that may
have been. As post-boomers we'd been rudely kicked from our razor
scooters, the lot of us risen with bloodied shins and forearms, sensitive
to the slightest touch and even sunlight. Our reward for getting up: a
slap across the face. Yes, we'd been lucky to have stumbled across that
brief era of good fortune, to have ridden the final crest of an economic
wave that had kicked up in the 1980's, a self-organizing swell of
indulgence that broke abruptly and hard upon the ground without
warning—(some say)—although the *ex post facto* consensus was, had
we been looking beyond the crest we would have seen the precipitous
end just ahead. Many did and many called it out. The majority of us,
however, simply refused to pay attention. And what a difficult landing
it was. Geoffrey, the Screaming information architect with whom I'd
been in contact again in my never-ending quest for work, had taken up
sharing his loft out of financial desperation with one of his several
boyfriends, even though, as he said, "I don't love his ass one small bit."
With disappointment registering as loudly as traffic zooming by on the

streets, Geoffrey summed up the era thusly: "This is not the world I was led to believe I would inherit." And so at the time it seemed perfectly acceptable to be riddled with annoyance and filled with such righteousness as I felt with the Hiring Manager staring at me obliquely, me feeling deserving and wanting to believe I was being denied some inalienable right. But what did I know. The not-so-distant future would write an ever nastier economic phase than that one—putrid, rot-filled and incomprehensible as it would be. But it was nothing I could presage at the time; nobody ever knows what lies ahead. (And, oh, how our nostalgic whining would be trampled by those greater, forthcoming, ascendant truths.)

"No," I said to the Hiring Manager, I didn't have any direct QA experience. I told him that my interaction with RDMS was really only second-hand because it was a segment of the project plan I was tracking but, regrettably, "That's it."

The Hiring Manager nervously tapped the tip of his mechanical pencil on top of my resume before speaking again. He suggested we wrap up the interview, "unless you have anything else you'd like to add?" He apologized that the actual responsibilities of the job were so inconsistent with the job posting; with a wink he promised he'd look into it. He smiled and stood up, revealing a sagging gut on what was an otherwise youthful frame. "Thanks for coming in, Hugo." He held out his hand. "Best of luck."

I feigned a smile.

Best of luck!
On your way!
Bonne chance!

So went my days post-Emily, post-boom, post-contract from hell, and pre-whatever lay next. Stuart didn't have any contracts that were suitable for me: "It's all pretty senior stuff," he'd said, "but I'll keep an eye out." I sent out dozens of resumes into the abyss; I managed to get a handful of mixed-review phone screenings followed by three failed in-person interviews before turning utterly disenchanted and deciding that I needed a change of perspective. My father had been calling more frequently after I was laid off from E-MERGE and he hadn't been entirely convinced that I was actually working during the contract from hell. No matter how strongly I insisted that a contract was nearly the same thing as a job, only it didn't last as long, he couldn't quite grasp the concept. (*"You mean like a temp job?"*... *"Yes, Pop, like a temp job."*) He always capped off his calls with a *"Why don't you come visit,"* and so as I sat through my series of hapless interviews, the mismatch of my skillset to the sparse opportunities rattled like a nickel in a beggar's cup and my father's suggestion eventually took hold. Free food, free lodging; a mini pseudo-staycation whose only expenses were an airplane ticket and having to endure a weeklong dousing of religious pixie dust. It beat the hell out of interviewing.

* * *

"Well ain't this a surprise," declared Polly when I called from my cell phone around dinner time. "Dwight," she called into the house. "Guess who's coming to visit?" Then after a pause, "No-o-o…it's your boy, Darryl."

"Hugo," I said with annoyance. "My name is Hugo."

"Hey boy," my father said happily after he picked up the telephone receiver. I could hear the TV running in the background with a baseball game. "When you coming?"

"Tomorrow morning."

"Tomorrow morning?"

"That ok?"

"Of course it's ok. Everything all right, boy?"

"Yes, Pop, it's all good. I just thought I'd come out for a few days."

"When do you get in?"

"Seven o'clock."

"Ouch. Your momma's gonna have to pick you up. That's too early for me."

"Stepma."

"Boy boy boy…"

"She's not my Ma."

"I know, boy. I just want you to be family is all."

"Well, she is family. But she's not my Ma. And don't worry, I'll take a taxi."

"Good enough for me…Oh, it's hot as blazes," he warned. "Summer went and dragged itself to the very end."

"Great. Can't wait."

"Me, too, boy. Outside of the heat, we'll all be happy to see you."

* * *

Little baby Josefina de JesuCristo; Mahatma Gandhi in cross-stitch plaid; Buddha Child in teeny braids—whatever she was—greeted my sleepy visage at the front door early the next morning. "Hey Trish," I said, holding my hand out. She feigned terror, shrieked and ran to the protection of her mother, who stood nearby.

"Oh, TriciaBee," her mother laughed as she pulled the little girl close. Polly gave me a hug and then stepped out of the way.

"Hey there, boy," my father said. He grabbed me into a hug and then took a step back. "Flight okay?"

"Just fine. One Nyquil and a whiskey and water; next thing, we're touching down."

"Sounds like a fine way to fly."

"You want breakfast, hon?" Polly asked. "Can't believe you're here all of a sudden," she said as she wandered down the center hall to the kitchen, the rest of us following behind. "Seems like we just talked to you."

"You did."

"Well, you know what I mean." Then she went off onto her maternal ramble about the various options available for breakfast: what she'd planned on cooking but what she could cook instead, what my father liked on weekday mornings versus what he liked on Saturday versus Sunday, options if I wanted something different...

"Anything is fine," I said. "You got coffee?"

She laughed sharply. "Coffee? If I don't got coffee I'll be out on the street."

"Now..." chided my father.

The freckled little Sancta Divina laughed, having no clue what she was laughing about. Near the kitchen counter she tugged on the hem of her mother's Dacron pullover. "Mommy?" Her voice was a poorly disguised whisper. "How long is the man going to stay here?"

* * *

My father wanted to know if everything was ok. "Sure now, boy?" he asked for the second time that morning.

"I'm sure, Pop."

We finally had some alone time together, just the two of us. Getting away from Polly and Tricia was no easy trick. Even after Little Miss Pop-Tarts and Pencils had gone off to school it seemed like she was back in the house, educated and all socialized, before you could barely finish a sentence.

"Now don't go talking smart about your sister like that," my father says. We were sitting calmly at the kitchen table, staying inside to keep cool. He was on his fourth cup of coffee, which, freakishly, seemed to have no affect on his metabolism. Polly was at the grocery store. The air conditioning was running on high; when it cycled off you could almost hear the humidity pawing at the windows outside trying to get in. "Things been tough lately," he said, "huh?"

"Yeah, they have, but I'll be fine."

"Too bad about that Emily. Just dumped you for no good reason?"

"She went to Mexico."

"What, is she looking for a beaner?"

"Don't talk like that, Pop."

"Well she's lookin' for something to go all the way to Mexico."

"I don't know what she's looking for. But I'm not talking about that. Don't use words like *beaner*. Jesus Christ."

"Well, don't be using *his* name while you're in this house unless it's out of gratitude."

"Fine fine."

"We'll have ourselves a truce while you're here."

"Whatever...You want more coffee?" I asked, scooting my chair out.

"Nah," he said.

A sample air of quiet fell between us before I added: "Pop, I've been thinking lately—." I leaned into the back of the chair and stared at the familiar stranger across the table. "I got a question for you."

"Shoot."

"How come you let Polly call me Darryl?"

"Ah, boy."

"I know, but Pop—."

"Well, for starters, it's your given name."

"I know that. But after we moved to Millville—."

"I know, boy, I know." He seldom wanted to talk about that period in our life. We never really shared anything more than snippets of conversation when it came to the topic of my Ma. *Very little* seemed the greatest amount of energy he could devote to discussing her. After he sold the farm and we moved to Millville he promised me that we were starting over, as if from scratch. We weren't forgetting my mother, he said, but we couldn't be tied to her loss any longer if we were going to make something for ourselves. "So," he had announced in a ceremonious voice, as we stood in the kitchen of the new house in Millville surrounded by boxes, open space, unfamiliarity and freshly laid kitchen tile, "Darryl Hugo Storm is heretofore known as Hugo Storm." Just like that (erroneous word choice aside) the past was severed. Recalling that era from his Florida kitchen, a tightened posture came over my father and he leaned his forearms into the table and cradled his coffee cup in his hands. The reason he started calling me Hugo, he confessed, is because after my mother died he couldn't bear to hear anyone call me Darryl. "Didn't matter who was saying it or who was calling you; I always only heard it in your Momma's voice, and I couldn't bear it. I had to move on, too. I wanted all of us to move on."

"But Polly comes along and I'm back to Darryl. How come you let her do it?"

He shrugged his shoulders dismissively. "That's marriage, boy. Some things you fight, some things you gotta let go of. You were baptized as Darryl and so she's gonna call you Darryl. End of sentence." He sat back in his chair. "Besides, it sounds different when she says it."

"You don't hear Ma's voice anymore?"

"Nah…" he said. "That was a different chapter, boy. *Long long* ago. Time takes care of some of the hurt." His gaze drifted backwards in time, off to a land that was probably now covered in parking lots. "She'll be gone twenty years next summer," he remarked quietly. "Seems like somebody else's life, sometimes."

* * *

I was a guest in Daddy and Polly's home and I behaved as such, even though they tried to convince me it was my home, too. That was sort of a ridiculous effort, though, since *my* room was actually the guest room/sewing room. No matter how hard I tried I could never picture my bedroom having a sewing machine tucked into a corner with a towel draped over it. Nor would I have chosen the wooly floral wallpaper that covered the walls above the plastic chair rail. Nor the Victorian lace nightlight that cast an artificial aqua-green light in front of the door, illuminating in the middle of the night a portal to somewhere strange and inescapable. The pull-out sofa that was *my* bed was manageable enough in short doses although I could feel here and there the metallic springs pressing up against the mattress pad. For me this sleeping arrangement was the hallmark of transiency. Each slow turn from side to side throughout the night reinforced the sense of visitor-ness. Even in sleep I knew this was not my bed. This was not my home. My first home was Buckshutem Road, although that was really only a sliver of home: somebody else's home, to borrow my father's mood. Following that was the house I think of as home: the house we lived in, all three of us, in Millville—Daddy, Alice and I. There is where we shook off our loss and started anew. When we moved there I did my best to pack up all the hazy memories I had of Buckshutem, my mother, and the farm, and leave them behind along with my name. It took Daddy leaving Jersey to fully start his life over again. Yet Alice, who seemed to suffer Ma's loss in silence, was more perpetual. She was a constant. She was a strange attractor if ever there was a strange one to be had. I loved Alice. She loved me back, and even though we were never mother and son we were true family.

As I lay in bed that first night in my father's house, no matter how many thoughts came to me of all that had transpired over the past couple of years work-wise and relationship-wise, my mind kept drifting back to Alice. The blue-green light of the nightlight beckoned me to travel beyond the door and visit that place of happiness all wound up in sorrow.

After Ma died and we moved to Millville, and Daddy started seeing Polly, and Trisha was born, and I moved to San Francisco and Daddy and his new family moved there to Orlando, Alice—bless her heart, but dammit—didn't want to be a burden. She wanted Daddy and his family to have some privacy. "Ah'll go live with Bernadette in Laredo," she announced as the family was planning the move south. Bernadette was Alice's sister, widowed nearly ten years prior. Both women were getting old, nearing 80, and neither was in the prime of health. "We'll take care of each other," she said. "I don't need your wife looking after me. Bernadette'll do just fine. She'll watch after me and I'll watch after her. You go be with your family on your own now." A year or so after I moved to San Francisco, Daddy'd been in Orlando for just a little while and Alice, according to a letter she hand-wrote me for my birthday, was doing all right in Texas: *"Hotter than blazes...,"* she said in her lilting penmanship, full of awkward, craggily swirls. *"...Tarantulas the size of snapping turtles...I'm 'bout halfway to California, I figure. Maybe I'll make it there yet, boy."* Some time between Halloween and Thanksgiving Daddy calls me up, his voice choked up with tears: "Boy," he says, "it's your Aunt Alice. She's gone." From there Polly took the phone over and let me know what had happened, the old guy was too upset to talk. Alice was out front sweeping the porch then she headed down the front walk toward the sidewalk. When she got to the juncture of the walk and the sidewalk she stopped and just stood there, looking casually left and right like she was expecting someone. Bernadette saw her through the living room window and then went to the front door, wondering what Alice was doing. She called out to Alice. Once. Twice. Alice just stood there, a searching gaze across her face. Bernadette called her name a third and then fourth time, and at that point Alice turned around. Leaning against the broom for support, she held out her left hand like she was reaching for Bernadette to come and get her. Then, the moment Bernadette set off down the sidewalk Alice bent down at the knees and fell onto the dusty stones that edged the sidewalk. "And that was it," Polly told me. "The Lord took her away on the wings of a warm Laredo wind."

I always felt bad for Alice. It seemed like she died out of place, a stranger. Good thing she was with her sister, but still it wasn't her home. Then I realized that I don't think Alice ever had a home. Like me at my father's place in Orlando, she was a perennial guest.

Lying on the strange sofa bed in the strange room in my old man's unfamiliar house, the thought of dying somewhere unfamiliar terrified me. The sense of being a guest was overwhelming. With eerie green light casting a glow throughout the bedroom, I pulled the thin woven blanket up over my head and urged myself to sleep.

* * *

Early autumn swarmed over the Florida suburbanside in early September of 2001. On the last days of my visit I watched as the heat and humidity gently wore away. The air conditioner was turned off, windows were opened. I had extended my long weekend in Orlando into nearly two weeks. It was the longest I'd ever spent with my father and The Steps. It could be trying being in that household for too long a period of time, so by September 10th I was plenty ready to get on the plane and head back to San Francisco.

"Sure you don't want to stick around another day or two?" Polly asked kindly in the morning as I was getting set to leave. "It's been nice having you. Been way too long since we seen you for this long a stretch."

"I'd love to stick around," I told her, "but at some point I've gotta get back and find a job."

Only the second half of that statement was true. Well, I lie. It's true that I didn't want to stick around, but at the same time it was nice to see them. I felt good about having spent that much time with them. I'm not sure we got along any better than we ever did, but there was something that felt healing about the trip. Maybe I'd grown up a little bit in the past year, or maybe it was recent events. Maybe simply it was the sense of having a place called home to come home to. Even if, as my step-sister frequently warned, "It ain't your house. It be mine."

"*Is*," I told her repeatedly. "Is. Is. It *is* your house."

* * *

On September 10th I landed at SFO early in the evening. I took a taxi home to Langton Street, unwedged twelve days of mail jammed into my mailbox, got some carry-out Thai food for dinner, turned on the TV and sank into the strange quiet of being alone and at…home.

In the morning, of course, I awoke to a very different universe.

-13-

JESUS SWEDE
&
THE JUNIOR CONSULTANT FROM CLEVELAND

It was a not uncommon February morning in the City. Chilly by San Francisco standards; probably in the low 50's, damp, dreary. Rain fell in flashes that filled gutters faster than they could drain, leaving liquid street corners all throughout town. The morning commute was sluggish; buses slogged along filled with water-logged commuters toward downtown towers that looked dreary and sleepy-eyed beneath the grey skies. The whip of the wind was sharp; carrying an open umbrella was a foolishness that guaranteed a trip to Walgreen's at lunch time to hunt down another five dollar, throw-away device. In the subway stations there was some respite from the conditions, some hint of warmth, grotesque as it may have been, as swarms of bodies converged on platforms or emerged from foggy cars.

My new morning commute in that era of different living came courtesy of a diligent if disorganized software security division at a large firm in Oakland. (*Share no names, spread no secrets,* I was told.) They had hired me as a contractor through The Swarthmore Group, Stuart's firm, to do project coordinator work similar to what I had done at the power company. It was a nine-month contract and, for a while at least, it promised a return to a modicum of stability in my life. To get to work I took BART, the metro rail system that served the greater Bay Area. I boarded each day at the underground station at Civic Center, above which swarmed a heaving trough of grizzled humanity, and arrived at a small cocoon of high-rises in central Oakland fifteen minutes later. With ten minutes or so walking time on either end of the journey, my commute required just enough effort to keep the blood flowing and lasted just long enough to allow me time to reflect.

I was grateful for the work, since I desperately needed to recover from the state of near-pennilessness I'd reached after 9/11. There was no work to be found after the attacks. Any spark of employment opportunity that might have existed before I went to Florida to see my family disappeared like a photon in flight. Job requisitions were cut instantly and across the board as companies hovered in breathless states to see if the stock markets would mimic the plight of the World Trade Center buildings. Prior to that, on my contract from hell, I'd been living paycheck to paycheck, barely able to keep my emergency fund in the black while paying my mortgage, my taxes, and of course that enduring gift I owed the IRS after my fabled and painful foray into stock options. So it was with extreme gratitude and a mild faith in the miraculous that I wandered down into the bowels of Civic Center on that crappy, rainy, cold February day to catch the Oakland-bound train to go to work.

In the vast anemic lobby of the BART station, City workers were heading in to fill the surrounding government buildings and the gold-domed City Hall. They shuffled disinterestedly past the common underground elements—a flower seller, a newspaper seller, a mediocre guitarist playing for nickels and pennies, bundled up homeless sleeping in corners. They skirted gate jumpers and petitioners, and, as though it were instinctual, completely ignored a folding table manned by two figures in dress clothes. On the table there was a stack of books resting in a neat arrangement, with one propped up for display beside a good-sized sign that read in red letters, STRESS TEST. One of the table manners, a young guy, was seated and talking devotedly with a young woman. The other manner, a young woman a little bit older than me, stood out front on guard, she a false lure, a chatterer, a huckster of faith at the gates to the bridge of salvation. "Good morning. *Good morning.* Good morning, hello...Good morning!" The tone of her voice aimed to be soothing but it echoed in the dirty tiled place with an edge as sharp as the wicked wind outside.

The voice was familiar. As I passed in front of the woman I took a look at her face and had to stop in my tracks. "Glynnis?" It was Glynnis Hoffmeister, the usability and human factors expert from goFORTH, one the banes of my former existence.

She swallowed and tried to look away, then she looked me in the eye. She forced a smile. If ever there was a candidate in need of saving, I'm sure I fit her bill. Her forehead twitched a little as she held out a pamphlet. "Stress test?"

Glynnis had cut her hair and it had a streaks of brown highlights, as though she were trying to soften her image. "Hello Hugo," she said.

"Wh-what—?" I couldn't finish the question. Was it too large or was the answer simply too obvious?

"I'm on the Bridge," she said softly. Confidently.

I resisted all urges to tell her, No you're *not* on the Bridge, you're in the underground. But instead I asked politely, "How are you?"

"I'm doing well," she said. "When I realized what I'd gotten involved in—how caring so much for something with so little meaning had led me to unhappiness—I decided to make a change."

"Are you working these days?"

"I have a different calling now."

"I see."

"I'm sure you'll find something humorous about my condition. Something curious. Something to ridicule. But I'm on the way to finding my true self, Hugo. What about you?"

"I'm good."

"Are you burdened? Debt-laden? Still single?"

"N-no."

"Are you happy?"

"Sure I'm happy."

"That sounded sarcastic, Hugo. Sarcasm is a sign of unhappiness. You've always been sarcastic."

"I'm doing fine, Glynnis."

"If you say so."

"It's true."

"I'm glad for you, then. Can I interest you in—?" and she held out her brochure again.

"No, thanks. I have a train to catch. Big meeting today—."

"There will always be a train to catch, Hugo." She tried to lay a hand on my arm. I figured they must have rehearsed their rejections; went to class; read pamphlets; had online chat groups with clever titles like *Inverting the 'No'*. I avoided her touch and stepped away. "Good luck with yourself."

"You too." Unruffled, she turned away and went about tormenting other people passing by. *"Hello, good morning. Stressed? Hello!"* I crossed the lobby and slid my transit card into the gate and descended further into the City's stomach as Glynnis' voice got lost at the top of the stairs.

* * *

We were about a week into my new contract and I'd only met a handful of people on the project, so I went to the conference room early, wanting to make a good impression. The Project Manager on the engagement was a far cry from the one at the power company. This one was competent; beyond capable; in fact, he was such a thin-lipped master of project planning that he might possibly have been a savant. He'd taken a liking to me and had faith in my ability. He was exceedingly particular but promised to avoid the sort of nitpicking manipulation I endured at the power company. I wouldn't say that I necessarily liked the man but I was impressed by his commitment and his energy. His Director, who reported to a Vice President that would remain mostly unknown and unapproachable at first, was herself an avid survivalist and particularist. The Vice President, I would learn, cared less about the specifics of an implementation than about the fine luminescence with which her project staff could reflect their brilliance upon her. It was a different sort of self-servitude than that affected by James, the power company Vice President who loved to count pages. This one's hands-off approach flowed down to the overworked Director, her Project Manager, and the rest of the Team with such tremendous expectation that not only God but Jesus, Joseph, the Saints and the Apostles all resided in our daily details.

Working in semi-isolation as I was—my first week was an indoctrination into the methods, deliverables, modes, and processes of the Director and her effete yet indomitable Project Manager—I barely knew anyone. I was to be kept that way until I was well versed in the etiquette of the place and until we'd made sure that the finest detail of the project plan mapped so perfectly to every possible act of achievement and derailment that if the slightest aspect of the project went awry the entire effort, I was warned by the two of them, would unravel into a chaos of light storms and black hole-creation. If I'd been more astute in things corporate and political, I might have realized that the project, despite its atomic precision, was actually a mess.

The meeting for which I'd forgone conversion by Glynnis earlier that morning was the Phase II Technical Development Kick-off. The project had been forging along for nearly two years and was recently restructured with new objectives, new deliverables, and a significantly heftier budget after 9/11. Targets had been shifted and now the Team was commencing on the actual build of the security system. It was a new phase and therefore required a new kickoff meeting: Bigger crowds. More attention. A raft of new consultants and contractors. And all of us were gathering on that sloppy February day to christen Phase II in what would turn out to be one sorely undersized conference room.

I arrived before anybody else. I double checked the conference room number on a plaque outside the door, then checked the agenda I had just printed. There had been three updates to the electronic meeting notice in the days preceding the meeting, the latest of which arrived at 8pm the night before. I was fairly convinced I was in the right place, so I sat down on the far side of the table with a view of the door. As I sat doodling on my copy of the meeting agenda, a middle aged white woman carrying an armload of documentation entered the room and set the stack down hard upon the conference table. "Hello," she said tersely, as though the anticipation of an eight-month development schedule had already consumed her with exhaustion and stress. "You here for the PRV kickoff?"

"Yes," I said.

"PRV. Not BRB right? They sound alike. Business Resumption is in the room we *should* be in." The she muttered something about the incapacity of administrative assistants and meeting scheduling; she let various binders slam down on top of the table as she sorted through them.

"I'm in the right place," I said. "Thanks."

"You new?" she asked unceremoniously.

"Yep."

"I'm Janet."

"Hugo Storm. Swarthmore Group."

"Contractor, eh?"

"Yes."

"Who you working for?"

I told her the name of the Project Manager I was under, as well as the name of his Director.

"You're not the new process auditor, are you?" she asked with tangible note of contempt.

"Me? No. I'm doing project coordination."

"Hm."

"What do you do?" I asked.

"Technical liaison."

"Oh, right. What is that?"

She looked at me with bland affect. "Beats me. If you can figure it out you win a prize."

Five minutes after the scheduled start of the meeting the room started filling up. There were a few empty seats at the table, one of which was beside me. In walked a gorgeous young woman, one in whom it seemed the angels sang. She had long black hair that fell between her shoulder blades and a beautiful, white organic smile. I couldn't help but forget my purported reason for being in the room. She asked if she could sneak into the chair beside me.

"Of course."

She grinned, her smile giving off light.

"I'm Rebecca Sanchez." She offered her hand—soft white fingers, subtly painted nails—everything exquisite. "Are you by any chance—?"

"Hugo Storm."

"I thought so." She shook my hand gently. "Carol told me to keep an eye out for you."

Rebecca was one of a few contractors that Stuart had working in that division. It was a new conquest for him and he had instructed Carol, the account manager, to bring us all together and make us feel like a team. He wanted to build "presence." Luckily, Rebecca had been shifted onto our project—"just yesterday, in fact." My heart couldn't have been gladder, my gut no more anticipatory. After months of nothing fruitful on nearly every front of my life, there was no scenario more promising than that of the lovely ringless fingered one sitting beside me.

Five minutes more and the room was packed to standing room only. Rebecca leaned in and whispered, "They always start late here."

"There's a lot of people, too."

"Ohhh, yes." She raised her eyebrows suggestively and opened her notebook.

The Director and the Project Manager were seated side by side a few seats away from us. They were positioned slightly off-center so as to avoid looking the cliché of power brokers and also to give themselves an air of casualness. The Administrative Assistant came in while the Director was asking people to settle down. Poor woman, the Admin was a perpetual deer in headlights. She arrived in the meeting room as the last attendees strolled in, squeezing in where there was space. In a fluster she looked around at the large audience and announced loudly, "Sorry for the tight squeeze, everyone. We were supposed to have [*some other, larger conference room*] but [*insert crisis here*]. We'll just have to make do. Also, the agenda has changed slightly. I didn't have time to resend it before the meeting so I made a hard copy for everyone." She split the stack of photocopies into piles and handed a stack to the people on either side of her. "Take one and pass it along." Another small stack she flopped onto the center of the conference room table.

Someone asked from within the crowd, "Should we disregard the agenda from yesterday?"

"Yes," she said with a hint of fatigue in her voice.

"What about the documentation plan?" someone else asked.

"Still valid," she said. "Everything I sent out last night with the meeting update is the latest, except the Agenda."

"Do you know what version that is?"

"What what is?" she called into the crowd, emanating frustration.

"The documentation plan."

The Admin looked quizzically at the Director, who rifled through at a six-inch pile of documentation in front of her.

"2.2," the Director said authoritatively.

"N-no, no," interjected the Project Manager. "We renumbered at 3.0 last night so we could start the meeting fresh with even numbers."

The Director tilted her head: "3.0 it is."

"Is that the same one that was sent out yesterday morning?" someone hollered from the back.

The Project Manager stood up. He was a short man, a rotund man. He had a catalogue of minutia running through his head at all times, which often led to his own and others' confusion. He raised a hand. "Just a minute, people! We'll go over *all* of the documentation during the Documentation section of the meeting. Keep what you have and don't worry about versioning for right now." He sat back down in his seat. He was about five chairs away from me, just around the bend of the oval conference table. He looked at me and nodded very quickly as both a question (*"Agreed?"*) and also a request for validation (*"Did that go ok?"*). I nodded yes on all counts and half-smiled, aware of the many unfamiliar faces that were suddenly looking in my direction.

The first Agenda item of our 3-hour meeting was a statement of the purpose of the meeting, which was, the Director told everyone, to kick off the large and important new phase of what was a high profile and very "mission-critical" project. She followed up with a summary of the Agenda, in which she went into detail-ladened descriptions of every single item on the printed page.

The curious matter of who everyone was was addressed in the second agenda item, *Introductions*. A line of personal introductions snaked erratically around the room, starting with people at the conference table first then moving on to the people in scattered chairs and then the standing room only crowd, the order bouncing around as people overspoke on one another and hemmed and *uhm'd* and struggled to gracefully get a turn. We each stated our name, department and role on the project. When it had been my turn, I informed the reasonably age- and gender-diverse, yet scorchingly white, audience that my name was Hugo Storm. I was a project coordinator from the Swarthmore Group who was working for the Project Manager. Our Director wagged a pointed finger high and warned everyone, "Hugo is our task master. We're running this ship tight and fast. He is tracking deliverables and dates, so you better keep him apprised of what's going on. If you don't want to hear from the *VP*," she cautioned, "be sure to feed him your status and updates *on time*." Most everyone found her comments to be jovial but they made me want to excuse myself and go crawl out of my skin. As I looked around the room half-grinning and trying to look in one glance both menacing and kindly without looking retarded, my eyes fell on a young guy—really young; a kid almost. He was eagerly scratching notes in his notepad at the far end of the table. He would introduce himself as Todd. He would inform us that he was a process auditor from The Cincinnati Committee—.

"The *Cleveland Group*," the Project Manager corrected me during our first break in the meeting. We had gotten through *Introductions, Documentation Summary, Project Overview, Roles and Responsibilities, Tracking Mechanisms, Issues Resolution* and *Timeline* before the Director announced that she thought we could all use a bio break before diving into *System Overview*. "At least, I could use a break," she said trying to sound congenial. All sorts of muffled exultations rose from within the stifling room as people bolted out through the glass conference room door.

"He's a copious note taker," The Project Manager remarked confidentially of the young consultant after coming to sit down beside me. "Isn't he?"

"I think he captured every single word in shorthand."

"If he tries to talk to you, point him to me. He has explicit instructions to only talk to those people that either I or Sally (the

Director) pre-approve. If I want you to interface with him I'll let you know. It will not come from him. We have to work out the particulars of his engagement—that's our 3 o'clock, by the way." He winked and patted me on the back. "Fun fun."

Post-break, after the attendees had all re-assembled in the tired grey-blue conference room, the Director stood and elicited quiet. "Thank you all for getting back so quickly. At this point," she announced, "I'm going to turn the meeting over to Anders, our Technical Director. Anders is going to walk us through the System Design and provide an overview of the System Features."

Anders was a new face in the meeting crowd. He was known quietly within our project team as The Swede because he was hired over from a big firm in Stockholm prior to being given that project. He arrived in the conference room during the break, ready to assume center stage at his designated time. As the room went quiet Anders approached the projector screen, which had hung blank against the front wall for the first hour and a half of the meeting and now was filled with white light.

Anders was a decent looking guy with curly blonde hair that spilled down the back of his neck. He was dressed casually and sported a meticulously maintained blonde beard. His skin was clean and clear and creamy white and his eyes were nearly a crystalline blue.

"*Cheese a weed,*" Rebecca leaned in and whispered into my ear.

"What?" I whispered back. She scribbled the phrase on her notebook and pointed discreetly: *Jesus Swede.* Then she turned the page quickly so nobody would see it. She leaned in again to whisper in my ear, "He looks like Jesus, doesn't he?"

This girl was clearly a trouble-maker. Not wanting to look like the new kid disrupting the class, I pointed my pen to a spot on the Agenda, pretending to show her where we were, or provide some such masquerading charade for the benefit of anyone who might've been watching us. I looked back at Anders. Now that she'd brought it up, he did. his resemblance to a picture of Christ that Aunt Alice kept on the wall above her dresser was uncanny. Spooky actually.

But then he opened his mouth.

If Jesus Christ was a self-aggrandizing, condescending and pontificating technical überprick, then he had indeed resurrected in our lifetime and landed in our neighborhood. This guy was a jerk. Every other phrase out of his mouth was a jab—"Okay, kids," he'd start. *Kids.*

If you were foolish enough to ask a question he'd sneer or chortle as if to suggest that you were an idiot before digging into you. Case in point: "Toddy wants to know if—" started the Swede.

"Todd," the Junior Consultant from Cleveland corrected him in a loud, shaky voice.

"*Todd* wants to know if there's going to be Business input to the Functional Requirements. Well. Why don't we get through the Overview of the System first, and then at the end of my presentation, when we're looking at the Development Timeline we can address that question in specific. Suffice it to say, kids, the Point Verification Relay system has been so well thought out and designed that—well of course there will be opportunities for the Business to review it. But let's get a move on. I think we are all more interested in how the System is going to work than whether or not the Business is going to choose background colors for the user buttons."

Nearly an hour into the System Overview, which was more like a hyper-detailed mechanistic deconstruction of the logical data models that underscored discreet bits of the System's functionality, not to forget a glorification of the sheer brilliance of the Development Team, my head was spinning. All around the table, though, the words of the garrulous, good-looking stand-in from Stockholm were lapped up like puddles of milk spilt for a room full of cats. There wasn't a single inattentive eye, which astounded me. I felt like cutting myself to see if I was still alive. Unbeknownst to me until later that day as I was reviewing my notes, at 11:40 am I scribbled something scarcely legible on my notepad: "*I'm going slightly mad.*"

Still we slogged on. A large stack of documents—"This is the first of fifteen," Anders announced—was passed around the room. "Pursuant to Toddy's relevant yet—."

"Todd."

"Todd's relevant yet premature inquiry about the Business-slash-Technical project intercourse, the Technical Analysis Team will be producing each of these documents on roughly a two-a-week schedule. We will walk through each one of them in person, in a room such as this, so that everything—I repeat, *everything*—is crystal clear. Now, kids, if you look at page..."

Anders, it was clear, wished to be exalted. He looked the sort who would find it a perfectly worthy and appropriate venture to be laid upon a table, his privates draped with a satin sheet and his body surrounded by a sea of multi-colored tulips, rosebuds and candles as his unworthy minions of adoration danced in slow circles around him holding hands, chanting softly and extracting indulgence from the aura that his presence exuded. Keyboards, back-up tape drives, computer monitors, flash drives, cell phones and the rest of the techno-accoutrements which had been lain around the base of the table by devotees before the beginning of the pseudo-science dance would serve as an intellectual pyre, igniting the ingeniousness of the magnificent, curly blonde-haired man with a sculptured chest of finely trimmed brown hair—Icarus upon a slab of virtual life; the Messiah upon a technical altar. The slow undulations of the revolving crowd would increase in speed as candles burned and the chanting rose to a heated pitch. Hands would unclasp and arms would rise upwards. Fingers, fondling the tendrils of smoke and air above reveling heads, would decree him the Master. Voices would rise and wails would unfurl as the room turned steadily orgiastic.

A civilized if fatigued round of applause greeted the conclusion of the Jesus Swede's presentation, which snapped me out of my quick mental trip to never-ever land.

My God, I thought, clapping obligatorily, *I didn't hear a word he said*. I leaned over toward Rebecca: "I am so glad there are handouts."

She grinned.

Someone in the room tried to ask Anders a question as the projection screen went dark. Anders held up his hands. "I have a Development meeting to attend. If you have questions, email Janet Lane." He pointed to her. I looked over at the woman whom I'd met briefly before the start of the meeting. She vaguely smiled; it was a smile that said something like, *"Don't even think about it."*

The Director thanked Anders as he reached the door. She then announced it was time for another bio break, "After which we have a very important procedural topic to discuss, so I want you all to come back as quickly as you can. I know that we've run overtime, but for those of you that can stay, please do." Given that the meat of the meeting was overwith, it was clearly a desperate plea on her part, especially considering that the keynote speaker for the final portion of the meeting would be Todd, the Junior Process Audit Consultant from Cleveland.

"First off," Todd said to the room, which was barely a third full after the break. He was standing up front by the projector screen so people might see his small frame better. As well as his khakis. And his medium blue dress shirt. And his navy blue blazer with insignia buttons, the sleeves of which were just a tiny bit too long for his slender arms. "The provenance for this sort of modality comes from a body of work that was done over a period of years in the health services and financial services sectors. A summary of the results was published in the *Harvard Business Review* in October 1999." He raised the white projector screen to reveal a whiteboard on the wall, upon which he wrote with a weakened felt-tip pen, *HBR 10/99*, just like a little old school teacher. "Our study—."

"Yes, yes, Todd," interrupted the Director. "We're running short on time. If you have copies of the research we'd love to see it. Email it to Florida (*the overworked Admin, who rolled her eyes*) and she'll distribute it. In the interest of time, why don't you tell us about the kinds of assessment you'll be doing and the type of results you'll be presenting."

"Very well," he said. And he commenced presenting a string of incomprehensible facts and definitions, fed to us like drops of inflicted pain delivered through an IV tube. His twenty minutes of being front and center passed with the grace and lightness of a Germanic opera. "In closing—," he eventually concluded.

I glanced around the room and even my Project Manager was nearly comatose.

* * *

It was a difficult era, those first couple years after 9/11, made no easier by the absurdity of my days in Oakland. Of course one had to ask: difficult for whom? The San Franciscan who could still look up at his city skyline grateful that the Miami-bound jet whose target had been the Transamerica Pyramid housed no terrorists on board? The white guy who could more or less still hop a flight to anywhere without suspicion? The observer far removed from the physical scars of the events, who lost no one directly and yet still, in stirring subterranean emotions, found himself moving inward toward another new realm of silence?

In a way I was glad Emily wasn't around. There was something about her that I missed, and had been missing ever since she left, but had she been around on 9/11 that would have been the end of things. With each repeated slamming of the planes into the towers, the throes of the day would have overwhelmed her. I could only imagine her assuming a posture of increasing moral outrage that would quickly turn to self-blame and devastation, the tirade of her leftist dismissal of the State turning more and more unbearable. Better that she was gone. I presumed she was in some sunny spot, anyway, feet sunk into the sand, greedily oblivious or allowing herself only a brief period of shock from which she would escape as soon as the next round of tequila was poured.

As for me (and others, it was clear) I felt afloat on a directionless current. Before 9/11, my friend Trini, the Pakistani developer, had gotten a consulting contract that required him to commute from his place in South San Francisco to LA every other week. Every other Sunday night he would pack his suitcase before bed like many a roving technologist. Early on Monday he would kiss his wife and his infant daughter goodbye; he would taxi to the airport, spend a few days in meetings and presentations then return home to his two bedroom apartment later in the week. He called me in the early days of my Oakland project; he sounded desperate: "Hugo, are there any opportunities for me where you are? I have to find a new job. Something closer to home." His contract, he said, was killing him. He refused to fly to LA anymore; he was tired of the suspicious looks and being constantly pulled out of line for extra searches and questioning. He wouldn't dare use his cell phone while the plane was sitting at the gate. "I can only read *The Economist* or something frivolous like *People* magazine," he complained. "My wife even made me shave my moustache; she said I looked too much like a terrorist." It was too much strain for him, so instead of making the four-hour door-to-door trip in a plane he would get up at 3:00 in the morning and drive to Los Angeles so he could be there by ten, then drive home late after work at the end of the week. "They have been very supportive," he said of the company he was consulting through, "but I have had enough, Hugo. I am from a good family. We are respectable. We are well educated. Here everyone thinks we are Muslim. But we are Hindu, for heaven's sake. For generations—Hindu! We came here to escape persecution in our own country, and now I am being harassed for something I am *not*."

In general I wasn't a political person. I wasn't even really an aware person. I lived. I worked. I went out and spent money and drank too much and had some fun. I enjoyed the shameless luxury of being able to fret over immaterial things; I didn't have to worry about people thinking I was a terrorist. Like vast numbers of people, I was a *leave-the-details-of-running-the-place-to-someone-else* sort of person, unaware of the complicitness of my existence, taking the ease of my life for granted. September 11, 2001, however, forced me to change my view of things. As I sat in my darkened room watching the World Trade Center footage over and over, and later in listening to Trini's longing pleas, I realized that history was a living thing. It infused our days in ways both subtle and outright. Nixon's departure from the White House on my birthday; the space shuttle explosion; the falling of the Berlin wall—all of these things I'd lived through but I could only disaffectionately, disinterestedly, label them History. Before 9/11, History had been something lived by other people. Claims that *"History was made today..."* were a favorite rhetorical device of ridiculous politicians and easily excitable news commentators, and I usually found their claims dubious. But on the days following 9/11, as the skies remained silent with the absence of air traffic, you could hear in that silence a plainly spoken truth: History is not something that bursts onto a news headline one day and is then quickly filed away for subsequent revisions to the History books. History is a living wound. It's fire; vehemence; upheaval. Sometimes it's a single miraculous event performed by a simple individual; often it's a larger effort of collective will. But ultimately, more often than not, History is drowned in its own tears.

* * *

At three o'clock that afternoon, the Overly Efficient Project Manager and I had a meeting with the Hyperfocused Director and the Junior Consultant from Cleveland to figure out how best to integrate Todd's process audit Deliverables into our overall Project Plan. The four of us spent some time going over the Project Schedule and resolving where and how the young man would interface with the Business and Technology teams, most of whom didn't want him there in the first place. Said differently...in lieu of a collective decision making process, we adhered to the decisions that the Director had already made prior to the meeting, the purpose of which—the meeting, that is—was merely to offer the illusion of having had a discussion. The purpose, then, of the question and answer session, of the whiteboarding and the frantic note capture that had gone on for nearly 40 minutes, was simply show and posturing. This manner of interchange drove the Project Manager, who at that point was in a turmoil-induced sweat, nearly crazy.

Regardless the painful mechanism for getting there, we now had guidelines and parameters for the young business process savant to follow. We had Rules of Engagement and Reporting Requirements. We had Escalation Guidelines. We had a list of people that Toddy—sorry...Todd—was allowed to talk to. All things being relative, things went pretty well. At least until Jesus Swede came into the room. Late, of course. The sour look on his face made it plainly obvious that he felt his life was being disrupted. His belief that the Business was a distraction to the more meaningful technical efforts of his days would resound like church bells until the end of the project and likely continue onward ever further toward infinity. He refused to sit in the chair that the Project Manager dragged in for him from an adjacent office. "I prefer to stand," he said brusquely.

The Director told Anders that the Process Audit was going to include *all* aspects of the project, with the Business/Technology interface being a critical component of said audit.

"I disagree with the need for an Audit."

"We don't have a choice," said the Director. "Otherwise we end up evaluating our own processes against what Todd rightly calls Indefinable Reference Points. And if we fail that, then who knows what the end product will end up being."

This appeared to irritate the Swede inconsolably. "Elaborate."

The Director got up and pointed at the large sheets of adhesive white paper on her wall, where was written out in colored markers a list of the Junior Consultant's Deliverables, Tasks, Timeline, and all the rest. She set forth explaining how the act of, for instance, interviewing a technician and reviewing the decision making process behind Business Requirements set out in the Technical Documentation would provide Feedback Loops to the End User Evaluations performed by the Business as they figured how best to deploy and promote usage of the System and develop User Training Modules around it.

"As I think you're aware," Jesus Swede interrupted, "the PRV system has been meticulously designed down to the last detail. All you need is our Technical Specifications to build your training. As for the System itself, there isn't a single thing that has to be done to change the end product. The bottom line is, we're building. We know what the target is—this indefinable *IRP*, as he calls it. We defined that long before young Toddy arrived on the scene. Probably before he graduated high school."

The little boy jumped up and declared, "Now listen here—!"

The brilliantly unkind thing about Anders was that he couldn't begin to register how insulting he was. The Junior Consultant's face turned pinkish red, the color of Chioggia beets in Spring. The Director warned Anders that he was out of line.

"*I'm* out of line? I *know* how to run a technical project."

"Nobody's telling you how you to run things, Anders."

"You're right. Because this is a waste of time. I'm not going to disrupt my team with this ridiculous exercise. I have an application to build."

Having heard enough, he raised a hand and walked out of the room.

How I envied the ease of Anders' dismissal. How I wanted to hold up my own hand and say, *Enough.* I'd had enough of the IT industry. At first it had been good to me: it gave me a kick start on a professional life; it had given me the means to buy a place. Then it kicked me out on my ass. And now it had returned to me in the guise of that latest, droll punishment in Oakland. The truth was, I couldn't stand my work. Not the Anders's nor their Project Managers nor their Escalation Guidelines or their System Specifications. Not their obsessive Acronym and Capitalization FETISHES nor the intangibility of the things we built. I could no longer abide the fleetingness of how I spent my days.

* * *

"At least it's work," Angela said.

"But I can't stand it."

"Then find something else."

"I want to sell."

"Then go sell."

"What should I sell?"

"Hugo, we've been down this road before. If you're unhappy with your life, change it."

* * *

The dull, monotonous shriek of work carried on throughout summer as I aimlessly pondered my future. By summer's end, the NASDAQ was on its way toward a five year low, which seemed to me a relevant irony. The falling index seemed a mirror of the downward trajectory my own life; it was clear that it was time for a personal turnaround.

I had no idea what I was going to do with my life, though, so I went to see Stuart. If there was anyone who had an actionable perspective on things I figured it would be him. Treading carefully—I was still working for him, after all—I invited myself over to his office one evening at the end of a work week. When I got there he was sitting behind his desk, a modernist stretch of glass and metal on top of which rested various stacks of reading material. A copy of the *Wall Street Journal* was spread open in front of him and his eyes were smiling, as if he were savoring the typeset.

"Hey there," he said, staring at his newspaper. "What's up?"

"Nothing, I—."

He looked up and grinned. "You disrupt my Friday ritual for nothing?"

"No, not nothing. What're you reading?"

"The *Weekend Journal*. I live for this."

"For a newspaper?"

"It's an entire world in your hands, Hugo. It's—. Look—." He held out his hand; his fingertips were stained with a charcoal colored ink. "It rubs off on you."

"And this is your ritual?"

"It's how I like to end my week, yes. Ever read the wine reviews?"

"No."

"My favorite section is the real estate."

"Seriously?"

"I love to look. Fantasy mansions in Newport, Greenwich...Midtown co-ops..."

"Well, for those of you who can afford such things—."

"Yeah right." He let out what sounded like some sort of laugh. "What's up?"

"I need some advice."

"Shoot."

After some fawning expressions of gratitude for all the work he'd gotten me, some wide-angle and pre-emptive apologies, I stammered until I managed to get the actual words out of my mouth: "I'm sick of IT."

He looked at me blankly. "Seriously?"

"Yes."

"What brought this on?"

"It just—I don't know. No," I said, "I do know. I'm just sick of it. The intangibleness, the constant bugs, the mind-numbing details, the—." I pointed to his newspaper. "The lack of ink."

He nodded. "Got it."

"You do?"

"Can't say I blame you. Computers do amazing things. But working with them is like paving roads. Nobody gives a damn about your work until it falls apart."

"Exactly."

"So?"

"So I don't know," I said. "I'm struggling. How do I figure out where do I go next?"

"That depends on what you want to do."

"I want to sell."

"Okay. Everything on the planet has to be sold, so you literally have a world of opportunity available to you. Minus IT sales, since you're no longer interested."

"But I can't figure out *what* I want to sell. I don't want to just fall into something random again. That's how I ended up in software. It seems to me I have some choice, right? I know we're supposed to *live* our passion, but I don't think I have one."

"Screw passion," he said. "95% of the world's population doesn't have the luxury of living any *passion*. That's the biggest line of crap to come down the pike in a long time." He pointed a finger at me. "I'll tell you about passion, Hugo Storm. If you have no driving need in life—no deep-rooted desire to do good, no obsession, no, I don't know, urges—then simply embrace what you're good at. You don't have to turn into some over-zealous caricature on a mission from God in order to have a meaningful life."

"Yeah?"

"Look at me."

"But you're passionate about what you do."

"No I'm not, I'm aggressive. Do you think I really care about the work I do? Do you think it gives me some deep, fundamental gratification? Hardly. What I do I do *well* because the only thing I have to rely on is my reputation. Working hard is a means to an end, and that's it. I have a condo to maintain. I have a weekend house. I like to travel. I like to go out. I like good food. I like good wine. I like to be able to go anywhere, anytime—(work issues aside, of course). I like my top-of-the-line Mercedes." He raised his hands unapologetically. "The things I have and the things I like to do take money. That's the only reason I work as hard as I do. I could go live in a shack somewhere and never have to work a day in my life. But that's not the kind of life I want."

"Easy for you. You've already got plenty of—."
"No. It's not about money, Hugo. It's about quality of life. There's value in a life lived decently, simply and according to your abilities. You have to figure out what you're good it and what kind of life you want to lead. I'm talking realistically. We can't all be superstars or rich. But you can do what you do *well* and be happy with that." He scanned his newspaper and then folded it up quickly and held it out in front of him. He jabbed at the middle of the real estate section. "Look at this: an eight-room pre-war on Central Park West. 12th floor. East- and south-facing views. Six million. Fuck me."

I left Stuart's office no closer to knowing where I'd end up next but I felt better about things. Before I left his office I made three commitments to him: first, that I would always remember that it was a luxury to have some say in how I earned a living and to squander that luxury would be a shame; second, that I wouldn't bail on my contract with him without sufficient notice; and third, that if selling was what I really wanted to do, then I would sell anything, whatever it was, as long as I could put my hands around it and touch it, feel it, smell it or possibly even long for it.

* * *

On the topic of things I could put my hands around...my romantic life during the *Contract to End all Contracts* was largely an exercise in self-fulfillment. I had an on-again, off-again pseudo-dating thing with Rebecca Sanchez, who was separated from her husband of two years and was struggling to finalize a divorce from him. Not the brightest move on many levels—especially since we worked together, which was like doing a slow dance in the back of a church: it wasn't necessarily wrong, but it felt weird. We came close to the edge of a very slippery slope at one point when she thought she was pregnant. "No more without protection," she whispered harshly from across the table as we ate our morning bagels in the client's cafeteria. "My God, Hugo, I can *not* get pregnant." Soon after, she and I drifted away from the physical and became simply friends without any sexual benefits.

Later In October Rebecca and I spent an impromptu Saturday together. We had decided to take the freeway down to Highway 92 then head over the hills into Half Moon Bay and check out the annual Pumpkin Festival. Both of us needed a diversion: I was still avidly trying to find my higher professional calling; she was trying to ignore the annoying upward swirls of dust that were the fulminations of her soon-to-be ex-husband. On a self-indulgent note, I also wanted to show off my vanity license plates. Ever since I'd bought my car I'd been wanting vanity plates. So on my 28th birthday I went to the DMV and registered myself for a gift, *HugoSF*. It was a cheap but lasting thrill, and I affixed the plates to my Beemer in the garage before heading out to pick Rebecca up.

"This traffic *sucks*," she shouted out the car window as we slogged our way down the Half Moon highway on a two-lane road that was a solid line of cars heading in the direction of town. We both laughed, recognizing the ridiculousness of our endeavor: a quaint pumpkin festival in a coastal town just outside the City. The first bright cold days of winter. A modest return of optimism to our wedge of the land. Naturally people would be out in droves.

"Let's turn around," she said.

"Then what?"

She shrugged and stretched her arm out the window, slicing the sharp breeze with her hand. "Go to the park? Get lunch. I don't care, let's just wander around. Anything beats sitting in this mess."

"Works for me." I made an abrupt u-turn on the winding downslope of the highway and in half an hour we were back in town, in Golden Gate Park, doing exactly what Rebecca had suggested. The park is a marvelous place of refuge, a vast wilderness within the City pockmarked with places to hang out and either educate yourself or do nothing. It's like a magnificent country estate with museums. Rebecca and I wandered through the perfectly sculpted Japanese Tea Garden, ambled about the humid conservatory, checked out art in the Legion of Honor, then drove to the far end of the park and had a late, late lunch with a view of the Pacific. If we hadn't committed to only being friends—"At least until we get our mutual shit together," she suggested—I might have started falling for her. I could tell the same thing might have been rummaging through her mind as well. At one point in the Legion of Honor I put my arm around her shoulder and we stood silently looking at a tall portrait of a woman like the one Grace Kelly sat staring at in the movie *Vertigo*. Rebecca looked over at me. She smiled. She leaned in a little bit closer.

Evening arrived quickly, so it was pitch dark by the time we got back to her house. She was renting a small place in the Sunset, a vast flat neighborhood in the western part of the City where every avenue looks the same and the actual sunset is seldom seem on account of the constant fog. "Wanna come in?" she asked.

"I'm tempted," I said. "But I think I'll go home."

"I understand." She gave me a kiss on the cheek and got out of the car. I waited until she was inside the house and had turned on a few lights before I drove away.

I drove through the congested, grid-like Sunset district then picked up Portola to head over Twin Peaks toward my side of town. The sky above San Francisco was a lonely, steely dark blue that night. On the great swerve at the top of Market Street the lights of downtown and the eastern hills of the City came into view. Windows were illuminated in yellow-golden light and from a distance the entire setting seemed like life in miniature, a fantasy playset etched from a block of dark matter by an elaborate knife of willful yet random creativity. Just then the car descended down the winding asphalt road toward the Oz-like city, past flat matter houses lining glossy streets. The bright wide corridor of Market Street bisected the body of the City like a spine, a busy line painted on life's dark torso by countless hands of moving light. The lure of the City is sometimes unfightable and she can easily absorb you once you are all of a sudden in her midst: the buildings, busy sidewalks, chatter, clatter, traffic and voices...

In no time I was on the littered streets of the Mission making my way toward the even grungier streets that surrounded my loft on Langton Place. Such was SOMA, littered with bodies like heaps huddled in building doorways, shadows within the shadows. There were nights when my neighborhood felt like the moon, and this was one of those.

Once inside my loft I popped open a Stella, filled a glass, shaved the foam off at the rim of the glass with the back edge of a knife the way I'd seen it done in bars. After tooling around the internet for a while—I'd been intrigued by the rising housing costs in the City and was curious as to what lofts like mine were going for these days—I logged into email and saw a message from MDodger@..., aka Emily Dodger, aka my Emily:

hey hugo. i'm back for a while. wanted to say hi, see you how u r...

--Em

She'd been out of touch since she dumped me. I didn't know where she'd been, and although sometimes I thought I didn't care, there was a jealous part within me that wanted to know who she was with and what she was doing.

I left her message open, unsure of how I wanted to respond. I got another beer from the fridge and went over to the sofa. I plunked myself down and set the beer on a side table in the spot where I used to keep a picture of the two us, taken when we went whale watching outside the Golden Gate. It was freezing cold that day on the water and the waves were choppy and brusque. Frigid seawater splashed everywhere and there was very little cover on the boat where you could stay dry. A handful of passengers got sick and spent the bulk of the trip hanging over the back edge of the boat. To everyone's disappointment, we ended up not seeing see a single whale in over two hours of doddling around the Pacific. We ended up cruising around the Farallons for some damp strain of time and then rode our dismay along with the afternoon fog back into port at Fisherman's Wharf. No whales. Not a single one. Not even a fish. Just puke and a cluster of islands covered in bird shit.

I laid a series of overlapping rings with the wet base of the beer glass on the side table. *"Just like that,"* I thought to myself, stamping each damp ring. Emily and I were just like that. "A waste of time."

* * *

"At least she was a good learning experience," said Angela. while her wife was in the kitchen. She and Tamara, who would suspend her contempt for me during the holiday season and even (was it possible?) treat me with acceptance in times beyond, had invited me over for Thanksgiving dinner. The two of us were sitting in the rustic living room of the couple's classic 2-1 Berkeley bungalow.

"Do you have to have a smart response to everything?" I replied.

Angela threw her hands up. Headlights from passing cars danced in the bay window behind her. With her hands raised it looked like she was giving off sparks from her fingertips. "Fine," she said, "I yield."

"Don't yield to him." Tamara set down a plate of nuts. She had happened into the room at just the opportune time. "Hugo, if there's one person in the world whose opinion you should respect, it's hers."

"Who said I don't respect it?"

"You with your defensive tone of voice."

"I wasn't being defensive, I was simply asking for a halt to the over-analysis of my private life."

"Then you shouldn't have brought it up."

Flummoxed, I took a handful of nuts.

"The polite thing for you to do is say thank you and then shut up." Tamara turned around. I watched in annoyance as she passed through the dining room and went into the kitchen.

Angela scooted in closer to me on the L-shaped denim sofa and wrapped an arm around me. She smelled faintly like warm sweet perfume and ginger ale and her torso was wrapped in a soft cozy sweater. She squeezed me and then kissed me on the cheek as if I were a plaything: "You're such an easy target, Hugo Storm."

"I can't help it if I'm sensitive."

"She's starting to like you."

"*That's* like?"

"You're in her territory. She's just letting you know who's boss."

"I see."

At the dinner table, after a thorough dissertation on the ills of living in a country where a president can be indicted for sexual acts, the topic of conversation drifted away from politics onto my less intriguing and muddled professional life. Tamara passed me a bowl of stuffing and suggested, "How about real estate."

"Great idea!" said Angela. "You're constantly talking about the market."

"Not because I want a career in it. As a homeowner I'm curious, but—."

"Well, why not?" insisted Tamara. "Any nimwad with half a brain and enough money to pay for the classes can get a real estate license. I know a woman; she's good with people, which must be the trick. She's smart: she offloads all the grunt work to an assistant and spends all of her time schmoozing and showing people property. In six weeks she earns what I make in one year. Six weeks."

"That so?"

"If you're half the salesman you claim you are," she said as she ladled brussel sprouts onto her plate, "you might do well."

* * *

It didn't take long to see the wisdom in Tamara's suggestion. Real estate was tangible. It had intrinsic value. It could be repainted or added onto; built up, torn down, everything right before your very own eyes or with your very own hands. There was plenty of it and demand was strong. According to Stuart it was about the only economic sector doing well at the time. "Well," he remarked longingly, "that and government contracting."

By Christmas I decided I would pursue real estate. In January I enrolled in a licensing course. I studied online at night after work and attended an in-person session with about thirty other potential agents every other Saturday. There were as many real estate agents in San Francisco, Stuart joked, as there were contract attorneys in DC. Competition was going to be stiff with so many hands shoved into what was ultimately a finite pie, but something about it felt right. Stuart thought favorably of my new career choice and reminded me that in the meantime I still had obligations with his company, and to his client.

By all calculations, by Spring I would be free. I set targets. I gave myself a date.

* * *

Valentine's weekend rolled around and Stuart called while Rebecca and I were slumming in the soft armchairs at Starbuck's during a break from the PRV project.

Ever since our confessional dinner a year and a half before, he'd become a friend. Mentor, advisor, pseudo-parent first. Then friend.

"Hey short-timer," he said. "Got plans tomorrow night?"

"It's Valentine's Day."

"I know. I'm having dinner at my mother's. Want to go?"

"To your mother's?"

"Do you have plans?"

"No," I said.

"Good. I don't celebrate Valentine's Day; I think it's a Hallmark holiday. But it was my parent's wedding anniversary, so ever since my father died she and I have Valentine's dinner together."

"That's nice," I said. "Weird. But nice."

"Well?"

"Who's going to be there? Just the three of us?"

"Plus Héctor."

"Who's Héctor?"

"He's somebody I want you to meet."

"Explain."

"Well number one," he sounded proud of himself, "he has a career. And number two," his voice went advisory, "he'd be good for you to know. He knows a lot of people."

* * *

"Is she mean?" I asked Stuart as he unloaded a case of wine from the trunk of his car. He'd parked in the white zone in front of his mother's apartment building, which was around the corner and just across the small Nob Hill park from Stuart's condo.

"No, she's not mean. She's very polite." He handed me the box. "In fact, my mother's politeness is both legendary and profound."

"Should I have brought flowers?"

"Only if you're trying to seduce her." He shut the trunk of his car. "Take the wine inside and wait for me in the lobby. I'm going to park and I'll be back over."

Mimi Piers lived at the apex of California Street in a simple, eight-story white building with trimmed, potted evergreens at the entrance. Its unpretentious adornment allowed the building to blend into the background of that central City hilltop almost without notice; its subtle presence gave the building a gracious feeling. There was a doorman, an African-American gentleman named Fred, who stood watch underneath a canopy that extended almost to the sidewalk's edge. He had been at the front door as long as Stuart could remember. He greeted residents and oversaw the flow of traffic in and out of the building. When it rained he took shelter in the marble lobby, which lay behind an exquisite iron gate, the building's chief ostentation. Fred held the door open for me as I went inside to wait. Unlike the plain exterior of the building, the entrance lobby was a marbled masterpiece of Old World moneyism. It was imposing yet restrained; somewhat cold; and it had a way of putting you in your place. From all I'd heard, Mimi Piers was a deceptively delicate-looking force to be reckoned with. Children were off-limits as a discussion topic, Stuart had told me in no uncertain terms: his mother accepted his sexuality without judgment but she was constantly encouraging him to find a decent partner and a surrogate so he could carry on the family line. ("Or you could have a marriage of convenience like your uncle did," she'd said. "It's less honest, of course...") As I sat in the lobby looking at the reflection of myself in a tall gilded mirror, I couldn't imagine coming to this place as someone's potential son-in-law. Emily's parents were a couple of Santa Cruz hippies, and although I never met them it would have been legions easier meeting them over magic brownies on the boardwalk than in a place like Mimi Piers'.

After Stuart came back we headed to the elevator in the back of the lobby and got in. I asked him if his mother had met Héctor.

He nodded.

"Does she like him?"

He nodded.

"She met any of your other flings?"

He nodded. "Regrettably."

Stuart, it turns out, had brought Alejandro, the forklift driving cowboy, to dinner at Mimi's apartment one evening around Christmas a couple years back. As he told it, at the door to the building Fred greeted Stuart by name and wished him a Merry Christmas. He nodded to Alejandro out of courtesy. In the lobby of the building, the wooden heels of Alejandro's cowboy boots made a baritone clapping noise as the two of them walked to the elevator. "Tread lightly on Mother's hardwood floors with those boots," Stuart advised.

"Should I take them off?"

"No, you don't have to. Just be gentle in the foyer and the kitchen. She has rugs everywhere else."

Mimi was her usual pleasant self when she greeted them at the door. "I like your boots," she said to Alejandro after she introduced herself. "They're very handsome."

"*Gracias, Señora.*"

Mimi, true to Stuart's description, was exceedingly polite. She also had flawless posture. As the three of them sat in the living room getting acquainted before dinner, she sat perfectly upright on the edge of an armchair. Her white hair rested without incident on the tips of her slender shoulders. She wore a clean checkered apron, like a well-to-do Betty Crocker, and sipped a glass of white wine decanted from one of the bottles Stuart had brought. She inquired about Alejandro's family and his upbringing in Mexico. Normally she wouldn't ask such a thing of one of Stuart's boyfriends, but on this night she inquired pointedly: "What is it you do, Alex?"

"I work in Fremont."

"Is that so? Doing what?"

"I move equipments in a factory over there."

"I see," Mimi said. She consumed the information as though it were bits of the salted snacks set out in the fine china bowl on the coffee table in front of them: nothing inspired, just so. "Are you a US citizen?"

"Green card," he said. "I am eligible to apply next year."

"For citizenship?"

"Yes."

"And will you?"

"I think so."

"That's very nice," she concluded with stunning dispassion.

As she spoke those words, soft pink lights illuminated the façade of Grace Cathedral, which dominated the view from the western end of the living room. Across the street from the cathedral, multicolored Christmas lights adorned the London plane trees in the park, which had been pruned for winter down to their gnarly bulbous branch ends. Stuart excused himself for a moment and stood at the window looking at the lights. This view, which he had seen from those same windows throughout his childhood, was his favorite view of San Francisco: the park filled with red, pink, green, yellow and blue lights—a lively luminescent winter wonderland. He motioned for Alejandro to come look. As the two of them stood like children staring out the window, Mimi left them and went into the kitchen to check on dinner.

Later, during dinner at the fine cherry dining table, Mimi, trying to find a connection to this latest in a string of unsuitable suitors for her son, related an unsolicited parable about truth, work and economics. "Stuart's grandfather drove a wagon when he was young..." So began the story that Stuart had heard some variation of all throughout his life. Mimi focused her gaze on Alejandro. "Pop-pop, which is what we called him, was studying accounting in San Francisco back in the early 1900's. Like many young men, all he wanted was a steady job in a reliable field so he could get married, take care of a family, buy a small house. But while he was in school he had to work. He had to pay his tuition and help support his parents. So he got a part-time job driving a supply wagon for a purveyor of building materials. It didn't pay a great deal, and he didn't get the best routes because he was just a junior driver. But Stuart's grandfather was a garrulous sort; he was very good at connecting with people. He could talk to anyone. Stuart has a lot of his grandfather in him; less so his father, although at times—. In any event, during Pop-pop's wagon runs he met people from all over town. Well. One day, with graduation nearing, his entire world changed. Of course I'm talking about the earthquake of 1906.

With the City smoldering and his bookkeeping school burnt to its foundation, Pop-pop took notice of all the people living in lean-to's and tents throughout the City. In many cases these people still had homes but they were uninhabitable or badly damaged. The people who had to tear down or repair their houses—what were they going to do? What would Pop-pop do? (He who was lucky that his family's small house was on a hill far from downtown.) What did Pop-pop do?" she repeated. She held a hand out to Stuart, drawing out from him a reluctant response.

"You finish the story, Mother."

"He created a place to let the people store their belongings," said Mimi. "He convinced his employer to loan him wagons from work and to rent him the extra space that he had in a warehouse over in—well, it's probably now the Mission District. Pop-pop gathered together the other drivers and hired a few men to help with heavy lifting. They moved people's belongings to the warehouse; inventoried everything; and guaranteed them that their belongings would be safe until they were able to rebuild their homes. And there was borne one of the first storage unit businesses in the country. Naturally, once people had their things back they didn't need the storage any longer. That wouldn't come into vogue until late in the Century. (Pop-pop was a visionary). After that, he took what he'd learned in his accounting classes and in his recent experience as a small business owner, and he started working on the City's reconstruction. He realized through all of that that he could do more in life than simply hold a job. He didn't have to survive, he could *succeed*. He could build something. And he did. Tell him, Stuart."

Stuart looked at Alejandro and said, "My grandfather built this building. He lived in what's now the doorman's apartment on the first floor. Eventually he was able to buy the whole building. This is where my mother was raised, and where I was raised. *Entendiste todo?*"

"*Mas o menos. Lo importante, sí.*"

"My point is this," Mimi concluded. "Succeeding is about responding to people's needs. Stuart's grandfather saw a need in people and he capitalized on that." She looked at Alejandro with a mix of compassion and encouragement. "In the long run it doesn't matter that you drive a truck for a living."

"Forklift," Stuart corrected.

"What?"

"It's the short, squat tractor-like thing with two prongs."

"I know what a forklift is, dear. They use them in warehouses."

"*Exacto.*"

"Well—." Mimi paused. "It doesn't matter what you do for a living, what matters is what you *do* with what you do for a living." She addressed her son: "Did that make sense?"

"Ask him."

"Did that make sense?" she asked Alejandro.

"What matters is your life," he replied.

"W-well." Mimi gently tilted her head. "As long as there's some ambition behind it."

* * *

"He's younger than I anticipated," Mimi Piers said of my appearance as I stood beside Stuart in the penthouse foyer with his mother staring me directly in the face. She was dressed up as if she were going to a cocktail party. She parted her lips in a deliberate and well-intentioned grin and held out her hand. "I'm just teasing of course. It's nice to meet you, Hugo. Happy Valentine's Day."

"Happy Valentine's Day," I replied.

"How nice of your boss to bring you by for dinner."

"I'm not his boss for long, Mother." Stuart took my overcoat from my arm and hung it in the closet by the front door. "Hugo's getting his real estate license."

"How wonderful," she exclaimed. "Stuart's father and grandfather were in real estate. On the construction side."

She led the way down a short paneled corridor into the living room, where the three of us sat in an elegant seating group in front of a fireplace eating shrimp cocktail and drinking pink champagne. Héctor, Stuart informed us, was on his way; he was driving up from the peninsula.

"So, Hugo, you're solo tonight," Mimi remarked with a friendly and playful air. "No…significant other?"

"He's straight, Mother."

She looked at her son. "The term still applies, dear."

"I had a girlfriend for a while," I told Mimi, "but I'm not really dating anyone right now."

Mimi focused her gaze on me. "That's too bad." I was seated on a plush loveseat next to Stuart. Mimi was seated on a matching loveseat directly across from me, on the other side of the coffee table. Each time I leaned down to take a shrimp she would do the same and our eyes would meet and our flaccid pink crustaceans would touch edges as we swiped them in opposite directions in the ruddy seafood sauce. "There's nothing wrong with a young man playing the field," Mimi said aloud.

"Except when it comes to me," Stuart lamented.

"I said *young*, sweetheart." Mimi winked and took a sip of her bubbly rosé. Then she asked seductively, "Would you like to see the rest of the apartment, Hugo?"

In time we returned to the living room, after Mimi's slow-paced, meticulous tour of her fastidiously maintained and elegant condominium. Stuart was lounging on the loveseat tinkering busily with his phone and ignoring us. He took up the whole loveseat with his body so I sat down next to Mimi. "You could get a fortune for this place," I told her.

"Oh, my dear, I could never sell this place. This is my home."

"Well," I suggested, "one day your *estate* could make a fortune—"

"No no. I'm trying to convince Stuart to move in after I die. I would love to see the apartment continue on."

"Next topic," muttered Stuart.

She shook her head. "Stubborn like his father."

"Héctor's here," he announced, still looking at his phone.

"I didn't hear the phone ring," said Mimi.

Stuart held up his cell phone and said, "Text, Mother. He sent a text."

Mimi raised her brow as though she were slightly wearied by the new wave of technical revolution unfurling around her. She was disinterested in devices. In her luxe penthouse she remained happily a conscientious objector.

Stuart stood up. "Be right back."

"Fred can let him in," his mother said sternly.

"Nevertheless." He kissed her on the cheek and left the apartment.

Mimi liked Stuart's new "friend" very much. She told me this as we sat in the living room alone together. "Hopefully this one will last. He speaks English *and* he's a professional."

"Professional what?"

"I don't recall. Marketing, public policy—that sort of thing."

"And he's legal?" I asked.

"What do you mean?"

"Well, I—."

"Oh! Unlike the others, you mean. Oh, my word. Thirty percent of the state is Hispanic, and they don't all wash dishes or cut lawns because they don't have papers. Trust me. He's been introduced to countless professionals over the years—men and women of every background and persuasion—but no. He's like his grandfather. I've never been able to figure out if it's compassion, or empathy—. Maybe guilt?" She demurred. "Who knows. Stuart has always been guarded about having money. His grandfather was the same way. As he got older, my father softened; he started to worry about people; he started being drawn to people who had nothing. He let his feelings seep into his business and he made some very bad decisions. If it wasn't for my husband, who took over the business and turned things around, we might have lost everything." Mimi went quiet for a moment and delicately skewered an olive from a bowl on the table. Then she smiled politely, her lips pursed around the tangy fruit. She chewed it gently and swallowed and wiped the corner of her mouth with a cloth cocktail napkin. "I've said too much."

"No, no," I insisted.

"It's the sparkling wine." She grinned then went back on topic: "I like Héctor. He was raised in New York City, I think Stuart said. One of his parents is from Venezuela, the other is Colombian. I can never remember which is from which. Anyway, he's a handsome man; just delightful. I think he plays the piano." She skewered another olive. "And thank *God* he has his own money."

Stuart returned to the living room moments later. Walking slightly behind him was a good looking, middle-aged Latino in an impeccable business suit and perfect shoes.

I looked over at Mimi, who rose elegantly from beside me like an aging movie star. She stepped around the coffee table and held out her hands. Héctor took Mimi's hands and greeted her with a kiss on both cheeks. He let go and Mimi said, "Welcome welcome," her voice brimming with a mother's long-overdue delight.

"Hugo," Stuart said to me once the two of them had separated, "this is Héctor. Héctor," he announced, "this is Hugo. My mother's gigolo."

-14-

EVERY ENDING BEGINS ANEW

In the visions I held when I was younger, California was a reclining beauty sprawled across the edge of the bed of America. She lay like a treat of flesh and desire whose youth had been spent on a horde of tedious lovers, men who came to spray their seed on her pale unblemished torso, which in its prime had been insatiable and heaving with hunger. In my imaginings, my California lay draped in white sheets like the foam of the sea rolling over her coast. In my dreams I snuck in from the other side of the bed and slid beneath the sheets, cozying my way in until I was lying beside her, my chest pressed up against the warm flesh of her back, my arm wrapped around her breasts in an embrace.

In the California I encountered, the land was a woman of incomprehensible beauty who kept the tattered corners of her life's history in scrapbooks on a bookshelf beside the bed, spilling dust and sequestering secrets. Hints of her glorious past would come to reveal themselves in the sudden undulations of her back as a new lover arrived to explore and renew with techniques that had languished in someone else's tales of sentient mastery. My California, I discovered, was a husbandless widow writhing with newfound desire. She was a middle aged mistress. She was—.

* * *

The last meaningless detail I ever captured on a spreadsheet was in April 2003. My overefficient, angst-driven Project Manager took me out for a drink along with half a dozen members of the project team to a noisy bar near the office on my last day as a contractor. The bar was a professionals' hangout, a high-end, modern-styled place with dark wenge woods, hard low stools, grey walls, and a beautiful staff devoid of any depth of personality. The only natural light coming into the place came through draped windows in the front that captured whatever angle of evening sun wasn't blocked by the high rises of central Oakland. There were men and women of reasonable means—or at least of leverage—and of every ethnic and racial persuasion, jammed into the space. Their ambitions for career, house and spouse were like a dandy's obsession for matching shoes, belt and watch. They all wanted the biggest, newest, most expensive whatever, in order that they might prevail in the war of licentious envy. They were driven by the lust of the latest sexiest ad bearing naked women and men revealing hints of pubic hair. They hungered for what the celebrities had (drove, wore, carried, flashed). For them a nicely creased and tailored shirt didn't merit hanging in some cheap rented closet, it needed a walk-in room of its own in a single-family residence whose renovation cost more than the neighbors', more than they could ever afford if it hadn't been for 0% down and bargain-basement, adjustable rate mortgages.

And they were all potential clients of mine.

Cha-ching.

I was finished with my real estate classes and only had to take the licensing exam before becoming a full-fledged agent. I'd been ghosting a few agents from a local agency on weekends to get a sense of how the work was done, who their clients were—the practical psychology of the overall exchange. What I was discovering was that they were a needy and greedy lot, these new future clients of mine, buyers and sellers alike. The former feared being taken advantage of yet would willingly throw away truckloads of money they didn't have; the latter felt entitled to their bidding wars and newfound riches. It was a seller's market; it was a rising market. The mild euphoria, the sense of a rising tide, helped supplant the social hangover from the internet bust and eased our collective depression over 9/11. Real estate had become the new ether.

I looked around at the small crowd that had gathered on my behalf. Rebecca Sanchez was there, relying heavily on Pink Cosmos to keep the endless monologue about her recently completed divorce well-lubricated. The ever-conscientious Director was there briefly: she had one mineral water, wished me luck then fled to pick up her children from daycare. The remainder were decent people, kind people, some of them interesting people, but people I hadn't bothered to get to know because I was bound up in displeasure and probably, partly (erroneously) blamed them. Soon they would be a forgotten memory, a price that had had to be paid along the way to something different. I had lined up work with Noe Realtors, in the City. Assuming I passed my licensing exam, which seemed certain, I was going to be brought on as an agent in their main office in Noe Valley, a quaint and pricey bedroom community on the south side of San Francisco. I would start May 1st, after taking a few weeks off to decompress and visit my father and his two disciples of Jesus before I began what I'd begun referring to as Phase Three.

The Hypervigilant Project Manager raised his arm and wrapped it around my shoulder. He offered a toast on my behalf—"To Hugo, may he sell lots of houses!"—and I drank blissfully, cordially, greedily, snarkily, and in thoughts of undying liberation with regard to the new road ahead.

* * *

Time flew.

Not that that was a revelation.

But had you asked me on the day that Daddy and Alice drove me to the airport in Philadelphia if I thought ten years could pass so quickly, the answer would've been a resounding no. It had been nearly three and a half years since I'd gotten laid off from E-MERGE at the bitter end of the boom; sixteen months since I'd started selling real estate; ten years in total that I'd been in San Francisco. I was turning thirty years old in just over a month and I had no idea what I was going to do to celebrate. I had two buyers who were ready to bid their lives away on houses, and we were hearing offers on another listing that Tuesday after the holiday. My August 9th birthday, when all of this activity would come due, was promising to be a busy week.

"Let's celebrate your birthday here," Stuart suggested. He'd invited Tangela, as I called my Angela and her Tamara, and me up to his place in Bodega Bay to spend the long 4th of July weekend. Héctor was there, too; he had installed himself in Stuart's life and the recipient was willing and even seemed delighted. I'd contemplated bringing a girl named Lisa with me, but we'd only gone out a few times and although we had a good time I was preoccupied with work and she seemed to be looking for a boyfriend who'd give up all of his time for her. I wouldn't say I'd turned into a workaholic, but I worked odd hours and long hours, and my weekends were seldom free. I needed a more reciprocal relationship in my life, one where I could do what I needed to do and not have a lot of obligations or restrictions. As usual, I was looking for companionship but I wasn't ready for a steady girlfriend.

I stood staring at the seemingly endless ocean outside the picture window in the living room of Stuart's getaway.

"Well?" asked Stuart.

"I think it's a great idea," Angela said from her reclined position on the sofa.

Stuart came and stood next to me at the window. "Is that a yes from you or an *I don't care?*"

"Yes," I said. "Yes. That'd be fun."

"You seem preoccupied," he said. "What's going on?"

I squinted as flickers of light bounced off the waves and in through the glass. I looked at him and surprised even myself with my answer: I was thinking about Emily.

* * *

I ended up doing the unthinkable: I worked clear through my 30th birthday. The impromptu celebration in Bodega had been all I needed, though. Angela baked me an angel food cake; Héctor took us all out to dinner. In lieu of gifts they each told stories about the first time they met me. In exchange I proffered my most vivid memories of them. The shocked look on Héctor's face when he heard that Stuart had slept with Angela was worth photographing. (Luckily we avoided the larger circumstances surrounding the trip to Seville.) As I sat at my desk in the office drawing up an offer for a client on my birthday, I sat back for a minute and thought about it. That little celebration had been enough. It was perfect. Certainly it was far more grown up than my 21st, which found me heaving in the alley behind Slo Club at four o'clock in the morning.

* * *

The following winter consumed the City as it typically did: rain married the wind and their union with the grey sky yielded days of seemingly endless darkness. Then all of a sudden the sky would explode into bright white light and blue skies, with huge puffs of clouds residing in view but always in the far distance—so far and so beautiful and so high that they obscured nothing.

In the first few months of 2005, during winter's dance with discordance, I got a phone call from Héctor. He lived in a house on the peninsula and he wanted to put it on the market at the peak of Spring buying season. He said he was interested in me being the listing agent.

"Seriously?" I said.

"Of course you'll have to *persuade* me. I want to hear your marketing ideas, staging, the whole *enchilada*."

"Absolutely."

Héctor's home was a 3 bedroom, 3 and a half bath hacienda-style house on half an acre in the western end of Palo Alto. It was a beautiful house in an incredible neighborhood. I studied up on comps in the area, did some other research and then drove down to Héctor's place to give him my tailored schpiel in his living room. As I started talking, Héctor leaned back into an overstuffed chair. A large stone fireplace dominated the wall behind him. His feet, which were ensconced in $300 shoes, rested on large imported clay tiles from Mexico. Try as I might to divorce my sense of awe over the rich from my own need to achieve and obtain, I couldn't help but be drawn in by lustful admiration of what this man had. (All family money, it turned out. But families don't start with money: someone, somewhere along the line, has to earn it. Someone has to maintain it and carry it forward.) I was eager for his business; I wanted his endorsement. So I presented my ideas. We talked about the selling points. We talked competition and comps and the risks and opportunities of selling a premium property in a crowded market. Then we stopped talking. After a moment of silence Héctor nodded his head. "Sold," he said. The listing was mine. At an asking price of 1.8 million it would be the biggest listing I'd ever gotten.

I followed Héctor into the large, comfortable kitchen where he opened a bottle of champagne and poured us both a glass, the bubbles spilling casually over the rim. "Let's sell this place," he said.

"Will do. It's a great house."

"I know. Time to move on, though. You can't keep the past alive forever."

"Cheers to that." I raised my glass and asked him what he was going to do next.

He shrugged his shoulders coyly. "I'm going to stay out of the market until things cool down. There will be some bargains coming up down the road. I'll wait until then."

"Why not get another place and flip it?"

He shook his head. "Too much work. I have enough to keep me busy already."

We headed back into the living room and sat down.

"So where are you going to live?" I asked.

"I'm moving into the City."

"You're going to rent?"

"Not exactly. I have my sights on a flat on Nob Hill."

"I thought you weren't going to buy."

He grinned.

And then I remembered I can be slow to hook things together sometimes. "Oh, no kidding?"

"Yes, no kidding."

Come Spring, Héctor would be living in Stuart's condominium, just around the corner from his grand old mother-in-law, Mimi Piers.

* * *

Almost as soon as it went on the market, Héctor's house sold. It went for 2.1 million, which was three hundred thousand above asking. The bidding war was intense and, for me at least, exciting. The entire process required an incredible amount of work, and Héctor was a demanding client, but in the end it was a thrill. The actual signing of the closing papers left me jittery. After subtracting the agency's share of the commission, I walked away with a check for $55,000.

For one sale.

I was in heaven.

"Better sock it away," Héctor warned.

* * *

Call it the lure of the bright California sky, the gentle hum of Spring. Maybe it was a feeling that I could allow myself, after working for two years without a break, to take some time and relax. Perhaps it was the feeling that my life had finally righted itself. Whatever it was, something urged me to get in my car and drive. I checked my calendar, my client list, my pending items. There was nothing that screamed for attention so I packed a weekend bag and called Nelly, the office manager, and told her that I was taking a few days off.

"Where you going, Hugo?" she asked.

"For a drive."

"Where to?"

"Santa Cruz. Monterey. I'm not really sure. I'll just kind of stop when I feel like it."

"Nice."

I turned off everything in the loft and headed out back to the garage. Once in my car, I leaned my head against the headrest and closed my eyes. *Thank God,* I thought, *for a strong market. Thank God for Stuart Piers. Thank God I was out of the technology field. Thank*

God for all that had transpired over the past few years—good and bad, mean or delicious.

I drove the few crusty SOMA blocks to the freeway on-ramp and took 280 headed west toward the coast. With my phone off and the radio silent, the only person I had to talk to was me. Not that I discussed with myself the sharp curving slope of the freeway as it dropped down toward the coastal town of Pacifica and became almost without warning a two lane road with traffic lights. Nor did I remark out loud on the wending topography, not even as I passed through the craggy pines of Moss Beach and then encountered the standard brief slowdown as traffic lolled its way through Half Moon Bay. There was only silence inside the car, broken by a coastal wind blowing in through the open windows. Once south of Half Moon, past the new housing developments and a luxury hotel, the slender undulating tar of Highway One turned into a limitless path through thousands of acres of coastal quietness. On one side were cliffs dropping off to the turbulent sea, on the other hills that rolled upwards into low mountains or extended like waves of green and brown earth into the heartland.

This was the California of my imaginings. The one I'd remembered from the movies. The one that was easy to forget exists when you're confined to city streets and either fail, or are unable, to venture outside the urban domain.

With a descending sun as my guiding light off the right side of the car, I headed south on the sparsely populated road, passing fewer cars than anticipated in that day and age of overcrowded everything. A couple hours south of San Francisco, as the sun sat perched in waiting above the horizon, ready to make its final arc of the day, I pulled into the Davenport Roadhouse Inn. In the wide downstairs restaurant I sat at a simple wooden table for two to indulge in a dinner for one while reading the slender pages of a local news and arts paper. In an adjoining room a guitarist entertained locals sitting at a heavy, carved wooden bar. The waitress, who was about my father's age and moved from table to table as if the whole of her life's experience had involved taking care of people who walked through those doors, asked how far I was headed.

"Monterey, I guess. Maybe further."

"It's going to be dark driving that far down Highway One." She set down a bread plate and a glass of water in front of me. "You in a hurry?"

"Nope."

"Might as well spend the night here."

"Where's there to stay?"

"Upstairs," she chirped. "Nice rooms with a view." She tilted her head toward the front of the restaurant. "The hostess can help you. I'm sure there's something."

"Sounds like a good idea," I said.

She scribbled down my order for a glass of wine and then she vanished, while outside the window the sun kissed the lip of the earth.

* * *

After dinner I paid for a room and then sat at the bar with a whiskey that shimmied through every neuron in my body, which had a pleasant doubling effect on the already slowed-down pace of the place. The guitarist played an array of Irish songs and other folksy, country-sounding music that added a warming buzz. The bar was decidedly local but it was also placeless; it seemed it could have existed anywhere. You could have transported the old room from its singular spot along the California coast and set it down in another state; in another country; given it a different language and changed everyone's names; it would have remained unchanged and somehow perfect.

I drank my whiskey slowly. The guitarist finished his final song. He set his guitar down and nodded in acknowledgment of the few hands of applause. As he sorted the bills in his tip basket I thanked the bartender and headed upstairs to my room.

The rooms of the Davenport Inn were reached through a wooden outside porch that wrapped around two sides of the building. As I walked up to my room after leaving the bar, I noticed that the sky was full of stars, a canopy of glitter that stopped at the dark border of the sea. In a narrow bedroom above the restaurant I took a hot shower, wrapped myself in a thick terry robe that was hanging on the bathroom door, then I climbed into bed and let myself drift off to sleep with a feeling of absolute weightlessness.

Morning came dressed in a dusting of fog as noises of the restaurant's early shift drifted up through the floor. Occasional traffic scurried along the highway in front of the inn. The rising sun coming over the hills cast a slanted light in through the window. Just beyond, the dark shades of the ocean started softening into familiar tones of blue. After dressing myself in yesterday's clothes I headed downstairs and had some breakfast. With no obligations beyond an eleven o'clock checkout time, I then wandered across the road to a path that cut through a grove of coastal trees. Beyond the small grove lay a set of train tracks which, to my right, curved inland toward the City and to my left formed a straight shot heading south. Across the tracks the path diverged. One branch headed to a wide grassy bluff, the other wended its way through boulders down the side of the low cliff toward the beach. I opted for the latter route.

Hundreds of miles of the Pacific Coast had similar craggy inlets covered in ashen sand like that one. Large clumps of brown sea-faring weeds littered the beach, complicated in their individual composition yet looking like abandoned oceanic microworlds tossed along the sand. Overhead, a flock of birds, seven in all, flew in tandem down the coast. That northern California beach was so unlike the beach I'd known in New Jersey. Back in Jersey, where literally miles of asphalt or cement boardwalks gave way to pale, raked sand abutting turbid water, the seashore was a long familiar stretch, thick with the noises and voices of humanity. There, bodies blossomed underneath the white sun as music spilled out from open arcades. Real life got put on hold when you ventured to the seashore during the summer. Your mediocre world lay suspended, dormant and forgotten, while you thrived on a day of escape with your friends. Reality was a backpack you left on the sand, and when the day was done you slung that bag full of doubts and boredoms onto your sun-cooked back as you headed to the car for the hushed and always disappointing ride back inland.

In Davenport, by contrast, the sand was cold and thick, chilled overnight by a fog bank that receded further out into the sea as daylight warmed the coast. That sand carried in it the imprints of a different sort of existence, a very different approach to living; it insisted that you spill open your backpack and inventory all of your things.

I had taken my shoes and socks off before I started walking and I couldn't help but think of Alice, who once, years and years before, had said she wanted to put her toes in the California sand one day. About midway across the isolated beach, I stopped and faced the ocean. Low waves broke with their grey-green mist rising above the foamy collision of water and the rocky sand. Perennial winds blew across the ocean's surface and carried the scent of cold sunshine in every one of their molecules, which landed in gentle gusts on my face and hands as I shuffled my feet into the brisk, briny sand. I raised my arms in deference to a memory from a terrible time in my youth and I let the rising wind wrap itself around me in an embrace.

"It ain't LA," I said out loud to Alice and my mother, "but what do you ladies think?"

* * *

In winter the sparsely numbered taxicabs of San Francisco fill up almost the moment they take to the streets. All the more so when the wind blows rain at your waist. To catch a cab at the end of a dark wet workday is akin to witnessing the Virgin Mary ascend the steps of a Muni station: the odds are not in your favor. (Well, one has to disclaim that with the Halloween exclusion, a day on which there are many such visions overtaking the City. If you've seen the Castro at Halloween you know what I mean.)

It was hard to believe we were back in a season of rain again. Harder still to believe that we were at the halfway mark of the first decade of the 21st century. As always, work consumed nearly everything. Ever since selling Héctor's house, I'd seen little of Tangela and the two men, Hector and Stuart, though we managed to keep in touch through email. I was gladdened to know that the four of them were going to be my collective dinner date that night. It was long overdue, like always, but at least we were getting together again. We were all ensconced in living our respective lives, in reconciling our breathless pasts with the easier air of better economic times. Such was the promise, at least: a temporary breather. The constant flow of real estate transactions was forcing new energy into the country's outlook; the stock markets were not so dynamic, but after the difficult landing when they crashed after the boom they no doubt needed to relax a little bit. Take in some air. Find their way. Here and there were published articles announcing a familiar villain: *the bubble*. This time word was that there was a housing bubble. This time, as we were so good at doing, we continued onward, silently, heads down, playing our part in the endless cycle of promise and renewal, pretending we were paying attention. Stuart, with his pulse on seemingly everything, advised me to "Earn now." Not knowing what he meant I went about my work, buying and selling dreams, brokering financing through my connections, lifting, I believed, the condition of so many other people's lives.

With my car in for servicing, I tried to snag a cab in front of my loft to go to the restaurant but it was hopeless. Unfortunately the taxi gods had abandoned me. After ten or fifteen minutes of loitering on the corner of Langton and Folsom, I started wandering up 7th Street toward Mission, figuring the odds were better heading in that direction. Walking nearly backwards in the rain, I kept my eyes focused on the shiny blur of oncoming traffic in search of that magical white *available* light atop a cab. Every now and then an elusive yellow-bodied sedan would pass by, its belly full of black-clad passengers, the rain on its windows creating a sort of postmodern stained glass.

Wet from the sideways blowing rain, I eventually gave up. I crossed Mission Street and resigned myself to the less glamorous alternative: the 14 bus, a roving homeless shelter, a juvenile hall on wheels. The *bueno* of this bus line was the frequency with which it ran. The *malo* was the bus itself. Behind the bus stop, which doubled as homeless housing, a bulky and brooding new Federal building was being built. Work on the massive, alienating edifice was done for the day, halted as part of the end of the laboring week. The skeletal behemoth cast a nighttime shadow over the bus stand, on the outside of which stood the commoners like myself, the ones who couldn't stand the bodily stench and litter contained within the glass-protected shell of the bus stop and who chose to witness the rain firsthand instead.

I shoved two begrudging dollars into the receptacle as I boarded the next 14 that arrived. The interior reeked of unmentionable odors. The front half of the double bus was packed solid with people. The back half was filled with marijuana smoke. To add to the ambience, somebody had puked the shiny pink contents of their stomach onto the rear stairwell. The windows were all open to vanquish the smell, which only served to distribute the stench more thoroughly throughout the traveling hookah and to allow raindrops to flurry into the bus with chilling discomfort.

Twenty minutes later, after enduring endless stops and jolts and inhaling enough second-hand weed to make me feel light-headed, I arrived at 20th and Mission, heart of the busy, bustling Latino district. The sidewalks were boisterous despite the weather. With rain falling and the wind whipping at gangly branches of the one or two scraggly trees poised along the block, assorted members of society lingered beneath the shelter of doorways or commercial awnings, awaiting entrance to a club or restaurant, looking to buy or sell drugs, begging for a handout...whatever.

My foot landed in a puddle as I stepped off the bus. (I let that affront pass calmly.) As I crossed the street in pursuit of the night's destination, my umbrella got sucked up and inverted by the wind, its slender batwing bones snapped at the joints. (I let it go.) Any other sort of reunion, any other group of people, I might have bagged it all and headed back home. But these were my friends. Stuart and Héctor were nestled snugly in Nob Hill with their private millions and no mortgages. Angela and Tamara resided in wedded, East Bay lesbian bliss. My own relationship status was at that moment *off-again*, but I wasn't worried. The few promising starts I'd had had ended in failure; nothing crashing or dramatic, it's just that none of them was sustainable. One day, I knew, once that latest swell of great fortune had rescinded, once a new wave rose and another fell, as I bore my own weight along a porous sinking sidewalk, I would one day bring my girlfriend, fiancée, or wife—yes it could, and it would, eventually happen—to one of those gatherings.

All things to all persons in their due course.

I looked up at the bouncing white lights above the restaurant sign to make sure I was in the right place. Through the gap in the rustic wooden doors came the sound of some loud jazzy island *Son*, its rapid-fire brass and drums imbuing the Cuban restaurant within with a sexy, hyperfriendly heartbeat. Desire drove me forward and I stepped inside, where familiar faces, somewhere within the densely seated crowd, awaited me.

The aroma in the place was of garlic and roasting meat. The room itself, with tall ceilings and walls painted a deep embracing blue, was hot like a sauna, packed with people on low benches dining at communal tables. Unharried young waitresses in short skirts and blouses weaved between the tables taking orders and serving food.

From within that midst arose a hand that gave a short lateral wave, left and then back to the right again. I looked more closely. It was Stuart waving me over. Nestled in the center of the room—but of course, how could they be seated anywhere else—were my four friends.

I squeezed my way in through the crowd and stretched out my hands to greet them.

"Smoke a little weed?" Angela joked as she hugged me.

"I took the bus," I had to shout.

I leaned down and gave Tamara a peck on the cheek. Héctor stood and we shook hands across the narrow table. Stuart stood beside him wearing a suit, and as I shook his hand he pulled me toward him and grabbed me by the shoulders. His grip was immobilizing, as firm as ever. "You look great!" he said loudly, then planted a kiss on my cheek.

I wedged myself in between Angela and her wife. I put my hand on Angela's knee and she smiled. She gave me a kiss on the cheek and hugged me and I imagined that it had only been last week that we last saw each other, or last met each other, last lingered in such familiar, fragile bliss.

After shedding my raincoat and siphoning off some of Angela's tequila, my shoulders relaxed and I became recharged and at ease. The warm bench felt like a seat at the family table and the four faces surrounding me were my favorite relations.

Delighted for all we had at the moment, and breathing in the aromas and anticipations of everything that lay beyond—good, bad or even wearying—I grinned at my beloved and said to her affectionately, "Is this one unbelievable kind of a life, or what."

Made in the USA
Charleston, SC
24 July 2011